DEERHAVEN
PINES

Diana McRae

Bella
BOOKS
2012

Bella Books, Inc.
P.O. Box 10543
Tallahassee, FL 32302

Printed in the United States of America on acid-free paper
First published 2012

Editor: Katherine V. Forrest
Cover Designer: Linda Callaghan

ISBN 13: 978-1-59493-288-5

For Carolyn,
librarian par excellence.

And for Jaslo,
a brilliant writer who knows ghosts.
Beautiful.

About the Author

Diana McRae is the author of *All the Muscle You Need*. She works as a librarian and is devoted to her wife and three children.

CHAPTER ONE

Sula set one foot down in the snow outside her car and the white powder melted into a puddle where her soft leather boot came to rest. Despite a windchill factor of minus twenty that night, she wore nothing but a long, wine-colored raincoat over her blouse and tight black jeans. Sula Smith's body generated its own heat. Only her tiny nipples responded to the cold, becoming hard and erect under rose silk and red purple nylon.

Secure in her natural warmth, Sula locked the door of her Jeep Cherokee, and glided across the wintry parking lot. The neon sign, "Wildflowers," flashed on whenever the words, "Finest Food, Best Company," blinked out. Sula considered herself more discriminating about food and more selective about companionship than whoever had dreamed up that slogan, but she made regular visits to the establishment and usually departed satisfied.

Bursting through the heavy doors like a displaced August breeze, Sula squared her shoulders, bracing for the general appraisal her appearance in Wildflowers' lounge always generated. Members of the women's community around the Sierra Nevada town of Sonora could account for each of their own. But hardly any of them knew who Sula was or from where she came. Tonight, as usual, they stared their full before returning to drinks and conversation.

"Hello, Murphy," said Sula, in a rich alto voice familiar to every woman in the room. Their familiarity with her vocal quality had nothing to do with Sula personally. Sula possessed the vocal quality of those butchy movie stars from the '40s: Hepburn, Davis, Crawford; and the women at Wildflowers had seen all their films.

Sula looked nothing like those tailored bygone beauties, however. Blessed with a wild aureole of black wavy hair, vivid red lips and cheeks, and snow-white skin, Sula reminded the crowd at Wildflowers of Briar Rose or Snow White in a child's picture book. They felt free to weave stories featuring Sula as the romantic lead, without thinking of her as very real.

"Good evening, Sula," answered handsome Pat Murphy, wearing one of her trademark leather vests. Murphy was one woman who did know where Sula lived but she would never tell.

Murphy had been selected by Sula one night five months ago, and Murphy's gait had been lighter ever since as she made her way to a barstool at Wildflowers each evening. "Have a seat," Murphy invited.

"Maybe later. Right now, I need a hot meal," Sula said, stopping to give the woman a quick hug and inhale the rich smell of damp tanned hide rising from Murphy's suede vest. The women of the Gold Country loved animals, but they didn't mind wearing their hides either.

"Don't forget what I told you," Sula whispered into Murphy's sleek dark hair. She moved away with an encouraging nod. Murphy smiled into her glass of Corona.

"What did she tell you?" demanded Francie Flarety, Murphy's date for the evening. Francie had donned the obligatory plaid shirt, but she couldn't disguise a voluptuous figure so she wore it well.

Murphy looked away. Her smile became self-conscious. "She said I had excellent manual dexterity," she said. "And that it would take me far in life."

"That was it? Those were her words of wisdom?"

"She told me more than that but it was private." Murphy blushed but plowed on to say, "Ever since then, I've been thinking about going to dental school. I always wanted to be an orthodontist. Did I ever mention that? It's almost as though Sula knew."

"Come on, Murphy," protested Francie. "She's not a fortune-teller. She's probably a straight woman who likes to go slumming. We shouldn't even let her hang out with us until she pays her dues."

"What dues do we pay?" demanded Murphy. "You mean listening to the same thirty-five-year-old women describe their lousy relationships with their parents over and over again? Watching our friends teeter between Wildflowers and the Recovery House? That's our choice of poison, but Sula's exempt from those dues. Besides," Murphy broke into a grin, "take my word for it, Francie, she's not straight." Murphy continued grinning into the lemon-tinted liquid in front of her until Francie cracked a smile.

"She's had you under her spell for five months now," Francie commented. "And you know what, Murphy? I have to admit it's an improvement." They linked hands for a minute until Murphy decided to signal for another bowl of pretzels.

"I've never known an orthodontist," mused Francie. "I guess that's why I still have a gap between my two front teeth." The two women looked at each other and giggled.

****

Poised to enter the dining room, Sula rotated her hips sensuously under her raincoat. Then, she hung her raincoat on a loaded brass coatrack, ran her fingers down her own warm body, and aimed for a table where three women in their late twenties sat eating spinach salads dressed with yogurt and sprinkled with bacon-flavored bits of soy. The women looked up.

"May I join you?" Sula inquired. She felt a natural lick of anxiety at putting herself in a position where she could be questioned about her identity. On the other hand, no woman asked very many questions when approached by Sula. The warmth on Sula's face won her a place wherever she chose to go.

Sure enough, the intellectual-looking one, a blonde in white ski pants and a white cashmere sweater, smiled and replied, "Sure, sit down and introduce yourself. My name's Lilah."

The other two stopped chewing long enough to greet Sula and offer their names. Sula murmured pleasantries, all the while maintaining eye contact with Lilah, who, as luck would have it, was the one Sula had targeted after scanning the room. She inched her chair closer to Lilah's so that Lilah would eventually become conscious of the heat radiating off Sula's body and the electricity crackling from her hair. Lilah was just Sula's type, smart and gentle-looking but with a passionate energy smoldering behind her light hazel eyes.

Ordering the Wildflowers' complete dinner, Sula choose eggplant Parmesan as an entree. For a first course, she gobbled a quarter loaf of buttery garlic bread laced with cheese and chives. Sula didn't eat often but when she did, she ate a lot. The server brought breadsticks and Sula took several. She'd order hot chocolate with her dessert so for now she drank only water.

Sula waited for the right opportunity to interview Lilah. She couldn't afford to be too obvious about her immediate attraction to the light-haired woman. If Sula's reputation around Sonora were to suffer, if the women began to label her an opportunist or a letch, she would have to drive much further for her nights out.

"What do you do for a living?" Sula asked Lilah after a decent interval.

"I'm a soils analyst. I work for the Forest Department," Lilah informed her. Perfect. A woman of science, someone who could take care of herself. "What do you do?" Lilah asked in return. All three women leaned forward to catch her reply.

"Oh, a little of everything." If the vagueness of Sula's reply irritated her three companions at the table, they accepted it with polite silence. Soon, main courses arrived to distract the dinner party from pondering Sula's vocation.

At nine p.m., dancing began in the lounge. A local band, Heather and the Heartthrobs, sang nonsexist oldies backed up by piano and electric guitar. Sula knew she wouldn't be able to endure the din and the edited lyrics for long, so she asked Lilah for the first dance. Lilah hesitated, not so smitten by Sula's various charms that she didn't stop to think before agreeing to dance with a virtual stranger. But, Lilah put her dessert fork down and replied, "Why not?"

"Why not?" repeated Sula. "I promise you've got a lot to gain and nothing to lose." Lilah stood up, as graceful as Sula would have guessed. Lilah's friends appeared puzzled by Sula's cryptic promise, but Lilah laughed and bowed in a courtly manner.

Once they swayed in each other's arms on the dance floor, Sula registered the fact that Lilah was tall, almost as tall as she herself. The two of them pushed and shoved at first, jockeying over who would lead, but by their third dance, they worked out a compromise consisting of smooth transitions from one segment of the dance to another with each partner leading every other portion of the sequence. Casual observers would not have been able to testify as to which woman directed the other's steps. They made the best of an eclectic set of renditions: "He's (She's) So Fine," "Unchained Melody", and "Anything Goes."

"It's chilly in here but not when I'm next to you," commented Lilah. "Your hands are so warm."

"Have you seen the movie, *Body Heat*?" inquired Sula, and the corners of her ruby lips turned up.

"I don't see many movies, and I don't have a VCR," Lilah replied. "I'm the outdoorsy type."

"Well, try to see *Body Heat* if you get a chance. It's erotic." Sula put her mouth near Lilah's ear and whispered, "It's about a woman who's hot, the same way I am." Sula stepped back to assess the effect of her remark. Even though she knew that most women weren't as forward as she, Sula never tried to check herself. Her boldness worked to her advantage except when she ran into prudish women, and she didn't date prudes anyway.

"You're a pistol, aren't you?" Lilah laughed. Sula didn't respond to the laughter but instead continued to concentrate her considerable emotional energies on Lilah.

This would be the turning point in their encounter. If Lilah didn't back away, Sula would not be lonely that night. Sula stepped back and held out her slender white arms. Lilah glided forward. Done. When the music started again, Lilah's pubic bone skimmed Sula's jeans and her mouth landed near Sula's ear so that her breath rustled waves of dark hair and sent a chill down Sula's spine.

When the band struck up a chorus of "Twist and Shout," they decided to leave.

"If you like the outdoors, you'll love my home," Sula submitted to Lilah, trying to encourage the tall, light-footed woman to throw caution to the wind. Soon they found themselves negotiating the remainder of the evening.

"Where is it that you live?" asked Lilah. If Sula had been ambivalent about her pursuit, she would have evaded the question. But Sula wanted Lilah, wanted her tonight.

"Near Deerhaven Pines," Sula answered. Anyone in the Sierras would be familiar with the picturesque town of Deerhaven Pines, situated on Highway 68. The Stanislaus River ran through the outskirts of town, forming a wide, sandy beach just past the bridge. A main street lined with gold rush-era buildings, an all-purpose grocery store, post office, saloon, bank and a folk art and antique store, had been refurbished at the end of the 1980s. Sula tried not to be embarrassed by the knowledge that Lilah must know you had to have a great deal of money to live "near Deerhaven Pines."

Tourists came from everywhere in the western United States to stay at the $350 per night Deerhaven Pines Hotel, decorated with exposed oak beams and ceramic tiles painted with Sierra flora. The distinctive trees and crags framed by picture windows throughout the hotel pleased city-weary eyes, and dull palates were inspired by the unique French/Californian cuisine, pretending to be gold rush-era food, that visitors sampled in the restaurant on the hotel's bottom floor.

"Come let me show you," she urged Lilah. A reckless lift of Lilah's eyebrows encouraged Sula's growing belief that this encounter would end happily.

"Okay, let's go to your place. I'd love to see it," said Lilah.

Wildflowers' customers, she knew, weren't as cautious about going home with strangers as the women denizens of Sonora's cowboy bars. The cowboys sometimes got rough, but nobody in Sonora had ever heard of a lesbian rapist or a lesbian serial killer. Women might fear being bored or irritated by casual pickups, but they didn't fear death or violence.

Once they reached the highway, Sula sped through the lightly falling snow with confidence. Sula possessed excellent reflexes along with a four-wheel-drive vehicle and supernatural good luck. In the absence of friends and acquaintances, Lilah grew shyer, but Sula found her to be a clear thinker with a sense of humor. Lilah turned out to be political, a liberal, but she soon sensed that Sula was not interested in causes or dogma. After a while they settled into talking about the earth and her mysteries. Their relationships with Mother Earth differed but Lilah had no way of knowing that. Sula could only reveal so much.

Upon reaching Wolf's Creek, the town closest to Deerhaven Pines, the Jeep traveled Main Street at the speed limit since Sula could not afford a run-in with Sheriff Phil Morton, a pawn of her enemy, local minister Reverend Were. After passing the "You have just left Wolf's Creek" sign, they picked up speed even though the Jeep's nose pointed windward. Sula made a left on Brown Bear Road and a right on Jane Copley Lane, bypassing Deerhaven Pines itself. Lilah stirred uneasily in her seatbelt as if wondering how far from Sonora they had come. She'd watched groves of snowy Douglas firs and sugar pines go by for many minutes.

"Do you have a condo out this way?" asked Lilah, shifting in the passenger seat to face Sula.

"No. I live in a big house. It's a fascinating place. You'll love it." ˎ

"Is the house in one of the developments?"

"There are no housing developments where I live," answered Sula.

Massive gold and black wrought iron gates rose before them, eliminating the need for an explanation. The crest over the topmost archway gave away the address.

"You live at Deerhaven Forest Hall?" gasped Lilah.

"The Hall has been my family's home for four generations," Sula told her astounded date. She waved when she noticed movement to her right. William Roe had been watching from the gatehouse for her arrival. He waved back at Sula, opening both gates for her. Watching the intimidating gates swing open, Lilah didn't speak again until they'd cruised through and were heading down the drive.

"I don't go out very often," said Sula. "So, when I do, Will worries about me. That's why he's here at the entrance to the grounds. I wish he'd just go to bed." Sula wanted to explain this aspect of her life to her guest. She didn't want Lilah to think she needed anyone to look after her.

"Are you one of the Windsor family, Sula?" Lilah questioned.

"No. I'm a Smith. We belong here just as much as the Windsors, but we aren't well known." Sula parked and patted Lilah's hand.

Numbly, Lilah followed Sula out of the darkened garage. They trod a pathway which seemed to be kept clear of snow by some radiant heating device. Lilah hoped that Sula wouldn't make her enter the house by the stately mahogany doors in front and, as if responding to Lilah's timidity, Sula led the way around the building to a side entrance screened with a long trellis. They entered through a broad back door and passed through a huge farm kitchen hung with brass cooking implements and dried foodstuffs.

Inside the forest house's public rooms, Lilah caught a glimpse of lavish paintings and opulent antique furniture adorning huge high-ceilinged rooms with intricate parquet floors. Their traverse through the remarkable mansion felt like an eternity to Lilah. Her heart began pumping wildly and her knees had grown weak. Until this dalliance with Sula Smith, Lilah had avoided adventure, preferring from the very beginning to get good grades, enough sleep, and later, a nice steady paycheck. Why did I agree to this? she asked herself, although she knew the answer to her own question.

"These are my apartments," Sula finally announced. She turned on electrical lights that had the quality of candles inside smoked glass lanterns. The soft glow revealed a richly appointed bedroom, study and a small perfect kitchen. "There are no windows, only skylights, because we're toward the center of the house," Sula explained.

Lilah looked upward. High above, she could see storm clouds and through one pane of glass, a swath of laser bright Sierra stars.

Sula's expression softened. "I did the right thing bringing you here, Lilah. You're perfect. You look beautiful in this light." Sula moved closer and held out a hand in an inviting but supplicating gesture.

Wishing her heart would slow itself, Lilah paused. She could hear herself breathing. Without making a conscious decision, she slipped her hand into Sula's and felt an intense heat radiate up her arm and into her chest. The fire spread into her breasts until they both throbbed and the fire inside them hungered for more of the fuel that fed it. And here was Sula to provide the fodder.

Unbuttoning her shirt, Sula exposed small, pale breasts pulled taut by tiny, hard, pink nipples. Sula moved closer to Lilah, removed the parka which hid Lilah's hair, the color of a snow-maiden's, pulled up her sweatshirt and yanked up Lilah's blouse and undershirt. Sula took one small breast, soft as new snow, into her mouth. As Sula raised her mouth to Lilah's, she brushed her aching nipples against the other woman's until four hard knots burned with pleasure between them.

Sula raised a hand and touched that sweet area where Lilah's tempered body melded into the soft tender curves of her thighs. Their hips swayed in a reflex grinding motion. Sula grasped Lilah by the waist and pressed the woman's pubic bone against hers. Lilah answered with a sweet, high moan.

When Sula felt her face flaming, she knew her mouth would have turned a fiery color. Lilah's mouth was the ointment for her lips. Lilah slid a cool and delicate tongue along Sula's teeth and Sula shivered.

The room grew hot, and they both secreted a clear, clean liquid that lubricated the private parts of their bodies and minds. Added to the heat, the scent, the texture, were the violent tremors of two lovers coming together as strangers.

Eventually, the two tall women, dark and fair, tumbled onto clean cotton under rich satin, and the fineness of the fabrics eased their descent into deeper, rougher sensations. Sula circled backward so that her mouth could envelop Lilah's innermost hidden scarlet hood. She thrust her tongue down and down and down. They held back and let go by infinite degrees.

"Oh, my God," Lilah panted. She imagined being torn apart by rutting beasts, crazed by the frenzy of their lovemaking. Discordant thunder sounded and then faded.

"What was that noise?" cried Lilah. "And what's that over there? On the wall. Could that be blood?" A blood-red hue had flooded Lilah's brain sometime during their lovemaking. The redness before her eyes might have come from straining the vessels and veins in her brain to their breaking point with primitive rapture, but now that her eyes were open, she saw real blood dripping down the walls around them.

"The acoustics in this house are strange," offered Sula, touching Lilah's naked flesh with one finger to paint shivers of spent passion. "And the construction of the building can produce unusual visual effects."

When Lilah looked again, the viscous red substance on the wall had disappeared. No more roaring broke the silence. Lilah shifted onto one shoulder so that she could look up into the face of the woman she'd made her lover and gasped. Sula's wild beauty seemed to have intensified. Enraptured, Lilah reached out to touch the white skin and black hair.

"My God, what are you?" Lilah choked. "A witch?"

"No," murmured Sula. "A librarian."

CHAPTER TWO

"Do you have a story about two girls who meet a ghost?" asked Lesley Rosen, age nine. The children's librarian, a young woman with lavender eye makeup and a spun-gold coiffure, giggled and covered her mouth. Her badge read, "Barbara Blathen, Children's Services." Barb's seventies look was "in" in library circles that year, 1984.

"We stock the standard fare," Barb informed Lesley with all the blitheness of a children's librarian. "The one about the escaped mental patient with a hook instead of a hand. That old chestnut where a high school guy loans his letterman's jacket to a girl who turns out to have been killed in a car crash years ago. Go look on those shelves labeled 'spooky,' over there, under the picture of Casper."

Lesley found herself unable to muster any interest in hooks

or football jackets. "Well, never mind," she answered, with great politeness. "Do you have *Socks* by Beverly Cleary, instead?"

"We certainly do," replied the librarian, smiling approvingly. "I'll get the book for you."

Barbara Blathen wore braces, Lesley noted. The Rosens' library couldn't seem to retain the same children's librarian from one month to another. Library management sent out a different *Services As Needed* employee every other week or so.

Mr. and Mrs. Rosen took their daughter to the West Hollywood Branch of the Los Angeles Public Library every other Thursday. Mr. Rosen favored nonfiction on topics such as McCarthy-era politics and baseball history. Mrs. Rosen read women's fiction about poor but worthy young ladies who met strange brooding men in New York penthouses or provincial villages in Western Europe. Eva Rosen didn't quibble over time or place as long as the romance turned rocky and then ended in marriage.

The Rosen family routine concluded with a visit to MacTavish's Ice Cream Parlor where they sat in a red vinyl booth. They scanned their menus on each visit and considered the specials. The Rosens liked experimenting with flavor combinations, cashews with butterscotch, dark chocolate dust sprinkled over peach sherbet, cherry syrup and marshmallows. By the time their server arrived, she would find the Rosens immersed in reading fiction or nonfiction, depending upon their proclivity. The three of them ordered different sundaes so that they could compare. The night she checked out *Socks*, Lesley asked for Rocky Road with caramel and white candy sprinkles.

"Any good?" Mr. Rosen asked Lesley as she spooned black, tan and white richness from a bowl shaped like flower petals. Lesley knew his question pertained to the book, not the ice cream.

"*Socks* seems like an excellent piece of writing," Lesley pronounced. Mr. Rosen nodded and scooped up a bite of her sundae.

"Give me *Socks* when you're done," said Mrs. Rosen, looking up from a novel with a castle on the cover and a dark handsome man wearing thigh-high boots. "I love the funny things that cats do."

"God bless the library," commented Mr. Rosen in utter contentment.

****

Year 2002

Night after night, terrible beasts pursued and sometimes devoured Ryan in his dreams. Last month, however, the hairy fiends who prowled his unconscious departed without so much as a goodbye snarl. Whether these nocturnal apparitions fled as a result of the lactose-free diet that his pediatrician prescribed, or for developmental reasons, his mother couldn't say.

"Tell me a ghost story," Ryan asked and grinned, charming his mother with the very gray-eyed gaze he inherited from the Windsors. He'd never ventured such a request before.

"Ghosts?" Lesley Rosen Windsor, aged twenty-seven, queried with concern. Would a frightening story reactivate the demons in Ryan's dreams? Her husband, Michael, twenty-four years Ryan's senior, still awoke in the dark, screaming, sobbing, thrashing.

Michael's night terrors had been bad lately and for a reason. These past months had been a period of disequilibria for the Windsor family. Michael's mother, Cosette, lay under a broad silk canopy in the Windsor family home, dying of a cancer that caused her mind to wander. She mumbled about ghosts who sat at the foot of her bed reciting stories about dead Windsors. The ghosts invited her to join them.

Lesley knew about Cosette Windsor's illness third-hand. Lesley had been married to Michael Windsor for nine years and had never met his family of origin or been to the house in the Gold Country where Michael grew up. The Windsors refused to accept Michael and Lesley's marriage when they heard that she was half Jewish and from a plebian family, and Michael remained estranged from them. Michael's brother, Kelvin telephoned on the sly to report on their mother's condition. Lesley dreaded Kelvin's surreptitious calls detailing Cosette Windsor's descent into infirmity and madness because Michael became more distressed with each call. She never knew when to expect a call from Kelvin because Kelvin, who also didn't accept Lesley, called

Michael at work.

Strangely, Cosette Windsor's dementia served a purpose. Kelvin Windsor admitted that Cosette enjoyed the ghostly visitations, enjoyed them more than life itself now that life amounted to a gnawing pain in her bones and brain. The Windsor ghosts comforted Cosette, and she looked forward to joining their ranks. Having never met her husband's mother, Lesley didn't know what to think of this latter-day spiritualism. So how should she handle Ryan's request? To have Ryan, the youngest Windsor, express a sudden interest in the occult could almost be viewed as a family proclivity. Lesley couldn't decide whether to discourage or inform him.

"Go ahead, Mommy," Ryan urged. "Tell me a story about a haunted person."

Lesley sighed, recalling a ghost story she'd heard somewhere."Once upon a time," she began. Did ghost stories begin that way? Lesley's own mother told her fairy tales, only fairy tales.

"When?" asked Ryan, never a fan of fairy stories. Lesley reconsidered her opening.

"Over a hundred years ago, in a far away place," Lesley told him, to clarify time and setting.

Ryan held up a finger. "What place?" he questioned.

"Maybe not so far away," Lesley corrected herself. "Northeast of here but this side of the Sierras."

"Okay," pronounced Ryan.

"Deep in the forest, there lived a greedy man named Simon Chalmers." Why did this story spring to her lips as though she'd learned the words by heart? Lesley didn't know but she continued without effort.

"When he was a young man, Simon Chalmers rode in a fine black carriage drawn by fawn-colored stallions, and he attended lantern-lit parties at fancy houses owned by Astors and Vanderbilts. Simon grew accustomed to lavish ways but when the elder Mr. Chalmers died, Simon discovered that his father left none of the fortune that Simon had expected.

"After his father's death, Simon lived a dissolute existence, accepting favors from the gay blades and empty-headed women he used to squire about New York City in his elegant trap. Money from his former companions paid for the upkeep of his livery but nothing more. This untenured phase of his life brought him no joy but, at the point when his lack of satisfaction deepened into the velvet maroon of despair, Simon heard rumors that might provide him with a way out of penury.

"Word came to New York City of golden riches for the taking in a place called California. Simon borrowed enough money to stake a claim in the Mother Lode country and went there and bought a mine called the Golden Buck. The Golden Buck soon yielded plenty. Simon Chalmers' descendents still profit from the mine's bounty. His progeny endow foundations and oversee corporations, and more, but I digress. Back to Simon.

"Everything in this life pales and even being wealthy paled for Simon. To brighten his days in the Gold Country, Simon sent for a certain Mary Dunne, a slight but tall young woman with shiny light-brown hair, and he married her. Simon knew Mary, although not well, when he lived in New York. Mary's father supported five daughters and hoped to expand his mercantile operations. He considered himself lucky to palm Mary off on a rich man who would assume the cost of her upkeep and possibly loan money to the Dunnes.

"Mary Dunne proved a loving and competent wife, but her life at Chalmers House could not be deemed tranquil. A dark fate awaited Simon Chalmers, and Mary, a nice woman but fragile, proved unequal to the task of warding off Simon's dark destiny. You see, the spirits who inhabited the hills above the Golden Buck Mine decided that they would prevail upon Simon to carry out a sacred mission in exchange for proffering him his sinecure. Simon learned, through the medium of dreams, that the spirits expected him to lay down his life for their cause should the need arise. And the need arose. Simon died for them, in the end.

"You may be wondering how this tale qualifies as a ghost story, Ryan. I'm about to explain. You see, Simon's shade still walks the oaken floors of the house he built beneath the Golden Buck. He still carries the stout wooden cane, topped by a fierce brown she-bear's head, the stick that supported him in life. Upon Simon's demise, the higher powers condemned him to spend all eternity overseeing his daughter and any child born of his line. So, he conveyed to his daughter the need for her to pursue the spirit's mission or die.

"*Champion the Hue! Champion the Hue! Champion the Hue!*" Lesley chanted until she bit her lips to kill the phrase. She noticed her son gaping at her in astonishment.

"I've never heard you talk like this before," commented Ryan. "When did you memorize this story?"

Lesley reached for a Kleenex from the box on Ryan's nightstand and wiped her forehead. "I don't remember where I learned the story," she told him.

"What happened to Simon Chalmers' ghost?" asked Ryan, leaning forward, his gray eyes silver with eagerness.

Lesley began to speak but made herself halt.

"I can't remember anything more about him," she said. "I'll tell you the rest tomorrow."

What a strange reverie! She really *didn't* know any more about Simon Chalmers. Why had her knowledge of the story ended? The medium but not the source of the saga, Lesley found herself at a loss for words when transmission of the story got cut off. For all she knew, she might never dredge the end of the story from her consciousness.

"Why don't I sing while you fall asleep?" Lesley offered, and began. Ryan's eyes closed and he grew still. Lesley crept from the room.

Without premeditation, she went to the huge mahogany china cabinet in the dining room. Lesley's family ate in the kitchen almost exclusively, and she always served meals on Aztec-pattern stoneware, microwave and dishwasher safe. They never used the Windsor family china. Lesley opened the cabinet and extracted a large platter.

Vines and tiny gold flowers embellished the dish and the two-part family motto appeared on either side. "Choose Your Affinity," she read in ornate Old English lettering near the bottom rim. Upon deciphering the topmost phrase, Lesley felt the piece of china rattle in her hands. "Champion the Hue," she pronounced. Lesley would swear that she'd never really paid attention to the wording on her formal dinnerware but maybe she was wrong. Maybe she'd fashioned the ghost story for Ryan out of the Windsor family motto. Deep in thought, Lesley returned to Ryan's room to check on her son.

When the front door slammed, Ryan awoke and attempted to curl into a ball to protect his sleep. Michael must be home from his job at the Lawrence Livermore Laboratory, Lesley thought. She found him in the kitchen, pacing, head tilted, looking damp and sweaty.

"Ryan just drifted off," she stated, treating him like a typical concerned dad. Michael's relationship with his son consisted mostly of competing with the boy for Lesley's time and attention, but she liked to help him maintain the pretense of fatherhood.

"I want an omelet," Michael whined, "with ham, chilies and Monterey Jack cheese."

Lesley didn't ask where he'd been during the evening. Michael hated being pinned down by having to answer questions about his day. Sometimes he volunteered information but not often. Lesley prepared Michael's late supper with the deft motions she'd learned from cooking programs on public television. Loquacious tonight, Michael discussed his workday at the lab and the conference he'd been chosen to spearhead. When they first started dating, Michael had told Lesley that he'd been accepted to Veterinary School at U.C. Davis. The morning after their wedding, Michael announced that he'd accepted a job as Senior Technician at the Livermore Lab instead. Lesley worried about her son's father coming into proximity with lethal, loose rocketing particles, especially after seeing the movie *Silkwood* on DVD. She wished herself married to an animal doctor, the one Michael had promised he'd be.

When Michael laid down his fork, the kitchen became quiet. Lesley rinsed plate, glass and utensils. She sensed that she shouldn't ask questions of Michael right now. He rubbed his hands together as though warming them over a fire. His eyes flicked back and forth as if between two people who might yell at him.

"You didn't answer when I called you today," he accused.

"Ryan's class gave a bake sale. I helped the kids set up and make change. Pauline worked with me."

"Just send money next time. I want you to pick up the phone

when I call."

"I like helping at school, Michael. You work long hours. I need company now and then."

"There's no reason you should need people outside the family," Michael stated. "The Windsors stick together."

"Ryan and I don't have any family except you, Michael," argued Lesley, aware even as she spoke that a reasonable response to her would not seem reasonable to Michael.

"You always talk back when I tell you how things should be," he complained, his posture dejected. Lesley wondered how her life had come to this. Her own sweet, dry little parents, dead since her teenage years, would never have condoned their daughter living with a spouse who believed in the concept of "backtalk." Her parents loved discussion, and discussion, Lesley realized, constituted the antithesis of backtalk.

"I'm worried about my mother, and you care more about selling cupcakes than you do about me," Michael grumbled.

"Michael!" cried Lesley, glancing back to make sure they hadn't woken Ryan with their bickering. Then, the whirring sound of the phone cut off her retort. Lesley picked up the phone and the brother-in-law who declined to make her acquaintance asked to speak with Michael.

****

In the Gold Country, not so far away, a bear-headed cane slid across the Windsor's oaken floors. Simon Chalmers glided up to and through Cosette Windsor's thick oak door. The cane didn't catch the edge of the fringed carpet that stretched away across the floor. Simon proceeded to Cosette's bedside.

"I am here for you, my dear," he said, in his formal Victorian fashion, with a rising inflection.

CHAPTER THREE

The phone call unpleasantly interrupted Michael's dinner. Lesley could tell that Kelvin was imploring Michael to visit Deerhaven Forest Hall; the family home in which Michael had not set foot for ten years. Cosette Windsor's doctor had informed the family that Cosette could not last more than a few days and this might be Michael's last chance to see his mother. Kelvin would need help with the funeral arrangements after their mother died. Michael's father, Kelvin said, seemed prostrate with grief and anguish.

In her living will, Cosette had stated that she refused to leave Deerhaven Forest Hall for a hospital no matter what the circumstances. She wanted to hear nothing about her prognosis, preferring to deteriorate at home without hearing an exact definition of how or when she would die. The family respected her wishes. As his wife lay dying, Russell, her husband, lingered in the bedroom next to his wife's sickroom, worrying about disease and death. Russell loved Cosette to distraction and claimed he didn't really want to go on living without her. He wanted her last days and hours for himself alone. He resented sharing her with doctors, his sons, and the spectral presence of the family ghosts. Kelvin, on the other hand, insisted that Michael should come to the aid of his father and bid goodbye to his mother.

"I can't get away. You'll have to go to Deerhaven Forest Hall," Michael informed Lesley after hanging up and wiping his face and neck with a pocket handkerchief. "My mother is dying and I need you to be there."

"Me?" asked Lesley, gaping at him. "I can't go to your family's house without you, Michael. I don't know those people. I'd just be in the way."

"Mother wants to see my son," mumbled Michael. "She's always wanted to see the boy." Lesley stared at him in amazement.

"Michael! You've always told me that they didn't even know that Ryan existed. What are you talking about?"

"Well," Michael admitted with a frown, "I might have misled you about my mother. I called her when Ryan was born and she was real glad."

"Do you really mean to tell me that your mother wanted to see Ryan all along?" responded Lesley. "Oh, Michael. The poor thing! We should take Ryan to Deerhaven Forest Hall tomorrow!"

"I said I can't go with you," barked Michael and then, in a tone of false sincerity, he added, "My conference opens tomorrow morning, and I could lose my job if I don't show. *Power of the Neutron in the Twenty-first Century*. Participants have flown in from all over the country. I'm on call around the clock for the next four days."

"Michael, your mother's dying! Surely they can find someone to fill in for you." Michael's face contorted with shame and belligerence. His weak gray eyes filled with tears. Lesley accepted, in that moment, the fact that Michael did not have the emotional fortitude to be present at his mother's deathbed.

"Okay," Lesley relented, "I'll go. But how do I know your family will accept me after all these years?" She faltered, remembering that he'd misrepresented his mother's feelings about Ryan. Michael licked his lips.

"My father and my brother have come around," Michael confessed. "They're glad I'm a family man. And, I guess I should have told you, but they all wanted me to bring you to Deerhaven Forest Hall."

"You mean, none of them object to meeting me and Ryan?" Lesley demanded, stunned.

Michael emitted an exaggerated sigh. "The truth is," replied Michael, "I've always told them you didn't want to meet them."

Lesley stared at him in horror.

"You lied to me and to them?" she cried. "Why, Michael, why?"

"I was afraid they wouldn't know how to act with you. You're half Jewish and they're Christian. They're old-fashioned. You might have left me when you realized how narrow-minded a family I came from."

"Michael! That's absurd!"

"I was wrong. I realize that now. The family minister confused me about you and them. He convinced me that I should never introduce you. He's the one who's anti-Semitic. He also hoped I'd marry a local girl. I never should have listened to him."

The phone began ringing, as if to spare Michael further confession. Michael answered and his face soon collapsed into lines of despair.

"Oh, God. Oh, no," he moaned. "Christ, Kelvin. She went so fast."

"Your mother?" asked Lesley.

Michael nodded, a thick film of gray tears turning his eyes to an oil slick. Lesley attempted to stroke her husband's fine soft brown hair, but, Michael, stiff even in grief, ducked her gesture of comfort. He paused to listen to his brother on the other end of the line and when he replied, his voice sounded gruff and defensive.

"I can't come home for a few days," said Michael. "I'd risk losing my job. My wife, Lesley, will leave immediately and bring our son. Just make sure you take care of everything at the house before they get there. Tell Mrs. Woolf that I don't want my wife and child getting any nasty shocks."

Reeling with mild shock over the death of the unknown woman who she might have learned to love, Lesley wondered about her husband's odd admonition, then dismissed it.

"You're very sure that they want me there at a time like this?" Lesley asked. Her husband hung up and sat staring into dead air. Lesley put the kettle on the stove and lit a burner.

"My father and brother are overwhelmed with grief. You and Ryan will have to help with arrangements." He looked at her for the first time, scrutinizing her. "She doesn't want to be buried in the churchyard where my brother attends services. As an outsider, you won't be involved with in-fighting and such. I'll meet you there in four days."

Michael buried his face in his arms. Lesley heard him muttering. She thought at first that he spoke to himself, and then became aware that his words were directed to her. "They'll want you to take part in the changes at the Hall. They'll want you to but you're mine. Make sure you let them know you're on my side."

"Of course I'm on your side," Lesley said to placate him. "Let me make you a cup of tea," she offered.

He grimaced and clenched his fists. "I don't need tea. My mother's dead, and I'm going out for a drink. If you need me, call the Schooner Tavern."

Michael exited the house with another resounding slam.

Michael didn't drink alcohol on a regular basis but when he did, Lesley dreaded the results. Under the influence of alcohol, he babbled the kind of strange, loathsome tales he endured in his nightmares. Lesley could see no alternative but to pack for Deerhaven Forest Hall. Michael deserved her support at this terrible time and if her visit to the Hall would give him peace of mind, then she would go.

Alone in the quiet kitchen, Lesley contemplated how little she regretted departing from her and Michael's home for a few days. The Windsors' house in Blackhawk, an exclusive gated community just outside the San Francisco Bay Area, resembled every other Blackhawk dwelling, more or less. Lesley despised living a redundant life in a replicated house. Michael's suburban aspirations had indentured her. The day that Lesley and Michael returned from their Hawaiian honeymoon, he'd brought her here, to 66 Calle Diablo, and informed her that they'd be adopting the Blackhawk lifestyle, complete with association fees and swimming pool maintenance contract.

How had she come to marry a man who would buy a house with no mature trees? When they met, Michael had told her alluring stories of a rustic place nestled in old woods, his family's home. He'd implied that he and Lesley would live in that house. She had pictured in her mind a rough-hewn mountain lodging built for some eccentric ancestor of the Windsors, hidden in the dark sap-scented Sierra forest, surrounded by a mattress tick of pine needles which cushioned the family's footsteps.

After they took up residence in Blackhawk, Lesley had begged to visit Deerhaven Forest Hall but, when pressed, Michael announced that he would never again darken its doorstep and admitted that his parents would probably not open the door for him if he did. He told her for the first time that his family objected to him marrying out of his faith. He'd been lying about his family's reservations, of course. All this time, she lived among ornamental fruit trees in redwood containers rather than trees with many rings.

She did not understand many of her husband's idiosyncrasies. Why would Michael be comfortable with her meeting his family now that his mother no longer lived? Did they know that he'd kept her sequestered? What if they thought she'd spurned their company all these years? Didn't Michael worry that she'd feel awkward introducing herself to his family while he remained in Danville? Lesley thought about her husband's lack of character and sighed. No, he wouldn't worry about what she might endure at the hands of his family so long as he didn't have to face them himself.

Although Lesley wanted to remain true to her ill-considered marriage vows, her husband became more weak and erratic every day. She and Ryan constituted the least of his worries. His mother's death had significance because it affected him.

His existence minute to minute revolved around avoiding unpleasantness. A bad bout of the hiccups made him suicidal. Nasal congestion impelled him to drug himself into a stupor that verged on overdose. Lesley hoped she could help him weather his mother's death but she feared for him.

CHAPTER FOUR

The position of librarian commanded utmost respect among the staff at Deerhaven Forest Hall. Jane, the young master's new bride, dared not utter more than a "Good morning," "Good day," "Good evening," when she beheld the erudite raven-haired beauty who held the position. The head of the family, Daniel Windsor, could be numbered among the most powerful men in the thirty-first state, but librarian Ursula Smith reigned supreme in his household.

Miss Smith's power emanated from the septagonal domed room at the center of the house, a Minotaur's labyrinth thanks to its profusion of tall oak bookcases. Remarkably clear glass had been imported from Italy to create large sparkling library windows from which occupants could admire the beauty of nature without venturing outside. In Ursula Smith's domain, windows graced the ring of seven rooms from so high above that they seemed to catch the rays of Heaven direct from the source.

California's economic depression of the 1870s had become a distasteful distant memory in this, the year of our Lord 1894, and the Windsors were flush with riches and land. A lavish bridal suite had been created before Jane Copley arrived from Scotland to marry the Windsors' youngest son, John Bennett. Jane appreciated their extravagance but the lavish furnishings, the finery and sumptuous meals, made Jane feel awkward, and she preferred to spend her days outdoors, riding the sweet-tempered bay mare that John Bennett had given her as a wedding present.

"I always helped my father manage the animals and fields at Copley Manor," Jane explained to John Bennett. "I cannot thrive without fresh air." For the time being, her husband pretended to understand. Although he paraded his marriage to all and sundry, John Bennett wished his new wife out from underfoot as much as possible.

From the day of her magnificent wedding in late August through October, when dry leaves and pine needles wafted through the shafts of forest light, Jane enjoyed her sojourn in Deerhaven Pines. By day, she roamed the woods, under Scotch pines, cedar trees and black oaks. By night, she sewed quilts and finery. John Bennett rarely saw her except in the dark or sitting in an ornate flowered armchair by lantern light. This suited them both.

None of the Windsors commented upon the fact that, although she was fair of face, Jane would have to be considered a gawky girl. She dreaded the changing of the season when she would be housebound and her confinement would allow many opportunities for her husband to observe the gaucherie that might cause him to scorn her. She supposed that he couldn't send her back, after making her his wife, but she feared the confinement of winter anyway.

How Jane wished she could be as elegant as Belle Corlieau Windsor, John Bennett's mother, or his two sisters-in-law, Eleanor and Julia! They wore heavy silk gowns that flowed out from them as they walked and the folds of their skirts swished like summer river water over granite. Jane's plaid riding skirts and white blouses made her look like a governess to the family. Not only did she lack their style, none of her new relatives' sureness and confident airs rubbed off on Jane. The eeriness of residing in a house where the center, located in the library, could not be penetrated and whose rooms seemed to shift in size and location, distressed Jane. She dreamed about ghosts who whispered instructions concerning care of the Hall. They also muttered threats, although not, curiously enough, threats against her. The spirit voices impugned the more cultivated women in the house, Belle, Eleanor and Julia. Jane often remembered a small portion of what the ghosts told her but never enough to repeat to any other living soul.

Jane would have to name fear as the key component of her existence at Deerhaven Forest Hall.

****

For most Californians, 1895 began as a good year. California flourished as settlers continued flocking from the four corners of the earth to make their fortunes in agriculture and industry. By the fall of that year, however, signs that they faced a long winter sobered the pioneers. The snows came early to Deerhaven Forest Hall. By early November, blizzards left the treetops blanketed with heavy drifts. When the sun did occasionally shine, massive deposits of snow melted, slid from the house's peaked roofs, and thumped when they hit the ground. Inside the houses of gold-rich people, maids laid hardwood fires in the houses' huge hearths and stoked them night and day. The ladies of the house were expected to perform winter chores, polishing silver, readying clothes and gear for spring, inventorying foodstuffs, candle making. The women of the house appreciated Jane's skill with a needle now, rather than viewing her stitchery as recreation.

Despite the proliferation of women's work, Jane grew bored. She could no longer wander the lush meadows and somber Sierra forest. All of the ladies magazines purchased in London before her embarking for New York, Jane had long since committed to memory. Jane needed something to fresh to read but her timidity presented an obstacle.

****

The idea of braving a trip to the library and facing Ursula Smith terrified her more than the prospect of dining with John Bennett and his entire family. For that matter, she might not be the only one to quail in the librarian's presence. The Windsors' behavior gave Jane reason to believe that they too might feel intimidated by the well-favored scholar who moved so assuredly among her tomes and maps. Jane noticed that the Windsors never entered the library after dark, and during the day, only in pairs.

One evening, Jane's pitch of boredom grew overwhelming. She fixed upon a plan born of desperation. She, first, begged a morning of slumber the next day. Her two forbidding sisters -in-law agreed that Jane should have an interlude of rest. She slept late, slipping out from under the goose down covers well after John Bennett had risen and left for town with his brothers. Breakfast on the sideboard had grown cold, but Jane relished sitting at the expansive dining room table alone with her bowl of gluey oatmeal laden with coarse brown sugar. She loved oatmeal. The bacon, sausage and fried fish favored by the Windsors made her a touch queasy every breakfast time.

After breakfasting, Jane heated water and washed her hair. Next came, fresh underclothing, laundered by Giselle, a disapproving housemaid who seemed to hover upstairs for the purpose of making Jane feel clumsy and out of place. A new lavender dress, ordered from Atwell & Co., made Jane feel as well turned out as possible. She dried her long brown curls and tucked them into a pearly comb that had been a present from her mother on her sixteenth birthday.

Traversing the house on her way to the library, Jane almost turned back many times. Her father-in-law, Stuart, regularly urged her to partake of the family's diverse collection of books but what kind of a reception awaited her? Would the librarian let Jane walk away with the treasures she superintended? Jane didn't know what the sentiments of a librarian might be toward those who sought to remove books from her domain.

Not knowing how one gained admittance to the library, Jane

circled searching for an entrance. She finally located a wide door so well hung that the eye could barely discern the frame. The library door, thick oak with a heavy brass handle, weighed and measured more than the other doors in the house. This door would withstand sleet and hail as well as the front doors that the architect designed to sustain actual assaults by those elements. Jane used both hands to grasp the handle, turn it, and shove open the portal to the Windsor family's storehouse of history, literature and languages.

"I've been wondering when you would get here!" came a throaty voice with a trace of laughter affixed to every syllable.

Jane's eyes searched for the speaker but the light from the high clear windows momentarily blinded her. The windows must be angled in such a way that they did not trap the drifts of snow from winter storms. When Jane's vision cleared, she could see clouds and Sierra light high above.

"Who might you be?" called Jane, not recognizing the bold voice that addressed her. Jane's vision cleared before the speaker could reply and there stood the librarian.

"Hello. We've barely met so let me introduce myself. I am Ursula Smith, Librarian. My rooms are in the library's southernmost corner, and I never take meals at the family's table. So I've not yet had the pleasure of a profound conversation with you, Jane Copley Windsor. Well, better late than never, as Livy first observed. Welcome to my provenance."

Jane could only nod. Ursula held out her hand and waited until Jane slipped a small white hand into the sinewy but graceful one proffered.

The librarian's rose-red lips curled up at the corners as if she had discovered some secret bit of humor that permanently affected her countenance. Miss Smith's brilliant blue eyes flashed with obvious mischief. Jane had never known a woman who shook hands or, for that matter, a woman who exhibited such natural vigor.

"What can I do for you?" asked Ursula, balancing on one foot and then another within her closely silhouetted black dress, as if enjoying the motion of her own lithe body.

"I..." Jane stumbled. She experienced a strange intuition

that the librarian's question pertained to something more than reading material. Jane felt as though Ursula could help her in some way if she could only fix upon how to solicit the librarian's assistance.

"I came for something to read," said Jane. While she usually worried that people would think her a "harum-scarum young woman" as her mother used to say, she faced the opposite problem now. She felt as though she were being overly proper and priggish, in the eyes of the librarian and, indeed, Ursula responded with a broad grin.

"You're a reader then? That's more than I can say for the other two."

"The other two?" Jane didn't understand what she meant. "The other two wives. They make an uninspiring duet do they not?" Ursula laughed irreverently.

Jane stood rooted in horror at the woman's audacity. She hadn't even acknowledged to herself how greatly and how often her new sisters-in-law oppressed her. Eleanor and Julia Windsor counted as kin now. She should guard against granting even tacit approval to the librarian's impertinence and disrespect.

"I love to read," Jane replied in an earnest tone that brooked no further lapses in decorum. "Can you recommend a book that I might borrow to pass the time these chilly afternoons?" Ursula's smile shifted to an expression of deep concentration. The woman seemed to take a request for one of her volumes with great seriousness. Wheeling, the librarian commenced walking briskly across the room. Palms out, Ursula laid her hands upon the glossy light wood of the wall. The outline of a door appeared and, as Jane watched, the door became a reality and swung open on noiseless but real hinges. Ursula signaled Jane to follow.

They circumnavigated many shelves laden with beautiful leather-bound volumes, some of which matched, others that must have been chosen on an individual basis. Occasionally, the shelves exhibited pieces of art, including artifacts that Jane couldn't even begin to name. Near the statue of a Greek woman with long wavy tresses and lascivious flesh, Ursula halted. The librarian slid a narrow ladder on oiled gears to the spot she had chosen and climbed halfway up the wall, reading the lettering on the spines of the books.

"Are you partial to the work of Mr. George Sand? The French author who wrote *Lelia and The Haunted Pool*?" asked the librarian.

"I've read *Indiana* and I liked that piece of work very much, although there were those in the congregation of my church at home in Scotland who found the subject matter too indelicate for a woman to read."

"Ha!" laughed Ursula. "How droll. You see, Mr. George Sand is one of the gentle sex. She's one of us, Jane. And here's a book she wrote for you!" Ursula handed her a thick pamphlet entitled simply, *Marie*. "You won't find this missive in any other library in California," Ursula promised.

"Why, thank you, Miss Smith."

"You may call me Ursula," replied the librarian. "And I refuse to call you Mrs. Windsor." Ursula swung off the stairs so that her layers of skirts flared to reveal bare feet and ankles. Jane averted her eyes. Jane must have surprised the librarian before she had finished with her morning ablutions.

Seemingly oblivious to Jane's embarrassment, Ursula strode to a cabinet hewn from a glossy variety of wood, orange in hue with many knots, that Jane didn't recognize. Unlocking the compartment, Ursula extracted another book. This was a slim volume with a blue ribbon and peculiar seal.

"Take this book also. I would like you to read it. Pray don't let any of the others set their eyes upon it, however." Ursula stood back, appraising Jane.

"Hide something from John Bennett?" Jane asked, startled.

"That's right. You wouldn't want me chastised, would you?"

"Oh, no," gasped Jane. "I'm sorry, Ursula. I will put this book in my chest of drawers and read the piece at night after John Bennett leaves to visit the Stag's Horn." Ursula gifted Jane with another bright, almost giddy, smile. "Should I send word by one of the maids before I visit here again?" Jane asked.

"Certainly not!" exclaimed Ursula. "Never hesitate to visit

me and the library. You and I are going to be the closest of friends. I have a feeling that you're the one for whom I've been waiting since the day I accepted this post."

Not knowing what she should say in response, Jane clutched the books in both hands, nodded, and ran.

CHAPTER FIVE

The next morning as the sun rose over Mount Diablo and began to warm Blackhawk, Lesley awoke filled with both dread and exhilaration. She sensed the possibility that what awaited her at Deerhaven Forest Hall might change her life. Would the change be for the better or worse? Michael had never come home the night before. The bedclothes on his side of the bed remained tucked.

Sipping coffee in her tidy kitchen, Lesley stared at the proscribed backyard that came with a Blackhawk home, seeing instead a Sierra forest. She should be preparing for this trip but the task presented difficulties. Michael hadn't been clear about how long Lesley would be expected to stay, and he'd never conveyed a hint about his family's lifestyle. Lesley didn't even know how to dress, casual or formal. The only thing that seemed clear was that she needed to explain Ryan's absence from school. When the clock over the stove read eight, Lesley picked up the phone and called the school's office manager. When nagging anxiety forced her feet in circles, she placed another call.

"Pauline? I know you're getting everyone ready for school, but I want to tell you something."

"Lesley! You sound tired," replied Pauline.

"Michael's mother died yesterday," Lesley told her friend. "He didn't take it very well." She summoned a wife's loyalty and continued in a more traditional vein. "Michael's quite grief-stricken. Anyway, he wants us to visit his family and help with funeral arrangements."

"He wants you to meet his family? Now?" Pauline exclaimed in surprise.

Lesley winced at how clearly eccentric her family must seem to her friend. "Yes. He's reversed everything he ever told me about their feelings toward me. I'll explain when I see you. Meanwhile, we're leaving for Deerhaven Forest Hall, that's the name of his family's cabin in the Sierras. I'm going to take off as soon as I get Ryan up and give him breakfast." Lesley didn't stop to explain that she didn't feel eager to face her husband in whatever state he might be in this morning.

"And Michael's going with you?" asked Pauline, her tone conveying that she was still floundering over the change in family dynamics.

"No," Lesley admitted. "He says he can't leave town because of a major conference he's spearheading."

"Oh, my God! You're going to meet his family without him?" Pauline's voice trailed away as if she were remembering that she should be circumspect about Michael's habits and actions. By defending him these past years, Lesley had given Pauline the message that discussing Michael was off limits.

"I called the office at Del Mar School, but could you talk to Ryan's teacher for me?"

"Sure," answered Pauline.

After a pause, Lesley said, "Pauline, if I ask you a favor will you not give Dan the impression that I think Michael is unstable?" Pauline's husband worked at the Lawrence Laboratory also, as a department supervisor.

"Sure, Lesley. I'll be discreet. What is it?"

"Could you find out from Dan whether the conference that Michael told me about is for real?"

"I'll take care of it," said sturdy, faithful, Pauline and asked no more questions.

"One last favor?"

"Name it," answered Pauline.

"If we're not back soon…" Lesley began and then hesitated. What would their prolonged absence imply? "I'll call and tell you what's going on or you might call me. Here's the number at Michael's family home. I got it off a phone bill years ago. You have the number. Probably you should wait until I call you. The rest of the Windsors could be as…well, as reserved as Michael."

Pauline knew what Lesley meant to say. She would be counting on Pauline to send help if she and Ryan got waylaid. Pauline knew enough about Michael to question what might be waiting at his family's home. Lesley gave her friend the address of the house for good measure.

"Are you sure you want to do this, Lesley?" asked Pauline, sounding strained. "You take care of yourself and Ryan."

"I'll do my best," promised Lesley. "I'll talk to you soon."

"Keep your cell phone charged," ordered Pauline and they hung up.

Should she have allowed herself to say more? The weight of handling Michael's aberrant emotional life grew more intense every day. She didn't know if she felt ready to admit what she suspected, that her marriage to Michael would have to end. No, not today, not with Michael driven by grief over the death of the mother from whom he'd been separated all these years. But someday.

After eating Cheerios and packing bags, Lesley and Ryan drove away from Blackhawk in their white Lexus van, a variation on the vehicle driven by every Blackhawk parent.

"Where are we?" Ryan asked in awe as they mounted Altamont Pass. "Are those windmills?" Lesley explained that the windmills were a source of power for the Bay Area. He knew nothing about such things since Michael never let them stray this far from home. Thick fog eddied over the pass, pushed by a wind from the valley beyond, impeding the car's progress. Lesley entertained her son with light local history, since he'd developed a taste for fanciful tales.

"A great battle occurred on this pass, according to Native Californians. Psychics say that the ghosts of warriors who were killed still appear sometimes. They scare drivers into veering off the road, or so they say."

"I thought it was something like that," said Ryan with childlike acceptance of an alternate reality. "There was a man in the fog waving to us. Then, he wasn't there. He was wearing feathers and strips of fur."

Lesley gripped the steering wheel tighter. Since when did Ryan imagine things like this? She hoped his terrible nightmares would remain at bay but Ryan's fog-induced vision didn't seem like a good omen.

"The crown of the hill and the heavy fog make this place look like a good spot for an alien spaceship to land, don't they?" Lesley joked. Ryan smiled and nodded, but Lesley could tell that he was thinking about the indigenous soldier in the fog.

They stopped at several historical markers and then ate a pancake lunch in a small farm town bounded by a bend in the highway. After purchasing Big Red gum to keep their ears from popping, they headed toward the mountains. Because the month was November, not many tourists joined them on the road even though this route dead-ended at Yosemite National Park. Trucks loaded with winter vegetables or bales of hay rumbled in the slow lane. A few cold-weather campers, a group that didn't dress as well as skiers, sped past.

Deerhaven Forest Hall, that house with the cumbersome name, lay beside the Stanislaus River, high in the Gold Country. Lesley liked the terrain. Mariposa pines and mighty redwoods ringed silvery-green meadows crisscrossed with small silver streams. Resting in the forest and next to the river, boulders with veins of quartz, like diamond necklaces, glittered. They pulled over and slogged down to the water where they spied beads and globs of ore, beautiful to look upon, the color of dreams. Lesley explained that bangles of gold lay submerged in the streams and rivers, waiting to excite the eye of the greedy. Then, she told him the composition of fool's gold and that the mineral bore no relation to the booty that drew miners from the East. The hills around Deerhaven Forest Hall still hid real gold but no one knew where.

The trip to Deerhaven Forest Hall required that travelers from the San Francisco Bay Area adapt rather than endure. The trip didn't last long but the high Sierra foothills bore little similarity to suburban Danville. When Lesley and Ryan stopped for drinks in the tiny hamlet of Wolf's Creek that, on Michael's map, looked like the nearest town to Deerhaven Forest Hall, excepting a tiny spot marked "Deerhaven Pines," they breathed wilder, less civilized air.

Resuming their drive, Lesley and Ryan passed resort housing and skiers' cabins until they came to the cluster of upscale services, which turned out to be Deerhaven Pines. A green and white sign announced that the surrounding woods bore the same name. Lesley rolled down the window so they could enjoy the piney fragrance. Within minutes, they came to a paved forest lane marked "Deerhaven Forest Hall Road, Private Property, Trespassers Will Be Prosecuted." Lesley signaled the turn with trepidation, feeling like a trespasser, wondering if they would be welcomed or run off with a shotgun.

Ryan grew silent as they sailed under tall trees laden with needles browned by the long year. When they drew up to artfully rendered but sturdy wrought iron gates, woven into a mosaic that made the house a fortress, Ryan gasped. He swiveled in his seatbelt, turning to Lesley.

"Is that where Daddy grew up? How did he get out of there?" Ryan cried.

"They open the gates when someone wants to get out," Lesley told him in a reassuring tone. As she spoke, an older man in a plaid flannel coat emerged from what looked like a gatehouse and held up his hand in a "halt" gesture. When Lesley stopped the car, he came to the driver's side window.

"Good morning, madam and sir," he greeted them, removing a thick flannel cap with earflaps. "If you identify yourself and state your business, I'll be happy to admit you." He spoke with a slight British accent, as if recruited for his position from a Brontë novel. From what kind of a place did Michael come?

"Is this Deerhaven Forest Hall?" asked Lesley, hoping she'd come to the wrong place.

"I'm William Roe. I work for the Windsors, and my father before me worked for the family too." He waited for her to respond.

"I'm Lesley Windsor and this is my son, Ryan. I've come to join my husband's family for Cosette Windsor's funeral."

William Roe peered at her and then studied Ryan. His creased, liver-spotted face broke into a beaming smile.

"The boy's the spitting image of his father. We'll have you up to the house in no time, Mrs. Windsor," he promised.

"Please call me Lesley," she began, but he was already halfway to the cabin that housed whatever mechanism opened the gates. The gates glided open and she guided the car through and down the drive. Before yesterday, Michael could have sprung from any kind of dwelling and now this!

Judging by the name, Lesley expected Deerhaven Forest Hall to combine elements of the John Muir House in Martinez and the Ahwanee Hotel in Yosemite but the actual structure resembled nothing Lesley had ever seen. This example of Victoriana could not be called typical by any stretch of the imagination. The height and complexity of the rises, roofs and crenulated roof befitted a city house not a forest dwelling. A strange white beam seemed to emanate from the sky onto the housetop although the light might just as easily have originated within the house, shooting skyward. A Frank Lloyd Wright color scheme made the house appear to have been constructed from natural elements, not a characteristic of its architectural period.

"Daddy's house is pretty," Ryan commented in awe, "and bigger than anybody else's."

"This is quite an adventure," Lesley agreed.

They left the car under a stand of tall pines rather than usurping space in the garage, or maybe to make a quick getaway if necessary, and trod the driveway hand in hand to a door the color of forest loam.

When Ryan pressed a button adorned by an engraved brass plate reading "Windsor," they heard a gong sound deep within the recesses of the house. Ryan stood at Lesley's side, staring at a brass knocker shaped like a deer's head. He looked like a baby crow confronting the first shiny object in his experience and his gray eyes grew large and dark with anticipation when the door began to quiver.

A regal white-haired lady wearing a flimsy white robe trimmed with white satin answered their ring. Lesley felt herself blush when she realized that she'd roused the woman, probably the housekeeper, from her bed. The entire household would be upset by the recent death within these walls. No wonder that the woman in white chose to sleep late. Before Lesley could apologize for the intrusion, however, a serene smile lit the pale lady's face.

"You must be Ryan," she exclaimed in a slight but melodious voice. "I'd know you anywhere. Come in, both of you."

"Thank you," Lesley responded, squeezing Ryan's hand.

"You must be Lesley," said their hostess. "I've waited so long to meet you." Another incandescent smile from the drowsy woman gave Lesley the impression of great warmth despite her colorless aspect.

"And you are?" Lesley asked.

"I am Cosette Windsor," the woman introduced herself. "I'm your grandmother, Ryan, darling."

She turned, indicating that they should follow, and Ryan plunged into the darkness of the foyer, following in his grandma's wake.

"Ryan, no! Ryan, come back!" Lesley called. She ran into the house, pursuing her son and her dead mother-in-law.

Inside the huge dimly lit foyer, Lesley froze like a deer in a gun's sights and considered her options. Multiple exits from the entryway presented themselves and choosing between three different doors confused Lesley for a moment. When a startled exclamation issued from the left, Lesley's paralysis lifted. She bolted through the leftmost door and toward the sound.

Down a hallway paneled in somber wood, Lesley sought her child. Several more dark doors presented themselves, but she chose her way by intuition. When she burst through a mahogany swinging door, a commodious kitchen lay before her. Lesley observed a dizzying profusion of copper cookware, dried spices and foodstuffs but the room was empty of people. A set of hinges creaked far across the kitchen and Lesley guessed that Ryan might have been spirited through that door.

On the other side, Lesley found a work area or pantry, lined with polished counters laden with cooking receptacles, a utilitarian place. The door on the opposite side lay open and led to a dining room. Darting around a freestanding serving cart, Lesley jogged into a huge formal banquet room. Portraits adorned the walls but Lesley didn't stop to look at them. Tall candelabra decorated a table large enough to seat thirty.

"Ryan!" called Lesley. That she'd allowed him to be stolen by a white phantom, claiming to be his deceased grandmother, appalled her more as the seconds sped by. Where was her son? What would she tell the police if she didn't find him? Heart pounding, she pressed onward.

Just beyond the dining room, a gleaming parquet floor under a domed ceiling marked the area as a ballroom or convention place. Two broad hallways connected at this terminal point in the house. A sixth sense guided Lesley to the right. With no further regard for propriety, she threw open the door to each room she passed. Four doors down the hall, in a morning room decorated with laces and delicate china, Ryan sat on a fragile stool, which was decorated with a filmy skirt. His concerned expression cleared when he spotted Lesley in the doorway. He rose and ran to her.

"Grandma wanted me to come with her, but I waited for you catch up," said Ryan.

"Where did Grandma go?" asked Lesley. The bright feminine room, filled with bric-a-brac, reflected an owner with a lively mind. Was the owner gone for good? Was this Cosette's room in life?

"Grandma said that our ancestors were calling and she had to go talk with them," Ryan reported. "Meeting me made her happy," he added.

"Oh, Ryan," gasped Lesley. She sank to her knees and

drew her gray-eyed boy into a fervent embrace. Ryan put his arms, thin but strengthened by hours of schoolyard ball games, around her shoulders. The bizarre events surrounding their arrival at Deerhaven Forest Hall exacerbated Lesley's normal level of anxiety, the high-anxiety person she'd become when she lost both her parents so suddenly. Lesley struggled to restrain herself from clutching Ryan too tightly. When she found herself alone, she knew she'd be tempted to take the medication that her physician prescribed for times of stress.

"Hello, there!" called a woman's voice, not sweet and whispery like Cosette's, but clear and sprightly. Lesley turned to see a young woman lounging in the doorway. Like a fairy tale princess, she flaunted skin as white as snow, cheeks as red as roses, and wavy hair as black as coal. A cordial smile from the woman reassured Lesley that she bore them no ill will. Her beautifully textured flesh and mundane everyday garments seemed quite substantial, nothing ghostly about this attractive person.

"Hello, I'm Lesley Windsor and this is my son, Ryan. We..." Lesley faltered and then concluded with, "We let ourselves in."

"Well, you're entitled," the woman replied, her mouth curving at the corners with some inner amusement. "You can't enter this house unless you're entitled or invited."

What strange wording, thought Lesley. She redoubled her hold on Ryan.

"Who are you," she inquired.

"I'm sorry. I assumed you'd know me. I'm Sula."

"Do you live here? Or work here?"

"Both," said Sula as though the answer were self-evident. She didn't dress like someone employed as a domestic worker, but who could tell with a family as strange as the Windsors?

"What is it that you do?" asked Lesley.

"I'm the librarian," replied Sula. "The Windsors maintain a large, private library of local history material and artifacts. I'll take you on a tour once you've settled in. There's nothing like visiting the library to help you see the point." She had an odd way with words, but the librarian was so pretty and winning that Lesley trusted her.

"I'd love to see the library," Lesley responded. Ryan, hiding behind Lesley's skirts, smiled at the librarian and then ducked his head again.

"See me. Anytime," Sula instructed. "Would you like to meet your father-in-law? Russell has been lying down since last night but he rang for tea about half an hour ago. I think he might be feeling better."

"Thank you, Sula," Lesley answered with gratitude.

Sula ushered Lesley and Ryan to a comfortable parlor furnished with sofas, chairs and a television.

"Wait here. I'll have the housekeeper, Mrs. Woolf, fetch Russell," said Sula.

Soon, an older lady, Mrs. Woolf presumably, appeared with an elderly gentleman in tow. Without offering an apology or introduction, she shoved the old man into an armchair and snatched his feet off the ground, propping them on an embroidered footstool. Lesley stared at the old man in wonder. Russell Windsor resembled her husband so strongly that Lesley would have recognized him anywhere.

"I'm the Windsor's housekeeper," the thick-muscled, squint-eyed woman allowed with a grudging air. "You can call me Mrs. Woolf."

Ryan huddled against Lesley, silent, eyes wide. Lesley saw that her father-in-law didn't seem to notice the housekeeper's unpleasant behavior. He stared into space as though waiting for someone else to arrive.

Mrs. Woolf's lip curled. "He can't help you much. I'm sure you understand," pronounced the housekeeper without any show of sympathy.

"Is my brother-in-law, Kelvin, at home?" Lesley asked. "He's phoned on a regular basis to tell us about Mrs. Windsor's condition."

"You must have been worried something terrible," Mrs. Woolf snapped in a biting, sarcastic tone. "She lay there week after week asking to see her grandson but no! You wouldn't allow it. Michael's told me how cold you are. Well, she's dead and never seen her grandchild. I will do my duty and turn the house over to you, but I will not pretend to like it. I despise turning her house over to you. There, I've spoke my piece. Don't think you can fire me, either. I go with the Hall. It's that kind of house."

Mrs. Woolf sucked a gusty breath through her teeth. Ryan whimpered.

"You talked with Michael? Recently?" Lesley asked, faint with tension but determined to respond.

"Of course. I talk with Michael every time he comes," Mrs. Woolf replied, eyes gleaming with spite.

"Could you remind me when Michael last slept here?" inquired Lesley. Pride prevented her from asking other questions.

"Only a few weeks ago," snorted Mrs. Woolf. "Don't you and he talk at all?"

"I got confused. I'm very tired," explained Lesley. Her mind reeled.

"You Bay Area folk lead hectic lives." Mrs. Woolf spat the words. "Probably don't know whether you're coming or going from one day to the next."

"Where are you from?" Lesley asked to divert her.

"I was raised in Wolf's Creek, but I'm not going back there. This job is mine and I intend to stay. The last Mrs. Windsor made me a promise."

"Why, certainly," Lesley murmured.

The housekeeper didn't look appeased. "I have honest work to do. You keep your eye on him," ordered Mrs. Woolf, pointing to Russell Windsor. "It's about time you looked after someone in this family."

"Ryan and I will take him to his room after we talk awhile," said Lesley, eager for the housekeeper to go.

A nasty smile played upon Mrs. Woolf's lips. "Take care not to speak ill of the dead. We get unusual visitors here at Deerhaven Forest Hall and they're easily offended. Now that Mrs. Windsor's passed on, she'll visit in spirit form if she chooses."

"She already has," exclaimed Ryan.

Lesley quieted her son with a glance but not before Mrs. Woolf's eyes began to gleam. "You've seen her? I never thought she'd be back so soon. Her last hours were hard."

"Ryan must be mistaken," said Lesley.

"It was my grandma," Ryan insisted. "She was very nice."

Mrs. Woolf emitted a throaty laugh. "So! You've met your grandmother already. Your mother can't keep you from her now. She'll come and go as she pleases," pronounced Mrs. Woolf and loped from the room in satisfaction.

"I've seen her today too," said a thin forlorn voice. "She told me to watch out for our children," reported Russell. "From where she dwells now, she can see that all three of our children may be in peril."

"Grandpa?" said Ryan, startled by the voice.

Three children? Lesley didn't dare question the number. Her father-in-law looked too frail to interrogate about anything, but she wondered what he meant. Russell lapsed back into a dazed state, and Lesley decided she should not tire him with introductions. Ryan took a seat beside his grandfather, and Lesley was surprised when the old man reached out and patted the boy.

When Ryan grew restless from sitting too long beside the subdued old man, Lesley plucked a copy of *Pride and Prejudice* off a bookshelf and read out loud. Although Russell Windsor's eyes didn't move, Lesley hoped her reading soothed the grieving old man. When Ryan's attention wandered at the end of Chapter Two, Lesley decided to seek her brother-in-law. She opened the door, calling, "Hello! Hello!" and eventually, a young woman in a neat black dress came in response.

"Is Kelvin Windsor home yet?" Lesley asked.

"Kelvin has gone into Wolf's Creek to do some shopping," said the houseworker, who asked to be called Lena. "He won't be returning soon because he has one of his political meetings at the Grange Hall this evening."

"Did he mention that he was expecting me?" Lesley asked, no longer sure of anything.

The household worker, a Latino woman of about twenty-five, cast down her eyes. "I don't know, ma'am."

"That's all right, Lena," said Lesley. "I can take care of myself and Ryan. Will you take Mr. Windsor to his room?"

With a nod, the maid helped Russell to his feet. The old man swayed but his gray eyes grew more resolute. "It's been good to meet you," he told her in a sweet voice. Lesley got a sense of his usual gentlemanly demeanor. "You have nice manners and a good reading voice. And my heart is lighter because you're with us, Ryan, my dear."

He stepped toward Lesley. "Cosette asked me to make sure that I placed this heirloom directly into your hands, Lesley. Mrs. Woolf covets the thing but it's yours by right." Russell fished in his pocket and drew forth a pendant on a chain. He held the clumsy necklace aloft until Lesley extended her hand. When Russell dropped the piece into her outstretched palm, Lesley felt a shiver of dread or exhilaration. She didn't know which.

"Thank you, Russell," said Lesley, "and I thank Cosette." She examined her gift. An intricate swirl, like a logo, highlighted the words, "Champion the Hue." Her least favorite of the family mottoes, Lesley thought. On the obverse side, Lesley found the figure of a running wolf. What should she do with the thing? She looked up to find Russell staring at her. Lesley forced herself to smile.

"What should I do with the necklace, Russell? Wear it or put it in a bank vault?"

"Cosette recommends that you consult Michael for the wisdom to use the necklace well," Russell reported. A small but peaceful smile came to Russell's lips. "I think you'll do well, dear. You don't seem like the woman Michael described. Michael is prone to present things in the bleakest possible light, and I think this is one of those instances. I'll see you in the morning."

"I'll take Mr. Windsor back to his room and sit with him for a while," promised Lena. "No need for you to trouble yourself on your first day here at the Hall." She led the old man away.

Each encounter left Lesley confused. Ryan gazed at her, waiting for direction. Although she felt glad that they'd been left to her own devices, Lesley realized that she didn't even know where they would be sleeping. Mrs. Woolf seemed inclined to offer hostility rather than hospitality. Ryan needed a short nap but where should he lie down? Lesley felt almost thankful when she spotted a shadow that reminded her of Cosette Windsor. When the shadow slipped along the wall, Lesley and Ryan followed the shade.

They arrived at a cheerful Victorian bedroom with southern light. The guide, who might have been Cosette Windsor, evaporated at the door. Inside, a large poster bed draped with a pink and blue wedding-band quilt awaited Lesley, and a trundle bed with a crazy quilt would be perfect for Ryan.

"Let's both take a quick nap," Lesley suggested. "When we wake up, we'll go into town. After we get something for dinner, we'll try to find Uncle Kelvin."

She tucked Ryan under the soft colorful quilt and lay down on the big bed. Ryan fell asleep but tension and worry overrode Lesley's fatigue. Her husband's lies, omissions and deceit, ran through Lesley's mind. She began by examining Michael's story that his family was so violently anti-Semitic that they could not accept a half-Jewish wife or a quarter-Jewish grandchild. None of them had suggested any such thing. They resented Lesley only because they believed that she'd shunned them. That Michael would use her heritage as an excuse to keep her away from his family confused and sickened her.

Next, she thought about Michael's portrayal of his upbringing. He'd always billed himself as an unloved younger son in a crumbling old house in the woods. No detail of Michael's story corresponded to reality. Michael's family seemed attached to him, and this house could only be described as a magnificent estate.

Who knew what other "discrepancies" would surface? Russell's reference to a sibling never mentioned by Michael suggested a new and outlandish falsehood.

Having saved the strangest thought for last, Lesley contemplated the woman who'd introduced herself as Cosette Windsor. Up until today, Lesley wouldn't have been able to say whether or not she believed in ghosts. Now, perhaps, she'd seen one. Either she'd gone crazy or ghosts existed, and Lesley knew she wasn't crazy. Unnerved but not insane. Therefore, she must believe in ghosts. Could the ghost of Cosette Windsor be a threat to her son? Lesley didn't think so, somehow, and she trusted her judgment enough to drift off to sleep.

Sleep proved hard to sustain in Deerhaven Forest Hall. Eerie screams woke Lesley and Ryan. The sounds came from above their heads, far enough away to be muted by distance and density. Darkness had fallen and enveloped the Hall. A madwoman in the attic, of course they would have a madwoman locked in their attic. Although she'd adjusted to the apparition at the front door, Lesley didn't relish meeting the screamer in the attic.

"What's that?" Ryan questioned her. "Does someone need help?"

We do, thought Lesley, but she remained calm for Ryan. "I think we should leave that up to Mrs. Woolf or Grandpa," she told him. "We need to leave for town so we can find Uncle Kelvin. Come along with me and don't stop no matter what you see."

"Is Grandma going to walk us to the door?" asked Ryan.

"I don't think so," Lesley answered.

Minutes later, Cosette Windsor's pendant thudded against her breastbone as Lesley fled from her husband's haunted house.

CHAPTER SIX

They departed Deerhaven Forest Hall through the wide front doors. Lesley walked to her van, staying only a pace behind Ryan. As she opened the van's side door to strap her son into his seatbelt, William Roe approached. The weathered gatekeeper carried a flat-edged shovel over one shoulder but looked as though he meant no harm.

"We're just leaving," said Lesley.

The man followed her to the driver's side, looking as though he intended to speak. The wrinkled corners of his mouth puckered into a smile. "How do you find things at the Hall?" he asked with the eagerness of a natural gossip.

Lesley knew and liked his type. The intimate details of other peoples' existences had provided hours of pleasure for Lesley's parents and their neighbors. Michael disapproved of expressing interest in one's fellow human beings and did not allow Lesley to engage in the tawdry habit of informal speech and casual talk.

"I met my father-in-law," replied Lesley. "He's quite tired though, from his ordeal. Ryan and I are heading to Wolf's Creek to track Kelvin down. He's attending a meeting at the Grange Hall."

Roe put down his shovel and took off his hat. Appearing to debate how much he should say, he cleared his throat. "I know Michael and Kelvin like they're my own boys. They went on many a trip into the woods with my oldest son, Brian, and me. Brian will be taking over for me when I'm so old I have to stay inside. You'll be able to depend on Brian, ma'am. He's solid as hardwood."

William Roe paused for breath, and Lesley tried to fashion a reply. Ryan laughed in amazement at the proliferation of words. "How nice that your son wants to fill your niche," Lesley answered.

"I just want to say that I'm glad Brian will be working for you. I'm glad you and Michael will be installed in the Hall. I'm not speaking against Kelvin himself, but I don't trust his associates. He always had bad taste in friends, even as a boy. Michael seems to have got lucky when he met you."

"Thank you," replied Lesley. "But I think you might be mistaken about the length of our stay. Ryan and I are only here until after the funeral. Michael will join us in a few days. Then, we'll be returning home."

William Roe, head tilted to one side, looked unconvinced. "A Mrs. Windsor always resides at the Hall," he told her with a trace of stubbornness shadowing his pleasant, husky voice. As if he'd settled the matter with this single statement, William Roe stepped back and motioned her to start the engine.

"Don't worry about living here, ma'am. It'll be a good life for you and your son. Let's all give thanks that Michael's the oldest son and has brought home such a nice family."

Michael, the oldest son? He'd told Lesley many times that his older brother, Kelvin, made his life miserable throughout his childhood. Lesley filed this glitch away with the rest of them.

"I'll be back before nine o'clock," said Lesley and backed away.

"Don't be out too late. The running of the Hall requires

time and attention. You'll see. Don't be worried about the acreage outside the Hall though. I'll assist you with whatever you need."

"That is kind of you," Lesley replied, too disoriented to argue. After closing the windows and locking the van's doors, she pivoted her car and headed toward the gates.

"Maybe he'll take me on a trip into the woods," Ryan commented as they cruised the long drive.

Lesley looked over at her son, sitting erect in his shoulder harness. Until now, Ryan would have cowered at the thought of entering dark trees. Her child's habitual fears seemed to be receding. She wished she could say the same for her own. Her thoughts drifted to the whereabouts of the pills she carried with her as a safety cushion. Had she packed them? Yes. She'd secured the pillbox in the outside pocket of her shoulder bag.

"I wonder how far into the woods we could go," mused Ryan, sounding untroubled by ghost or groundskeeper, "and still get back before dark."

"I don't know. You learn how to pace yourself," Lesley told him.

This time, as they passed through town, Lesley and Ryan admired Deerhaven Pines' Main Street. A beautiful hotel, combining elements of Victorian architecture with a more contemporary use of the setting's natural beauty and building materials, rose from behind a long autumn lawn suitable for crochet and gentle strolls. Everything in Deerhaven Pines looked upscale but not pretentious.

When they reached Wolf's Creek, their surroundings changed. Wolf's Creek advertised a population of 12,867 but Lesley couldn't imagine where most of the citizens lived. Inelegant wooden stores and one-story houses lined either side of Highway 72 that bisected the town.

Lesley stopped at Culpert's Grocery Store and, approaching a man at the register, explained that she and her son needed directions to the Wolf's Creek Grange Hall. The aproned man, wearing a knitted ski cap indoors, narrowed his tiny black eyes, assessing her and Ryan.

"You're looking to attend the Reverend's meeting?" he asked, nodding at his messy bulletin board. A banner draped above the other notices read PURITI in large block letters, and in small type, *People Unified in Repelling the Intrusion of Troublesome Influences*. The location and date followed, *Wolf's Creek Grange Hall, November 3rd. Protect the purity of your community—Champion the Hue. Dessert and coffee provided by Wolf's Creek Community Church, Reverend Cooper Were, Minister*. Lesley stood transfixed by the phrase she'd recited to Ryan just last evening, a Windsor family motto. She'd thought the phrase floated up from her own unconscious but now the words surfaced everywhere. "Champion the Hue," she murmured. Ryan sent her a quizzical look.

"Are you or aren't you on your way to the PURITI meeting?" the grocer demanded, his beady eyes hostile.

"Yes," replied Lesley. "I think so. Can you tell me what the phrase on the poster means? Champion the Hue? What is the Hue?"

"The Hue means what the Reverend believes in. The colors of the rainbow I guess. You just abide by what the Reverend says and don't ask questions. Why are you headed to the meeting if you need to question the Reverend's mission?"

"I'm looking for my brother-in-law, actually. Kelvin Windsor?" Lesley knew that in a community this small, the man behind the counter would probably know Kelvin. Sure enough, his face softened.

"Kelvin? Sure. He and the Reverend are thick as thieves. Pleased to meet you, Mrs. Windsor. I'm Ted Culpert. I know you folks at the Hall will most likely keep ordering your groceries from Barr's Provisionary over in Deerhaven, but please keep in mind that I'd happy to beat their prices. There's no reason I couldn't make deliveries to the Hall. Call me any time, Sundays, holidays, whatever."

His change in attitude made Lesley uneasy. "I'm afraid you've misunderstood, Mr. Culpert. I'm only visiting Deerhaven Forest Hall to attend my mother-in-law's funeral. My husband and I will be returning to the Bay Area afterward."

His tiny eyes narrowed until they disappeared along with the false smile he'd produced to punctuate his sales pitch. "Who will run the Hall if not you?" he asked. "Michael is the oldest son and you say you're his wife. Your place is at Deerhaven Forest Hall. You would have known that when you chose to marry Michael Windsor."

Lesley felt that he expected a comment on his statement.

"The family employs a housekeeper, a Mrs. Woolf," Lesley pointed out. "I'm sure she'll keep things up."

"There needs to be a Mrs. Windsor at the Hall," Mr. Culpert corrected her. "Cosette Windsor had grand ideas about eating, she never ordered from me, but she was a good lady and the Hall has been well run. You just try and live up to her standards."

"It's very touching that my husband's mother was so well-loved by the community," said Lesley, assuming that affection for Cosette Windsor must be why everyone seemed dead set on retaining her as the new Mrs. Windsor. The storekeeper put his hands in his pockets as though protecting them from the contagion of Lesley's foreign thought processes. Further conversation seemed futile. "Would you mind directing me to the Grange Hall?" Lesley asked. Ted Culpert threw up his hands and gave her street directions.

The Grange Hall, a huge wooden barn a few blocks from the highway, didn't turn out to be hard to locate. Lesley parked the van under tall pines and headed through a parking lot crowded with big-wheeled pickups, and large older cars decorated with bumper stickers that read, "Native Californian," "The Second Amendment Lives," and "Strive for PURITI." Held open by anvils serving as doorstops, the barn doors leaked heat. Lesley could feel the lost warmth dissipating in the chilly evening air. Men in cowboy boots and tight, faded jeans milled outside, drinking beer from aluminum cans or coffee out of Styrofoam cups.

"How will we know which one is Uncle Kelvin?" whispered Ryan.

"We'll ask somebody," Lesley whispered back.

Women in the lobby urged Lesley to sign the guest book, but she excused herself to look for Kelvin. He must be inside the sealed auditorium. Closed doors with steel push bars, like the ones at Ryan's elementary school, admitted only a gleam of light.

The crowd behind the doors gave a raucous cheer and then the group chanted something in unison. Ryan helped Lesley press the bar.

Inside the auditorium, she joined a huge, fractious crowd. Only a few women and children circulated among hundreds of men. Long tables bearing coffee and cookies lined the walls and ice chests filled with beer and soda cans rested underneath the nearest tables. At the front, six men sat behind a trestle table on an elevated stage. A tall man, dressed in black, stark as a deciduous tree in November, tapped the shiny head of a microphone to make it bark. The crowd fell quiet in a second's time.

"Good evening, sisters and brothers. Let us pray," the man began. Hands clasped in prayer, the congregation recited with him. "Let us entreat you, oh Father of Original Sin, to save our community from the blight that is blackening our souls and poisoning our children."

"Save our children from depravity!" the dark man thundered. "The devil lurks in every corner. We must be vigilant! May God have mercy on our souls and deliver us from evil."

Ryan clung to Lesley's hand. What was the nature of this congregation? If this was a prayer meeting, why didn't they meet at a church? The people on the floor began chanting, crying, and moaning.

"Let's leave," begged Ryan.

"All right," Lesley agreed. She took one last look around. "Ryan! Doesn't that guy up there on the stage look a lot like Daddy?"

Ryan craned his neck. "Is that Daddy?" he asked.

"No, honey. That must be Uncle Kelvin. People who are brothers sometimes look a lot alike." Her son had no experience with kinship. "We'll introduce ourselves soon," she promised. The tenor of the meeting discomfited Lesley enough that she led Ryan back into the lobby.

Outside the auditorium, Lesley looked for anything that might clarify the Reverend Were's mission. PURITI members glanced at her and Ryan without smiling. On a big bulletin board near the restrooms, Lesley spotted a poster headed, "PURITI=PURITY." Purity sounded ominous rather than agreeable in this context. A young blond man, too reminiscent of a Nazi Youth for Lesley's taste, smiled at her from the poster. A caption read, "Stamp out moral impurity in our community. Support old-fashioned family values. Goal: 100% PURITI Membership, Year 2002." Michael, registered as a Republican, could stomach phrases such as "family values" but Lesley mistrusted ambiguous jargon. The "family values" set in Blackhawk drove fancier cars than anyone else. Their cars sported fewer bumper stickers than those of this group, but their hostility toward those less privileged than themselves reminded her of the assembly in the Grange Hall tonight.

"Ryan, let's be careful what we say around these people. Remember, we don't know them yet."

"All right," Ryan agreed without question. A rhythmic chant in a minor key rolled down the corridor. "What's that?" Ryan cried. They returned to the main meeting room and found the PURITI members speaking in unison. Oddly enough, considering that Lesley felt no affinity with the group, their words echoed her own.

"Champion the Hue," the crowd recited. "Champion the Hue." What did this phrase mean?

"Uncle Kelvin?" she heard Ryan say. Looking up, she saw Michael's brother, coming toward them.

"You must be Lesley," he said. "And you're Ryan. I've seen pictures of you two. Nice to meet you. Why don't we head back to Deerhaven Forest Hall?"

Lesley opened her mouth to reply but she couldn't make a sound. The room swam and she fought for air. Champion the Hue! Champion the Hue!

"Why do they keep repeating the Windsor family motto?" Lesley gasped. The question seemed all-important.

Kelvin Windsor, his dark, handsome face knitted with concern, moved closer to Lesley and Ryan.

"They took the words from our family crest. The Windsors founded this community, and Reverend Were insists that members of the community live by the Windsors' creed."

Champion the Hue! The words overwhelmed Lesley's senses so profoundly that other thoughts choked in her brain.

Although she'd never fainted in her life, Lesley felt herself losing consciousness. Crying out to Ryan, her knees buckled, she sank to the floor, and everything went black.

CHAPTER SEVEN

From the comfort of an upstairs window seat in Deerhaven Forest Hall, Jane Windsor watched light snow fall. She'd finished *Marie* by George Sand only a few minutes before, and she needed time to savor the stimulating prose and novel ideas. After reviewing the pamphlet, a thought occurred to Jane. To acquire new reading material, she would need to venture into the library once again and face the formidable, the audaciously beautiful Ursula Smith. She shivered and pulled her shawl tighter around her shoulders.

What must the brilliant librarian think of her? As winter set in, Jane's sisters-in-law, Eleanor and Julia, had felt free to launch oblique but derogatory comments on Jane's shortcomings. "Do try to stand upright, Jane. Your spine will soften into that inferior posture if you let it do so. Look at how regally our mother carries herself," added Eleanor, always picture perfect.

"A lady should be able to instruct the servants in the preparation and serving of standard fare and French cuisine," supplied Julia upon discovering that Jane often sneaked into the scullery to steal herself a bit of food. "You can't allow your staff to have the upper hand in the kitchen. The Scottish diet is very plain, I've heard. Is that true, Jane? Perhaps you should spend a few days observing our butler, Mr. Collier, and surreptitiously acquire some of his skill. Just remember to be discreet, Jane, and don't let Collier start feeling superior. You'll never be the mistress of your own household if you cannot earn the respect of your servants."

Julia and Eleanor planned to marry and leave Deerhaven Forest Hall to run their husbands' homes. They both aspired to suitors with money and titles, and the family entertained prospective husbands on a regular basis. Only Jane, of the three women, would remain at Deerhaven Forest Hall and someday assume responsibility for running the house. Jane's heart sank at the idea. Being trapped inside the house so much of the time would be a fate worse than death.

"I must have something to read," she told herself. "I should not sit here and fret about what I cannot change." With that resolve, Jane picked up the pamphlet she'd borrowed from Ursula Smith and tried to remember the obstacle course that led to the library. Although she expected to get lost, Jane found her way with ease and arrived at the library door in only minutes.

Entering the library's vestibule, Jane took time to admire the seven lofty slices of ceiling and the strange bright windows. The library had been outfitted with furniture made from a glossy red wood that Jane had never seen in Scotland or America. The librarian did not appear at first so Jane roamed an aisle, reading and absorbing the gilt titles on the spines of the volumes. All the wisdom of the ages seemed to rest upon these remarkable red-hued shelves, Jane marveled. If only she could live here, under the sparkly panes, and fill herself with alluring words and newborn ideas.

"You've come back!" called a voice so vibrant that Jane recognized the speaker at once. She shaded her eyes and spied the tall, lithe form of the librarian, Ursula Smith.

"I've finished *Marie*," answered Jane, feeling insubstantial in contrast to the librarian. "I've brought it back. Thank you."

Miss Smith slipped closer to Jane. "Well?" the librarian asked, as if issuing a challenge. "Did you like it or not?"

Jane blushed. "Very much. I cannot thank you enough," she answered, ducking her head. She forced herself to raise her face and not cower in front of the librarian.

Miss Smith's face had fallen as though Jane's answer disappointed her. "Let me give you another work. Perhaps this next piece of writing will set your tongue afire. I do so look forward to literary discussion."

The librarian sped back into the catacombs and returned with a book bound in rich green Moroccan leather. Proffering the volume with both hands, Miss Smith's eyes never left Jane's crimson face.

"*Frankenstein*," Jane read from the cover. "Whatever could this be?" She knew John Bennett would not approve her partaking of subversive literature. The George Sand, she had hidden in her dressing table although she couldn't say why.

"Mary Wollenstonecraft Shelley has written a work which is both a monster story and a work of philosophy," explained Miss Smith. "I look forward to discussing the finer points, should you be so inclined."

Jane nodded, not wanting to commit herself with words. As she struggled to produce some small shred of conversation, Jane heard a fierce roaring, coming from a distance.

"They've returned," Ursula Smith uttered with a cry. "Will they ever cease plaguing us?" Miss Smith grabbed Jane's arm and pulled her into the maze of library shelving.

"Who's back? Who's here?" asked Jane, fingers gripping the borrowed book, her heart racing.

The two women, long-skirted but nimble, turned corner after corner until they entered a passageway that ended in a door to the outside. Jane hesitated. John Bennett would be angry if he heard she had left the house when she should have been taking part in the winter's domestic duties. Since cold had set in, John Bennett's tongue had developed a rough side. Instead of a gentle rebuke, Jane's transgressions provoked threats and lengthy humiliating remonstrations. Ursula's Smith's voice interrupted Jane's internal debate.

"Don't just stand there, Jane! You'll miss the excitement! You must seize this opportunity. A married woman during winter needs any stimulation she can get."

Jane had no time to wonder about the librarian's insinuation. Ursula's eyes, blue as a summer sky, sparkled with suppressed good humor. Choosing a midnight blue wrapper that made her blue eyes even more brilliant, Ursula unlocked the door. So lively and inviting was the librarian's demeanor that Jane grabbed boots and cloak and rushed outside in Miss Smith's wake.

"Not that way!" hissed Ursula, seeing that Jane meant to head for the front drive. The librarian led Jane down the snowy garden path and into thickets beaded with ice crystals. They emerged near the front gate where thick piney boughs screened them from sight.

Within their line of sight, a gaunt cleric holding a knotty stick aloft in prayer, led a crowd of unruly ranchers and miners amassed on the front gardens of Deerhaven Forest Hall. "The Lord is my shepherd," they began, "I shall not want." Jane felt her lips shape the twenty-third psalm with them until Ursula gave her a rude thump between the shoulders.

"Wait until you see what comes after this nice display of piety," Ursula whispered. "Don't be misled. Their leader is a man of iniquity and his followers not much better. Never let them into the Hall."

The minister encouraged his pack of worshippers to chant along with him as he finished his Bible verses and continued free form. "Save our children from darkness!" he screamed. The assembly answered with a scream and then the ministerial figure continued. "Depravity lurks in every corner. We must maintain a constant vigil to ward her away. May God have mercy on our souls and deliver us from the evil in our midst."

"What does he mean by salvation from darkness?" asked Jane, confused and fearful. "Does he fear the people who lived in these mountains before us? The ones with dark faces? I have heard them called Miwok."

"No," replied Ursula. "The Miwok are a kindly and hospitable people. Reverend Chaney hopes to convert them into Christians and, by the by, into cheap labor for his mines."

"To whom does he refer, then?" inquired Jane.

"A vague evil," Ursula answered. "Chaney claims he will reveal the particular face of evil when the time is ripe."

"Do the Windsors subscribe to Reverend Chaney's idea that the devil is loose in Deerhaven Pines?" inquired Jane.

The librarian's face grew graver. "The Windsors publicly endorse the Purity Party, as the Reverend calls his not-very-pure-minded group," the librarian replied in a cautious tone.

"Why would the Windsors associate themselves with Reverend Chaney?" asked Jane.

"Chaney wields a great deal of power," answered Ursula, her breath a spray of chiffon in the chill air. "The Windsors curry his favor in order to secure their standing in the community. Your husband's family has a great deal at stake. They have inherited the job of protecting something valuable and dangerous."

"I didn't know," whispered Jane. "What is it? What's hidden within the walls of Deerhaven Forest Hall?"

"Librarians have a sworn duty to answer any request for information but I cannot answer the one you just put to me. Each person must discover the secret of Deerhaven Pines for his or her own self." Her full red mouth twitched as if she were swallowing a smile as she spoke. "Still, I might perhaps dispense the merest hint." With these words, Ursula stepped closer to Jane.

What happened next, Jane could never remember with any clarity. Soft lips brushed Jane's cheeks, maybe they touched her lips. If she were to be honest, she would admit that her mouth sought the librarian's. Ladies kissed each other, of course, but this experience did not in any way replicate the pecks Jane had exchanged with family and friends. Jane did not feel awkward and clumsy the way she did in John Bennett's company. Her knees went weak and her cheeks blazed with queer warmth.

CHAPTER EIGHT

"Mommy! Mommy!" cried Ryan, his wails penetrating her unconscious.

Lesley opened her eyes. She lay on the floor of the Wolf's Creek Grange Hall. Michael's brother squatted at her side, slapping Lesley's wrist to revive her. Kelvin Windsor resembled Michael but his gray eyes were flecked with black, like coarsely ground pepper. Michael would have been cringing with embarrassment over Lesley's unbecoming lapse of consciousness, but Kelvin looked concerned.

"Are you ill, Lesley?" asked Kelvin.

"I can't imagine what came over me," said Lesley, although the minute the words came out of her mouth she wondered if hearing the phrase "Champion the Hue," could have overwhelmed her senses. Too prevalent in her life these last two days, the motto made her uneasy, almost sick.

"The altitude affects some people like this," suggested Kelvin.

"What's altitude?" asked Ryan, never a child to suppress a question. "Is it like attitude?"

"No." Kelvin smiled. "Altitude is the height of a place in relation to sea level. Coming to the mountains can make you giddy for a few days. But don't worry about it, Ryan. It usually doesn't bother kids."

"Are there bad altitudes?" asked Ryan. "Like bad attitudes?"

"No," Kelvin answered. "No connection." He put his arm around the boy's shoulders, and Ryan surprised Lesley by pulling away with a stiff formality. "You doing any better?" Kelvin asked Lesley.

"I'm fine now, thank you," Lesley told him, still sitting on the cold plank floor and brushing her slacks.

"What brought you to tonight's meeting?" Kelvin inquired. "I expected you to go straight to the house."

"We did," Lesley answered, eager to get acquainted with her newfound brother-in-law.

"Grandma met us at the door," supplied Ryan, stepping back to appraise his uncle's reaction.

"Ryan, cool it," said Lesley, "we'll talk about it later." The old woman at the door could have been anyone, perhaps a crazy person employed by the family. She hoped Kelvin would ignore Ryan's remark.

"Many things are possible at Deerhaven Forest Hall," said Kelvin, with ease. "My mother has always wanted to meet you, Ryan. That's probably why she came back so soon."

"So soon?" Lesley stuttered.

"In spirit," Kelvin replied, and said no more.

"I wish we'd known your mother when she was alive," Lesley told him.

Kelvin glanced at her with curiosity but asked no questions. Passersby stared at her as she sat on the floor with Kelvin and her son arranged around her. Lesley stood up and found herself feeling stable.

"I'm glad you're here now," Kelvin replied. "Having you join us will help."

"Your mother's memory lives on in the house and in her children," said Lesley, producing the only words of comfort that struck her as uncontroversial. Everything she considered saying took on a strange coloration because of their encounter with the lately deceased Cosette Windsor.

"Thank you for your sympathy," said Kelvin. "Let's get going. We shouldn't leave Dad much longer. I'll tell the Reverend Were that I'm cutting out early."

"Will the Reverend Were be conducting the funeral services for your mother?" asked Lesley.

Kelvin grimaced.

"No. Mother asked that Bill Patterson, pastor of the Sonora Unitarian Church, deliver her eulogy. When Mother attended church, that was where she went." Once again, Lesley did not feel inclined to ask follow-up questions. After explaining his departure to several men at the head table, Kelvin rejoined Lesley with the imposing, angular, dark minister at his side.

"Welcome to Deerhaven Forest Hall, Mrs. Windsor, young Mr. Windsor," said the Reverend Were in a sonorous tone. The Reverend held out a bony hand for Lesley to shake, and she resisted the temptation to put her hands behind her back. Ryan seemed to have no compunction and did that very thing. The Reverend stood with hand extended to the boy for several long seconds and then shrugged.

"I hope you and your son will consider taking an active role in the church and familiarize yourselves with the worthy goals of PURITI. Only with one hundred percent participation by community members can we eliminate the stain of evil in our midst."

Never had Lesley been around so peculiar an evangelist. "What evil are you talking about?" she asked, bolder than she would have expected.

"Undue and subversive influences, Mrs. Windsor. I recognize them when they appear. My job is to serve as watchdog for the congregation." The gobbledygook nature of his reply left Lesley with no response.

"Thanks for leaving the meeting to greet my sister-in-law," said Kelvin to break an awkward silence. "We'll let you get back now, Reverend." The minister gazed at Lesley and Ryan for a moment, nodded, and returned to his flock.

They decided that Lesley would follow Kelvin's Land Rover so she wouldn't risk getting lost in the darkness. Lesley and Ryan followed Kelvin out to the parking lot. The gathering twilight made Lesley nervous. When high-pitched squeaking noises and frantic motion broke out as they walked underneath a big oak, Lesley jumped and reached over to protect Ryan.

The unexpected distraction galvanized Kelvin Windsor. Without time for contemplation, Kelvin pulled a small but lethal-looking revolver from under his jacket. Aiming his pistol at the oak, he pulled the trigger and a shot rang out. Ryan screamed as a fat, brown squirrel fell dead out of the branches. The animal's tiny legs flailed in agony and then went still.

Lesley pulled her son away from the scene of violence. Once Ryan calmed down, Lesley would speak with Kelvin. She assumed that her brother-in-law would be upset about harming a small innocent nut-gatherer but, looking up from her distressed child, Lesley caught sight of something that made her freeze. A smile played on the lips of Michael's brother! Dismay overcame her. No one survives childhood without meeting a bully who delights in torturing small creatures but still Lesley was shocked to learn that her brother-in-law might be one. She looked again but Kelvin's face already conveyed appropriate concern, a civilized mask. Shaken, Lesley grasped Ryan's hand.

"Uncle Kelvin will take care of the little squirrel's body," Lesley told her son. "Let's hurry to the car, Ryan. It's getting cold."

"I'll go get a shovel from inside," said Kelvin in a kind and reasonable voice, "and give the poor creature a proper burial. Why don't you two wait in your car?" He sounded like the most solicitous of uncles. Lesley shelved her speculations about Kelvin's true nature until she found time to sort her thoughts. Years of accommodating Michael's depression and episodes of erratic behavior served to blunt Lesley's natural reaction to Kelvin's behavior.

By the time they left Wolf's Creek for Deerhaven Forest Hall, night shrouded everything. The mountains lurked behind clumpy shadows shaped like frightened people curled upon the ground. Lesley checked to make sure she'd locked the car doors and rolled the windows up. Forests, rocks, turbulent streams, unknown forces of nature had always menaced pioneers in the darkened Gold Country and Lesley and Ryan were tenderfoots unequal to the terrain.

At Deerhaven Forest Hall, Mrs. Woolf and Lena appeared to offer dinner or drinks to Kelvin. Each greeted Lesley and her son with a courtesy they'd not displayed earlier. On their earlier arrival, only Cosette had been truly welcoming. What was she thinking? Lesley must stop assuming that she'd met Michael's mother. Even though the popular belief in these parts seemed to substantiate the idea that Cosette had returned as a ghost, the woman had died yesterday. Lesley needed to keep her bearings. Up until now, dead was dead, as far as Lesley knew.

"I'll check on my father and see if he can join us," Kelvin told Lesley, speaking a little too fast. "I'll leave you in Mrs. Woolf's capable hands." Kelvin left with a nervous flourish of his hand. He no longer seemed comfortable with Lesley as though he knew he'd betrayed himself to her with that secret, sadistic smile that shouldn't have been there.

Mrs. Woolf gave no indication that she'd spoken with outright hostility only hours earlier. After learning that Lesley and Ryan had eaten only corn chips and fruit purchased at Culpert's Grocery Store this evening, the housekeeper brought Lesley and Ryan a supper of home-baked bread, cold fried chicken and marinated green beans. Lesley would not have expected the abrasive housekeeper to come up with such delicious fare. Ryan ate with relish but Lesley, discomfited by the day's events, made only a token attempt. When they'd finished, Lena appeared to remove their plates. The household functioned with efficiency in spite of Cosette's absence, Lesley noted.

"Father hasn't been able to sleep," announced Kelvin when he reappeared, leading a bleary Russell Windsor.

The older man's face beamed at the sight of Lesley and Ryan.

Lesley hoped that Russell's apparent sweetness didn't mask the same depravity she'd glimpsed on Kelvin's face. She needed to trust at least one person in the Windsor family.

"I'm so happy to see you," Lesley told her father-in-law with sincerity.

He still couldn't take his eyes off Ryan. "Another branch on the family tree," stated Russell. With this segue, Russell began entertaining Ryan with a child's-eye view of the family genealogy. Kelvin assisted when the old man's memory or energy flagged. Ryan interjected the occasional question to clarify a date or establish his relationship to a historical personage. Russell reminded Lesley of Michael during their courtship, kind and confiding, almost what Lesley would describe as innocent. Kelvin Windsor seemed benign in this setting. Kelvin's cold-blooded murder of a small, furry creature seemed almost unreal.

"Dad has a scrapbook with reprints of newspaper articles that concern the family," said Kelvin, the pace of his speech slowed by a liberal infusion of brandy. "There are quite a few sites on the Internet that concern our family and Deerhaven Forest Hall. Technology is so amazing. Total strangers all over the world have access to our secrets and our history."

Why did I never think to look on the Internet for information about Michael? Lesley thought. She knew the answer, of course. She used to trust her husband. Russell's meandering family history began to lull Lesley to sleep, and she listened less closely.

"The San Francisco *Alta California* ran an article on September 19, 1852 which profiled our relative, Nathaniel Tinsley, who built the first suspension bridge over Wolf's Creek," Russell recalled. "You can still find the remains of the bridge, spanning the wild waters at the far boundary of Wolf's Creek, near where the creek separates the town from Deerhaven Pines. Two granite disks that Tinsley left imbedded in a black oak near the water used to have great significance to our family. I can't remember what the significance is, though."

****

Russell took an imperceptible sip from his snifter. Ryan snuggled against Lesley.

"I'll take Ryan to see that bridge while we're here," Lesley promised Russell. He beamed at the two of them. "Maybe we can figure out what the disks mean to our family."

"Cosette will be so pleased that you're finally taking an interest," Russell murmured, his eyes blinking back tears.

Lesley felt the impulse to defend herself, but she exercised restraint. She rose and asked permission to phone home, explaining that her cell phone and laptop didn't work around Deerhaven Forest Hall. Michael hadn't answered any of her calls.

"He's probably still entertaining visitors to the conference. I'll call him in the morning," Lesley told his family. She would have loved to call Pauline, but she didn't want to be overheard questioning Michael's whereabouts.

"You must be tired, Father. I'll call Mrs. Woolf," said Kelvin.

"I'm hoping your mother will visit me in my room," mumbled Russell, attempting to rise. "I'll be waiting."

"Yes," Kelvin answered. "You wait in your room and get some rest." He turned to Lesley. "Lena will show you and Ryan to your room. She'll make sure you have all the comforts of home."

Lena led Lesley and Ryan to a bedroom that, she assured Lesley, had been thoroughly cleaned and outfitted with the house's best linen. A fire had been lit in the bedroom to ward away the chill. Before the housemaid departed for the night, she offered to bring a hot toddy for Lesley and a cup of hot chocolate for Ryan, but Lesley couldn't wait to be alone with her son.

"Ring if there's anything you need, Mrs. Windsor," said Lena. "You'll find a pull cord in your bedroom that sounds in my room." Lesley didn't envy Lena her job. After Lena departed, Lesley turned the brass stick key to lock the door.

A huge, canopied bed with white lace bed linens occupied the center of the room. Not Michael's style. Ryan fell asleep in a child's sleigh bed under an eastward-facing window, just his style. Kissing her sleeping child's rosy face, Lesley pulled the shade aside and peered out into the chilly darkness. A radiant moon illuminated the sky so that Lesley could make out the tree line and even follow the movements of a nocturnal animal leaping into the woods. In the distance, the forbidding treacherous Sierras, with their snowy peaks and passes, angular and layered, subsumed the landscape.

Lesley unpacked flannel pajamas and also a beautiful embroidered cotton nightgown. She'd packed for any eventuality. The blue striped pajamas would have served her well this cold evening but Lesley folded her traveling clothes and put on the white gown instead. Dimming the lamp by her bedside, she slipped under the heavy covers and lay with eyes open, thinking about the Windsors. A roar from outside made her think about the wind, a "torrent of darkness among the gusty trees," a line she'd memorized in elementary school although she couldn't remember the rest of the poem.

The wind created a tidal hum among the tree boughs and eventually lulled Lesley toward sleep.

Owwwhh! A long, anguished wail interrupted the sounds of night in Deerhaven Forest Hall. Ryan stirred in his sleep. Could that unearthly sound be Russell, thought Lesley. Keening his loss? No, the sound must have come from a woman's throat.

Slipping out from under the sheets and goose down comforter, Lesley made for the armoire to get her dressing gown. Another terrible prolonged scream stopped her in her tracks. Ryan moaned. Both times, the sound issued from right over their heads. Lena had described the rooms above as attic storage space.

"The attic attracts rats and squirrels no matter how often we fumigate," Kelvin had mentioned in passing. "Don't be frightened if you hear scratching or thumping. It's just rodents hiding from the cold." Unmindful of ghosts or relatives, Lesley felt drawn to seek the source of the wild lamenting.

"Ryan," Lesley called softly. She couldn't leave her son alone in a strange house. The boy turned over and lay still.

"I'll sit with him, my dear," came a voice, calm, thin, sweet. Lesley whirled. Cosette Windsor stood by the door, dressed in floor-length nightclothes, hands folded. Ryan's grandmother looked younger, by a good ten years, than when she'd greeted them at the front door earlier in the day.

"But you aren't really here," Lesley faltered. "It would be like leaving him alone."

"He's not alone as long as I'm with him," promised Cosette.

Owwwhh, came the long, sad shriek. In that instant, Lesley made a decision she would never have foreseen. She decided to trust the ghost of Cosette Windsor.

"I'll be back in a few minutes," cried Lesley as if leaving instructions for a living babysitter. Rushing for the door, Lesley felt Cosette pass her, heading for Ryan's bedside. Lesley turned the key in its spindle and left her sleeping son protected by the spirit of his grandmother.

The sconces in the hall, turned down for the night, shone dully. Lesley's abbreviated house tour hadn't included the entrance to the attic floor but instinct guided her. A left turn took her into a hallway where she found a guest bathroom, a linen closet, the upstairs laundry and finally, the stairway that must lead to the upper story. Taking a deep breath for courage, Lesley raced up the stairs.

"Lesley!" called a low, musical voice from the landing. Halfway up the first rise of stairs, Lesley turned. The beautiful librarian, Sula Smith, stood at the bottom of the steps.

"Will you come with me, Sula? I heard someone crying in the attic!" Lesley continued mounting the stairs.

"I'm not allowed above the second floor," Sula called. "And you can't go up either. A terrible disaster awaits any woman who goes too far up the stairs in Deerhaven Forest Hall. My mother assured me that I would be in peril should I tread those stairs, and my mother never lied."

"Then I'll go. I'll be fine. Wait for me there."

A woman's cry issued once again from the floor above. They must really have a madwoman stashed in the attic, thought Lesley. As if the presence of ghosts weren't enough of an oddity. *I hope she doesn't turn out to be Russell's first wife, confined all these years above his head. Or Michael's first wife,* she thought, *living here among his family.*

"Lesley, come back!" Sula implored. The librarian sounded

perturbed, desperate to force Lesley back. Gathering courage, without knowing why, Lesley hurried her steps.

"I'll be down when I've made sure whoever's up there doesn't need me," Lesley exclaimed, as she lost sight of Sula's upturned face. The pendant hanging from her neck took on a life of its own, throbbing like a human heart ripped from a still living body. Lesley sensed the pendant giving her the strength to face whatever lay upstairs. It wanted her to proceed.

At the top of the stairs, Lesley grasped the oversize antique doorknob. The door was locked. Panting, Lesley leaned against the door to catch her breath and think. At this slight pressure, the heavy oak door slid open with no noise or friction. Lesley waited for her eyes to adjust to the Sierra moonlight streaming in through a rent in the clouds and spilling onto the plank floor under dome windows in the roof. When she regained her vision, Lesley flicked on lights shaped like candles in dim old-fashioned sconces.

She looked around and saw an entry hall, outfitted like a doctor's waiting room. The place struck Lesley as unattic-like. Whitewashed maple floorboards gleamed in the lamplight. An attic floor would be made of pine or inexpensive subflooring.

New cries issued from behind a heavy door with well-polished brass fittings. Pushing the door open, Lesley emerged into well-appointed rooms. A figure in tidy white clothes, a nurse's uniform perhaps, careened toward Lesley. Although garbed in white, she was not a ghost. Her heavy tread identified her as a corporeal being.

"How did you get in? You can't come in here," the woman protested.

"I heard someone crying," said Lesley. "So I came up the stairs to see if anyone needs my help."

"How did you get in?" the woman demanded. "I always double lock the door at the bottom of the stairs, and I've already turned the security system on." The woman's eyes narrowed.

"The door wasn't locked, and I don't know anything about a security system," Lesley contradicted her. "Who are you? My father-in-law didn't mention you."

"My name is Valerie Kemsley. I'm a registered nurse,

employed by Russell Windsor. Is he the father-in-law you keep mentioning? He never mentioned entertaining a daughter-in-law."

"I'm Michael's wife, Lesley. This is my first visit to Deerhaven Forest Hall." A moan interrupted their introductions. The piteous quality of the sound drew Lesley toward the next room.

"Stop!" shouted the nurse. Lesley charged past the white-uniformed figure into a sickroom furnished with maple furniture and pallid impressionist prints. A person lay under the pale comforter, someone too small to create a large mound. The occupant of the bed writhed as if in pain.

"Are you all right?" asked Lesley, stepping closer. A woman with long, wavy dark hair and huge, gray eyes sat up.

"I'm dying," said the gray-eyed woman. As though her own life might be at stake, Lesley clutched her heart, almost fainting for the second time that evening. A weird fever coursed throughout her body, heating her veins. Gripping the back of a ladder-back chair for support, Lesley gathered small shreds of bravery that she hadn't known she possessed.

"I can't let you die," Lesley told her. She had never spoken so sincerely in her life. This woman must live. The pendant around Lesley's neck burned, inflaming the tender skin above her breasts.

"She's not going to die," the nurse interjected.

"Yes. I am. I sense death."

"It's a feeling," said the nurse with little sympathy.

"I'll save you," promised Lesley.

The dark-haired woman focused on Lesley fully for the first time. "Leave us alone, Valerie," requested the patient.

The nurse hesitated and the bedridden woman shot her a fierce look. Valerie Kemsley retreated, reluctance obvious in her demeanor. "I'll be right outside," said the nurse as though the woman might need protection from Lesley.

"Who are you?" asked the woman in the bed when the nurse was out of earshot.

"I'm Lesley. Lesley Windsor. Who are you?" The woman didn't answer, turning toward the wall. Lesley stood motionless until she gathered strength and turned to face Lesley again.

"The ancient words apply to you, then, Lesley," said the woman in a clear, bell-like voice. "Choose your affinity. I'm not allowed a choice but you get to make one."

Lesley's breathing accelerated. She took the pendant in her palm and her fingers closed around the engraved words, *"Champion the Hue."* Lesley sensed every particle of herself coming to life, fine brown hair growing longer, heart pumping hot, red blood, warm, pink skin meeting cool night air. After that moment, Lesley could tell that she'd changed. A sensation of fear had been gnawing at the base of her spine since the day her parents died. On bad days, the fear gave her a fierce neck ache. Suddenly, the sensation ceased, turned off like tap water.

"What's come over me?" Lesley whispered, although she knew. Not even a complete novice could mistake this rush of warmth and wanting. She'd fallen in love at first sight.

All other goals subsided as a new and novel goal emerged. Somehow, she must convince this woman to return her love. Sending the woman a wild, foolish grin of spontaneous and involuntary courtship, Lesley let loose of the pendant. She concentrated a warm smile on the gray-eyed object of her desire. Her ill-considered marriage to sad, unrelatable Michael Windsor faded to a poignant memory.

The woman in the bed did not answer Lesley's opening sally. "Get away from me!" responded Valerie's patient. The woman assumed a defensive posture as though Lesley might attack her.

"What?" choked Lesley.

"You're making me sicker," the woman accused. "You're killing me. Get out! Get away!

"Get out! Get out!" screamed the woman, in a frenzy.

"I would never hurt you," Lesley promised. Flooded with warm feeling as she was, the screams barely fazed Lesley.

"You are! You're hurting me," shouted the young woman. "Get out!"

Valerie Kemsley approached looking barely more hospitable than her patient. Lesley shook off the state of hazy euphoria induced by meeting the woman who lay before her. Winning this woman's love looked like an uphill battle to say the least. Oddly, though, Lesley continued to feel strong and optimistic.

"I think you should leave, Mrs. Windsor," ordered Valerie.

"Mrs. Windsor?" shouted the invalid woman. "She's dead! Evaporated! Her ghost came to me this afternoon, begging my forgiveness." The woman's fists clenched as she added, "I refused to forgive her! Even in death!'"

"That must have been Cosette Windsor who visited you," said Lesley. "I'm Lesley Windsor, Michael's wife."

"Married to Michael? Then you're my enemy. Get out!"

"I'll show you to the door, Mrs. Windsor," said Valerie, sounding more like a security guard than a nurse. The woman only thrashed and moaned. Lesley had to admit that further communication would be impossible. How strange that such a terrified person could extinguish Lesley's habitual fear and timidity.

At the stairway, Lesley turned to the nurse. "Who is she? Your patient. What's her name?"

"Why, she's your husband's younger sister. Rachel. Didn't you notice the resemblance?" A similarity between the heat-generating woman in the attic and Michael Windsor, cold and flat, would never have occurred to Lesley. Rachel's eyes did match Ryan's though. Michael's sister, thought Lesley. *Oh, my God.*

"Why does she live up here?" Lesley demanded. "What's wrong with her?"

Valerie shrank back.

"If Mr. Windsor didn't see fit to tell you about his sister, I don't know that I should say anything," she answered.

"How long have you worked here at Deerhaven Forest Hall? Do you know my husband?"

In answer, Valerie opened the door to the stairs, indicating that Lesley should leave. "Of course I know your husband. I consider myself a member of the Windsor household," replied Valerie. "I've taken care of Rachel for nine years, and I check Michael's health every time he visits," she added. Lesley's heart thudded.

"How often does my husband come here?" Lesley asked.

Valerie looked confused. "He's never here more than twice a month," said Valerie. "But you would know that, of course?"

Lesley marveled at the magnitude of Michael's duplicity. How could she have believed this many lies for nine years? Lesley kept her head erect, pretending a dignity she didn't feel.

"Thank you, Valerie. It's been a pleasure meeting you," she said and plunged down the stairs.

Pacing the richly colored runners in the hallway below, the house librarian looked relieved to see Lesley emerge from the upper rooms. "Are you all right?" demanded Sula. "I shouldn't have let you go upstairs alone." The librarian put a long slender arm around Lesley. Lesley mustered a smile, resolving to forget her loss of faith in Michael and focus upon the exhilaration of her newfound strength and love.

"Don't you want to know who lives up there?" asked Lesley.

"No. I don't want to become an accomplice to whatever they have going on up there."

"All right, Sula," Lesley answered. "I will need to tell you some time, though."

"Maybe tomorrow. I'll think about it." The dazzling librarian frowned with the distress of confronting what she'd never faced before. Sula Smith took her mother's caveats with an absolute seriousness that impressed Lesley.

Even though nothing tangible had befallen her upstairs, Lesley felt entirely different. She had gone upstairs a frightened naive young wife and come down a woman with a passion.

"I'm okay, Sula," insisted Lesley.

Sula wrinkled her brow, studying Lesley as though she were a reference book with fine print. "If anything bad happens as a result of your trip upstairs," said Sula, "come to the library. I have ways to protect you and your son."

Sula walked Lesley to her bedroom, bade her lock the door, and headed away leaving Lesley to admire the librarian's Greta Garbo stride. Lesley entered the bedroom where she found Cosette Windsor sitting in a rocking chair beside Ryan's bed. Cosette stood up as Lesley moved toward the sleeping boy.

"Ryan woke up for a few minutes and we had a chance to

get better acquainted," Cosette whispered. "I sang him back to sleep."

"Was he scared?" Lesley asked.

"No, my dear. He wasn't a bit frightened. There's a bond between us that death cannot sever. Get some sleep now. You've come a long way today." Cosette drifted out of the room.

Lesley noticed that her bedclothes had been smoothed and the coverlet folded back. Perhaps the painstaking care of her bed was Cosette's work. Or did the ghost of Ryan's grandma have the power to move animate objects? Lesley tried to remember under what rules ghosts operated. A tapestry drew her attention. The threads portrayed men on horseback and, surrounding them, wiry hounds in a pack. The antique cloth appeared to re-create a medieval castle's wall hanging until Lesley analyzed the content. The hounds weren't baying at wild game or woodland quarry. The dogs cowered before two tall, dark, human forms, awful robed men with livid, yellow eyes. The tapestry's horses too, shied from the dark human figures.

The tableau puzzled Lesley. The artist had positioned a large female deer with huge, intelligent eyes in the exact center of the picture. The doe's eyes seemed to look back and forth at two male deer on either side of her. Heavy symmetrical horns with serifs, curved and unbroken, crowned the bucks' noble heads. What message did the doe's eyes convey? Behind the perspicuous deer, trees with near-human countenances looked out over the scene. Hunters and hounds provided an audience for the doe and her consorts, perhaps nothing more. The trees invited Lesley to decode the artist's vision that, in her current overstimulated frame of mind, Lesley couldn't manage. This needle-and-thimbled landscape, strangely reminiscent of the woods near Deerhaven Pines, troubled Lesley but she might never know why. The artist probably died long ago.

The pendant, gift of her dead mother-in-law, throbbed at the base of Lesley's throat as if the thing emanated electrical impulses. When Lesley turned her attention from the strange wall hanging, the pendant ceased to bother her. Slipping under the covers, Lesley turned down her bedside lamp.

She felt as tired and battered as though she'd arrived at

Deerhaven Forest Hall by horse-drawn coach. She lay awake in the darkness reviewing the last sixteen hours. Under any other circumstances, the most memorable person she had met during the day would have been Sula. Lesley had never met a woman as ravishing as Sula Smith. But the pale, oval face and luminous eyes of her newly discovered sister-in-law, Rachel Windsor, obscured Lesley's memory of the beautiful librarian.

How could a woman evoke these kinds of feelings? She had never felt this way about Michael, even before he became the tormented soul he was now. Her spirit of passion had lain dormant until it came alive at the sight of Michael's sister. What would this do to her life? Although she knew that some people desired sex with people of their own gender, she didn't think there were any of those people in Danville. She doubted she knew any. Too many internal changes may have rocked her being to allow her to return home. Ryan too would be affected by Lesley's new choices, whether she succeeded in attaining the woman she desired or not.

Lesley slept fitfully all night, tossing like the wind-tossed limbs of the tall pines outside, and conscious that she could no longer consider herself a normal woman. She feared that Ryan might suffer if someone discovered his mother's hidden deviance; this became her greatest worry as the hours crept past. Fleeing Deerhaven Forest Hall seemed like the only reasonable course of action. Perversely, what made Lesley long to stay was the same agitated, ailing person from whom she knew she should extract herself.

What malady kept Rachel under a nurse's supervision in the secluded top story of her parents' isolated estate house? Toward morning, when the wind quieted, Lesley made herself face the likely answer. Madness. Rachel must be as mad as Brontë's madwoman in the attic. And Lesley cared only for her. No Rochester would be able to incite Lesley. Even lunacy would not keep her from pursuing the woman with whom God clearly meant her to share her life. For the first time ever, Lesley felt religious.

****

Six years before Queen Victoria concluded her reign with a majestic funeral procession through London, a time when convention dictated the lives of the middle class, young Jane Windsor grappled with the concept of love between women. Like Lesley Windsor would discover so many years later, Jane distrusted the powerful urges she'd discovered within herself. Unlike Lesley, Jane did not know for sure whether any other living human being was likewise afflicted. Except for Ursula Smith.

The Reverend Chaney's revival meeting, earlier in the evening, had impressed Jane as evil in tone. Jane feared him. Everyone knew the Reverend to be a man of God, but he struck Jane as a threat to her own safety and that of the general population. She resolved to investigate the Reverend Chaney if the opportunity arose.

"I've become more intrepid since meeting you," Jane admitted to Ursula Smith. Moonlight illuminated the room in which Jane slept, the room she used when John Bennett visited San Francisco. The rays highlighted a blue, brown and gold wall hanging, a hunting scene but not a gory one. A doe stood at the center and seemed a benign presence. The doe's attitude encouraged the observer to focus upon two antlered bucks facing each other. A towering robed man, ochre-eyed, boded evil but Jane could tell that hope remained. The spirits of the trees promised safety. Those trees suggested the quality of mercy. If only Jane could sleep in this room every night, her sins would be washed away under the auspices of whoever made this tapestry.

"No God would condemn a person for the love in their heart," Jane concluded as she studied the tapestry one night. "If I felt love wash through me when Ursula Smith's lips touched my face, well then, there is more love in the world."

She wished she could share this certainty with the dear family she'd forsaken when she married John Bennett. Jane's little Scottish father possessed a deeply religious nature and a sweetness of spirit. Hugh Copley's God solicited human love. Her father would never reject her for loving another person, regardless of that person's gender. Jane knew the truth in her heart. Satisfied, she fell into a peaceful slumber. That night,

Jane dreamed of running through the meadows near Deerhaven Forest Hall so fast that she took off and flew like a Ruby-crowned Kinglet, warbling as she bobbed over brooks and trees. Liftoff and flight filled Jane with the exhilaration only enjoyed by a creature born to fly.

an uneaten bowl of oatmeal in front of him. Lesley resisted an impulse to kiss his shiny forehead as she used to do with her own father. How strange that she felt comfortable with the father that Michael took such pains to hide from her.

"Sausage, madam?" offered Mrs. Woolf, her lip curled as if she already knew that Lesley didn't eat meat.

"I'm a vegetarian," Lesley admitted, "and I prefer that Ryan not eat meat either."

Mrs. Woolf, a faint smirk scarring her face, answered, "Perhaps some Cream of Wheat, Mrs. Windsor?"

"I'll serve myself and Ryan," Lesley answered with unusual firmness. She could feel the presence of Rachel Windsor, upstairs. The memory of Rachel, vivid and powerful in Lesley's mind, buoyed her spirits. Little did she care that the patient lying above their heads might be demented and didn't like her. Lesley chose not to worry about the reasonableness of her feelings. She would be strong from now on. Whatever had weakened Lesley upon her parents' death remained at bay.

"You'll come with me to the funeral home, won't you?" inquired Russell.

"Certainly, if you'd like me to," said Lesley. "I wouldn't want to intrude. Will Kelvin be accompanying you?"

Russell glanced around the table and when he didn't see his son, looked to Mrs. Woolf for an answer.

"Mr. Kelvin is meeting with the Reverend Were for grief counseling," announced Mrs. Woolf. With a brief, tight smile in Lesley's direction, the housekeeper left the room.

"In that case, Russell, I'd be happy to go. Do you think I might ask the librarian to look after Ryan while we're gone?"

"I don't know," replied Russell, sounding tired and confused. "It's not really her job. She looks after the books and the library. I don't know how she feels about minding children." His eyes came to rest on his grandson and a smile brought some animation to his face.

"I'm sure she'd enjoy spending time with you, though, Ryan," said Russell with the carefulness of an old man who valued everyone left in his life. Ryan grinned at his prodigal grandfather.

CHAPTER NINE

By morning light, the tapestry faded to a prosaic piece of handicraft. The wind had died to an unimpressive whisper during the night. Lesley dressed in a loose white dress with sprigs of pink roses, a favorite of Michael's, and then reconsidered. Without stopping to analyze why, she changed into a different outfit, jeans and a jacket, as if making herself ready for any exigency. She had the sensation of having been warned that this day might require clothes that allowed freedom of movement. Should the lady lying upstairs need intervention, for whatever reason, Lesley would be ready.

Ryan rose fresh and cheerful from his first night's sleep in his father's childhood home. They dressed and went downstairs where they found Mrs. Woolf patrolling a buffet breakfast in the dining room. Russell Windsor sat slumped over a cup of coffee,

Footsteps sounded and the librarian appeared in the doorway. "I'd love a date with this guy!" said Sula Smith, wearing an emerald-green silk shirt and shiny black trousers. Her coloring made her a standout against the backdrop of the Victorian dining room furniture, huge dark breakfront and gleaming expanse of ebony tabletop. Lesley didn't blame Ryan for leaping to his feet and running to greet her.

"Good morning, Miss Smith," Ryan called, jumping up and down like a half-trained puppy.

Sula patted his head and picked up a china plate. "We'll spend the morning in the library, Ryan. I have work for you, returning books to their right places. We own fascinating books about the history of Deerhaven Pines. I'll help you read them."

"Do you have *Shivering Stories, Books I, II and III*?" asked Ryan. "Everyone in my class reads them, but I've been afraid to until now."

"I'm afraid I don't have *Shivering Stories* but we could read, *The Turn of the Screw*. It's terrifying."

"Oh, boy," shouted Ryan, bringing a smile to his grandfather's face.

"Phone call, Mrs. Windsor," called Lena from behind Lesley's shoulder.

Lesley excused herself and followed Lena to a room that must have been tended by Cosette Windsor's one time. A flowered nameplate over the desk read, "Cosette Atwell Windsor." Many pictures of the Windsor children decorated a shelf above the desk, Michael, Rachel and Kelvin, at various ages wearing riding clothes, costumes or formal dress. Rachel. She'd been here all along.

"Hello," said Lesley, expecting to hear Michael on the other end of the line.

"Is everything okay?" asked Lesley's friend, Pauline Walden.

"I think so," replied Lesley. "Michael's dad has adjusted to losing his wife better than Michael told me to expect. But, Pauline, Michael hasn't been honest with me about his family. He's lied to me about everything." She'd never spoken of Michael with such disloyalty. She waited for dread to seize her but nothing happened. Michael no longer deserved her loyalty, and Lesley felt clear-minded about what she should say and not say.

"The Windsors have wanted me to be a part of the family all these years," she told her friend. "They're not anti-Semitic and they're very kind." The story of meeting Michael's dead mother could wait, Lesley decided. Even Pauline's generosity of spirit and imagination might be strained by Lesley's report that she'd established a relationship with the ghost of her mother-in-law.

"I'm happy for you, Lesley," said Pauline. "It will be good for you and Ryan to be part of the family. Better later than never. How's Michael holding up?"

"I don't know," Lesley told her. "He wasn't home when I called last night. I left a voice-mail message at his office, but he hasn't returned my call. He probably entertained conference participants until late last night. Did you get around to checking with Dan about how the conference is going?"

"Lesley," Pauline sounded strained, "isn't Michael with you?"

"No. The last I heard, he couldn't get away from work until the day after tomorrow."

"Les, I don't know how to tell you this so I'll just say it. Dan told me that Michael turned the entire conference over to Frank Caravelle. Michael said that he planned to join you immediately. He hasn't been at work since day before yesterday. He left a note asking me to look after your house. I'm taking in your mail and feeding Ryan's guinea pig."

"Where could he be?" asked Lesley, flustered by Pauline's news.

"I know he's your husband, Les, but you've got to recognize the fact that Michael's functioning less and less well every day. I hope you'll watch out. A shattering event like the death of his mother could leave him in worse shape than ever."

"You might be right," she admitted. She and Pauline discussed Lesley's options. The two friends agreed that Pauline would call Lesley at Deerhaven Forest Hall if Michael turned up in Danville.

Afterward, Lesley sat in the sunlit room. Smiling and unsmiling, the Windsor children stared at her from their mother's photographs. If Michael had allowed her to visit Deerhaven Forest Hall, she would have smelled a rat when she spied these pictures. There sat Rachel, in every group portrait, a jewel in the setting, glowing in between her two complementary brothers.

No wonder that Michael had never wanted her at Deerhaven Forest Hall. His mother would have talked about her three children. Lesley would have learned that Michael came first in the birth order and that, as his wife, the family expected Lesley to assume the running of the Hall some day. Did he not want her filling his mother's shoes or, more likely, did he fear that she'd reject the role? Whatever his reasons for guarding his secrets all these years, she wondered why he'd decided to send her to Deerhaven Forest Hall at last. Maybe he hoped that Rachel would remain a captive in the attic and no one would mention her. Maybe he'd chosen not to come with her to let her adjust.

"Was that Michael calling?" asked Russell when Lesley returned to the dining room. She decided not to mention that she didn't know where to locate Michael. Michael might have gone into seclusion to grieve for his mother and, if so, he'd show up when he felt ready.

"No, it was just a friend," she told him. After breakfast, Lesley and Sula walked Ryan to the library. Sula treated them to an anecdotal history of the paintings and furniture they passed. Suddenly, Lesley stopped in her tracks, facing a massive old-fashioned portrait in blues and purples with a Sierra backdrop. The sitter's face glowed like the moon at night.

"Who posed for this?" Lesley asked Sula.

Sula mimicked the stiff Victorian posture of the woman in the portrait and then went limp with laughter. "I know she must look a bit like your husband," said Sula. "That's a Windsor wife, Jane Copley Windsor, painted in eighteen ninety-eight. She looks quite like Michael in the face, doesn't she? Michael is her distant descendant, of course. We have Jane's diaries in the library."

Lesley stood transfixed by the portrait. Jane Copley Windsor resembled Rachel more than she did Michael. Ryan, too, seemed captivated by the woman, or by the hundred-year-old purple clouds and shadowy peaks. He slipped a small dry hand into Lesley's.

"Who is she?" Ryan asked.

"An ancestor of yours and Daddy's," answered Lesley.

"She looks a little bit like Daddy," Ryan commented.

"Only a little, though," said Lesley, somehow uncomfortable with the topic of family resemblances.

"There's a Windsor look to all of them," agreed Sula. "Including you, young Mr. Windsor."

Ryan blushed and moved closer to Lesley. Sula must not have seen Rachel or, at least, not seen her for many years. If Sula saw Rachel Windsor, she would know who the portrait mirrored. Lesley felt relieved to learn that Sula had never been part of the conspiracy.

Lesley felt loath to leave the portrait of Jane Copley Windsor. That same face with the narrow straight nose and gray eyes hung in her mind's eye, waking or sleeping, but she couldn't stand gawking at the painted replica. They proceeded to the library entrance.

"What's that?" questioned Ryan, pointing to a piece of carved oak fretwork over the door. The curlicues, although intricate and asymmetrical, looked familiar to Lesley.

"That's the symbol of this library," Sula explained. When Ryan appeared bewildered, Sula added, "A logo. Like the Nike symbol on the side of kids' shoes is a logo."

"Mom!" cried Ryan in his little-professor voice as they walked through the library toward Sula's office. "Look at that light on that floor! It looks like the library's logo." The gray, swirling clouds of the night before had cleared and a thin, white November light sifted through the library's high glass windows. The refractions created curves and lines. Ryan might be right. The pattern of winter light projected onto the pale hardwood floor resembled the carved whorls above the door.

"I'll look at the library with you when I have more time," Lesley told her son. Ryan ran ahead to a paneled enclosure that Sula used for an office.

"Who are these old-fashioned ladies?" she heard Ryan asking the librarian.

"These are my ancestors, going all the way back to my great-great-grandmother, Ursula Smith," replied Sula. "That's Ursula in this oil painting. The next painting is my great-grandmother, Ursaline. That's my grandmother in this picture, Ursuletta. And this is my mother, Ursa."

"And each of them kept the name Smith?" asked Lesley, coming to the office door. "How unusual."

"Unusual women run in the family, Lesley," laughed Sula.

"Where is your mother now?" came Ryan's next question.

"My mother used to be the librarian here at Deerhaven Forest Hall," replied Sula in a cheery tone. "But she retired at an early age and moved to San Francisco. That's how I got my job."

"Who are these ladies?" asked Ryan. Lesley stepped into Sula's office in time to see him point to a bulletin board decked with pictures of young women, most of them displaying a tender look for the camera, some of them inscribed "To Sula..."

"Are they related to you?" Ryan inquired.

"Those are friends of mine who have visited the library," Sula answered.

There was only one word to describe the smile that played across Sula's lips, *roguish*. Lesley was witnessing an actual roguish grin, which she'd heretofore only read about. Sula does not match the stereotype of a librarian, thought Lesley, holding back a grin of her own.

CHAPTER TEN

"Did the deceased leave any written notes regarding our last farewell to her?" inquired Mr. Dekker of Ralph P. Dekker & Sons Funeral Home in Sonora.

Russell looked bewildered by the question.

"Did Cosette leave instructions for her funeral?" Lesley paraphrased.

"I know she'd want songs," Russell ventured, "but she never liked church music. How about some jazz? Duke Ellington? John Coltrane?"

Mr. Dekker, a man as gray as his corpses, with the look of a smoker in the terminal stages of cigarette inhalation, seemed taken aback by the deceased's taste in music. "That would be interesting," he replied, clipping his consonants. "Let's just run it by your minister."

"Cosette didn't have much interest in organized religion," mused Russell, oblivious to Mr. Dekker's discomfort. "Perhaps we won't have a minister. Perhaps our librarian would be willing to read a few poems by Emily Dickinson."

"You don't want a man of the cloth to preside over the services?" Dekker protested. "A librarian is going to deliver the eulogy?"

Russell tilted his head, considering.

"Wait a minute!" exclaimed Lesley, sitting up. "Kelvin mentioned that Cosette wanted Bill Patterson from the Sonora Unitarian Church to speak at the funeral."

Russell and Dekker both looked relieved.

"What a good idea," Russell commented. "Cosette met Reverend Patterson at a party and was quite impressed with him. He can juggle five oranges at a time, and the fellow does bird impressions as though he were a mockingbird in his former life." Russell smiled at this happy memory.

The funeral home director shifted in his seat, probably hoping that Reverend Patterson would restrict himself to reciting from the scriptures at the upcoming event.

Before yesterday, Lesley would have been too timid to interject her opinions on the funeral but when Dekker began to formalize his plans, Lesley tried to soften and humanize them. The gentle woman who sat on Ryan's bed last night would not want her friends and family subjected to a synthetic spectacle.

"I didn't know her, but I think she would like a poem by John Donne read, perhaps *Sweetest Love, I Do Not Go*. My husband told me that Cosette loved to read Donne for comfort."

Russell broke loose from his vacant state of grief and looked at Lesley for the first time. "Cosette did like John Donne. I'd forgotten that. You're so thoughtful, Lesley." His light-gray eyes teared. He reached over to pat her hand, his fingers soft, papery.

"I wish I'd been to Deerhaven Forest Hall sooner and knew more about Cosette," said Lesley.

Did she? Her life had grown complicated in the brief time since coming to the Hall. If she'd met Rachel Windsor on some other night, in some other place, would she have been smitten in the same way? The answer came to her on the heels of the question. Yes. She would have fallen for Rachel any time, under any circumstances.

What would Cosette Windsor think of Lesley's feelings for her daughter? Instead of guilt or panic, this question brought a sense of calm. Whatever Cosette might have believed in life, her mother-in-law had most likely transcended petty bigotries. Lesley returned her thoughts to the task at hand.

"We'll conclude with 'Jesu, Joy of Man's Desiring' as the guests exit the service," suggested Mr. Dekker with unwarranted hope, coughing into a stained white handkerchief.

"I think I'd prefer 'Somewhere Over the Rainbow,' an instrumental version," countered Russell, emboldened by Lesley's contributions. "Cosette loves that song." Satisfied with this final suggestion, Russell rose on unsteady legs. Lesley stood and took his arm.

"I'm sure it will be a very nice funeral," said Lesley, holding out her free hand to Dekker.

"I hope so," Dekker replied, his handshake limp and clammy. As if realizing he could have better phrased his reply, Dekker added, "Our clients always give us top-notch ratings. I intend to keep it that way."

The dead ones or the live ones, wondered Lesley, although she remained silent.

"Would Cosette be happy with the plans we've made?" Lesley asked, when they'd parted company with the depressed funeral home director.

"She'll find a way to let us know if she doesn't," answered Russell, his words clearer than at any time since Lesley met him. "Women who marry into the Windsor family remain at the Hall even after death, if the living need help or guidance. My grandmother helped Cosette with the running of the Hall when Cosette was a new bride." His face grew wistful. "I won't be able to see Cosette, but I expect you will. She'll want to tell you and our grandson the things she never had a chance to communicate before she died. Transmissions are limited, so I've always been told, but I expect you'll see her."

"Have you ever seen a ghost, Russell?" asked Lesley.

"No. I've never been part of cataclysmic events. I'll be left out of the hurly-burly to come. I was born to spend my life in peace. Young Ryan, though, might have vicissitudes. He may be at the center of strife now that he's taken residence at Deerhaven Forest Hall. He has that look about him. Don't worry, though, my dear, he's a strong boy."

"Russell, I get the impression that you've been misled. Ryan and I are here for the funeral, and for as long as you need us, but we're not moving here. We'll be returning home once we've made sure you're okay. Ryan can miss a little school, but he can't stay out of class indefinitely." Taking her eyes off the road for a second, Lesley saw a stubborn frown on the old man's face.

"There's always been a Mrs. Windsor at the Hall," Russell reminded her, just as Kelvin had. "It's time for Michael to come home. I don't like the way the world outside has treated him. I don't mean to pry but there's a nervous look in his eyes. It's been there for a few years. Now that we've met, I know it has nothing to do with you." Russell spoke with a sudden power in his voice, the way he must have sounded as a young man, when he added, "The three of you will be better off at the Hall."

Lesley sighed, hoping she wouldn't need to disappoint this sweet old man. The tiny but exquisite town of Deerhaven Pines lay in cool light-gold Sierra sunshine. Downtown Danville, while quaint, never looked so ethereal. Navigating the driveway leading to Deerhaven Forest Hall, Lesley scanned the front of the Hall in case Ryan had come out to watch for her. She half-expected to see Michael's car somewhere on the grounds, but when she pulled into the garage, a large dark building with cathedral ceilings, she realized that her husband had not arrived.

Inside the Hall, Lesley delivered Russell into the brusque hands of Mrs. Woolf, whom he didn't seem to mind. Lesley kept conversation with the housekeeper to a minimum and didn't ask for directions to the library. Two rooms later, she paused beside a portrait of an unsmiling lady with a high, ruffled collar, to consider the best route. No light shifted as Lesley stood thinking, but she became aware of a presence.

Cosette Atwell Windsor materialized in front of her but only partially, creating a diaphanous cloud in the corridor. The expression on Cosette's face could be read even in her present insubstantial state since Lesley's mother-in-law wore a look of anguish and panic. Lesley's heart began to race with terror.

"What is it, Cosette? What's the matter?" The ghost of Michael's mother attempted to speak and failed, finally pointing a filmy finger without a sound. Then, audio returned.

"The library. Run!" whispered Cosette.

Lesley flew down the hall with an incoherent cry of fear, knowing that Cosette wouldn't trick her. Something had gone wrong at the Hall and Lesley had left Ryan at its heart. An ominous silence greeted her as she searched for the library doors.

Should she go get Rachel for assistance? No, that was ridiculous. Rachel suffered from a disorder so debilitating she'd been locked away. As soon as she located the doors, Lesley took a deep breath and entered the library. The brilliance of the scene stunned her for a moment. The library windows transformed the outdoor sunlight into a rarer, finer color than could be found in nature. Desperate, Lesley employed heightened senses, ears sharpened with alarm. No sound came however much she strained to hear. The septagonal building appeared to be deserted.

"Ryan!" screamed Lesley, heedless of the well-known prohibition against raising your voice in the library. "Ryan! It's Mom. Are you here?"

Her words echoed back at her. The lack of sound provoked a terror so great that Lesley almost screamed again to end it. A sixth sense told Lesley that this fear would turn out to be real and terrible. Evil had visited the beautiful light-filled library in her absence, and she could only hope that Sula and Ryan had escaped the malevolence.

A weak moan obliterated that small hope.

Darting around glass and oak display cabinets, freestanding shelves and wall-mounted shelving, Lesley sought her son and the missing librarian. Eventually, she found one of them. Crumpled at the base of a Plexiglas case featuring a massive stuffed brown bear killed with a Winchester rifle at the dawn of the century, lay Lesley's little boy. Nothing about Ryan's person looked wrong, except for the slackness of his face and limbs. Lesley had never seen him lie so still. Her hands reached for him and in the process, she saw a discolored smudge on the Plexiglas which could only be blood.

Remembering that she shouldn't touch him before ascertaining the nature of his injuries, Lesley forced herself to hold back and look. Ryan's breathing generated a rattling noise and his respiration seemed shallow. When Lesley finally touched his smooth brown hair, she discovered what stilled him. Someone had shot her son in the head, above his left ear, and left him here, alone and untended. Lesley ran to the librarian's office and dialed 911.

When Lesley returned to him, Ryan's position seemed to have altered. He'd pulled one arm close to his body. As Lesley knelt closer, his eyes fluttered.

"Don't try to move, honey. The doctors are on their way." Ryan's eyes indicated his comprehension, but Lesley shouldn't encourage speech. Any movement could move the bullet deeper. Lesley laid soft hands on Ryan's shoulders to quiet him.

"She was crying," Ryan whispered.

"Shhh. What?" Lesley whispered back.

"The librarian. Sula. She was crying when they took her." Lesley had forgotten the librarian in her effort to fetch help for Ryan.

"Don't open your eyes, Ryan, just tell me who took her. Who did this to you?"

"I don't know," Ryan mumbled. "There was a big, wet hand over my eyes."

"That's okay, honey. Rest now, Ryan. The doctors will be here any time."

"Mom?" Lesley put her ear close to his mouth in order to hear. "Mom, I think Dad was with them. How could he? Why would he run away and leave me?"

Ryan grew silent and failed to respond even when Lesley broke down and called his name.

CHAPTER ELEVEN

The wait for medical assistance taxed Lesley's new emotional resilience even though paramedics and sheriff's department personnel appeared in a short time. A pair of uniformed sheriffs quizzed Lesley as paramedics examined her son. Her whole being remained fixed upon Ryan lying so limp and still.

"I don't know who did this," she told them, hoping she spoke the truth. Michael couldn't have been there. Even in his present confused state, he wouldn't allow anyone to harm his own son. "Ryan was under the care of the woman who runs this library," Lesley continued. "My son regained consciousness briefly and said that someone carried the librarian away against her will." This prompted a call for backup police presence.

Lesley could provide Sula's name but little other information about her. She suggested that the police officer locate Mrs. Woolf who knew much more about Lesley's family and their staff than did Lesley. The police officers refrained from questioning Lesley's lack of familiarity with her husband's family and their home.

The paramedics attached two plastic tubes to Ryan's thin white arm and taped a monitor over his heart. They immobilized his head with stiff padded planks. Lifting him onto a rolling gurney, they wheeled him through his grandparents' house, past the portraits and well-polished furniture, and out into the weak sunlight. Lena, and a woman Lesley hadn't met, who was wearing a floury apron as though she'd been baking, observed the gurney's progress in silence. Russell followed them outside. Tears trickled from the old man's eyes and he clutched a soggy handkerchief.

"I'm coming with you," said Russell, as he watched them load Ryan into the van. "William Roe will drive me in the Land Rover."

"Can I ride in the ambulance with my son?" asked Lesley.

"Maybe in front," said the taller, bearded paramedic.

"Mama," called Ryan. Every particle of Lesley strained toward the swaddled child, and she stepped toward him.

"Let his mother ride with the boy," barked the older woman paramedic. "We don't want him agitated." With that encouragement, Lesley scrambled to join Ryan. The two police officers climbed inside and took seats on a bench secured to the side.

The drive to the nearest hospital emergency room in Sonora felt interminable and made Lesley carsick. The ambulance took curves and turns at a fast clip. Entrusting Ryan to strangers felt wrong. Lesley wished she knew anything about gunshot wounds to the head.

The younger, red-haired sheriff asked many questions about the Windsors, her relationship to them and whether the recent death in that house could be related to today's incident. He wanted a comprehensive picture of life at the crime scene but Lesley couldn't answer most of his questions. Lesley admitted that she had never met Cosette Windsor. The sheriff turned to the subject of Sula Smith's disappearance.

"Was the librarian a married woman?" asked the older brown-faced sheriff.

"I don't know much about her," Lesley replied.

"Why would an individual family need their own librarian?" asked the redhead.

"I don't know," Lesley replied, stroking Ryan's free arm. "They have a lot of books and historical material. The family has always employed a librarian, even back in the eighteen hundreds."

"Do they have a large number of employees whose duties are that specialized?"

"They have a cook, a gardener, a housekeeper and a house cleaner," said Lesley, "although they might have more staff that I never met."

Once again, the officers glanced at each other and back at her. "How long have you and your husband been married?" asked the older man.

"Nine years," admitted Lesley, "but we didn't socialize with his family."

"Dad," murmured Ryan, his eyelids trembling. Lesley took his hand and pressed it within her own.

"Has the boy's father been notified?" asked a paramedic.

"I haven't tried to reach him yet," answered Lesley. "He might be in the area, but our cell phones don't work around here. Do you think a police officer could contact Ryan's uncle, Kelvin Windsor? I think Kelvin might be in Wolf's Creek being counseled by a minister, Reverend Were."

The police officer and the nearest paramedic looked startled.

"Are you familiar with the Reverend's work?" asked Lesley. No one responded for a very long time.

"He's what they call a fringe element," the quieter police officer said at last. "Or a hate-monger. He wants to get rid of 'unwholesome' elements in the community. Unfortunately, his idea of an unwholesome person includes everybody but himself and the white, male Bible-thumpers who do whatever he tells them." The officer bit his lip as though wishing he hadn't said so much. Lesley guessed he might be Native American and therefore not one of the Reverend's "in" group.

"Oh, dear," replied Lesley, not knowing what else to say. The squirrel, killed by Kelvin Windsor, scurried through her thoughts and hid in the branches of her mind.

"The Reverend Were wields a lot of power in this community," said the red-haired officer. "Someday there's going to be trouble between those who have kept their sanity and those who follow the Reverend Were." The officer shook his head. "It isn't going to be pretty!"

Lesley looked down at her stricken child and wondered if he might not, in some way, be a victim of the upcoming chasm of which the officer just spoke.

Before the officers could tell her more, the ambulance entered Sonora, turned on the siren, and raced to Sonora Sierra Hospital where they pulled up under a wide portico at the entrance to the emergency room. Lesley hurried to stay alongside her son as attendants wheeled him into an examining room. Bending over his small, white face, Lesley whispered, "Ryan, it's Mom, can you hear me?"

Ryan didn't respond. A thick woman in peach strode over to Lesley. "Dr. Gunther's on his way," the peachy nurse announced. "You're in luck. He's very good. He knows your family so he'll go the extra mile for you."

A doctor wearing green scrubs entered at a jog. His name badge read Dr. Bob Gunther. Gunther looked at Ryan's eyes and announced, "They're wide. There's still something going on in there." By "there" Lesley assumed he referred to her son's brain. "We need to start with x-rays to eliminate a skull fracture," he told her.

Lesley gulped nervously. Seeing her son in these surroundings tested her courage anew. The name 'Bob Gunther,' the look of the Dr. Frankenstein machine on a cart being trundled toward her son, the faded green paint, the other patients pacing, moaning, hiding their faces; every detail became etched in Lesley's mind. Instead of cowering, she marshaled her thoughts. Who put her son here? Anger flared in her breast. She would make sure that her son's assailant answered to her. Lesley felt her heart surge with a burst of courage she'd never before experienced, and her new valor shocked her by generating enough heat to warm the brooch around her neck, as though she'd become a forge. She lifted her necklace and swung the thing to cool it.

"We're going to do a CAT scan, Mrs. Windsor. Would you mind stepping out of the room? Sometimes we administer a mild sedative before proceeding with this test, but since—" Dr. Gunther looked down at a stainless steel clipboard to get the name, "Ryan is not conscious, we don't need medication." With that, the doctor turned away.

"Can I stay with my son?" asked Lesley. Green-suited Dr. Gunther gave Lesley an irritated frown.

"I think not," he answered with no further explanation.

Lesley Windsor of Blackhawk would have cowered before the arrogant physician but the changes in her internal makeup held. Lesley Windsor of Deerhaven Forest Hall cleared her throat with authority. Every instinct told Lesley not to leave Ryan alone.

"May I get a second opinion, please?" Lesley cried.

Dr. Gunther paused and stared at her, a supercilious lift of the upper lip contorting his handsome, heavy features. Lesley almost yielded to a dark despair and then, the door swung open, admitting fluorescent light from the hall. The place seemed less dingy in an instant.

"What's this?" inquired a low but melodious voice.

"The patient's mother is interfering with treatment," Dr. Gunther complained. "She refuses to allow a CAT scan."

"I just want to stay with my son," Lesley protested. "It's not that I don't want him to have the tests he needs."

"I'm Andy Riemer," said the doctor with the soothing voice. "I'll take over from here, Bob. Why don't you take the older man with chest pains, curtain six?"

"My pleasure," muttered Dr. Gunther as he slapped down the clipboard with Ryan's paperwork, and left.

"Let me explain why Dr. Gunther asked you to step aside for moment, Mrs. Windsor. Same as with traditional x-rays, we can't let anyone other than the patient be exposed to cathode rays. I'll let you know as soon as we're finished. Take a seat right outside the door. Or look through the window if you'd prefer to keep your eyes on your son."

Lesley squinted her eyes against the light in order to see the nicer doctor. With almost shoulder-length curly blond hair and dazzling blue eyes, wearing a traditional white doctor's coat over jeans, Dr. Andy Riemer looked as though he'd been acquired from central casting. In a movie, Dr. Riemer would turn out to be the bad one since he looked too good to be true.

"Thank you, Dr. Riemer," said Lesley. On second glance, Andy Riemer, despite his glamour, seemed intelligent and kind. "I know you'll do all you can," she said, "but you're a small hospital. Should I have Ryan flown to San Francisco or to Stanford Medical Center? Does he need an MRI? I know they're more accurate than a CAT scan. What would you do if he were your son?"

"I'd recommend transporting him to another facility if today weren't Thursday," Dr. Riemer replied.

"Thursday?" stammered Lesley.

"They bring the mobile MRI unit to our hospital on Monday and Thursday," Dr. Riemer explained. "I'd have to fly your son out any other day, but since we have the machine available, I'll take a look at the pictures and then decide. Keeping him here will be easier on his system. His pupils are wide and he's responsive on some levels. That means his brain is functioning. I don't see any overt signs of intracranial bleeding." He smiled and nodded encouragement.

Lesley made a brief attempt to return his smile. Andy Riemer laid gentle hands on Ryan's shoulders. Lesley left the room and found herself relaxing as they set up the machine. When they finished the procedure, they installed Ryan in a not-too-uncomfortable looking bed. A nurse informed Lesley that Russell needed reassurance from her.

Returning to the waiting room, Lesley found Russell staring at the swinging door beyond which lay his grandson. She took the seat next to him. Biting her lip for courage, Lesley conjured a few words of comfort to Russell. After that, her sense of time grew distorted. She couldn't remember whether it was early or late in the day. She could hear, in her mind, Ryan's sweet voice, asking, "Can't we go home now?"

Later, Dr. Riemer reappeared, his face set with grave

concern. Lesley's heart leaped in panic. Dr. Riemer led her and Russell to a cubicle and propped himself on his desk. Portraits of a golden retriever with a silly smile decorated his bookshelves. Lesley would have liked to protect Ryan's grandfather from the stress of Ryan's injury but she could tell that Russell, too, needed to hear what the doctor would say.

"The good news is that Ryan doesn't seem to have sustained major damage from the bullet wound you saw above his ear. The injury could almost be called a graze even though it's about a quarter of an inch deep." The doctor took a breath.

"The bad news is that Ryan has not regained consciousness, and we can't precisely tell you why. The human brain is well padded by the skull but still a fragile organ. Gunshot victims can lose consciousness from the trauma of what they've experienced, and I have a feeling that's the case here. On the other hand, Ryan's brain might have taken more of a jolt than we can determine."

"When will my grandson wake up?" quavered Russell. "We'll do anything it takes."

"Ryan could wake up any time," said the doctor, "or we might have to wait for any swelling in his brain to subside."

"What's the possibility that he'll never regain consciousness?" asked Lesley in tight firm voice she barely recognized as her own.

"I'm not going to entertain that possibility," answered Dr. Riemer. "Let's give him forty-eight hours. It's amazing what kids can shake off." Overwhelmed, Lesley couldn't think of a single further question to ask him.

"Here's my beeper number in case you need me in a hurry. Feel free to call any time." The doctor handed Lesley a card that she accepted with gratitude.

The day crept by like a surrealistic foreign film with no subtitles. Ryan did not open his eyes as Lesley prayed at his side. Russell Windsor sat with head bowed in the waiting room. Midway through the afternoon, Lesley bought two bags of Doritos and two cartons of chocolate milk. The old man should be receiving better nutrition but Lesley didn't want to leave Ryan. At dinnertime, Lesley took Russell to a pizza parlor near the hospital and ordered house salads and a thin cheese pizza.

The server brought them a complimentary pitcher of Coca-Cola and Lesley poured two frosty mugs, thinking of how Ryan would have enjoyed this meal. Her father-in-law, dazed with layers of grief, had spoken very little all day but now he stirred.

"I've never tasted a liquid so tart and bubbly," he commented.

Lesley almost smiled. Safe in his secluded mansion, Russell had been spared the experience of America's best-known beverages. "You don't have to drink the stuff, Russell," said Lesley in a gentle tone. "Would you like coffee or a glass of wine?"

"No. I like this very much," replied Russell. "Let's have Mrs. Woolf order some for the house." Lesley couldn't tell whether the old man was familiar with pizza but he chewed each bite carefully and asked whether Lesley could get the recipe for the cook at Deerhaven Forest Hall. Russell followed his pizza by eating a plateful of salad including the hot green peppers and black olives.

"An exceptional meal," he commented as Lesley walked him back to the hospital. Leaving Russell on a molded plastic chair to digest his dinner, Lesley returned to Ryan. Russell closed his eyes and went to sleep.

Ensconced in Ryan's room, Lesley used a credit card to call Pauline in Danville. As Lesley expected, her friend heard the news of Ryan's injury with shocked distress. Pauline viewed Ryan as an extension of her own family. After Pauline had processed the bad news a little, Lesley asked the question she must—Michael needed to be told about his son, regardless of her feelings about him.

"Have you checked whether Michael has been home? We still haven't been able to reach him."

"No one at work has heard from him, and I haven't seen his car at your house. Dan tells me that Michael picked up his messages by remote. He hasn't changed his voicemail greeting in a few days. Are you alone at the hospital? Should I drive up?"

Although she longed for the company of her friend, Lesley thought about the difficulty Pauline would encounter trying to arrange for care of her husband and children. Unbidden, Rachel Windsor's face rose before Lesley's eyes, and she wondered what Pauline would think of her strange new passion. Maybe she should forgo Pauline's company until she could absorb and interpret recent events, the shooting, the encounter with a ghost, meeting Rachel Windsor.

"It would be good to have you but I think I can manage," Lesley replied.

"Okay," said Pauline. "Call if you need me."

Afterward, though, Lesley felt bereft. No matter what happened, she vowed to keep her friendship with Pauline. She didn't want to gain Rachel but lose Pauline in the process. She wanted them both in her life, Rachel and her friend.

Pauline would understand, thought Lesley. If Pauline could understand Lesley's relationship with Michael, a messy piece of work, she would be able to accept what Lesley felt for Rachel, a sweeter thing. She didn't know the words for what she'd experienced last night at the top of the stairs at Deerhaven Forest Hall but when she found the words, she would tell Pauline.

Later that evening, dozing beside Ryan's bed, Lesley roused herself at the sound of footsteps. Dr. Riemer, still handsome as a soap opera actor playing doctor, strode over to Ryan and checked the monitors over the bed. He turned and, for the first time, she noticed that he wore a tuxedo. His teeth, when he smiled, matched the whiteness of his fluted shirt.

"He's not worse and that's a good sign," Dr. Riemer told her.

The thought occurred to Lesley that Dr. Riemer was a cup-half-full kind of guy, but she accepted his reassurance gratefully.

"We know from the CAT scan that he's not in immediate danger," the doctor continued. "I don't think an MRI would reveal anything further, in Ryan's case, so I feel comfortable leaving him here at Sonora Sierra. Let's see what a night's sleep does to heal those injured tissues." After answering Lesley's final questions with a charming solicitude, Dr. Riemer departed in a twinkle of cuff links.

Soon, William Roe appeared to chauffeur Russell home, and the hospital became quiet enough that Lesley could hear nothing but her son's respiration. She dozed in her chair and dreamed about a black-cloaked gunslinger chasing her toward the silhouette of a wooden suspension bridge. Silver bullets whizzed through a murky twilight and finally one lodged in her brain. The bullet put her to sleep. When Lesley awakened, she sensed a hostile presence. The shooter? No. Dr. Bob Gunther stood at the side of Ryan's bed and early morning sunlight streamed through the small high windows.

"Where are we?" Lesley murmured.

"The hospital," Dr. Gunther answered, helpful as ever.

Lesley's hands and forearms felt as though they were stuck to the plastic upholstery of the chair in which she'd slept. The brooch around Lesley's neck felt as though the metal might be searing her skin. Lesley pried loose her hands and picked up the necklace.

"Does this feel warm to you?" she asked the doctor, still groggy and disoriented.

Dr. Gunther took the proffered brooch from Lesley by reflex but his reaction brought her to a fully conscious state. The doctor acted as though a terrible electric shock were snaking up his arm. He dropped the necklace on Lesley's shirtfront.

"I need to get going. Don't call for me again after that trick," he muttered, his face contorted. Lesley went to Ryan's bedside. The brooch cooled and shrank.

Ryan's hair needed combing and a yellow disinfectant smear blemished his right cheek. His skin tone didn't seem bad, though, and he breathed lightly and without effort. Lesley extracted a plastic comb from her handbag and rearranged his hair. A wet paper towel took care of the discoloration on his face except under the cruel bandages.

"How's the patient?" called Dr. Riemer, entering the room. The doctor joined Lesley at Ryan's side and wrapped a blood pressure cuff around the boy's little arm.

"Shouldn't Ryan have woken up by now?" asked Lesley, knowing there might be no answer.

"I'd like to see him awake, but I'm no more worried than I was last night. Let's give him time." The doctor's tanned, unlined face turned toward Lesley. "Why don't you go home and get some rest. We'll call you if there's the slightest change."

"I don't feel comfortable leaving him," Lesley answered. "I'll be fine."

Dr. Riemer nodded his head in sympathy. "If you need anything, feel free to have me paged," he offered.

Lesley thanked him and he left her alone again to watch her son and try to ignore the monitors' electric dirge.

"Courage," she whispered to the ghost of her old timid self.

CHAPTER TWELVE

Lesley passed two long days in the gauzy realm of the hospital but on the morning of the third day, she left Ryan under medical supervision so that she could attend the funeral of her mother-in-law. No one had heard from Sula Smith and police feared the worst, but Lesley wasted no energy worrying about what might have become of the beautiful and charming librarian. With her son lingering in a coma, she could focus on nothing else.

As Lesley walked down the now-familiar corridor, 5-B, she wondered if she should have put her little blue and green plaid blanket over Ryan's legs. The day seemed chillier than she'd thought. Deciding the extra cover would be a good idea, Lesley turned and went back to room 537. A stately white-haired figure, maintaining perfect posture, occupied Lesley's plastic chair. The plaid tartan throw already lay over Ryan's legs.

"I'll be here while you're gone," said Cosette Windsor, in a sweet, reassuring tone. "Some spirits like to be present at their own funeral but I have no impulse to do so."

Lesley's eyes filled with unexpected tears. "How long will you be," she paused, searching for the right word, "around?"

"Don't worry, darling. I'll be here as long as you need me. We Windsors have staying power."

Assuming her mother-in-law to be a vaporous manifestation with no substance, Lesley resisted the impulse to put an arm around the old woman's shoulder. When Cosette reached over and took Lesley's hand, however, the ghost's fingers felt cool but solid.

"Will Michael be at your," Lesley paused again, unequal to the strangeness of this conversation. She started over. "Will Michael be at the services this morning?"

"I'm sorry, darling. I have no greater powers of prophesy than I did when I walked the earth. I've never been good at predicting other people's actions. Especially Michael's. His behavior was erratic even as a child."

Lesley would have liked to question Cosette about this disclosure but she needed to go. "Thank you for coming, Cosette," she said. Although her acceptance of Cosette's presence might be considered unnatural, leaving Ryan with his grandmother felt right and she left the hospital with a lighter heart.

The Sonora Unitarian Church turned out to be a new building shingled to create a rustic look. Large numbers of well-dressed funeral-goers made their way into the foyer where attendants handed out a program decorated with Emily Dickinson's poem No. 214, "Inebriate of Air—am I—" Lesley entered the church, scanning the crowd for Michael. Surely he wouldn't miss his own mother's funeral? Russell sat in the front pew, next to William Roe, but none of his three children had accompanied the old man. Lesley made her way to his side.

"Is Ryan awake?" Russell asked, hope lighting his faded gray eyes.

"Not yet," answered Lesley. "I left him at the hospital, in good hands." Russell nodded. As Duke Ellington's "Mood

Indigo" issued from the public address system, Ralph P. Dekker could be seen jogging frantically up and down the left-hand aisle, holding sheaves of paper bearing a portrait of Cosette Windsor. Desktop publishing meets the funeral industry, thought Lesley in distraction.

"Mr. Dekker tells me that his business has never handled a service as unusual as this one," whispered Russell. "He was upset when we couldn't tell him what family members would be attending." Russell leaned even closer. "I'm so glad you're here, my dear. Michael hasn't even called. He must be taking his mother's death very hard. And Kelvin has turned to religion in order to cope with his loss. The Reverend Were has been sheltering him."

"What about Rachel?" asked Lesley. "Didn't she want to be at her mother's funeral?"

Russell looked startled by Lesley's question. "I don't know how much Michael has told you about his sister," he ventured.

"Hardly anything," Lesley replied in a whisper.

"Rachel developed a mental illness during her college years and has never recovered. She suffers from neurasthenia. She's nearly paralyzed much of the time. On other rare occasions, she can be violent and abusive. A few doctors have diagnosed her as suffering from severe bipolar disorder. At any rate, she can be a threat to herself and others."

Since Cosette's funeral didn't seem like the right occasion for further questions, Lesley concentrated on the strains of "Honeysuckle Rose" wafting over the swelling crowd. She squeezed Russell's hand and thought about the deceased, a woman she'd never met in the flesh, now such a presence in her life.

The crowd, including an overflow of people standing at the back, fell silent. A pleasant-looking man with dark skin, wearing a casual suit, mounted the stairs in front. He looked down at the notes on his podium and spoke the words, "Sweetest love, I do not go, For weariness of thee..." Lesley's eyes filled with tears. Cosette would have loved the service, Lesley felt sure. Songs from mid-twentieth century composers concluded the memorial.

The first strains of "Somewhere Over the Rainbow" barely

brushed the ears of the chapel before a harsh din arose from outside. Turning in her pew, Lesley could make out moving forms behind the somber seatless mourners. Cries and shouting soon drowned out the piped music selected by Russell.

"Who would disrupt Cosette's funeral?" asked Russell, his voice shaky with dismay. "She was loved by everyone who knew her."

"Then it's probably people who didn't know her," Lesley answered. "Don't pay attention."

But when Russell got to his feet and started up the center aisle, Lesley followed him. They entered the outer vestibule and Lesley saw that the noise emanated from a surly-looking group on the lawn outside.

"Kelvin! Michael!" she heard Russell cry.

Lesley rushed forward. At the forefront of the crowd stood Kelvin Windsor and her husband. The heirloom pendant, began growing warm and heavy once again. Lesley pushed the thing aside and rubbed her irritated clavicle. The necklace might have seared her to the bone and yet she felt no impulse to remove the Windsor heirloom.

"Michael!" Lesley called, releasing the necklace so that the gold chain swung back and forth and resettled just below her throat. "Michael!"

"Champion the Hue! Champion the Hue!" chanted the unruly crowd. This slogan, so familiar to Lesley, also appeared on printed placards along with various other sentiments including "Lord, Save Our Family From Darkness," and "Deviants—Leave the Gold Country or Perish!"

"Michael!" Lesley called again, seeing him carried along with the crowd. Recognizing her voice at last, Michael turned and plowed his way through the throng. Her husband struck her as glassy-eyed, drugged by the crowd's strange energy.

"Les," Michael began and faltered.

"Michael, where have you been?" Lesley demanded.

Michael winced and stepped back. She must temper her words, Lesley told herself.

"Ryan is in the hospital," she told him, speaking in a calm voice loud enough that Michael could hear her over hum of the crowd. "He was shot. I've tried to reach you for the last three days."

"I've been tied up," said Michael, drawing near. Lesley noted his pallid skin and the tic that tugged his left eye scalpward every thirty seconds. "Tied up with business," he added. Neither Michael's stationary right eye or his busy left one met Lesley's. Nothing, thought Lesley, could excuse Michael's failure to inquire, with his first breath, about Ryan's condition.

"Dan Walden says you've been missing from work. They've put you on administrative leave." Lesley stared at Michael, hoping against logic that he would offer a reasonable explanation for his aberrant behavior, hoping he'd ask after their son.

Michael made slashing motions with his right hand. "I've lost my mother, Lesley. Without her, my family and me could be run off, lose the house and our land. Only the Reverend Were can help us maintain our reputation and keep what's ours. I need his support."

"Michael, I don't understand," Lesley replied, trying to sound calm and kind. "I'm so sorry about your loss. I wish you'd attended the funeral with me because I think you would have found comfort in the music and poems that your mother loved. What's going on with you? Why would you be worried about slander and about losing your property? What do these local politics have to do with your mother's death?"

"You wouldn't understand. Things come out. The community could exact retribution." Michael leaned forward and muttered, "There's rumors of homosexuality in the family."

Lesley felt her face turn crimson as though she'd done something incriminating. Then, she gasped. "Michael, you're talking nonsense. No one wants retribution against the Windsors. Look at the number of people who turned out for your mother's funeral."

"My mother was a good woman and a good wife. Not like you!"

"What do you mean? What are you talking about!"

"Oh, don't think I don't know. The Reverend Were could tell right away that you have ideas. You're not on my side."

"I've tried to make you happy—"

"You tried," he said, "but I'm miserable which means that you've failed. Divorce might be the only way out. I'll be compromised by becoming a divorced man but being married to you compromises me more. The Reverend Were would be happy to sever our bond."

Michael didn't even know the real reason he should divorce her, thought Lesley with a heavy heart. The idea that she'd fallen in love with someone else would never occur to him. As if recalling that Lesley had been convicted of nothing, Michael shrugged. "If you prove to be deserving, you'll become the permanent Windsor wife." Suddenly, his eyes fixed upon the medallion that hung around Lesley's neck.

"The Mark of the Hue!" he exclaimed. "You're wearing my mother's necklace. Does that mean you're ready to assume her place? I never thought you'd consider such a thing. I'll rethink, Lesley. I'll give you another chance."

"Take your mother's place?" Lesley stammered. "Michael, we never discussed moving to Deerhaven Pines. Are you so sure that you want to move back to your parents' house? And what does this pendant have to do with it?"

"Everything. The Guardian of Deerhaven Forest Hall wears that necklace. You have entered into the covenant. I'll take your act of fealty into consideration when I weigh the pros and cons of remaining your husband and letting you raise our son."

What craziness was this? Lesley thought. Russell stirred behind her. Michael rubbed his eyes with the back of his hand shook his head. "I'm sure you two will work this out," Russell argued. "You'll be happy at Deerhaven Forest Hall, Lesley. You're the family in residence now."

"Champion the Hue. Champion the Hue," the phrase continued to issue from the crowd. Michael's head swiveled.

"I have to go," Michael yelped. "I need to consult with the Reverend." He began to back away.

Lesley's heart sank.

"Michael, what's come over you? Your son is in the hospital. They don't know yet whether he's going to pull through. Ryan is hurt, Michael. You need to be with him."

"I have to go," shouted Michael. Sighting the Reverend Were, he lunged into the crowd.

"Michael, please!" cried Lesley.

"He's not himself," said Russell, taking her arm. "Give him some time."

Lesley turned and buried her head in her father-in-law's wool funeral jacket. "Michael is Ryan's father. How can he turn his back on his son? Does he even understand what's happened?"

"Pardon my son. Please," Russell entreated. "Windsor men don't always have the inner strength to conduct themselves with dignity." Russell's gray eyes grew moist. "The women do. If Cosette hadn't forgiven me for the pain I caused her in our youth, we would have missed the second half of our life together and they were good years."

Kelvin Windsor appeared from out of the crowd. "Dad! Hello, Lesley," he greeted them with an anxious smile. "I'm sorry I couldn't attend the services, Dad. Reverend Were feels that Michael and I should stay away from conventional places of worship. We need special guidance because of our position in his congregation. He will show us the true path. You'll see."

Lesley didn't know or care what Kelvin might mean. The necklace around her throat quivered like a caged squirrel.

Russell stared at his son, at a loss. "Will you be coming home soon?" he asked in a tentative, quavering voice.

"Champion the Hue! Champion the Hue!" Chants accompanied Kelvin's reply but his answer rang clear.

"Can't. Not today, Dad." Kelvin disappeared as quickly as his brother.

"You're right," admitted Russell. "They must both be undone by their mother's death."

"Let me walk you to your car," Lesley offered. They strolled to the edge of the parking lot and stood under a tall Ponderosa pine looking down at Tamarack Creek gurgling below.

"Michael told me what a devoted father you were when he was small," reflected Lesley. "You're very good to your sons. Their behavior has been strange since your wife died but you've been kind and understanding. I'll try to live up to the standard you've set." To her surprise, Russell's square chin sank toward his chest and he sighed.

"I was a terrible parent and a terrible husband for many years," he confessed. His earnestness touched Lesley. "My sons deserve tolerance from me."

"Do you want to tell me about those bad years?" Lesley asked.

"Not today, not here, with Cosette not even buried. We should go now." Cosette Windsor had asked that no family member watch her lowered into the ground. An anonymous cemetery worker would be the last to feel the heft and bulk of the mortal coil she'd lately shed.

"Will I see you at the hospital?" Lesley inquired.

"Yes, you will, dear." Russell started toward the long, black car where William Roe waited at the wheel, and then he turned to face Lesley. "I'm going to make sure that Michael doesn't make the same mistakes as me. I want him to enjoy his family while he's young." The old man's face looked limp, an old bird's nest sagging on a dry, gray, gnarled branch.

"Thank you, Russell. I appreciate your kindness," Lesley told him.

She watched Russell's car turn onto Wheelock Road, framed against massive oaks and big bush lupine, which contrasted with the darker hues of lichenous scab rock protruding through the thin skin of Sierra soil. Hoisted from its dais in the anteroom, Cosette's mahogany coffin rolled down the Sonora Unitarian Church's back concrete ramp toward a deep, dry, hole in the cooling earth to begin the process of commingling.

****

"Champion the Hue! Champion the Hue!" screamed the crowd outside Deerhaven Forest Hall. Jane Copley Windsor and the librarian, Ursula Smith, cringed behind heavy drapery at one of the compass points within the library.

"I can't believe they mean us any harm," whispered Jane. "They are Christian folk, and we are pure of heart. If they only understood the nature of our souls' communion, they would have respect and compassion for us. Should we pray, Ursula?"

"Our prayers would be blotted out by the coarse voice of Reverend Chaney. How could God hear us? How discouraging to see God smiling upon the Reverend's Purity Party while neglecting innocent women." Ursula's lips curled in scorn as she added, "Innocent women possessed of greater intellect than the Reverend's howling mob."

"I'm frightened of them, Ursula. My skin crawls when they chant as though their words are meant to threaten you and me." Jane dropped her eyes with habitual modesty. "I fear they mean to punish us for the magnitude of our love."

"Your fears may not be unfounded, my sweet Jane," replied Ursula. "We must be wary. Will John Bennett protect us? Will he forbid them to trespass on Windsor land?"

Jane hung her head. "I have dreaded confessing this to you, Ursula, but I believe that John Bennett sympathizes with Reverend Chaney and his congregation. He doesn't want me as a wife, never wanted me, and he senses that my affections have settled elsewhere."

"No great feat of intuition," laughed Ursula. Jane did not join in Ursula's merriment.

"The other morning, I looked into John Bennett's face, as I almost never do, and caught an expression I have never witnessed on another human countenance. What I saw was hate. He hates me, Ursula. Were he ever to discover that you are the object of my passion, he could prove dangerous to you."

Ursula's face grew stern. She squared her shoulders to reveal her true height. "No one ultimately defeats a librarian. All knowledge lies within the seven walls of our domain. Even the Windsors, whom we serve with the greatest devotion, should take care to tread lightly in the library. If we librarians chose to wield our power, the Windsors would fall. Deliver that threat to your husband, if he menaces you. Tell John Bennett, 'Take heed! The librarian knows where your family's arcane secrets lie buried. She has indexed and shelved the evidence against you.' I do not think your husband will challenge me. I could make him a pariah. His friend, the Reverend Chaney, would be fascinated and incensed by the fruits of genealogical research conducted in *my* archives."

Although Ursula's eyes glittered like crystals of impacted ice, which survive all summer long in the Sierra's highest elevations, the arm she slipped around Jane's shoulders felt heavy and warm, better than a goose down quilt. Jane moved closer, resting her head against Ursula Smith so that she could inhale the sweet papery perfume clinging to Ursula's dull librarian's garb. Jane's breathing slowed to a peaceful pace. Ursula and her books would vanquish those who swore to champion the Hue, that army of darkness mustering under the tall pines outside Deerhaven Forest Hall. Yes, goodness and Ursula would triumph in the end.

CHAPTER THIRTEEN

Sula remembered nothing after being kidnapped. They had handled her without care; her body still bore the bruises inflicted by their ungentle hands. From her prison in the darkness, Sula could hear the Stanislaus River thunder past, the same sound of white water audible from the library windows. They had administered drugs through her food or water; perhaps they injected her with sedatives while she slumbered. She hadn't stood for days and her tongue flicked back and forth over dry lips. Sula wished she knew how the drugs were being administered but she couldn't think well. How could she fight what she didn't understand?

"Evil bastards," Sula whispered. Her muscles spasmed, protesting the prolonged period of inactivity. Although Sula enjoyed being in a supine position under other circumstances, right now she hungered for altitude. Lying this low wasn't good for a tall woman who normally held her head high. Bodily fluids pooled in her shoulders, buttocks and calves.

As Sula's mind drifted to the river's timpani, she dreamed about women. Women she'd tasted and women she'd never met greeted Sula with hypnotic seductive gestures. None of them withheld their affection. Their caresses warmed her skin long after they evaporated and left her alone in the dark. The smiles that played across Sula's face confused her captors, if only she'd known.

****

Days into her captivity, a muffled thump far off signaled someone's arrival. Sula's semicomatose state did not prevent her from cataloguing noises. Footsteps and voices sounded within the building, too many to sort out. The door to Sula's prison room opened with a distinctive scrape. Footsteps crossed the room and her lunchtime bowl of what Sula termed "gruel" hit the bedside table.

"You're a pretty girl," said a nasty voice, thin but deep. This man's appearance usually coincided with Sula's most alert state. "A pretty girl like you should take care of her looks, not molder and pale in the dark. You're plenty smart too. Why not act smart?"

"I won't give you what you want," replied Sula. "Leave me alone. You're wasting your breath." She stopped, hoping he'd think she fainted. She waited a few minutes but heard no departing footsteps. Since he hadn't paid attention to her pretended faint, Sula decided to try a different tack.

"ARE YOU THE REVEREND WERE?" she screamed, out of the blackness in which she lay. Silence. She hadn't managed to startle a response from the thready bass voice.

"Your tricks won't gain you anything, Madame Librarian. Sooner or later, you'll beg to be one of us. Once you've acknowledged the error of your ways, you'll hunger for absolution. I'm offering you salvation. This hidey-hole provides the perfect setting for a transformative moment, wouldn't you say?"

"Solitude replenishes," returned Sula, trying to resist being brainwashed by recalling the details of her stay at the Fruitful Arbor Bed-and-Breakfast in Jackson. The eyebrows of the proprietress arched in a delicious parabola. If Sula escaped this dark confinement, she planned to make a room reservation. Over wine and cheese, she would openly admire those black eyebrows and investigate their Morse code of lifts and shivers. Sula had a feeling that the woman would give her a discount on the honeymoon suite. Then, an icky voice broke through Sula's reverie.

"We could make you talk if we employed the old-fashioned methods. Once the sharpened instruments of our Lord cut your flesh you'd tell us anything. A few permanent marks on that perfect face and you'd be begging for mercy. Alas, those techniques are beneath us."

"Yeah, right," Sula answered. "I know why you haven't butchered me. You're afraid of the ancient stories. You know about the old magic. I'll bet you've heard that if you sacrifice an innocent person in an evil cause, your pulpit will be destroyed. Death itself can be reversed. You can't kill me. I might find a way to come back and haunt you." Sula's giddy laughter made her tormentor snarl.

"You've read too much of the swill in your library," he hissed. "There's nothing keeping you from harm but our good graces and the mercy of the Lord. I suggest you mend your ways. We need the knowledge you possess before we can convict the deviants and defectives who have thus far gone unpunished. You've read the Bible enough to know that our time will come." A sneer thinned the man's voice even further as he added, "You'll be our disciple before you leave this room. Trust me."

Hunger overwhelmed Sula. She leaned over, picked up her spoon, and took a bite of tasteless mush. Sula could sense him watching her and heard his soft, thin laugh.

Once he'd left the room, Sula considered her captors' demands. She tried to analyze their words and actions. She didn't doubt that they could turn violent. They'd shot Lesley Windsor's beautiful little boy, after all, when he tried to shield her from their bullets. That alone proved that they were evil beyond measure. She could still hear Ryan Windsor moaning, "Mom!

Mom, help me." Her thoughts began to blur and fade. Realizing she'd been drugged once again, Sula acknowledged that every bit of food and drink with which they supplied her might be saturated with a chemical element that stole her consciousness. What should she do? She couldn't go without food and drink altogether but that would be the only way to regain her senses. She relinquished conscious thought but as she sunk into the netherworld, one phrase played over and over in her mind.

"Champion the Hue," her interrogators repeated over and over.

What would championing the Hue entail? thought Sula. She couldn't imagine. She'd never understood the Windsor family motto. "Hue" implied color but this group seemed affiliated with the dark. She must deny them. A librarian never championed darkness or intellectual blindness. Intellectual freedom would always be her creed. *Lux eterna*, muttered Sula. She'd always liked those words. She savored the words, but they segued in her fuzzy brain to the words, Luck be a lady. Words to live by, Sula thought.

****

Switching on some modern music, Lesley turned the wheels of her Lexus toward the hospital. The music helped banish the melancholy of Cosette's funeral but when Lesley pulled up at a stop sign on Coulter Pine Road, the Beatles faded. She glanced at the radio dials but the LCD readout still glowed. Lesley looked over and found Cosette Windsor in the seat next to her. The shade of her mother-in-law, vivid as the pedestrians crossing the road in front of her, sat with brows knitted.

"Ryan?" cried Lesley, heart in her throat.

Cosette reached over to comfort her. "Ryan's just fine. His nice doctor is with him," Cosette told her. "Could you pull over, dear?"

"What is it, Cosette?" asked Lesley, parking under a woody valley oak.

"Lesley, would you mind leaving Ryan in my care for a while longer? I'll see that no harm comes to him. His medical care is excellent. I have complete faith in Dr. Andy Riemer. You do too, don't you?"

Lesley nodded. "Cosette, why shouldn't I go to the hospital? It's not that I don't trust you, but my place is with Ryan."

The ghost beside Lesley lowered her glowing face and appeared to fight back tears if, indeed, ghosts cry. Lesley leaned toward the passenger seat, asking, "What do you want? Just tell me and I'll try to help."

"One of my children needs you," said Cosette.

"Michael? Do I need to help Michael?" Lesley asked.

"I don't mean Michael. It's my daughter, Rachel. She needs you, Lesley. Please. I wronged her many years ago, and I want to make amends." Cosette looked into Lesley's eyes with a steady, knowing gaze.

By the time Lesley blinked, Cosette no longer occupied the seat beside her. Lesley sat with her hands affixed to the steering wheel, thinking. Then, she started the engine and pulled into the street in the direction of Deerhaven Pines. At the Wolf's Creek boundary, Lesley decelerated. She'd come to fear the residents of Wolf's Creek, from Sheriff Phil Morton to the powerful Reverend Were. She didn't want to fall into their hands by receiving a speeding ticket. A sigh of relief escaped her when she passed the sign reading, "Entering Deerhaven Forest."

Still traveling at a moderate pace, Lesley observed the woodlands surrounding Deerhaven Forest Hall, a rich profusion of digger pines, interior live oaks, blue oak, poison oak, buckeye, chamise and redbud. When she emerged from the woods, she observed the tiny town of Deerhaven Pines sunning itself in a weak November light whose cool lucidity forecast the approaching Sierra winter. Not until she turned down the main drive to Deerhaven Forest Hall, did Lesley see and hear anything amiss.

"Champion the Hue! Champion the Hue!" The throng's guttural chant penetrated her car, and she experienced a twinge of the same sickness that had assailed her at the Grange Hall in Wolf's Creek. Lesley gripped the steering wheel tighter. Were Michael and Kelvin among the mob outside their own gates?

Yes, she could make out Michael's trim figure and the ominous Picassoesque silhouette of Reverend Were.

The crowd at the gates spotted Lesley's car and, to her horror, they raised fists and clubs in her direction. Didn't Michael recognize the Lexus? Wouldn't he protect her against these besotted strangers? The chanting, and Lesley's reaction to the words, increased in intensity as she drew closer. She regretted coming back to Deerhaven Forest Hall. This errand made no sense. With a small child lying in the hospital hovering between life and death, she could not afford to take risks. Quickly rotating the steering wheel, tires screeching, she turned back toward the town of Deerhaven Pines. But how could she face Cosette if she abandoned her mission? How would she answer her own conscience if any harm came to Rachel Windsor?

Out of sight of the crowd, she drove her van off the road and hid the vehicle behind chaparral, under pines and oak. Screened by trees, Lesley jogged back, following an orbicular course, and emerged near the Hall's rear entrance. The tall, spiked stakes surrounding the property seemed far enough apart for a slight woman like her to slip past. She held her breath and squeezed through the bars. Considering how to proceed, she scanned the Hall's roofline. "Hold on, Rachel! I'm coming," she murmured.

Gathering her courage, she removed the pumps she'd worn to the funeral and sprinted across the back lawns. By the time she reached the rear patio and grasped the door handles, her feet had grown numb, and she wished that she owned gloves. She slipped her shoes back on and relaxed when she found the kitchens deserted. Her luck held as she progressed forward. She met neither Mrs. Woolf nor anyone else as she traveled the length of the house. She started upstairs.

After a short visit to her sitting room where she swiftly changed into trousers and boots, Lesley checked the hallway and headed for the next flight of stairs and Rachel's suite. Contrary to what she expected, she found the bottom door unlocked.

"Rachel!" Lesley called as she took the stairs two at a time. "Rachel! Valerie! Are you there?" Lesley flew into Rachel's apartment and came to an abrupt halt, putting a hand to her throat.

"Valerie, where are you?" screamed Lesley. "Help!"

On the spartan dais in the center of the attic room, lay Rachel, in a crumpled ball, her dark brown hair streaming wildly. Rachel whistled through small white teeth like a fawn scared beyond reason.

"Valerie," called Lesley, but Rachel's attendant did not answer.

Lesley gathered Rachel in her arms. "You'll be fine," she murmured in the same voice she used to soothe away Ryan's and Michael's bad dreams. Her sister-in-law's small intakes of breath became more regular. Once Rachel grew calm, her eyes widened into broad smudges of soot-gray and she sat up and shoved Lesley away with steely arms.

"Are you the one who's going to kill me?" Rachel cried. "Are you with them?" She flung her feet over the side of the bed and tried to rise but her knees buckled and she pitched forward. Lesley grasped Rachel's shoulders to steady her.

"Your mother sent me to help you," Lesley told her. "Cosette knew you needed help." Rachel shook her head like a wildflower in a violent wind. "Cosette is dead. Her spirit visited me and said we'd not meet again. My father told me she died of brain cancer. So, she couldn't have sent you. If you're here to kill me, go ahead and do it. If my mother were alive, that would be her wish! She's wanted me dead since I was very young."

Lesley stared at Rachel Windsor in confusion. Could Rachel be talking about the dear departed Cosette whose spirit treated Lesley with such love and care?

"Champion the Hue! Champion the Hue!" came the audible threats from the rabble outside. Lesley didn't have time to psychoanalyze Rachel with the crowd coming nearer and nearer. Lesley ran to the window. Dark shapes milled upon the well-tended front lawns, many holding banners and placards that they waved above their heads.

"Rachel! I'm Lesley. Here to help you. Your mother wants me to protect you from the crowd on the lawn. I'm sure of it." She tugged at the wild-eyed woman. "Will you come with me? Trust me? My heart is in the right place." Rachel's gray eyes assessed

Lesley and some deep-felt emotion made Rachel's eyelids close and then open. Her eyes expressed a new softness.

"I will do whatever you say, Lesley. Where do you think we should go?"

"Anywhere but here. Can you walk, Rachel?" She didn't think she could carry Rachel even though the other woman was small and slight. The odious cries from the lawn swelled. Maybe Lesley could support Rachel enough to propel her out of the house on her own two feet. Where there's a will there's a way, Lesley's parents always said.

Lesley put both arms under Rachel's arms and, with knees bent, hoisted the young woman to her feet. Rachel swayed but found her footing. With Lesley supporting a portion of Rachel's weight, they threaded their way toward the door. The stairs seemed insurmountable but Lesley found that she could slide Rachel's feet from riser to riser. In that fashion, they reached the landing and confronted the hallway and the lower staircase.

Breathing hard with exertion, Lesley steadied herself by concentrating on Rachel's nearness. They must hurry toward the sheltering woods. But how would they get there undetected? Lesley could not shoulder Rachel's weight and still make good progress. A sprinkling of sweat, from fear or overexertion, broke out at the base of her throat.

"Rachel!" an authoritative voice called from the hall doorway. It was Valerie, Rachel's nurse. Never had Lesley welcomed company so much.

"Up here, Valerie," Lesley cried.

"Valerie," called Rachel in a weak voice. "Valerie, help us!" Rachel attempted to move forward and signal Valerie but she could not walk unsupported. As Rachel teetered on her feet, Lesley caught her and they slumped against the wall. Rachel's nurse hurried to join them.

"Valerie!" Lesley cried. "We need to leave the Hall before Reverend Were's mob overtakes us. Will you help me take Rachel to the woods?"

"Do you really think the Reverend's group could be a threat to you?" returned Valerie. "We could very well endanger Rachel's health by moving her."

"We have to take the chance," said Lesley with surprising conviction. She'd always been wishy-washy in the face of another's authority but not today. Valerie shrugged, ascended the stairs, and grasped Rachel's elbow. Lesley sighed with relief.

"Rachel will be fine," Lesley told Valerie, "I promise." She believed that Cosette would not let Rachel come to harm.

"I'm not taking responsibility," gasped Valerie, "No responsibility whatsoever. I could have my license revoked."

"She's my sister-in-law," said Lesley. "I'll take responsibility."

They escorted Rachel through empty corridors and down to the expansive entryway. Sunlight slanted through high windows illuminating a painting. The curving lines, weather and season symbols, odd familiar faces that Lesley couldn't quite place; she'd seen them before. The entry's walls formed a septagon, like the library. The etching on the oak floor in this area also appeared in the library. She wished they weren't in such a terrible hurry. The pendant around Lesley's neck throbbed and grew warm as if signaling the significance of the painting. Should she be paying more attention? Maybe she would come back here, stand in the entryway, and decipher the clues. The weight of all that Lesley didn't understand, on balance, seemed greater than the fragile weight of the woman who leaned against her.

"We can't just hide in the woods," Valerie remarked from Rachel's other side. "What are we going to do?"

"Leave by the back door and run for cover," said Lesley. "Then, we'll circle back to my car and take off." She glanced over at Rachel's stern attendant, thankful for her muscled hands and the authority conferred by her position as nurse. "Are you with us?" Lesley asked. "You're not too afraid of the crowd to help Rachel, are you?"

"I'm not afraid," pronounced Valerie. Lesley smiled with gratitude. Valerie nodded at Lesley through a cloud of Rachel's shiny, dark hair, streaming in the air currents created by their headlong flight.

"Let's go!" shouted Lesley, flinging open the back doors. They each half-lifted Rachel and burst onto the patio, lit by cool rays of sun. Crossing the bricked surface in seconds, Lesley and

Valerie found themselves slowed by Rachel's dragging feet. The brown detritus of fall sucked at the soles of their shoes.

"Don't let them get me," moaned Rachel.

For all Lesley knew, Rachel hadn't seen the light of day in years. "You're okay," Lesley soothed Rachel, "they haven't come around the side of the building. They don't know we're here."

She spoke too soon. Rude voices and the sound of booted feet pierced the backyard silence. "Oh, my God," Lesley exclaimed. "Hurry, Valerie." She could only hope the high weeds and brush would camouflage them for a while.

"Reverend! Brethren! Here! This way!" shouted Valerie.

"What are you doing?" Lesley cried.

"Alerting my Holy Commander," barked Valerie. "For years, I have watchdogged the Windsor family and witnessed them countenancing evil. Now, the day of reckoning is at hand. I will no longer pretend to serve this defective girl, this weak vessel of all that blights our world."

"Are you talking about Rachel?" asked Lesley.

The attendant's hard features answered Lesley more directly than words.

In a lightning dive, Lesley kicked at the attendant's heavy shoes and then her knees. Valerie pitched forward, landing on her stomach. The nurse turned with fingers arched as if to claw at Lesley and then Rachel. Lesley raked at Valerie with her own good right hand. Valerie possessed far greater physical strength than Lesley but scarlet blood saved her from the nurse. Blood poured from a gash in Valerie's forehead and ran down into her mouth. The nurse gagged and bent to wipe her face.

Lesley snatched off the leather belt she wore and tied the leather strap around Valerie's legs so that the binding bit the nurse's flesh. This tactic would not deter the nurse for more than a few minutes but Lesley would maximize every second. She glanced up at Rachel. To Lesley's relief, Rachel stood, wavering on her own two feet. Ignoring the caretaker who'd betrayed her, Rachel looked to Lesley for direction. Lesley retook Rachel's arm and dragged her toward the waiting oaks. Lesley didn't look back, couldn't hear a thing over the pounding of her own heart.

With every step, Rachel grew surer-footed, and Lesley took

heart at her companion's progress. Whatever problem caused Rachel to remain housebound, perhaps this crisis would give her the strength to transcend it. When the trees welcomed them, Rachel walked on her own, grasping slender trunks for support. By the time they reached full shade, Lesley halted and Rachel collapsed onto the ground.

"You've been great, Rachel," commented Lesley, feeling shy and unsure. Had their flight from the Reverend proved herself to Rachel?

"Thank you," Rachel returned in a flat voice. She took one quick look at Lesley. "You're really Michael's wife, Lesley?"

"Yes," Lesley replied, pleased that Rachel remembered her first name.

"I saw him with the Reverend's mob. Should you leave me here and go to him?"

"I'm divorcing your brother," Lesley announced, more sharply than she intended.

"Oh. I see," answered Rachel and asked no more questions. Surprisingly, Rachel's mind took a practical turn. "Lesley, can you go back and take a look at the house? Are they coming this way or standing outside the house again?"

Lesley crept to the tree line. "They're swarming inside the Hall. Oh, Rachel, your home! I'm so sorry."

Rachel pulled herself into a sitting position. "They've gone inside Deerhaven Forest Hall? No! There's no way they could."

"What do you mean?" asked Lesley, confused.

"No one can enter Deerhaven Forest Hall without permission. Therefore, no one who wishes the Windsors ill can get inside." Rachel paused for breath.

"You're wrong, Rachel," interrupted Lesley. "Someone broke into the Hall and shot my son."

Rachel's gray eyes went black with horror.

"How is your son?" gasped Rachel. "My nephew."

"He's going to be all right," said Lesley, forcing herself to sound sure. "Don't be upset."

"Don't be upset? The Hall has been invaded! Your son shot! I don't think you understand the implications." Rachel struggled to rise, grasping the trunk of a smooth and aromatic toyon.

Perfume rose from where Rachel's small hands alighted upon the tree's light gray bark.

"What do you mean?" demanded Lesley.

"The person who injured your son had to have been asked inside the Hall by a Windsor. The looters going through the doors right now also had to have been invited."

"Invited?" Lesley repeated.

"A Windsor granted them permission to go inside," stated Rachel. "They would never have gained admittance otherwise. Those who erected the Hall decreed that no outsider should be able to enter without permission."

"Could Michael have let those people inside?" Lesley queried. "I don't know what kind of crazy thing Michael might do in his present state. He's mesmerized by the Reverend Were."

"Michael? I don't think he's the turncoat. He's weak and probably a pawn in the game. More likely, my father let them in! His role as master of the Hall corrupted his soul years ago. I can attest to that!"

Before Lesley could question Rachel, hard cries rose from the field outside their haven of oaks and pines. Lesley snatched Rachel's arm. "Come with me! Valerie will have told the Reverend and his mob that we're heading for my car. We'll go the opposite direction to the river."

Lesley led Rachel in the direction of the Stanislaus. Stumbling through brush and trees, she strained to hear running water. Rachel kept pace, propelled by Lesley, but the river eluded them. None of Lesley's Girl Scout tricks—assessing the angle of the sun, noting the trees' growth patterns, paying attention to which side of the large boulders grew moss—helped orient her.

"Do you have any idea whether we're going in the right direction?" Lesley panted.

"I'm not sure," Rachel replied. "When I was a girl, I played in these woods but that was long ago." Rachel closed her eyes and listened. "Let's head this way."

They trod over pine needles, in, out and under stands of trees. When they came up against a dense stand of manzanita, Lesley and Rachel stood perplexed. Rachel's excessive panting betrayed her lack of physical stamina. When lost, remain where you are until help arrives, Lesley had been taught. So much for her bank of knowledge! Staying put would give Reverend Were the opportunity to ensnare them.

As Lesley pondered their next move, help arrived on tiny hooves. A family of neat, tan deer floated by, sailing over bushes, creating only the faintest rustling of dry leaves. They're probably heading for water, thought Lesley. "This way, Rachel!" she exclaimed and squeezed them between dull red manzanita limbs, in the wake of the deer.

They reached the crest of a hill and headed down. From inside a hollow filled with California buckeyes, Lesley watched their cloven-footed guides mount the next rise and disappear. She and Rachel followed.

"Water!" said Lesley.

"Men!" cried Rachel, pointing in the direction from which they'd come.

Whirling, Lesley saw a crowd of about fifteen or twenty people. Most wore colors, probably the flannel shirts that had been common among the group at the Grange Hall. A figure in white, one in red, and a tall form dressed in black, trailed the pack.

"Lean on me, Rachel. We can make it to the river!" Lesley dragged Rachel downhill, toward the frothy, sparkling water of the Stanislaus. They stumbled at a fast clip as the vegetation turned to Indian rhubarb, miner's lettuce and white alder.

The Stanislaus River lay before them. Near the riverbank, Lesley found Rachel a seat under an alder and surveyed the gravelly beach, hoping for help to appear. If the county sheriff were here, the mob would be arrested for trespassing on Windsor property. Or would the sheriff prove to be no more than a servant of the Reverend Were? Lesley mounted a huge river rock from where she could see a long stretch of river. No one emerged from the woods, for the moment.

Lesley scrambled to formulate a plan of escape. Trees, fast water, sipping deer, what would serve to provide help for her and Rachel? Her eyes finally settled upon a massive piece of knobby bark bobbing between two large pieces of granite near the shore. Too large to have come from a local tree, the bark boat must have sailed from a higher elevation. Lesley climbed back to where Rachel waited.

"Don't be frightened but I think we should escape by river," she told her companion. Rachel looked white and alarmed but she put a hand on the ground and pushed, attempting to boost herself to her feet. "Take both my hands," said Lesley, reaching for Rachel.

The bark stayed moored until Lesley seated Rachel upon it. Then, Lesley hauled the wooden craft free and stepped aboard. The bark sank to the rocky bottom, wetting Rachel's shoes and clothes. Rachel remained silent as Lesley labored to launch them. A few more tries proved that the makeshift boat would not support two. Gritting her teeth against the cold, Lesley shoved the bark bearing Rachel into the water and slid into the current, holding on with both hands. The bark, once extricated, carried Lesley downstream like the tail of a fish.

"Mrs. Windsor!" came an ominous shriek, too virulent to be wind or water. She craned her neck and saw their pursuers gathered at water's edge.

The Reverend Were, razor-thin, looking like a black stiletto jammed handle-first into the beach, pointed a forbidding finger at her. At the same time, the river bore them back toward the shore. Lesley observed with horror that the white blur she'd observed was her father-in-law, Russell Windsor. In between the minister and the old man, wearing red, stood Sula Smith, the missing librarian.

"Russell! Sula!" Lesley screamed.

"They're with me," thundered Reverend Were. "Everyone stands with me. Join us, Mrs. Windsor. Your husband will be restored. We will pray for your son's recovery. God listens to the prayers of many. Join us."

Clinging with frantic fingers to her insubstantial wooden craft, Lesley wondered whether the Reverend might, in fact, be harmless. What did he want from her? Although her feet had begun to freeze in the end-of-autumn Sierra runoff, Lesley's brain had not yet gone numb. She devised a test.

"All right. I'm going to let go of Rachel and swim to shore," Lesley shouted. "We can rescue her farther downstream."

The Reverend sliced the air with his knife-tip of a hand. "No," he called. "Bring us that young woman. She needs our guidance. Rachel Windsor embodies the darkness that allures Satan. Evil will come to Deerhaven Pines, Wolf's Creek, and beyond, if this foul-spirited woman is not cleansed by our love."

The word love resonated over the unruly water like an obscenity. Lesley had never heard the sweetest of endearments so perverted.

"Go to hell," Lesley screamed. "The river will save us."

As if responding to Lesley's urgency and faith, the current dragged her boat to the right, veering away from the shore. Delivered into the river's main stream, the bark boat sped forward and down a chute created by granite rocks on either side. Racing white water propelled them.

"Hold on, Rachel!" screamed Lesley. The water's crash and boom drowned her human voice after that, and the spray obscured her view of Rachel.

****

"Death to witches! Death to witches!" clamored harsh, ugly voices outside the front doors. Ursa and Jane crept forward, climbed on a window bench and peered through the heavy mauve drapery. Jane shuddered when her eyes beheld a writhing clump of townspeople led by a dark-gowned cleric, tall as his church spire.

"They can't come in," Ursa reassured Jane.

"Why not?" asked Jane, trembling. She would bear a child in the spring and she feared for her safety as she never had before. No matter how hideous and violent her poor bairn's conception had been, Jane already loved him without reserve. "What makes you think they won't come inside?" she repeated.

"No enemy can enter Deerhaven Forest Hall unless invited by a family member. This decree came down from the Hall's architect, Simon Chalmers. Good Simon Chalmers constructed the Hall according to the dictates of a higher being with whom he communicated all his life. The deity, who visited Simon in the form of a golden buck, promised him sanctuary for himself and his progeny. A golden buck appeared in Simon's dreams and assured him that an invitation would be required for admittance to the Hall."

"Did Deerhaven Forest Hall keep Simon Chalmers safe from danger?"

"I cannot say. Simon Chalmers died a strange death in the jaws of terrible he-wolf but not within the Hall. Mr. Chalmers' only child, a daughter, married Gordon Windsor and the Windsors have held Deerhaven Forest Hall and the revenues from his mine, the Golden Buck, ever since."

"So you believe we're safe inside these walls," said Jane.

"I know we are. Enemies have tested the golden buck's covenant several times in Windsor history and found that they could not invade Deerhaven Forest Hall."

A mighty crash sounded. The two women looked deep into each other's eyes and joined hands.

"Where are John Bennett, his brothers and his father?" asked Ursa, her voice suddenly sharp. "I saw Belle, Eleanor and Julia in the drawing room this morning. Can every one of them have failed to hear this commotion?"

"They took the carriage into Wolf's Creek," replied Jane. "They mean to purchase goods for the family's Christmas celebration. I remained behind so that we could be with each other."

Ursula's wide mouth softened and she touched Jane's cheek with her ivory librarian's hand so adept at finding the right passages. Ursula's fondness and Jane's pleasure did not, however, find further expression. A new tumult brought them to their feet.

"Ursula!" cried Jane. "They have penetrated the Hall!"

"I can tell you one thing," said Ursula, her face grim, all traces of sentiment wiped away. "This invasion means that at least one of the party who rode away in the Windsor carriage this morning has betrayed the sanctity of the Hall. A Windsor invited these marauders."

"Do you think they'll come to the library? Would they trifle with two harmless women who like to read and study with each other?" Ursula's eyes met Jane's.

"They might suspect that we enjoy more than reading and, for that reason, I fear we might be their quarry." Ursula pinched her temples as if her head hurt.

Jane squared her shoulders and turned to face the library entrance, guarded by two lions that, being cast in bronze, could offer them no protection. The two women heard the massive front doors of Deerhaven Forest Hall thunder on heavy hinges, followed by loathsome shrieks in the corridors.

"May the strength of our love protect us," prayed Jane.

CHAPTER FOURTEEN

Water filled Lesley's mouth, fresh Stanislaus foam. When she opened her eyes, Lesley saw huge pines and an icy blue sky. The river whirled around her as she treaded water to keep herself afloat. She'd arrived at a wide dam created by tree trunks. Spitting and choking, she gasped, inhaling a bodyful of pure Sierra air and, in an instant, the day's events sprang into focus.

"Rachel! Rachel!" Lesley called. The bark boat could not have traveled past the logjam but Lesley didn't see any sign of her beloved sister-in-law. Had the river swallowed Rachel? Lesley breaststroked toward the bank until she could touch bottom with her feet and, rising, trod globular slippery river rocks, stumbling and dunking herself in last year's snow melt.

The Stanislaus River chilled and bruised Lesley's flesh but the current helped carry her to shore. Collapsing on the bank, physically taxed, Lesley tried to marshal her thoughts. Downstream, upstream, which way should she turn? She addressed the running water, calling "Which way?" but the noisy water offered no reply. Waterlogged and verging on hysteria, Lesley turned northeast and began retracing her recent plummet.

As Lesley trudged along the riverside, she assessed the dismal circumstances that brought her to these banks. Her husband had almost surely turned against her, she'd accepted that hard truth, but that was only the beginning. Kelvin Windsor served the Reverend Were also and must also be counted as an enemy. Other betrayers included those whom she'd considered friends, Russell Windsor and the librarian, Sula Smith. With her own eyes, Lesley had observed them standing at the Reverend Were's side. They'd watched as he threatened her and Rachel and neither intervened. The only person in Deerhaven Pines that Lesley could trust, Cosette Windsor, had no more substance than river mist. That person had been buried that day. Rachel, however attractive, remained an unknown commodity in the trustworthiness category.

At meadow's end, most of the land navigable by foot disappeared, and Lesley picked her way along a bank littered with big boulders, sapling trees and a narrow pipe that paralleled the river. She spotted a man-made structure, like miniature train tracks, pinned to the cliffs above. Based on Michael's descriptions, Lesley guessed that this tunnel and track must be an open flume, a trolley used to move miners and equipment in gold rush days. The construction of modern tunnels had made flumes obsolete but Michael and his brother had traversed the old tracks as children. Lesley thought about climbing the steep, eroding hill to walk the flume but discarded the idea when earth and shale cascaded from above with no apparent provocation. She continued along the water's edge. White water foamed at her feet, wetting her leather Doc Martens.

Around a bend, the river canyon widened again. A swaying suspension bridge suggested that there might be people nearby and, although she didn't like idea of trusting strangers, any one of whom might be one of Reverend Were's converts, Lesley called out, "Is there anyone there?" She heard the bridge's creak and clang in the absence of human utterance. Lesley shivered as a cool breeze whipped at her damp clothing.

Lesley continued her tour of the historic Stanislaus River with growing despair. Beyond the bridge, she encountered clear evidence of sluice mining. The miners flumed water out of a small creek, held in a small pool above the slope, and then released downward. The slurry of dirt and water would have been sluiced in boxes with the hope of finding gold in screens. When Lesley came closer, she found disintegrating sluice boxes in the flat work area alongside rusting metal implements she couldn't identify.

Rounding another bend, Lesley caught her breath in wonder at the sight of a small meadow ringed with alders and pine. The forest-green woods and purple mountains glowed like an impressionist painting. Even in her distress, Lesley could not ignore nature's artful use of color. "I'll bring Ryan here," she promised herself, "and Rachel, too." Going forth from that lovely site, Lesley entered a serene stretch of river canopied with lacy foliage.

Puffy white clouds, innocent of treacherous raindrops, floated high over the pools she passed. At one point along the banks, incense cedars, yellow pines, big leaf maples, willows, Oregon ash, live oak and digger pines, shielded an incongruous fig tree. Lesley marveled at the wealth of trees. At last a sudden movement rewarded her exertions. She caught a glimpse of red against the green earth and trees, a cloak, a hood. Lesley's heart thudded with gladness. Rachel!

"Rachel," Lesley cried, running as fast as she could.

Rachel Windsor lay beside ponderous stones, her arms around the rocks; damp hair trailing toward her waist like tendrils of vine after a winter storm. Although Rachel's eyes remained closed, something about the definite positioning of her hands on the granite told Lesley that Rachel lived. Lesley knelt beside her.

Rubbing the young woman's downy temples, Lesley murmured encouragement, promising Rachel comfort and companionship, not that she knew whether Rachel wanted comfort or companionship from her. Rachel moaned and river water dribbled down her chin. Wiping Rachel's face with her camisole, Lesley smiled down at the woman.

"Who are you who offers me company and support?" groaned Rachel, her eyes open at last. "I don't know you."

"It's Lesley. Lesley Windsor, Michael's wife. We entered the river to escape from Reverend Were but we're all right. You're going to be all right." Lesley pumped her sister-in-law's hand as though congratulating her on a speedy recovery.

"Are they after us?" asked Rachel, struggling to sit.

"I don't know," admitted Lesley. "The weather looks like it might be turning bad, which might slow them down. We should find shelter and talk about what to do."

"Shelter. Yes," repeated Rachel, scanning their surroundings. "Where can we go?"

"I have an idea," Lesley replied. "I saw a beautiful meadow on my way here. The woods behind the clearing would give us cover. Let's go back there and see if we can construct a lean-to under the trees." Lesley stood and held out her hands to Rachel who slipped small, cold fingers into Lesley's warmer grip, and Lesley pulled her to her feet.

The rigorous float down the river had depleted Rachel's reserves and the dripping woman could not walk unsupported. Summoning a strength she didn't know she possessed, Lesley almost carried her sister-in-law. Their trek seemed endless, punctuated with stops so that Lesley could listen for the presence of their enemies. They encountered no living being as they struggled onward, not even a deer or chipmunk. Eventually, the sun disappeared behind a platoon of dark oncoming clouds but when they came to the meadow, Rachel stirred enough to whisper, "How wonderful this place seems! I've been up and down the river but I've never been here."

Just past the tree line, Lesley let Rachel slide onto a smooth boulder and sank down beside her, safe for the moment. Her worries crept back into her consciousness. Lesley shut her eyes and willed Cosette to appear and reassure her that Ryan didn't need his mother, but no soft white apparition materialized and Lesley contented herself with inner solace. She turned and peered into the woods. Black oaks lined what might be a path leading away from the river.

"Rachel! Let's take that trail. Maybe we'll find someone who can help us. I'll help you along the way."

Supporting Rachel against her, Lesley led them deeper into the woods. The darker their surroundings, the thicker the green and vermilion mosses, mistletoe and dry branches above their heads, the better protected Lesley felt. The vegetation would shield them from discovery.

"It's dark," moaned Rachel, faintly, as if to herself.

"We'll be there soon," Lesley replied, although she knew no more about where they might be headed than Rachel. Lesley's heart grew lighter even as the woods obscured the last dregs of light.

The darkness didn't last. Illumination filtered through the branches as soon as the light behind them disappeared. In front of them, at the edge of a new meadow, they found a place with color and composition as brilliant as in the clearing near the river.

"I can tell that we'll be safe here for a while," Lesley told Rachel.

"What's that?" asked Rachel, wincing as she lifted her arm. Where Rachel pointed, Lesley saw a stark granite boulder that might be the back of a carved obelisk, something fashioned by human hands. Rachel and Lesley approached the monument and studied the graceful, gray cut-stone. A smooth surface, untouched by wind or weather, met their fingers when they touched the rock's surface. Rounding the boulder, Lesley drew a breath in shock.

Here lies Dame Ursula Smith, Librarian,
November 14, 1922
She lies next to her companion of the heart,
Mistress Jane Copley Windsor, January 14, 1906
"Where did your Christ come from?...
From God and a woman. Man had nothing to do with him."

"A grave," stated Lesley. "One of your ancestors is buried

here. And one of your family librarian's ancestors, assuming that Ursula must have been related to Sula Smith."

Rachel studied the inscription, biting her lip. "Who buried them so far from home?"

"Maybe Sula knows," said Lesley but, thinking of Sula's betrayal, she added, "I'll never ask her, though. Not since learning that she's joined the Reverend Were."

"Sula was a small girl when I last saw her," said Rachel. "She never came upstairs. Sula's mother, Ursa, seemed like a nice woman, though. And smart." Rachel straightened suddenly. "Lesley!" she cried. "Could that be an empty house? Over there!"

Lesley shielded her eyes and looked. A neat, wood cabin, surrounded by gold flowers, late bloomers, sat waiting across the grasses. Later, Lesley would wonder why she never worried that the cabin might be inhabited. She didn't pause before entering but reached for the front doorknob as if by habit but discovered that the knob didn't turn. The last occupants had locked the door before departing. Lesley sat Rachel on the porch swing and strode back down the steps. As if she knew the cabin's owners and could anticipate them, Lesley ran her hand under the lip of the porch floor. Immediately, she discovered a metal box and extracted the key.

When the cabin's heavy oak door swung open, Lesley couldn't believe her eyes. Hidden behind rough-hewn outside walls, the interior gleamed like a diamond set in tarnished brass. Victorian furniture and oil paintings gave the front rooms a rich antique effect lightened by pale wood, cream-colored wallpaper and skylights that must be a more recent addition. Lesley searched the house and discovered two neat bedrooms at the back and a modern bathroom. The last occupants had provided soap, towels and toilet paper, as though this could be a guest cabin. The kitchen, stocked with non-perishable goods, would provide them with a camp meal of some kind, pancake mix, syrup and canned soup.

"Rachel, this house is perfect. Someone takes care of the place but they haven't been here for a while. The heat and electricity work, though. We may as well spend the night. By morning, you and I can decide where we'll go for help. For now, why don't you take a hot bath? I'll bring you a glass of the good whiskey I saw in the kitchen, and you'll feel better in no time."

Shivering and white, Rachel nodded gratefully. Rising to her feet, she swayed, reached out, and found Lesley's arm to stabilize herself. Lesley guided her to the larger bedroom, graced by a polished sleigh bed. Powdery snow made a sudden appearance at the picture window that framed the winter woods behind them. Lowering Rachel to the cherry-colored quilt, Lesley remarked, "Maybe you should rest before you do anything else."

"Yes," murmured Rachel.

Lesley removed Rachel's damp stockings and shoes and covered the weak, young woman with a soft wool blanket from a chest at the foot of the bed. Rachel closed her eyes and appeared to fall asleep in seconds. Lesley left the room, shutting the door behind her.

In the kitchen, Lesley poured herself a larger glass of liquor than she'd ever consumed. Rachel wasn't the only one who felt weak and shaky. As a daughter, a wife, and even as a mother, Lesley had never assumed the level of responsibility she'd taken upon herself since arriving at Deerhaven Forest Hall, and she needed to analyze how to proceed. With no way to help Ryan at the moment, Rachel's health would seem to be her primary concern. Lesley debated whether she should strike out and find a doctor to check Rachel's condition but leaving an invalid alone in the snowy woods didn't make sense. Lesley could only hope that she would be equal to whatever care Rachel might require. Taking a sip of burning liquor, Lesley voiced her other, private, concern.

"What will I do when Rachel gets better? She'll figure out how I feel about her and despise me. My crush on her is getting worse. Just the idea of looking at her body makes me feel like I could faint. God help me." Lesley took a long swallow and then decided that alcohol was not a good idea. She put her drink aside and roamed the house, inventorying their shelter's contents, especially the many pictures of women displayed in frames and photograph albums.

When an ancient photograph of two unsmiling women preserved in a mahogany-and-baize frame caught her eye, Lesley picked it up. The faces looked in some way familiar. Their poses did not look wooden. Looking closer, she amended her original assessment to "almost sensual." The faces tilted toward each other, and the women's lips communicated something intimate in their forced neutrality.

"The photograph was taken in this cottage," breathed Lesley, when she noted the women's surroundings. The cabin looked different in black and white but the furnishings hadn't changed very much. Lesley put down the picture and inspected the room. There it was! Covered with heavy brocade, she spotted the harp she'd seen standing near the two women.

Lesley went to the bedroom door and glanced at Rachel. With one long, white arm flung above her head, hair streaming wildly across the ancient linen, Rachel slept like the dead. Closing the door behind her, Lesley went to the harp, removed the cover, and sat down. She knew how to play a few chords. Arranging her fingers on the strings, she played the first strains of "Greensleeves" and began to sing, "Alas my love, you do me wrong to cast me out discourteously. When I have loved you, oh so long, delighting in your company."

The song would seem to be a comment on her husband, Michael, but Michael had become more of a ghost to Lesley than his mother ever would be. The music did not have anything to do with Michael. Lesley felt as though she were singing to Rachel whom she hadn't loved for all that long, who slept and couldn't hear the music. "Greensleeves" must be a love song, Lesley realized. The words meant nothing. The music said everything.

****

After the invasion of Deerhaven Forest Hall by the Reverend Chaney and his followers, Jane and Ursula fled to the beautiful little wood cabin that Ursula had commissioned from a local builder. They could not stay there, though, so near to the forces of evil. They realized for the first time that their love would never be countenanced by anyone, not the community, not the church, not their families. The only plan that would save them, would cost them each other. They only cared about each other but fortune intervened and stole the element of their lives most precious to them.

"Alas my love, you do me wrong to cast me out discourteously. When I have loved you, oh so long, delighting in your company," Ursula sang, her sinewy fingers plucking the harp strings with skill and melancholy.

Tears sprang to Jane's eyes at the sound of her lover's notes. "Ursula, my darling Ursula. Don't attribute such a thing to me, even in jest. As if I would ever cast you out! The world conspires to wrest you from me! I have not cast you out! Far from it! How can fate be so cruel as to take away the only person I have ever loved!" Ursula, no longer reserved in her expressions of affection and sympathy, flew from her stool and took Jane in her arms.

"I must go," Ursula choked. "My presence is a threat to you."

"Maybe I should flee to England with you, Ursula. We have read about Londoners, women, who live with each other."

"You cannot! Your husband and his family would pursue us. You would be in constant peril. No matter how onerous, you must remain and make your life here. I pray to God that you will find some kind of contentment."

"Oh, Ursula," sobbed Jane.

"I know. I know," Ursula whispered. "But there is one whom you will come to love as well as me." Ursula stroked Jane's huge swollen belly, rubbing her soft cheek against Jane's. Jane's teeth clenched in anguish and a moan escaped her. "Think of the baby, Janie," whispered Ursula. "You will find comfort there. I know it."

"I hope so, Ursula, but the baby is a stranger who might even resemble its cursed father for all I know." The betrayals and tumult of the last terrible months had left Jane a harder person than the innocent girl who came to Deerhaven Forest Hall expecting to marry an honest and honorable person.

"Jane!" reproved Ursula. "Your child will be a wonder and a blessing. I know it in my bones."

"I know it, too," Jane replied, attempting a smile. "This baby will be my comfort as the long years pass. I will think of you walking the snowy London streets or visiting the English countryside on a balmy summer day, and I'll make it into a story for my child. I'll fill her mind with the magic that you have taught me."

Ursula caught both of Jane's hands. "Someday, when your husband and the Reverend Chaney have gone to their just reward, I will return. Until then, Jane, I entrust the library to you. Do not even speculate as to the true nature of our library's secrets. That would be dangerous. The library houses treasures more valuable than jewels or precious metals, and you must protect the contents on faith."

"I will," Jane promised. "And my baby will become the library's constable also."

"No, Jane. Your child will be a Windsor and owes an allegiance to the Windsor family. The Windsors must be protected from the heavy burden of librarianship. The Windsors have no aptitude for librarianship. The Windsors exhibit, in any case, no aptitude for library work. Do not turn the library keys over to anyone but me or my appointed successor." Ursula drew from her haversack a massive ring dangling long brass keys and handed them to Jane.

"What shall I do with these keys?" asked Jane. The cold brass made her shiver. The ring's weight bruised her fingers. Jane looked into Ursula's hooded blue eyes for warmth and strength.

"I will tell you enough that you can act in my stead while I am absent. Listen carefully, Jane. If you meet a traveler whose need is great, you must unlock the inner doors and let them journey to the center of the library. In the library's concealed vaults lies salvation for certain victims of the world's malevolence. Just don't go inside the matrix yourself. You would find yourself in great peril."

"Tell me more, Ursula," urged Jane, although her heart quailed.

"You must come to understand the meaning of the septagon," stated Ursula. "Sevens are important to librarians. We do not put our confidence in easy, even numbers." Jane nodded, rapt with concentration now. Little did Jane know that, in the long, lonely years to come, the furtherance of Ursula's noble mission would consume, sustain, and comfort her.

"Seven," Jane recited as her lesson began.

****

"Seven," a woman's voice announced. After days of being attended by men, the woman's voice came as a great comfort to Sula. Unlike the harsh communications from her previous captors, this woman's words suggested a kindlier nature. Sula always did better with women. No reason that this wouldn't be the case this time.

"Seven what?" Sula asked.

"It's seven o'clock at night," the voice responded. "You asked me for the time. Don't you remember?"

"I don't remember much," Sula replied. "Your comrades see to that."

"Are you hungry?" the deep but feminine voice questioned. "Do you want me to help you drink some soup?"

Fighting the cumulative effect of tranquilizers and straining against her bonds, Sula rose on one elbow. Her prison room remained dark at all times. She couldn't see her new jailer, but a slight sibilance in the woman's speech rang a bell in Sula's muzzy brain.

"Who are you?" Sula demanded. "Don't I know you?"

"It's Valerie, Miss Smith. We rarely met, but I worked in the house with you. The Windsors didn't want anyone to know why they needed me at Deerhaven Forest Hall but I will tell you now. I took care of Rachel Windsor. She never went away to the hospital like they told everyone. They've kept her in the attic all these years. She is a deviant."

"That was Rachel in the attic?" moaned Sula. "Oh, my God. I thought she attended an East Coast boarding school. I played with her when we were little."

"They didn't know what to do with her. The world would be cruel to her, they thought. They did the best they could for the poor, addled creature. She never stopped saying she wanted to marry a woman. You can't let a person like that loose on her own. I've nursed her for many years."

"Ah," said Sula. "Yes. I recognize your voice. How could you help them keep their daughter a prisoner? What were you thinking?"

"Rachel is a madwoman. Driven out of her mind by the devil's whisperings."

The attendant used "s's" liberally, thought Sula, considering she had a definite problem pronouncing them. "You believe Rachel Windsor to be possessed?" asked Sula. "My God! You're a nurse. You can't really think that!"

"I've seen that girl bargaining with the Prince of Darkness. The Reverend Were says that her parents made a pact with the devil. The Windsors gave their daughter to the devil in exchange for worldly goods and favors."

Despite the darkness and the effect of being misused these last few days, Sula snorted with laughter. Then, she fell serious. "There is no devil unless you put arrogant, aberrant ministers into that category."

"The devil spoke through the lips of Rachel Windsor. I heard his evil words often enough!"

"I was told that Rachel developed adolescent schizophrenia," Sula admitted. "And that they'd put her into a humane institution after she finished boarding school. The Windsors told me that Rachel would have to remain in restraints until she made a recovery. Why would they want me to believe that story?"

"You should be scared of her! She should never live among decent folk. Not with her evil frowns and foul language. It's only prayer that's saved me from being struck down dead by her curses and spells."

"Maybe she felt hostile toward you for helping to keep her a prisoner in the attic," Sula suggested. "Although I'm sure you thought you were doing your best," she added, not wanting to alienate the nurse.

"I tried to do my small part for that poor, wretched soul," returned the attendant. "My hands carried out God's will. Now I do my best for you, by carrying out the Reverend Were's orders. The Reverend conveys his divine plan to us on a daily basis."

"How reassuring," commented Sula. She sighed. "What's your name again?"

"Valerie. Mrs. Valerie Kemsley. Mr. Kemsley is deceased."

"I'm sorry," Sula responded.

"Don't be. He was a drunk and a womanizer. His flatbed truck smashed into a yellow 1990 Cadillac Seville on Pelton Mine Road, and they measured his blood alcohol level at point two something after the crash. He was wearing bathing trunks under his pants. In January! The day after a fierce blizzard. No underwear anywhere in the wreckage! That's between Mr. Kemsley and his Maker but that man never left my home without flannel boxers, I promise you that. So where did he lose them? I ask you."

"You're not the kind of woman to overlook a piece of laundry," Sula guessed.

"Certainly not. I don't condone unseemliness and lasciviousness in myself or others. You being a librarian, would understand that."

"Yes," agreed Sula. "I wrote my graduate thesis on Victorian literature. How's that for respectability?" She spared Valerie the full title of her thesis, *The Effect of Sexual Repression on Mid-Victorian Era Women's Fiction.*

"Excuse me?" said Valerie. "I'm not familiar with theses."

"Just digressing," Sula told her. "I'm feeling sick, actually. Does your offer of soup still stand?"

"Of course. You deserve to be treated as one of the unsentenced. The Reverend tells me that you haven't been found guilty of anything yet. You might be an innocent. If so, you deserve decent treatment. Here, have some soup."

Valerie spoon-fed Sula tepid tomato soup with a delicacy that warmed the librarian. Sula admired a woman with manual dexterity.

"I can't let you have too much soup," said Valerie after a time. "They want you to drink all your chocolate. The Reverend insists. You'd better save room." Prior to this disclosure, Sula hadn't been able to figure out how her captors administered the tranquilizers that kept her unconscious. Now that she knew, Sula retained a large mouthful of chocolate until Valerie departed and spit the liquid behind her cot. Later, Sula slept but not as profoundly as before.

She woke to the sound of river water, clearer of mind than

in the previous days. Valerie had not returned but Sula could recall every moment of the nurse's previous visit. Valerie's idle indiscretions had revealed a lot.

At last, the nurse's plodding footsteps sounded in the room. "Miss Smith," spoke Valerie. "I've come to take you to the bathroom."

Sula tried to recall how she'd executed bodily functions before Valerie's tenure but she could not, a merciful amnesia.

When Valerie offered to put her under the shower for a brief wash, Sula accepted with gratitude. The weak, lukewarm shower invigorated her more than she would have thought possible. Sula shook her wet hair, trying to clear her mind.

"Let's get you into this nice, dry sweatsuit, Miss Smith," said Valerie. "It's a men's extra large. The Reverend's own."

Ugh, thought Sula, but when the soft cotton caressed her skin, she almost thanked the Reverend. Valerie hummed a hymn that Sula identified as "Nearer My God to Thee."

"You have a beautiful voice," commented Sula, determined to divert the attendant's loyalties.

"Why, thank you, Miss Smith," Valerie returned. "I raise my voice to God and He is the most gracious audience of all."

"Call me Sula," Sula murmured. "No reason for us to be formal. After all, I'm not paying for your excellent nursing skills. I assume you're doing this out of the kindness of your heart."

"True," giggled Valerie. "No one else will be available to take care of you until the Reverend comes out of seclusion."

"The Reverend Were has gone into seclusion?" said Sula.

"Yes. The Reverend experienced a spectral visitation, and he must contemplate the significance. He has retired to his lodge in Wolf's Creek."

"Was the spirit who visited the Reverend a friendly soul?" asked Sula, trying to find out as much as possible.

"That I can't say," said Valerie and paused. The nurse walked toward the door and tried the handle to make sure no one could overhear. Her rough voice lowered several notches. "The visit was from my former employer, she who just died, Mrs. Cosette Windsor. He hasn't said what Mrs. Windsor wanted with him.

She never said *boo* to him in life."

"How interesting," Sula volunteered.

"Very interesting," replied Valerie. "You probably read a lot in library school. Am I right? Perhaps you can answer the question that keeps popping into my head. It's this. Mrs. Cosette Windsor was not a nice woman, to my way of thinking, not nice at all. When Miss Rachel was about fourteen, Mrs. Windsor realized that Rachel must be shut away. She told me flat-out that Rachel must be depraved. But Cosette Windsor changed her mind when she got old and Miss Rachel grew into her twenties. Mrs. Cosette Windsor heard her daughter babbling vile thoughts and screaming about obscene acts just as always but she told me, 'Don't think ill of poor Rachel. Put the blame on me.' Well, if Cosette Windsor was to blame for Rachel Windsor's devilment, then she's probably gone straight to hell now she's dead."

"I'm not sure there's a hell," ventured Sula. "Although I know there's a heaven."

Valerie Kemsley stared at her, deep in thought. "I don't know, myself. But my question is...why would a man of God such as Reverend Were receive a visitor who's been relegated to the flames? I've given that man my allegiance. I've entrusted him with my almighty soul. Could I have been deluded all this time? What do you think, Miss Smith, I mean, Sula?"

"That depends," mused Sula. "I've read many philosophers' speculations on the afterlife."

"I knew it," breathed Valerie. "Tell me what you think."

Sula couldn't believe her luck! Divisions in the Reverend's ranks! If Cosette Windsor had really appeared to the odious minister, Sula thanked Cosette for her trouble. A few quick tears sprang to Sula's eyes. She'd missed the funeral of that kind sensible woman, and she would always regret not being there.

"I'd understand the situation better if you could describe Rachel Windsor's delusions." Sula held her breath for the answer. She needed to know why the Reverend directed so much vitriol at Rachel Windsor. She cringed at the memory of Rachel and Lesley Windsor plunging into the roiling Stanislaus to escape Reverend Were. The Reverend had used her as a prop to scare the two women.

Valerie drew so close that Sula could smell chocolate on her breath. "Perversion. Rachel's delusions involved perversion starting at an early age," came Valerie's Hershey-flavored derogation. "That girl imagined herself doing unspeakable things with other girls. Rachel begged her mother to let her loose so she'd be free to hound and harass decent women until they committed acts of degradation with her. Later, Rachel claimed she wanted nothing more than to attend college but I knew the truth. I'd heard too much about what she imagined doing with women. Oh, the sickness of her imaginings would curl your hair!"

"Really!" exclaimed Sula. "How did Cosette Windsor react to Rachel's sexual orientation?"

"As I told you, they did the fitting thing originally and confined Rachel in those rooms at the top of the Hall. They knew the girl should be punished. I knew I was doing God's work helping them keep her from the world. Mrs. Windsor lost her resolve later, though. Near the end of her life, Cosette Windsor argued that her daughter's perversion should be tolerated. She had come to believe that the fault lay with the world outside. By then, of course, Rachel Windsor had become even softer in the head. She offered to do anything at all to buy her freedom. Mr. Russell Windsor feared what the county's social services would say about Rachel if she went out into the world, even though Mr. Windsor also came to condone his daughter lusting after women! The two of them became the worst kind of liberals. Mr. Windsor didn't think Rachel could survive out in the world, she didn't even have a Social Security number after all, so he wanted her kept at the Hall. Her mother went so far as to beg Mr. Windsor to set Rachel free."

Valerie shook her head. "Just think! Acting as though there was nothing wrong with the girl! Imagine! Acting as though the world outside should be considered more dangerous than Rachel Windsor! The world will never be ready for her type."

"Not this world, maybe," whispered Sula, sickened by what she'd just learned. "Damn it! I can't believe I obeyed the Windsor strictures. My mother insisted that I adhere to their wishes, but I should have gone upstairs. I could have helped the whole family come to terms."

"Come to terms with what?" demanded Valerie.

"The problem in the attic," murmured Sula, and feigned a swoon into unconsciousness.

CHAPTER FIFTEEN

"Help! Help! The Devil!"

Horrible shrieks from the back room brought Lesley to her feet, and she sprinted across the living room, bursting through the bedroom door in time to see Rachel flailing against the bedclothes. Their refuge in the meadow cottage seemed to have brought Rachel no peace.

Soft lazy snowflakes drifted past the bedroom window and the afternoon light washed the cozy room in a tranquil gray light. She looked around for the devil but, to Lesley's relief, no fire-engine-colored lord of the underworld lurked within sight. Hurrying to the bed, Lesley sat down beside Rachel. From long experience with dreamers plagued by demons, she bent and took Rachel in her arms.

"The Devil," moaned Rachel.

Did the same incubus who tormented Lesley's husband in his nightmares pursue his sister too? The Windsors seemed to harbor family fiends who hounded their dreams by night.

"There is no devil here," Lesley crooned to Rachel. "Look around this house. You can sense goodness and mercy encircling us as surely as the walls and roof."

"You're right," returned Rachel. "I'm probably safer here than I have been for years."

Lesley let Rachel return to rest upon her pillow. She patted Rachel's long, soft, white fingers.

"We've escaped every danger so far," said Lesley. Looking at Rachel's face, filled with mild trust and faith, Lesley ventured saying, "and I'm beginning to believe that forces of good exist and that they're on our side The spirits of your mother and of the women who built this house want us to triumph over our enemies. I know they do."

Rachel's wide expressive mouth turned down at each corner. "My mother confined me in her attic from the age of fourteen on. Dead or alive, I don't want her help."

Lesley considered Rachel's accusation. "I think Cosette got caught up in something she didn't understand," Lesley responded. "She regrets what she did. She wants the best for you. I think she'd do anything to make amends with you. Can you forgive her?"

"No," stated Rachel flatly. "Some things are unforgivable."

"Maybe," acknowledged Lesley, "but people aren't. Sometimes people change so radically, they deserve to be forgiven their past transgressions."

"People who intentionally inflict terrible harm and suffering? You're wrong, Lesley. My mother—I find her unforgivable."

"Nothing can excuse what she did to you," said Lesley, "but will you allow that she might have been misled and mistaken?"

"Why would you want me to forgive the woman who imprisoned and reviled me?" countered Rachel, eyes black. "You didn't know her. I did."

"My impression of her is different than yours," Lesley acknowledged. "Could she have changed by the end of her life?

Maybe she would have tried to atone for what she did, if she'd lived longer."

Rachel looked full into Lesley's eyes for the first time. Her Windsor eyes went from black to gray. She took a deep, sad breath. "For you, I'll try to remember my mother in a charitable light," she vowed in a shaky but decided tone. "I would like to leave bitterness behind even though I don't know how."

"That's all I ask," responded Lesley.

"I've never met anyone like you," murmured Rachel. She gazed at Lesley intently and then her mouth tightened again. "He married you, after all." Rachel's river-gray eyes, a bewitching variation on Michael's cold orbs and Ryan's keen little peepers, studied Lesley with what seemed like calculation.

"I no longer consider myself married to your brother," Lesley stated, without conscious thought. Rachel stared with an intensity that made Lesley shiver. She's going to figure out that I lost my mind the second I met her, Lesley thought in despair. She waited, fearing she would soon see Rachel's face seized with repulsion. A gradual melting of expression signaled that Rachel's appraisal had not turned against her.

Then, she identified Rachel's look. Lesley herself had worn that same concentrated expression since she first climbed the upper staircase at Deerhaven Forest Hall and entered Rachel's rooms.

Could she be this lucky? Lucky enough to have Rachel return her feelings? There must be a catch. Rachel hadn't known many people. Maybe she was staring at Lesley with romance in her eyes because no one else had ever been available. Still, this newly minted emotion felt more real to Lesley than all the hackneyed stories of heterosexual love she'd read all her life.

Rachel's pale cheeks blazed like a crop of bright new roses. Touching her own, Lesley found them also ablaze. Lesley wiped her palms on her pants, considering what to say next.

Rachel spoke before her. "The devil has done his work here," she groaned. "I can tell by the way that I feel. My mother warned me years ago that I'm not normal. I can't be around normal people."

In a burst of intuition stronger than any in her life, Lesley divined the nature of Rachel's "illness," the reason for her years of imprisonment and agony. Outrage blocked Lesley's rational thought processes. Her hands reached for Rachel and gripped the other woman with unmaternal passion, nothing like her former ministrations.

"I've always been the most normal mom in Blackhawk School's PTA, 'normal' in every way, but I want you more than I've ever wanted anything except my son's recovery." Drowning in the feminine version of the Windsor gray gaze, Lesley felt herself anchored by her hold on Rachel's arms. Nothing could cool her lips and cheeks except one kind of balm. Eyebrows knitted with trepidation, Lesley leaned forward and touched her mouth to Rachel's.

Only weeks ago, if she'd been asked what two women in love did with each other's bodies, Lesley would have been hard-pressed to answer. Once her lips met Rachel's, though, the knowledge came in such entirety that Lesley cried out with revelation. Her mouth and Rachel's grew together and their tongues found a way into the core of their bodies and minds. When Rachel moved her tongue, the earth moved and a red mare of passion which Lesley rode bareback, galloped between her legs.

"How could this happen?" asked Rachel, an indefinite time later, as they lay gasping for air. "I never thought I would fall in love with a living woman, and I always assumed that if I did, she would run from me."

"I've been waiting for this all my life," murmured Lesley. "I've been too afraid even to imagine the possibility. Then, I saw your face and everything seemed possible. Oh, Rachel. You'd never run from me, would you? Please."

Hanging on Lesley's every word, Rachel shook her head in wonder. "What about my brother, Lesley. Did you love him? If you loved him, what happened? Why are you here with me, like this?"

How could Lesley explain the metamorphosis she'd undergone since coming to Deerhaven Pines? "I told myself I loved him," she answered. "I think I did, in a way. Michael never cared for me. I see that now. He wanted someone to make a life for him so he wouldn't have to make one for himself. He wanted someone too weak to leave him, and I was that person. Please don't think less of me." A new thought occurred to Lesley. "He wasn't to blame, Rachel. I must have been holding myself back from him all these years. Waiting for you!"

"Do you love Michael, Rachel? You must. He's your brother. I'm sorry I was so blunt. He…" she glanced at Rachel's face and continued, "he hasn't behaved well since Ryan was injured. You might not believe it, but I've wondered if Michael might have had something to do with Ryan being shot. He's fallen under the spell of that monster, Reverend Were."

"I loved Michael and Kelvin more than anyone when we were children but that love died. I begged them to help me escape from Deerhaven Forest Hall, and do you want to know what Michael said? I can repeat his words verbatim: 'Mother explained what is wrong with you. Your freedom would embarrass us. It's better for everyone if you're presumed dead or locked up for life. Then, Kelvin added, 'You've read *The Well of Loneliness*. Your life would be filled with hairy-lipped women, dildos and empty rooms, if we let you loose.' They both laughed at that, Lesley. They found me and my imprisonment funny."

"I believe you, Rachel. Your brothers weren't good enough for you. They aren't good enough for me."

"Thank you for not pressing me to forgive those two. I will never be a big enough believer in redemption to forget those words. Michael and Kelvin mean nothing to me."

For the first time, Lesley realized how strong the former prisoner of Deerhaven Forest Hall must be to have survived complete repudiation and then years of confinement.

"If Michael's no relation to you, then you aren't my sister-in-law," Lesley announced. "I hope you'll be something else to me."

Lesley's hand slid up Rachel's body and rested on one rounded breast. She felt a nipple stir under Rachel's shirt, and both her own breasts swelled in response, a sensation she would never forget. Retrieving her hand from contact with Rachel, Lesley snatched Rachel's hands and pressed them against her own chest in counter pressure.

"I won't be a sister-in-law to you," whispered Rachel. "Tell me what you think is my real title."

Without loosening her grip on Rachel's fine, shapely hands, Lesley considered. "You are everything to me," Lesley finally answered. "Maybe that's too much to capture in a single, ordinary word like husband or wife or lover."

"It's strange," mused Rachel. "After years of dreaming about you, I don't have the words for what I feel right now. I wouldn't know how to describe this or this. Or this!"

Rachel touched her and Lesley entered a sensual red locus where she'd never been before, a place with its own receptor organs and neural paths. Lesley's hands reached for Rachel's hidden recesses, the hair, skin, and tiny tongue between her legs, the soft underskin and nipples of her breasts, the cracks and creases bleached white by lack of exposure. Finally, Lesley's mind purpled and she lost conscious thought.

Much later, when Rachel weakened with exertion, Lesley still ached and burned. She could not stop grinding and stroking, the motions she'd learned in the unconscious state that overtook her hours ago. Embarrassed but desperate, Lesley clung to Rachel, letting her body beg for more.

"You'd think it was you and not me who'd been held prisoner all these years denied life and sex!" Rachel laughed with affection and replenishment.

"I can't get enough of you," Lesley confessed. "I can't stop."

"Lesley," said Rachel. "I don't know your body very well, however much I love it. Can I ask you if what we did together gave you the ultimate satisfaction? I'm not sure what the word would be but I knew when it happened."

"I have no way to know," admitted Lesley. "Sex with my husband made me numb. Sometimes I would cry afterward but he never noticed. He went right to sleep, after."

"I could tell you didn't know how to finish," said Rachel. "I have just enough bodily strength left within me to see if you can unlearn what came before."

Rachel never moved her electric body away from Lesley's. Handling Lesley like a treasured but sturdy doll, she rolled them both on their sides. Not knowing what came after this, Lesley waited for Rachel to take charge.

Furious concentration on her genitals did nothing for Lesley's pent-up state except to diffuse it. "Don't think," whispered Rachel, and Lesley exhaled the bad air. "Let me touch you."

Rachel's hands became all encompassing. Her fingers reached Lesley's legs, spine and neck at the same time. Rachel's lips grazed Lesley's face and breasts, belly and pubic hair. Soft hands massaged her feet and shoulders. Despite the generalized sensation of Rachel, the diffused state narrowed focus and Lesley felt her genitals widen and begin to throb as though building toward an explosion.

Rachel's thoroughness became an exquisite irritant. If Lesley had known her partner better, she would have screamed and ordered Rachel to hurry up. Long after Lesley's deep sighs became wracking, Rachel curled into a circle, becoming a globe, a world, between Lesley's legs. Beams of heavy sensation radiated from Lesley's core, down her legs, through her chest, into her feet, hands and scalp. Women's parts had never been so dense yet so liquid and volatile. Rachel became inexorable, burrowing under Lesley's delicate flesh until the ceaseless movements stirred an avalanche. Back arching, feet digging for a grip on reality, Lesley screamed without words and ordered Rachel, "Don't stop!"

Rachel's weight and command kept Lesley's body bucking and cascading for an eternity. Finally, Lesley realized that she wanted to stop, in fact, she had to stop. Rachel unwound her body and let loose of Lesley, surfacing from the mountains their bed had become. Both of them sat up, giddy with love and success.

"We're happy!" crowed Rachel. "We're happy as two people can be, in spite of everything."

Shyness overcame Lesley and she spoke softly. "Rachel, you've never been lovers with a woman."

"Not until today," Rachel replied.

"Then, how do you know so much about love and sex?" asked Lesley. She had known so little before today and learned so much from Rachel!

"I've had years to imagine the pleasure. Love and sex come from your heart but imagination must be what fuels the pump!

Otherwise, I couldn't have been with you. I'd have shriveled and become paralyzed by now."

"Here's to imagination!" cheered Lesley, feeling her confusion lift. "I wish mine were as good as yours. If it were, I'd have come and found you sooner. Oh, Rachel, if Ryan was all right, my life would seem too good to be true."

"Your son will be fine." Rachel stroked Lesley's slick naked back, instilling warmth and reassurance with her fingers. "He has to be. I can feel a space in my heart reserved for him."

"He will be okay," said Lesley. Cosette will take care of him, she thought without saying anything to Rachel. A surge of optimism flooded her.

"The three of us will live as a family. Ryan will love you, Rachel." Lesley smiled as she added, "and not just as an aunt. I want you to raise him with me. There's so much you and Ryan could give each other." Lesley wasted no time considering how they'd reached agreement on such a radical plan.

"I'd like that, Lesley, but we need to get back to Ryan. Where are we? I don't even know."

"We're down the river from Deerhaven Forest Hall," Lesley reminded Rachel. "We'll have to return to Deerhaven Forest Hall so I can drive us to the hospital."

"How will we escape the Reverend Were?" Rachel asked, her smile fading.

"I don't know. There must be sane people who will help us. We'll find them."

"Lesley, what will you do when you come face-to-face with Michael?"

"I have to make peace with him. Michael will remain in our lives. He's Ryan's father and your brother. He'll have no impact though. I've given him too many chances. He has no choice but to let me and Ryan go."

"If only Michael sees it that way," sighed Rachel. "In the meantime, just for this afternoon, imagine that everything will be easy from here on in. We emerged from the water, saw each other, and fell in love. The river cleansed us of everything but devotion and passion so we'll never know unhappiness or deceit."

"I hope all you say is true," said Lesley.

"Please excuse my language," asked Rachel. "Valerie told me that my vocabulary is out-of-date and affected. I've read too many paperback romance novels. My mother bought me books from Grady's Pharmacy in Deerhaven Pines. Mother didn't let me visit the library at the Hall. I've never read a book from our own library. Even raised on Valerie's gothic novels, I couldn't help thinking of physical love as involving two women. I changed the pronouns in my mind. Valerie used to slap me when I talked about love. She preferred hearing me scream like a demented person to hearing me discuss my concept of love."

"Rachel," said Lesley. "What brought on your fits and screaming? I don't understand. You're as sane as anyone I've ever met."

Rachel shrank and paled. "You would never believe me."

"I will believe you," Lesley promised.

Rachel studied her for several long minutes and sighed. "Ghosts tormented me. They gave me orders and their orders conflicted each other. Stay, leave, serve, champion, choose, abjure women, embrace women, beware women. I couldn't sort out what they said. I saw colors and shapes that probably weren't there. Do you think I'm insane? A madwoman who communicates with ghosts? Who screams so as not to hear their whisperings?"

"When I arrived at Deerhaven Forest Hall, I was met by someone." Lesley hesitated.

"Who?" asked Rachel.

"Your mother," Lesley replied. "She died the day before I came to the Hall but she opened the door for me and Ryan."

Rachel stared at Lesley, stricken. "Mother!" she repeated. "When I promised to speak kindly of my departed mother, I hadn't considered that she might return in spirit form but, of course, she would! They can all get back to that house. Promise me something, Lesley."

"Anything, Rachel," Lesley promised.

Rachel leaned forward, eyes trained on Lesley. "Don't be taken in by Cosette. I can't stand to think of you confiding in her, even now that she's dead. Please, Lesley."

Lesley reached for Rachel's hand in dismay. "Cosette has

been very good to me. I left Ryan in her care. Cosette sits with him right now, in the hospital. She's dead, Rachel. Can you give her a fresh start now that she's passed on?"

"I will never forgive her! She kept me prisoner because I needed to be with a woman. She left me in that room, prey to whispering ghosts, until I started acting like a crazy person. Don't you see, Lesley? She's your enemy too! It's our love she wanted to kill before it was born."

"Cosette was younger then. I think she'll understand now."

"No! She's still evil, dead or alive. Act like she isn't there and eventually she won't be. Promise me! I must be rid of her!" Rachel's gray eyes churned.

Lesley saw that she had no choice in this matter. "All right, Rachel. I won't respond if I see or hear from Cosette." Lesley's grief over this newest loss of her mother-in-law felt profound.

"Thank you, Lesley. Someday I'll make you understand."

"I think I do understand," Lesley replied, hardening her heart toward Cosette who had been a villain in the piece, after all.

Together, they searched the kitchen for food. They decided that someone had occupied the house as lately as the end of this last summer, based upon the dates stamped on cans and boxes. The refrigerator hummed but yielded little provender other than several jars of choice Beluga caviar. Lesley located pancake mix, sweet Basmati rice and many jars of peach preserves.

"There are still wild onions growing outside," said Lesley. "I'll pick some and make a savory rice dish. If we use everything we've found, we'll have a well-rounded meal."

While Rachel bathed, Lesley prepared their first meal together. By the time Rachel emerged, rosy and warm, November foliage in a crystal vase decorated the table. The main course, pancakes stuffed with caviar, complemented Lesley's oniony side dish. A preserved-peach cobbler lent the fragrance of carefree summer days to the chilly air. The two women ate like new lovers, anxious for fuel that they would each spend on the other, combustible dining.

Before night came on, Lesley explored the outbuildings where she found a lean-to stocked with firewood and a shed with winter provisions. Lesley gathered tinder and carried logs into the house. By dark, a sweet-smelling fire crackled in the living room. Draperies kept the cold and the wild forest at bay. Lesley and Rachel prepared hot chocolate, floating stale marshmallows in the rich brown brew, and sat on the living room sofa next to each other.

"It feels like this place was built for us," commented Rachel, voicing Lesley's thoughts.

"Who do you think lived here last?" Lesley wondered out loud. "Have you noticed the photographs and pictures?"

"No. Let me look." Rachel rose and went to a desk with a sea of standing frames. Picking up a first, Rachel examined the subjects with care.

"These people seem familiar," she told Lesley.

"Maybe you met them when you were growing up," Lesley suggested.

Rachel set down one photograph and picked up another. In the midst of sipping her chocolate, Lesley heard Rachel gasp.

"This is my Aunt Marie, she's dead. The woman with her is my Aunt Evelyn, who lives in France. They're my grandmother's sisters. Who put their pictures in this house?"

"I did," replied a gentle voice, familiar to Lesley.

"Cosette!" cried Lesley, without thinking.

"Mother!" Rachel exclaimed.

Beside the front door, stood Cosette Windsor, dressed in mourning gray. Rachel stared at the apparition with anger.

"Ryan?" choked Lesley.

"Ryan's resting. He's fine right now. Dr. Riemer is sitting with him."

"Lesley," said Rachel in a voice nothing like the soft reasonable tones of Lesley's lover.

"Rachel, your mother has been with Ryan. Can I ask about him?"

"You promised," Rachel reminded her. "Will you be like everyone else? If you betray me now, I'll go mad."

"I never would," Lesley assured her.

Lesley glanced at Cosette. At the sight of Cosette's tender smile, Lesley felt trapped between the ghost and her daughter.

"I came to warn you two about the Reverend Were and the Others working against you," Cosette pleaded, taking a step toward her daughter with arms extended.

"Don't listen," admonished Rachel. "Pretend she's not here, Lesley. She'll go away. If you find the strength to ignore them, ghosts disappear."

"Shouldn't we find out what she came to say?" Lesley asked desperately.

"She's full of lies and tricks. Don't trust her. Come here, Lesley. We'll hold each other until she loses form. If I must, I'll scream her away." Rachel held out her arms and Lesley could not help entering them.

"Lesley!" cried Cosette. "Your lives are in danger! Please listen. Rachel, I've tried to atone for what I did to you but I ran out of time on earth. I hope you will accept my help now."

"Alas, my love, you do me wrong," Rachel began singing.

Lesley watched Cosette waver and flicker, the ghost's serene countenance transformed into a distressed blur.

"Lesley! Please!" Cosette enjoined.

Lesley buried her face in Rachel's neck, drinking in the smell of her lover's freshly washed hair and skin. "I can't," she uttered.

"If you won't heed my warning," spoke Cosette, her voice charged with static like a telephone with a weak battery, "then stay in this house. This place used to be Jane's house, a safe place for women."

When Lesley raised her eyes, she found herself alone with Rachel in the cozy living room.

"And who but my Lady Greensleeves," finished Rachel. A log popped, breaking the silence.

****

The last dose of drug-laced hot chocolate ran down the wall next to Sula's bed and leaked through gaps in the rough floorboards. Her mind felt clearer already. She lay in the dark analyzing the woman she considered to be her target, Valerie Kemsley, Rachel Windsor's former nurse.

Valerie appeared to be malleable but might not be susceptible to Sula's standard machinations. She didn't know if she could get the woman to fall in love with her, which would be optimal. Valerie was a practical nurse, after all, and probably not prone to impetuous infatuations. Sula's appearance needed work, in any case, and her reserve of charm hovered at an all-time low ebb.

The most productive tactic would be to recruit the nurse. Valerie might be persuaded to reenlist in Sula's cause and desert PURITI now that her faith in the Reverend had been tested. But what should she use for an angle? She would have to stake out higher moral ground than the Reverend occupied, but she would have only a short time to create a high pitch of moral fervor in the stolid Valerie.

"Have you heard any news about my library?" Sula asked, the next time Valerie entered the room. "Knowledge is the greatest virtue. I'm sure you agree. If the whims of the obtuse desecrate the library, evil will be unleashed. Damaging a library is tantamount to destroying a temple, don't you think?" She could sense Valerie paying attention to this rhetorical gambit.

"I never thought about the library in quite that way," Valerie replied. "I've never raised my voice in a library, though. Never in all my years."

"So, how fares the library at Deerhaven Forest Hall? Do you know?"

"The Reverend directed his men to ransack the shelves," Valerie revealed. "He bade them root out works of Satan. They got bored before they'd browsed through many titles though. You have a good point, Miss Smith. They should never have questioned the authority of a professional librarian."

"Worse than that," said Sula, with studied gravity. "They have violated something valuable, even sacred. I've spent my life protecting the sanctity of the library. The Reverend's barbarian hoards disrupted the proper order of things. You believe in karma don't you? They will get their due!" She'd gone too far she suspected, but since Valerie had grown used to the heated oratory of Reverend Were, the nurse apparently didn't notice.

"I've always believed in the Dewey decimal system," said

Valerie, eagerly. "Practiced it since I was a schoolgirl. I admire a person who can lay their hands on the right book and pluck the title from the shelf. After vocational school, I put my textbooks in alphabetical order on a shelf at my mother's house. They're still sitting right there!"

"You have the instincts of a librarian," Sula complimented her.

"Why, I suppose I do," agreed Valerie. "I'm not a real well-educated woman but I respect book learning. I've never been one to fear the scholarly. Not like some people."

"Does the Reverend Were value education? Does he read much?"

"I don't think he does. I've heard him get critical about reading books that aren't the Bible. There's only one version of the Bible that the Reverend endorses. I have it at home. He told us to get rid of our King James because it sugarcoats the real message. That's what he said."

"The King James has always been my favorite," responded Sula. "The language is so beautiful." As a course requirement for the English Bible as Literature at U.C. Berkeley, Sula had, in fact, read and enjoyed the King James version of the Bible.

"You know what?" exclaimed Valerie. "I agree with you. Giving away my grandmother's leather-bound Bible with the names of the Houghs inscribed inside the front cover just killed me. I took great comfort from that book."

"That's a shame," Sula commiserated. She knew she should terminate this interaction while everything was going well, leaving Valerie hungry for further emotional arousal. "Thank you for telling me about the condition of the library. The best of humanity can be found within those quiet rooms." She felt maudlin tears form in her eyes. God, she was good. She reached out and slipped her hand into Valerie's. Valerie clasped Sula's strong tanned arm with fervor.

A small glow appeared in the dark room and not from the wall sconce. A red light illuminated the walls for a few seconds. Red light! She must have been more successful than she'd guessed.

"Doesn't it seem a little pink in here?" gasped Valerie.

"I often see red when I'm having a good time," Sula

murmured seductively. "It's probably neurological. Hasn't it ever happened to you before?" Sula knew, somehow, that she appeared to Valerie as a raven-haired beauty bathed in deep rose.

The nurse gaped. "Red," said Valerie. "I love this hue."

CHAPTER SIXTEEN

The consummation of her newfound passion left Lesley in a heady state. She didn't know whether she could fall asleep no matter how much she needed to rest. Rachel, on the other hand, because she'd been kept abed for years, grew exhausted. After dining, they had returned to the rumpled bed in the back room where, through the big, double-paned window, Lesley could still see snow drifting down in the dark. Lesley pulled the drapes to screen herself and Rachel from whatever lurked outside, and the thought crossed her mind that she should have taken this precaution earlier.

Cleaning the kitchen until the counters and pots gleamed and no stray crumb remained to entice woodland mice and squirrels indoors took the edge off her euphoria and Lesley walked into the bedroom again. Motionless under the covers,

Rachel barely seemed to be breathing. Lesley took Rachel's pulse and found the beat slow and strong. She studied her new loved one with respect and wonder. After surviving an aberrant childhood, sequestered from the world by a family who had been misguided if not downright malicious, Rachel could easily have turned out too damaged for intimacy but she'd seemed so intact during their lovemaking. How could Rachel bring such joy and wholeheartedness to love and sex after what she'd been through? Rachel had taken the lead when Lesley needed to be shown the way. Stooping, Lesley brushed fine strands of wavy brown hair off Rachel's face.

In a moment of clarity, she saw that Rachel's sexual orientation must be so ingrained that no amount of coercion could kill it. The steadfastness of Rachel's "tendency" helped assure Lesley that her own gayness, as well as their relationship, must be right and true. The other thing she guessed was that Rachel must have been loved as a small child. A human being who had received nothing but abuse couldn't have responded with the kind of unrestrained love that Rachel had just expressed. She possessed the resources to become a whole human being the minute that Lesley freed her from the confines of Deerhaven Forest Hall. Lesley wanted to believe that Cosette and Russell possessed redeeming qualities, that they'd loved their daughter in spite of the way they'd mistreated her. Concluding her ruminations, Lesley swayed with weariness.

Despite their recent intimacy, lying down beside the sleeping Rachel seemed presumptuous to Lesley but fear of marauders and cold overcame her reticence and Lesley sat down on the bed. Drawn to the warmth like a moth, she inched her way to Rachel's side, slipping a light arm over the small but substantial woman that she loved. Her last thoughts touched upon Ryan, her injured boy. She prayed that he rested well in the hospital bed where she'd left him.

When roused by a noise much later, Lesley moaned, turned over, and the brooch and chain conferred upon her swung free. Lesley opened her eyes. Groping for the pendant, she took the thing in her hand. The necklace burned and pulsed. Lesley looked down at the creamy platform of her breastbone where the brooch had been resting. A Celtic-like emblem emblazoned on Lesley's skin must have come from the metalwork on the necklace. The pattern reminded Lesley of the decorative device she'd seen at the Deerhaven Forest Hall library and inscribed on some of the Windsors' paintings.

What source of heat caused the pendant to grow hot? What could be the significance of the insignia? The pattern, now tattooed on her flesh, culminated in a focal point that appeared as a bright red prick in her skin. Distressed, she rubbed at the design with her finger.

Then, Lesley froze. She could hear a human voice calling out to her from the bleak, black forest in front of the house.

"Mother! I'm frightened. Come get me. It's dark out here. Mother, please!" The child's voice tugged at her heartstrings and Lesley sat up.

"Mother. Mother, please!" came another cry. Lesley slid out of bed with a backward glance at Rachel, curled like a small girl beneath the covers. What could a child be doing in the woods? The temperature had dropped since she'd gotten into bed. Lesley snatched up her coat and pulled it on over her nightgown. She stuck her bare feet into her soggy shoes. In the living room, Lesley realized that although the high-pitched voice carried well in the still night, the calls were coming from a distance.

"Mother!" called the voice.

"Ryan!" Lesley cried back. She could hear the child quite well now and she knew her son's voice. "Ryan!" She flung open the front door and ran out into the shadows of trees and mountains.

Lesley raced along the stone-lined path that led from the house to the gate, tore open the latch, and stumbled when she encountered the tall stiff meadow grass and boulders. Slowing, she picked her way in the direction of the river.

"Mother! Come get me! I'm frightened," she heard from the woods. A minor course adjustment pointed her toward the familiar voice.

"I'm coming, Ryan," she called. "Stay right there, honey!" Lesley reached the trees. "Where are you, Ryan? Tell me!"

"Mother! Is that you? Come get me!" he called.

She plunged into the undergrowth without caution. The

bushes became dense and thorny, and she could feel leaves and needles tear at her coat. Dry roots and vines snagged her shoes. Moonlight filtered through livid clouds, making the shadows of snow-bent tree branches look eerie. A tree's glowing fingers grabbed at Lesley's hair. The haunted foliage hindered her progress until her breathing became labored and frantic.

"Ryan!" she screamed.

"Mother? Can you come to me?" came an answering call.

Lesley beat her way through a stand of thorny vines and emerged into a moonlit sylvan glade. "This can't be real," Lesley told herself. "The place doesn't even look like the Gold Country." A larger-than-life sculpted deer decorated the scene. A winding stream reflected the night's Goya-light. The spectacle reminded her of Italian art or Grimm fairy tales, nothing American.

"Mother!" cried Ryan, stepping from behind the giant stag. "You're here! I have waited for so long!"

"Ryan?" Lesley halted. The boy's silhouette seemed taller than her son's. "Is that you?"

"My name is Richard," the boy replied. "I thought you were my mother. Who are you?"

"I'm Lesley Windsor. I have a son about your age, named Ryan. Where did you come from?"

"I come from Deerhaven Forest Hall," answered Richard.

Lesley considered him. The boy wore a fawn-colored suit, belted with soft leather straps, and a sweeping leather coat that hung to mid-calf and flared when he moved. He had been shod in laced boots that didn't look like any article of footwear a shoe store would sell a modern boy. *They can all get back to that house,* Rachel had said. Could they wander the woods also?

"Who is your mother? What's her name?" Lesley asked.

"Jane Copley Windsor," the boy answered.

"What year is this?" Lesley asked him. "Can you tell me?"

He tilted his curly head, a confused expression knitting his brows. "I cannot be certain. I have been trying to find my mother for ever so long. My death occurred in 1907. When my mother dies, she and I will be reunited and live forever in Heavenly Paradise." The boy's smile, dimpled and sweet like Ryan's, tugged at Lesley's heartstrings.

He's a ghost boy, Lesley thought, but he doesn't know what's happened since his death. His mother died a long time ago. Where is the spirit of his mother? Why wouldn't Richard's mother have joined him when she died? Lesley didn't know whether to tell the boy how many years had passed since his death.

"Why are you in the woods tonight?" she asked.

"I came from Deerhaven Forest Hall where I spent the day," Richard replied. "Lately, I do little except wander in the light upstairs but I thought I might meet my mother tonight if I followed the river downstream." He moved closer to Lesley as if for comfort. "Have you heard of her?" As he spoke, a remnant of the day sparked in Lesley's mind.

"Jane Copley Windsor, did you say?"

"That would be my mother's married name. John Bennett Windsor was my father, a cold man who conspired with ruthless and greedy zealots."

That was where she'd seen the name, Lesley realized. Jane Copley Windsor lay in her grave near where they stood. Lesley and Rachel had stumbled upon the headstone and read the inscription this afternoon. This chain of events could not be a coincidence. Lesley must be intended to show the poor lost boy the way to his mother's earthly resting place.

"Can you come with me, Richard?" asked Lesley. "There's something I should show you."

"Certainly. I would be happy to accompany you," the boy replied with courtly manners that would have dated him under any circumstances. No modern boy bowed like this one.

Downy snow sifted through the branches as they walked and Lesley's footsteps made a crunching sound as her shoes sunk through leaves lightly dusted with white. Gliding at her side, Richard progressed through the woods without a crunch. Other than her voice, Cosette had produced no sound either. Soon, Lesley would become an expert on ghostly visitations. Her own audible progress made her nervous since the noise she produced could alert enemies to her presence.

To Lesley's consternation, Richard could glide faster than she could walk. Stopping to catch her breath, Lesley braced herself against a stubby cedar tree. The aromatic incense cedar reminded her of dresser drawers, closets and hope chests, homey scents, which steadied her. She straightened, ready to proceed.

"Where are we going?" inquired the boy.

"To a place I discovered this afternoon. I think you might take comfort in going there."

Richard opened his ghostly lips to question her but shouts and shots interrupted them. If she'd been able to put an arm around the boy, Lesley would have done so. She settled for moving to his side.

They sped toward the wood's edge, Lesley struggling to keep up with Richard. Standing at the perimeter of the clearing, Lesley glanced over at the cabin. Smoke rising from the chimney mingled with snow falling on the roof. Anxiety pricked at Lesley's mind.

"Come this way, Richard," she ordered.

The boy hesitated. "Who are those creatures?" he asked, pointing toward the house. "Could they mean harm to us?"

"Creatures?" Lesley repeated. What did he mean? Foxes, deer?

"Those terrible black specters," Richard told her. "There."

Letting her eyes follow his pointing finger, Lesley spotted the creatures to which he referred and gasped in horror. "My God!" she exclaimed. Dark, larger-than-man-sized figures, traveling at an unnatural speed, moved as a band in a southerly direction. Their tall peaked heads appeared to prick at the snowy night air like burnt needles. After enduring so much, her child being injured, betrayal by her husband, ghostly revelations and the intensity of a woman's love, this sight presented one shock too many.

Lesley sank to her knees, regardless of the chilly, powdery snow on the ground. Richard knelt beside her. Reaching for him, Lesley felt her arms close around snowflakes and cold night air, nothing. She gagged.

"Are they so very dangerous then?" asked Richard. His sweet slightly British syllables revived her a little.

"I've never seen anything so frightening," she whispered. "Have you?"

"I cannot say. I may have seen creatures such as these before.

I have been waiting for my mother a long time. Sometimes, I meet lost people who speak of the dreadful cruelties to which they were subjected in life. They fear damnation, ghastly unending torment. Their spirits can be fearful. They are called the Others. Living souls in torment are drawn to them and do their bidding." The ghost boy shuddered.

"I'm sorry, Richard," she told him in lieu of physical comfort. Lesley rose and faced the horrible band. A bank of heavy clouds moved eastward and freed a strand of moonlight so that she could see them more clearly. A light-colored presence in the midst of the dark caught her eye and an appalling presentiment caused Lesley to run toward, rather than away from, the band.

"Come with me, Richard," she called over her shoulder. Without stopping to look back, she sprinted. She could never have matched the grisly group's phenomenal speed but she approached them on an angle. She drew near enough to distinguish one spectral figure from another but not close enough to alert them to her presence and then, she halted.

Faint screams escaped from the core of the band. A small pale, person hoisted between two grim figures flailed and struggled. Any human cries would be coming from the light woman they held captive. Rachel. Anguish flooded Lesley's brain.

"Rachel!" called Lesley, hysterical. She ran faster than she had since sixth grade, a time when she'd been fleet of foot and still wore pants to school. The distance between her and the supernatural guerrillas turned out to be an illusion. Her approach never caught their attention. The black band neither turned nor paused.

Just before they disappeared into denser woods on the downstream side of the clearing, Lesley drew close enough to scrutinize the dark assembly at closer range. Men, or spirits, wearing awful, billowing garb, composed the band. Although the black hue struck her as different, the cut of their clothing reminded Lesley of Ku Klux Klan members' formal attire even down to the hoods. Cosette wore vaporous wraps like a proper ghost. These black robes and hoods terrified Lesley. Then, among them, a shorter, dimmer figure, caught her eye. She knew him well.

"Michael! Is that you?" she shouted. "Michael, please. Don't do this. If you let your sister go, I'll do anything you want." She knew her pleas must sound weak and pitiful.

"Michael," she repeated. "I'll do anything." For a second, a vision of certain things Michael might ask her to do, things she'd resisted but barely, made her gag. She swallowed her fear. "Anything, Michael!" she yelled one more time. No one answered, not Michael, if he heard her, if he was there, or any other member of the party.

The black-hooded troupe hit the trees and melted into the dark boughs. Only one draped figure with spiked bonnet remained visible for a minute in the clearing. A menacing arm rose in the moonlight, signaling Lesley that her terms of surrender had been in some way understood and rejected. Then, the last clan member, Michael or not, took to the woods and Rachel disappeared with them.

"Richard!" called Lesley. She turned, expecting to find the ghost boy following at her heels but the clearing lay empty in the scant light. As she searched for Jane Copley Windsor's departed son, a new front of clouds closed in overhead. The snow turned icy and began to blow into her face. Any possibility of tracking Rachel or locating Richard evaporated. Alone, Lesley turned toward the only solace remaining, the beacon of light from the house at the clearing's end. A safe house for women, Cosette had said, but not safe enough to shield Rachel.

****

"You're a wizard, Madame Librarian!" breathed Valerie. "You know everything."

"I don't know everything," Sula replied with becoming modesty. "Librarians seem to know everything but they actually don't. What we do know is where to look things up. It amounts to the same thing as knowing everything unless one finds oneself stranded without resources."

Nurse Valerie stared at Sula in the gloom, her jaw slack with admiration.

In an effort to sway the loyalties of Valerie Kemsley, Sula had offered up a dose of local history. Her somewhat fictional oral history of hate groups in the Gold Country had impressed Valerie so much that it left her loath to identify with any such organization. By culminating with the surpassing evil of PURITI and the Reverend Were, although she'd tried to be subtle, Sula hoped she'd won the nurse's allegiance in time to save herself.

"Tell me," Sula asked. "Are the Reverend Were and his followers the ones who have been keeping me here?" If her campaign to alter Valerie's sentiments had been successful she would get an honest answer.

"Yes, they are," Valerie answered but not with conviction. "For the most part."

"Isn't it the Reverend who comes into this room? Was that him pumping me for information? I thought I recognized his voice."

"Yes. That was he."

"What did you mean 'for the most part?' Are you positive that he and his gang are the ones who captured me?" Sula asked.

Frowning, Valerie leaned forward in a confidential manner. "I've heard them talk about Others who help them. I don't recognize the names of the Others. They must not come from Wolf's Creek."

"Have you ever seen the Others?" quizzed Sula.

"No. And that's odd. I know everyone around here except for tourists and hippies."

"Did the Others participate in the shooting of Ryan Windsor?" asked Sula.

"I think so," said Valerie. "But I have a feeling that Reverend Were and the members of PURITI arranged everything that's happened. The shooting and the kidnapping could be pinned on the Others and nobody knows who they are."

Sula bit her lip with frustration. Who could be the Reverend's unknown cohorts? She hoped that the Reverend would maintain enough trust in Valerie to tell her the identity of the Others. All Sula's plans, of course, were contingent upon Valerie ending up with more loyalty to her than to the Reverend Were.

She rose to a sitting position and touched Valerie's neck, the soft vulnerable area under her hair, as though steadying herself.

Valerie's expression grew soft and silly with adoration. Sula's campaign seemed to be progressing with alacrity. The process resembled a tryst at Wildflowers and Valerie had become smitten with Sula as fast as any Wildflowers patron.

"Doesn't it feel as though we've known each other forever, Valerie? The unusual circumstances under which we met and the discovery that we have enemies in common have made our bond more intense. I'm so glad."

Valerie nodded agreement but with less enthusiasm than Sula would have liked. "I'm glad we're friends," she said, "but we have a lot of problems. You're a prisoner, the little boy in the hospital might die, and young Mrs. Windsor is on the loose with poor Rachel Windsor. I feel guilty about everything. What should we do?"

Sula had no choice but to test the strength of Valerie Kemsley's attachment to her. "I'm formulating a plan, Valerie. To begin with, I need to know where I am." Sula's captors had warned her against asking this question but Valerie answered without hesitation.

"You're upstairs in Deerhaven Forest Hall, of course. They've taken over the Hall. Mr. Russell Windsor is their servant. I thought you knew that much!"

"I thought the river's soundtrack sounded familiar but I wasn't sure," replied Sula. "I didn't believe I could be inside Deerhaven Forest Hall because I knew Russell Windsor would help me. We've always been close. He depends on my input and the resources of the library to guide his decisions."

"Decisions about life's spiritual dilemmas, you mean?"

"Well, no," admitted Sula. "I assist with his investments by subscribing to online databases and interpreting the data. And I evaluate every item he purchases. *Consumer Reports* is a bible to Russell. He's also quite neurotic about his health, and I provide reference material and recent journal articles to reassure him. Russell requires practical information more than divine prognostications. What have they done to him?"

"I think they must be drugging him. Without you and Cosette around to help him, he just eats and drinks whatever they give him."

"I'm going to make sure they don't take advantage of him much longer," vowed Sula.

"How capable you are!" said Valerie, and took both Sula's hands.

Valerie seemed to be a quick study. The nurse would be putting the moves on her soon, thought Sula. She needed to speed up the execution of her plan. With that thought in mind, she spoke out loud:

"We must fight the dark forces at work within Deerhaven Pines. Certain historical incidents and snippets of lore that I've read in the Windsor family archives might provide a solution to our problems. I can't recall the details, though. My mother enjoyed fuller access to the library than I have ever been granted. There are journals and diaries that I haven't seen since Mother left her post." Sula made sure that Valerie remained attentive before continuing.

"The ability to perform arcane reference search techniques isn't just handed to a librarian. These skills are acquired at great cost. Many never reach the pinnacle of a librarian's quest. My mother could be considered the Sir Edmund Percival Hillary of regional history, but I don't expect to attain her level of proficiency for years."

She sank back, fatigued. Her captor's drugs sapped her physical strength. She could only hope that these pharmacological agents hadn't drained so much color from her complexion that Valerie would become less enamored of her by daylight.

"How will you find the information we need?" asked Valerie, enthralled by the pursuit of knowledge.

Sula closed her eyes and attempted to dredge facts, history and peculiar philosophies out of her memory. Because of the drugs, perhaps, or because she was only a fledgling librarian, nothing but obscure images came to mind. Then, the solution presented itself. Her eyes flew open.

"There's only one thing to do!" she announced. "It's the first precept of librarianship and so obvious that I forgot!"

"What's that?" Valerie asked, riveted by Sula's epiphany.

"If you can't find the answer, call upon a higher authority," declared Sula.

"What does that mean?" asked Valerie.

"In this case," answered Sula, "it means we're going to call my mother! We can probably track her down at the California History Room of the San Francisco Public Library. That's where Mother volunteers now that she's retired. Mother hoped that she would never again see the inside of Deerhaven Forest Hall but we'll prevail upon her professional code of ethics."

"Ethics! Yes!" repeated Valerie.

"I'm so glad you agree, Valerie, because I need your help to get out of here. Do you have a cell phone?"

"I don't buy anything newfangled," Valerie answered to Sula's annoyance. She would have to hit the last gabby person in the United States without a cell phone.

"You have to get me to a phone without anyone finding out. The telephone in Cosette Windsor's study isn't on the same line as the rest of the house. We'll go there."

Valerie gaped at Sula with fear and amazement. "Take you to a phone!" she exclaimed. "I can't do that! If we get caught, they'll do something awful to us. You don't know what they do to people who go against them! You don't even want to know."

Sula would have liked to know but she didn't ask. "I must telephone for help, Valerie! We can't stop the Reverend without the aid of my mother. You'll love her. She's the canniest librarian you'll ever meet!"

"Oh, my!" said Valerie, clearly not convinced that she would enjoy meeting the dangerous-sounding Ursa Smith.

"And Mother's got a heart of gold," Sula reassured the nurse.

"How lovely," Valerie replied.

Sula ran her fingers back and forth across Valerie's rough palms.

"When would be the safest time to leave this room?" she murmured.

"I don't know," Valerie groaned, stupid with panic.

"We have to use the phone," Sula reminded her with infinite patience.

"Oh, God!" muttered Valerie, irritating Sula by invoking the

Reverend Were's supreme being. "I can't believe I'm doing this. I must be under a spell."

"You're a peach!" coaxed Sula.

Valerie Kemsley smiled back, appearing to appreciate this comparison to summer fruit. "Give me your hand," Valerie instructed. "I'll help you stand up. God willing, we won't meet anyone on our way to the phone and back."

"I'll take the blame if we do," promised Sula, not bothering to add, "Nothing ventured, nothing gained." Valerie didn't strike her as a natural adventurer.

CHAPTER SEVENTEEN

Pauline Walden unpacked nine bags of overpriced groceries purchased at the Blackhawk Market. The market charged at least twenty-five cents more per item than the local Safeway but you never had to wait in a check stand line. At the Blackhawk Market, a blue-aproned older man carried your bags out to the car. She'd become soft and she knew it, cushioned by her husband's wealth. Dan Walden designed operating systems for the nuclear arms industry but his salary was just gravy on top of the hefty pile of loot he'd been left by his grandfather.

Dan adored Pauline and enjoyed nothing better than using his money to spare her the slightest perturbation. The most exciting moment of Pauline's day often occurred when her son, Brent, arrived home from second grade, especially if Brent described a playground fight or a fellow student's academic debacle. The baby, Melly, spent almost every waking hour with her nanny, Mrs. Eutsy. Recently, Melly screamed every time Mrs. Eutsy attempted to place her in Pauline's arms. The process of trying to re-create a bond with her own baby would be humiliating. Pauline sighed.

Although Pauline avoided consuming fat during any of the day's prescribed meals, she fetched a pint carton of Double Rainbow Espresso Supreme ice cream from the freezer and extracted a spoon from the dishwasher. With practiced stealth, she pushed open the swinging door to the dining room. Neither Mrs. Eutsy nor the housekeeper, Ms. Mendoza, appeared on the horizon. Pauline spooned down three-quarters of the rich caffeine-laden dessert, stashed the remainder in the freezer, washed her spoon in the boiling water tap and returned the incriminating implement to the dishwasher. Then, she sat down at her custom-designed kitchen table and cried into her trembling hands. Why did she feel so furtive in her own home?

Under ordinary circumstances, she would have called her best friend, Lesley. Her friend always came through in a pinch, assuring Pauline that her life had meaning. Thinking of Lesley brought her a measure of optimism. She got up and searched her message drawer. Upon a hardware store receipt, she found the number for Sonora Sierra Hospital and Ryan's room number. She dialed the room direct. A confident male voice picked up the phone.

"Ryan Windsor's room. Dr. Andy Riemer speaking."

"Doctor? This is Pauline Walden, a friend of Lesley Windsor's. May I speak to Lesley or Michael?"

"Neither Mr. or Mrs. Windsor have visited the hospital since yesterday morning. They haven't been reachable at the local number they left. Have you spoken with them?"

"No, I haven't," she said in alarm. "I don't understand what's going on. Lesley would never leave Ryan in the hospital by himself. Michael's unpredictable but Lesley is definitely not."

"I will admit that we've been concerned that Ryan's mother hasn't been in attendance, given his age and the severity of his condition."

Pauline felt her anxiety rising. "Would it help if I drove up?"

she asked. "I could try to track Lesley down, and I could sit with Ryan."

"Mrs. Windsor listed you as an emergency contact so that would be great. Thanks for offering. Check in at the hospital admitting desk when you get here. They'll issue you a badge."

"Thank you, Dr. Riemer." Pauline tracked down Mrs. Eutsy and arranged for her children's care, packed an overnight bag, and got into the car.

As she crested the Altamont Pass, Pauline wondered what she might face in the Gold Country. Where could Lesley be? Had Michael run completely amuck after his mother's death? She remembered a strange story she'd heard from a schoolyard gossip one morning when dropping her son, Brent, off at school. She'd given the account little credence out of loyalty to Lesley but, unbidden, the woman's words came back to her.

"I've always thought little Ryan Windsor's father was a bit unstable," began Shirley Getterson in the standard lisp and lilt of a schoolyard gossip, "but now I've heard something truly distressing. I'm upset for the child. You see, my husband's sister is married to a police sergeant who works in San Francisco." Shirley's eyes had flicked to the faces of her very privileged listeners and she'd added a disclaimer. "Eliot's sister's husband came from a good family but he became estranged from them and joined the police force. You know how these things are!" A family member with a career in law enforcement didn't pass muster in Blackhawk and Shirley knew that.

"You were mentioning something about Michael Windsor?" prompted Kim Nelson, an airhead ex-flight attendant and a sucker for scandal.

"Yes! Officer Dietz sighted Michael Windsor in a dubious area of the city soliciting a filthy young man with tattoos and tight pants. Michael might be a homosexual or worse!"

These charges were so awful that the group fell silent. Pauline fumed but she hadn't officially been listening so she couldn't speak. The story gave Pauline pause, however. On some level, she'd always been wary of Michael and his moods, but the idea of him living a secret other life frightened her even more. She hoped she didn't regret her hasty decision to embark on this mission of mercy. Would she end up engaging in a distasteful scene with Michael? Only her devotion to Lesley and to Ryan, a trusting and intelligent boy who worshipped Pauline for slipping him the kind of candy he liked best, Starbursts, kept Pauline's foot on the gas pedal of her silver Jaguar.

****

At morning's first light, Lesley departed from the small house where she'd retreated after Rachel's abduction last night. She reached the Stanislaus River in much less time than the same walk had taken the day before since she no longer needed to slow her pace for Rachel. As she headed upstream, she kept an eye out for black-hooded men although she didn't know whether they roved the foothills in daylight.

The track narrowed and widened but she stayed at water's edge, using the river as a guide. Near a wide beach of beige sand that she hadn't noticed on her way downstream, a rapier-like church spire appeared behind the trees. The town of Wolf's Creek must sprawl toward the river at just this point. Instead of trying to reach Deerhaven Forest Hall before reporting Rachel's kidnapping, she decided to phone the county sheriff from Wolf's Creek. She scrambled up the slope away from the river.

Invigorated by the sight of rooftops, which suggested help near at hand, Lesley hurried toward the Gold Country hamlet. Imagining Rachel in the hands of black-hatted men spurred her to a faster pace. A hazy sun obscured any sure indication of time, but she estimated the hour to be around nine. Most citizens of Wolf's Creek would be up and about.

Eventually, a narrow street without a sidewalk meandered down to meet her. Ragtag vacation homes, Tahoe-style cabins with redwood decks and steep roofs, yellow and blue Swiss chalets, utilitarian rustic homes built from kits, occupied single, double, or triple lots. These residences, for the most part, looked deserted and she chose to pass them by, headed for the town proper. After a while, summer homes whose owners mercifully appeared to have solicited the assistance of a legitimate architect replaced the rinky-dink homes that Lesley had encountered on the outskirts of town. A plumbing contractor on his way to work stopped and offered her a ride. He conveyed Lesley several miles until she hit clusters of small businesses.

"You can let me off here," she told *J. Geddes, Plumber, Deerhaven Pines*, and hopped down from the cab of his truck. She hadn't hitchhiked since before her marriage, and, for a moment, she felt almost carefree, like the heedless college student she'd once been. Her ebullience faded in only a second as she scrutinized Wolf's Creek. A film of despair and discontent lay upon every building and business. She remembered liking the quaint look of Deerhaven Pines but Wolf's Creek, although Deerhaven Pine's nearest neighbor, evidenced none of the same charms. Deerhaven Pines recalled the romance of a bygone era. Wolf's Creek, although of the same vintage, suggested the shame of a crueler time as if the dual aspects of America's frontier past had been compartmentalized by the county assessors' map department.

Picking the first accessible storefront, she pivoted on the sidewalk to face the swinging glass front door. According to the sign on its door, Happy Flower Bakery had been open since seven in the morning. She plunged inside and asked to use the phone, contemplating buying a sticky bun and a cup of take-out coffee with the change in her pockets. The sour expressions on the faces of Mei Chun Liu, proprietor, and his co-worker, a teenager wearing a baker's hat embroidered with the name Damien, distracted her from the pastries.

"No phone," replied Mr. Liu. "Get out."

"Employees only," Damien added, his voice chilling. Lesley couldn't remember ever being subjected to so nasty a reception by total strangers, especially ones running a business. She backed out of the fragrant shop without another word.

At the Kierstead Meat Market, she watched Norman Kierstead, butcher, ferrying dripping cuts of beef from the meat locker to the glass display counter. The store opened at ten o'clock but Lesley jumped the gun by rapping on the door. She reassured herself that Mr. Kierstead would have to possess a pleasanter disposition than Mr. Liu next door. What were the odds on adjacent tradespeople turning out to be equally mean-spirited? The bulky butcher, attired in a classic white apron with bloodstains, over baggy brown trousers, positioned the last row of filets and plodded toward the storefront picture window where she stood, barely visible through the streaky red, white, and blue lettering advertising Kierstead's weekly specials. When Mr. Kierstead drew close enough to examine Lesley, he stopped in his tracks.

"You!" his rough cry shook the glass. "You get away from my door! Go!" He made shooing gestures with his meaty hands.

"I don't know you," called Lesley, stunned. "Do you know me?"

"The devil's companion," shouted Butcher Kierstead. "Don't come any closer. I'm calling the sheriff." He raised a fist and shook it. "I'm also going to call our minister, and he'll know what to do with you. Get away from my door, you monster!"

The butcher turned and ran back behind the counter, then returned with an oversize orange sheet of paper that he waved at her.

Lesley saw her own face in a photograph next to a snapshot of Rachel. The largest letters spelled, BEWARE. Block letters accused Lesley of kidnapping Rachel Windsor with malicious intent. The only other words that Lesley could make out read, "Call Chief Phil Morton, Wolf's Creek Sheriff's Department if you encounter one of these women." Kierstead's expression turned menacing. After the last few days' events, Lesley never doubted that Kierstead would call Sheriff Morton and anything that happened subsequent to that would not be beneficial to her. Lesley wheeled and ran, continuing down the block.

The last building on the block sported lime green paint and a flamingo as though the whole outfit had been transported from Florida by a rogue tornado. Erva Glasper Candles announced the oversize fluorescent sign. The flyer bearing Lesley's and Rachel's pictures had been scotch-taped inside the store's center window and this public accusation was the final straw. She could go nowhere in this town with anonymity. She needed to depart without delay. Bolting into the street, she looked for an escape route.

When a car with a real estate company logo pulled up and

the driver asked if she needed a ride, she accepted and leapt inside.

"Where're you heading, honey?" asked the agent, a fortyish woman with an elaborate stationary cascade of blond hair.

"Sonora Sierra Hospital," replied Lesley. "My son is a patient there." She could not stay away from Ryan's bed any longer. Her palms grew clammy at the thought that her son's condition might have deteriorated in her absence. In all his short life, she had never been away from Ryan for more than the length of a school day. Now, he'd lain in a hospital bed overnight without her. She tried to remain calm and convivial as the blond woman's car sped away from Wolf's Creek.

"Your boy is sick?" inquired the agent.

He had a bullet in his brain, thought Lesley in despair. "He was injured," she said, "but he's going to be okay."

"How old is the poor little thing?" asked the agent, dealing with Lesley as she would a prospective client.

"Nine," Lesley answered.

"Mine are grown," the agent volunteered and, to Lesley's relief, launched into an account of each child's progress through life, community college courses, dental hygiene training, sojourns in county jail, bouts with bipolar disorder, marriages that ended in divorce or bliss, parenthood, pyramid sales, home and recreational vehicle ownership.

"Here's my business card. Let me know if you decide to buy in the area," ordered the agent as Lesley thanked her for the ride and jumped out of the car.

Lesley sprinted through the pneumatic doors at the front entrance of Sonora Sierra Hospital. After inquiring at the front desk and finding Ryan's condition still listed as "critical but stable," she located a pay phone booth.

When the 911 operator answered the phone, Lesley blurted, "I'd like to report a kidnapping!" She would give them the real story of Rachel's kidnapping, up to a point.

"Who is missing?"

"Rachel Windsor of Deerhaven Forest Hall."

"Age?"

"I'm not sure," Lesley admitted. "She's in her twenties."

"Why do you believe that she was kidnapped," the operator asked with no real spark of interest. The 911 operator did not seem to be in the loop the way that every merchant in Wolf's Creek seemed to be.

"The sheriff's department thinks that I kidnapped her but I saw her carried away by a group of men."

"What men? And when?"

"The men wore black cloaks. I think the Reverend Were might be a party to the kidnapping although I don't know for sure. It was during the night. Probably about one or two in the morning."

"Can you give me your name, please?" asked the woman. Her voice had hardened with suspicion at the mention of Reverend Were.

"My name is Lesley Windsor. I'm Rachel's sister-in-law."

"Where are you now, Mrs. Windsor? My readout just gives the address of Sonora Sierra Hospital. I'd like an officer to meet with you and take a report."

Lesley hesitated. Her need to see her son and touch him had become overwhelming. She couldn't allow the police to show up too soon. "I'm at the hospital right now, and I need to visit my son. I could meet an officer at Deerhaven Forest Hall in an hour."

The operator insisted on recording the phone number and address of Deerhaven Forest Hall before allowing Lesley to hang up. Relieved that the police would be assisting her in retrieving Rachel, Lesley bolted across the lobby and into the elevator.

On Ryan's floor, she encountered a familiar nurse. The nurse's badge read, "Neil Horvath, Nursing Supervisor." At the sight of her, his face contorted with disdain but Lesley's brooch did not react to his presence. Neil Horvath looked like an annoying tightass but he must not be an evil Other. She would have to endure his icky, but not mystic, personality disorder.

"You haven't been to visit your son since the morning after he was admitted," Nurse Horvath stated with disapproval.

"That's right. How is Ryan?" Lesley asked.

"As I informed his father just a short time ago," Horvath began, emphasizing Michael's official title, "your son is holding his own."

"Michael came to see him?" she questioned, still eager to think well of Michael. "Is he here now?" she asked, feeling her chest constrict.

"I believe he left after spending time with your son. Your son, by the way, rests easier today. He moans less in his sleep."

"Thank God," whispered Lesley. "May I go to his room?"

"Certainly," answered the grim, peach-clad nurse. "I hope we'll see you later when Dr. Riemer makes his rounds."

"I hope so," said Lesley with forced sincerity. She brushed past the nurse who remained planted in the corridor, eyeing Lesley with disapproval.

Ryan lay in his room, alone. Lesley pulled up a vinyl-upholstered chair and sat, watching his gentle breathing and stroking his small motionless hands. What could Michael be thinking, leaving before consulting with her?

"Cosette?" Lesley called softly. "Cosette, are you around?" No answer came. She trusted that Cosette would appear should Ryan need assistance but her ghostly mother-in-law must have decided to respect Rachel's insistence that they not have contact. Ryan's peaceful presence proved steadying and she found herself increasingly sure that her son would be returned to good health. Such an insistent life force as Ryan's could not be quelled.

"Mrs. Windsor?" came a voice, soothing as anesthetic. Handsome Dr. Riemer stood at the foot of the bed.

"Dr. Riemer! How is Ryan?" Lesley dared not state her conviction that Ryan would recover.

"His condition has remained basically unchanged," replied Riemer. "We're playing a waiting game." He examined Ryan, touching the boy's pallid flesh with a delicacy that Lesley appreciated. Dr. Riemer's face grew graver as he examined Ryan. The door swung open and Nurse Horvath entered the room, but Lesley kept her attention focused on the man who would pronounce Ryan better or worse.

"Perhaps you should wait until his father is present to discuss the boy's treatment," suggested the nurse in an arch, judgmental tone.

"His father didn't say when he planned to return," said the doctor with no particular inflection. He turned to Lesley. "We might need to make a decision about Ryan's course of treatment, and we might need to make it soon. Why don't you give us your opinion right now, Mrs. Windsor."

"What do you mean, Doctor? I thought he was holding his own," Lesley said in alarm.

Doctor Riemer turned his trademark smile, a beacon of charm and sincerity, upon Lesley. He couldn't produce that smile if there were no hope, could he?

"It's always been a toss-up whether to transport the boy to a more sophisticated facility. Ryan's condition hasn't deteriorated markedly over the past couple of days but it hasn't improved either. The decision is whether to leave him here or to airlift him to a city hospital where he can be more closely monitored. I don't want to alarm you, Mrs. Windsor, but the services of a skilled pediatric neurosurgeon might be required. We'll want to make sure that we have access to a highly experienced practitioner. I was thinking of Delia Bevilacqua at UCSF."

"Yes. Absolutely," Lesley agreed.

"Are you and your husband in contact?" the doctor asked. "Can you discuss the options with him?" A nasty smirk played upon Nurse Horvath's lips.

"I'll try to track him down," promised Lesley, wondering where to start looking for Michael. The number of things she didn't know about her husband overwhelmed her.

After Dr. Riemer and his unpleasant co-worker departed, Lesley paced the room. How could she help her son? Scores of questions presented themselves and she could answer none. Then, she sensed an answer forming.

"Please, help me," Lesley murmured as though praying to an indeterminate someone. Somehow, Lesley's prayer distilled pure thought from the hospital's bacteria-laden air. The light in the room altered, hospital harsh turned to shimmering pale gray. A small figure, source of the clear, subtle emanations, now occupied the plastic armchair.

"Who are you?" Lesley demanded.

"I'm Jane," the visitor responded. "Jane Copley Windsor. I'm here to stay with your son while you attempt to remedy everything that's gone wrong."

Once again, Lesley found herself inclined toward accepting this offer of assistance from a ghost. A weird sureness that the hitherto unknown Jane Windsor, deceased, would take excellent care of Ryan descended upon her.

"Thank you, Jane. Pleased to meet you. Aren't you the mother of Richard Windsor?"

The ghost leveled a stare at Lesley. There was something Scottish about Jane even in death, a keen-eyed look.

"In life, I was the mother of Richard and Robin Windsor," she replied. "Now I am the mother of many, including this poor wee bairn in the bed here."

"I think I understand," said Lesley, choosing her words with care. "Where's Cosette?"

"Cosette understood that your relationship with her daughter forced you to end your affinity with her. She sends her blessings. So, I came instead. I hope you will choose to establish an affinity with me." Jane added, "You should be on your way. You have much to do."

Fatigue overwhelmed Lesley but she straightened her shoulders. "My..." Lesley paused, searching for the correct term but none came to mind. "My friend, Rachel Windsor, has been kidnapped by a man who calls himself a minister."

Jane nodded with gravity but no surprise. "That would be the Reverend Chaney's associate in this time," said Jane. "Can you tell me his name?"

"Reverend Were," Lesley supplied.

"Reverend Were might well be the instrument of Ryan's affliction," said Jane. "You have good reason to fear him."

"I'm very much afraid that Ryan's father might have been involved in the shooting," Lesley confessed. The ghost of Jane, fine hair under a neat cap, smoothed her vaporous skirt.

"He wouldn't be the first Windsor to misunderstand what it means to champion the Hue," said Jane.

"Champion the Hue?" Lesley repeated. "Like in the family motto?"

"Family mottoes have their roots in historical fact," replied Jane.

"What does the Windsors' motto mean?" asked Lesley.

Jane lifted her face to stare at Lesley once again. "Each generation must discover the meaning anew," she informed her in a gentle tone.

Lesley sensed that Jane could provide useful information. How might she extract what she needed to know?

"Deciphering the family motto won't help me undo all that's wrong," she said. "I need to understand what everyone is trying to accomplish and what they're trying to hide. Should I pursue my ex-husband, or look for Rachel, or confront the minister?"

"The mottoes should help," commented Jane.

"I'm not even sure who's good and who's bad," Lesley murmured. "So many people seem to have turned against me and Rachel for no reason."

"What of Sula, the descendant of my dearest friend, Ursula Smith?" Jane asked. "Why is Sula not here to assist in fighting those who are working against you?"

"Sula's missing, I'm afraid," replied Lesley.

Jane nodded. "I feared that they would take her. I see things, and I know some of what transpired. Do you plan to rescue her?"

"Are you sure she wasn't responsible for Ryan getting shot?" Lesley asked. "When I saw her last, she was with Reverend Were and his followers. Could she have joined their cause?"

Jane Copley Windsor looked shocked. "A descendant of Ursula's allow harm come to a child? Never! I see that you are too frightened to trust your good instincts, Lesley, my dear one. Sula would give her life to protect young Ryan. She quite obviously forfeited her freedom in the attempt. Sula is formidable, she is a librarian after all, but should Sula need a hand, you must be prepared to offer yours."

"What can I do to help Sula?" questioned Lesley. "I don't even know where to find her. Where should I start?"

"Where to start?" echoed Jane. "The only thing of which we can be sure is where to start."

"Where?"

"Where do you go to find everything? The library, of course. Every piece of this puzzle can be solved by using the library. But, since the librarian is not in residence, you will have to locate what you need without assistance."

"What is it that I need?" Lesley asked, bewildered.

"You need information about the occult," answered Jane. "To find it, you must suspend rational thought and move quickly. Temporal time is running out for you."

****

The trip down the back stairwell of Deerhaven Forest Hall seemed to take hours. Sula and Valerie froze with terror at every creak and rustle but they encountered no one. They found Cosette Windsor's study quiet and deserted. The telephone rested in its usual place on the late Cosette Windsor's desk, and a dial tone indicated that the instrument would work. Dialing an eleven-digit number by heart, Sula held her breath until a confident voice greeted her with, "California History Room, Ursa Smith."

"Mother!" Sula exclaimed. "I wouldn't have thought they'd let a volunteer answer the phone." Only when dealing with her mother did Sula nitpick in this way.

"They have several positions vacant right now. I'm on paid status. What can I do for you, darling?" Ursa never wasted time on idle chat.

"Mother, so much has gone wrong!" Sula relayed as much as she knew about the dire events of the last week.

Ursa remained silent for a moment on the other end of the line. "This relates to the library, Sula. As you know, the library attracts both good and evil and houses them both. Your job is to keep them in order. You'll notice that everything fell apart for the Windsors once you left your post. You're young, Sula, but the time has come for you to learn the magnitude of your responsibility."

"To this day, there's a lot I don't understand about the library at the Hall," Sula confessed. "They didn't cover what I needed to know when I got my MLS from Columbia. They stressed the technological areas of expertise. That's why I'm calling you. I need old-fashioned library skills."

"The library at Deerhaven Forest Hall is a depository for dark secrets and prodigious enlightenment," Ursa replied. "It's time you know the secrets."

"How are they catalogued?" asked Sula. "How do I unearth the secrets and the light?"

"The original librarian set up a unique filing system," Ursa informed her daughter. "It's now time you learned. Try to keep everything under control until I arrive. I'll leave the city at five o'clock. I can be there by eight or eight thirty."

"I'll meet you in the library," promised Sula. She smiled reassuringly at Valerie whose eyes darted back and forth in terror.

"One last thing," said Ursa.

"Yes?"

"Are there clouds or will it be clear tonight?"

"What?"

"Will the sky be clear tonight?" Ursa asked once again.

Sula consulted with Valerie. "There was a light snow during the night but the clouds have almost disappear," she reported.

"Ah! That's good," replied Ursa. "I'll show you why when I arrive there."

"What are you doing here?" called a harsh voice from the door.

Sula and Valerie whirled. A dark menacing figure with blazing yellow eyes blocked the only exit from the room. Mrs. Woolf! Minion of the Reverend Were! With all the mental dexterity of a librarian, Sula gathered her thoughts.

"I've got you now!" snarled Mrs. Woolf, hackles raised.

"No!" answered Sula. "I have the resources of the library at my fingertips. Checkmate! I've got you!" For good measure, she picked up Cosette Windsor's ornamental envelope opener to stab the wolf in the heart should the need arise.

CHAPTER EIGHTEEN

As Lesley stared at the dove-gray ghost of Jane Copley Windsor, preparing to leave Ryan in the ghost's keeping, her instincts told her that Jane represented the forces of good. But how could she be sure of anything? The pendant around Lesley's neck burned the fragile white skin above her bosom. Taking the brooch in one hand to spare her chest, she cried out. The necklace felt hot in her palm and seemed to grow both bigger and smaller. Lesley dropped the thing and the necklace came to rest upon her shirt. She hadn't been imagining its strange properties. The ornament on the end of the chain really did become warm and vibrant as if alive. Jane Windsor, dressed in period costume (well, not a costume, Lesley conceded, a long graceful skirt, tie-boots and soft jacket, had probably been part of the woman's regular wardrobe), gazed at the vibrant pendant.

"The necklace felt hot, just now," Lesley explained. "I don't understand why."

"In life, I wore that brooch," replied Jane, confounding Lesley. This physical bond between herself and a person long dead and buried brought home how strange a turn her life had taken.

"This might sound like an odd question," said Lesley, choosing her words with care, "but do you remember the necklace becoming heavy and warm, coursing with an energy not your own?"

"I do," returned Jane without hesitation. "Many a time I experienced just the sensation you mention. I never discovered the source of the brooch's emanations but I did become able to anticipate the phenomenon."

"Really?" said Lesley. She noticed that her use of the word confused the ghost. The usage must be modern. She smiled, encouraging Jane to continue.

"I could tell by the situation whether the necklace would be likely to...alter," Jane replied. "It seemed to me that the necklace grew warm and, how should I put this...less solid, is how I might describe it, when I entered into a situation where I needed to act on behalf of the family."

"Can you give me an example?" Lesley asked.

Jane considered. "While I lived, an evil person called himself a minister, the Reverend Chaney of whom I spoke earlier. Chaney became more and more of a threat to those I loved. In the end, he took everything I cared about from me."

"And he's related to the Reverend Were who leads a group of hate-mongers in this time?"

"I believe they could be related but how, I do not know," Jane answered. "If so, your Reverend Were may be capable of prodigious sin and evil."

"What did he do to you?" pursued Lesley.

"He and his followers brought about the death of my sweet young son, Richard. They drove my lover from these shores. What he did to me was so unspeakable that I cannot bring myself to recount the act. The Windsor family hid behind a cloak of secrecy after the Reverend Chaney's time, fearful that ignorance and bigotry might dishonor the family once again."

"How awful," breathed Lesley. A sudden thought brought a stab of pain. "Could the two ministers actually be in contact, Jane? In the same way that you and I can communicate? That would be awful! The Reverend Chaney killed your son. What if the Reverend Were put Ryan in this hospital bed? If there's a parallel, Ryan will die."

"Nothing is preordained," said Jane, stepping forward as though to comfort Lesley with the physical presence she'd possessed long ago. "Your choices will alter what happens and luck will come into play. Go to the library, Lesley. History and myth might be the best weapons at your disposal."

Lesley bent to kiss her son's soft, wavy, brown hair. His breath on her cheek reassured her that he only slept. Jane Copley Windsor promised not to leave Ryan untended, and Lesley forced herself to leave.

On her way to the parking lot, she informed the hospital staff that she could be reached at Deerhaven Forest Hall and that they should call her any time of the day or night. She missed the ability to use her cell phone more than she ever could have imagined.

Emerging from the heated building, she buttoned her jacket. Today's weak sun had burned off last night's snowfall but the air stung her cheeks, and she couldn't keep her footing in the wet parking lot. When she'd arrived at the hospital, she hadn't been able to figure out whether nonemergency visitors could utilize the short-term parking spaces so she'd left her van in the main parking lot. Approaching her car, she used the remote control to turn off the alarm. In the silence that followed the car alarm's beep, the sound of heavy rubber soles on wet gravelly asphalt alerted Lesley to the fact that someone followed her. Lesley froze, key ring in hand with the keys projecting through her fingers, the modern woman's version of brass knuckles.

Her stalker gave her no chance to use her keys in self-defense. Before Lesley could whirl and slash, the back of her head felt as if it were hit by lightning and the afternoon sun winked out. Her keys dropped, clinking and clanging, onto the slushy parking lot.

****

Jane Copley Windsor no longer possessed five senses, only two. She could use her eyes, although her vision went in and out of focus, and she could hear selected passages of sound and human voice. Touch, smell and taste departed when she left this mortal coil. Where she dwelt, she didn't need those three lost faculties but, inside Ryan Windsor's hospital room, she could have used the ability to gauge temperature. Ryan looked feverish all of a sudden, and pale blue.

Ever since Cosette Windsor's energies had been directed elsewhere, Jane had taken care of Ryan and Jane felt great affection for the boy. He looked so much like her first child that Jane could almost feel Ryan within the ghost of her womb. In this state of heightened attachment to the boy, Ryan's fever became palpable. Her concern, coupled with longing for her long-dead favorite son, a pain that haunted Jane the same way she haunted the Sierra foothills, helped her thoughts to coalesce. She must help Ryan. She must concentrate herself until she developed physical force.

In the warm, dry air of the hospital, her efforts had no visual affect. No steamy vapor in the shape of a woman appeared in the atmosphere like a ghost in a children's cartoon. Anyone in the room would have seen nothing. The spirit of Jane triumphed invisibly. Without leaving Ryan's bedside, she left the room and began combing Sonora Sierra Hospital. She brushed the faces of hospital personnel in order to check their identity.

Finally, she located Dr. Andy Riemer in the emergency room, tending a ten-year-old girl with cat scratches. Dr. Riemer finished treating his unhappy freckle-faced patient and launched into a lecture on respectful and careful treatment of domestic animals. To get his attention, Jane tapped him on the forehead. Looking puzzled, Dr. Riemer rubbed his temples, probably assuming that his sudden-onset "headache" could be alleviated by this measure. Jane knocked on his skull again. The doctor swiveled his head, either looking for the unseen specter who troubled him or hoping to work the kinks out of his neck.

"Ryan Windsor!" Jane shouted. No sound came forth. "Ryan needs you!" she screamed. Dr. Riemer's stunningly blue eyes widened. The cat molester's mom, helping her bandaged daughter with her jacket, failed to notice anything but the freckled peril looked around.

"Somebody's calling you!" she told Dr. Riemer.

"You'll have to excuse me," said Andy Riemer, his own voice, although audible and human, grown shaky with bewilderment. "There's a patient I have to check on." Massaging his temples as if he'd developed a headache, he hurried from the room and signed out of the emergency department. The triage nurse protested his departure but Riemer insisted that he needed to go. Jane wished she could thank the doctor for his willingness to trust his "intuition" but she didn't know if she would be allowed many more articulations before her exile from the earth became permanent. She followed behind as the doctor hurried to Ryan's side.

"His condition has deteriorated," Dr. Riemer reported to Nurse Neil Horvath and to Jane hovering near. "There must be minor intracranial bleeding." The doctor whipped out the names of medical tests, which Jane didn't recognize and gave orders she couldn't interpret.

Dr. Andy Riemer, a young man rooted in his own time, had no way of knowing what had really gone wrong with Ryan. As Ryan's family grew closer and closer to catastrophe, so did the boy. Jane hoped the doctor would be able to stave off a medical catastrophe until events intervened in the boy's favor. Although Riemer didn't know, his ability to sustain Ryan Windsor lay within himself. Twenty-first century medicine wouldn't be what saved the boy. Only Dr. Riemer's skill as a healer, an old and innate talent, might pull Ryan through. Jane wrung her fragile, filmy hands.

"Save the child, please, doctor," cried Jane. Ryan seemed to have become as much a part of Jane as her own Richard had been. Dr. Riemer looked up from his patient to see who'd spoken.

"We'll make sure this little boy hangs in for the duration, Neil," he answered, assuming that he'd heard the nurse urging him on. Following some atavistic impulse, Dr. Riemer laid his hands upon the unconscious boy to transmit his own strength and well-being. A slight breath of pink appeared in Ryan's cheeks and fingernails.

"What are doing to my son?" called a hoarse, unsteady voice.

Jane noticed an intrinsically handsome young man with disheveled hair and dirt-stained shiny clothing standing near the entrance to the room. Jane hadn't seen the man come inside the room. He must be Michael Windsor, Ryan's father! Jane recognized him at first glance and she knew from whom he was descended. The man, superficially, resembled his ancestor although the resemblance dissipated upon further observation. In Michael's ancestor, Jane's old nemesis, his appearance reflected his malignant soul. Michael, on the other hand, looked confused and broken but not evil.

"I'm glad you've come, Mr. Windsor," said Dr. Riemer. "I don't want to alarm you but we may need your consent to perform surgery on Ryan. It could be as soon as this afternoon. Would you mind remaining at the hospital until our specialists recommend how to proceed?"

"I can't," returned Michael Windsor. "I don't know why I came. They keep telling me one thing and then another. They whisper that I should champion the Hue. Then, they warn me that I have to choose an affinity." He clutched his head as if racked with pain. Jane feared Michael might be driven crazy before his wife got a chance to straighten things out. Windsors did succumb to madness now and again.

What should she do? Her search for Ryan's doctor had exhausted her ability to manifest physical energy. To help Michael, although she found herself without matter, she encircled him, hoping to quiet his spirit with her spiritual proximity. His brow relaxed for a second and then, he shook her off.

"Mr. Windsor!" Dr. Riemer expostulated. "You are responsible for making an informed decision about your child's treatment. How can you think about leaving your son in crisis?"

"I'm dangerous to him," gasped Michael. "I should go." The tiny rosebuds in Ryan's cheeks withered and blew away. Jane prayed for the power of common speech but these people couldn't hear her. Michael Windsor cocked his aching head, listening to the dark voices of Others.

"That boy is the devil's spawn!" Michael thundered suddenly. From somewhere inside his shiny clothing, still beaded with November drizzle, Michael extracted a gun and brandished the huge, silver weapon. "The devil's children must be extinguished," he roared.

"No!" screamed a woman that Jane didn't recognize, charging in from the corridor, dripping melting snow. "I won't let you hurt Ryan."

The woman was not a Windsor relative. Jane took heart. Perhaps a stranger could combat the destructive elements to which Windsors fell prey. For Ryan's sake, she prayed that this was so.

"Go away, Pauline!" shouted Michael. "I've told you a thousand times. Stay out of my family's business."

The well-groomed, blond woman took in the scene and her jaw tightened. "I'm Pauline Walden, Lesley's friend," she explained tersely to Dr. Riemer and his nurse. "We spoke earlier."

"Give me the gun, Michael!" said Pauline. "What have you done to Lesley, you bastard? Don't even think about using that gun. Dan and I will hunt you down and shoot you like a diseased skunk if you hurt your son. Dan collects real weapons. Remember?"

Michael leveled the gun at her and then lowered the pistol, hands shaking, eyebrows twitching. Everyone remained stationary, waiting for him to drop the gun. When he raised the ugly metal object again, he pointed the barrel at his son.

"Don't shoot, Windsor," ordered the doctor. Nurse Horvath cowered against the vinyl-papered wall, eyes covered. Riemer's voice attracted Michael's attention and the befuddled gunman readjusted his aim.

When Michael pulled the trigger, the room reverberated with the loud report. Andy Riemer gasped and fell. Nurse Horvath screamed. The small, sheet-covered figure in the bed did not respond to the commotion.

"This is driving me out of my mind," moaned Michael.

"Lesley won't stop hounding me. She offered her body to me in exchange for my sister. What kind of a woman would do that? I have to get rid of her. I'm going to Deerhaven Forest Hall. I have no choice."

"Leave Lesley alone," threatened Pauline, her voice strangled with fear, eyes fixed upon the doctor's prostrate body. The gun, swinging in Michael's hand, leapt into his fingers again. Strangely, Michael couldn't straighten the weapon, as though an invisible person were pressing the barrel toward the floor.

"I'm calling 911," announced Pauline, whipping out her cell phone. A voice informed her that she'd strayed out of range. She needn't have worried. Two uniformed hospital security guards burst into the room.

"He's got a gun," Pauline shrieked. The guards lunged forward but Michael ran out the door and down the corridor with a guard in pursuit. The other guard stooped to check the condition of Andy Riemer.

"He's breathing," said Nurse Horvath. "Call someone to attend to the patient too. He's running a fever."

"I'll be back," called Pauline, before the guard could detain her with questions. She must get to Deerhaven Forest Hall. Lesley's life dangled in the balance. Pauline felt charged with righteous energy, as she never had before. How many times had she warned Lesley that she should treat Michael as loose cannon, a time bomb waiting to explode? How terrifying to be proven right and to watch this nightmare unfold.

****

As soon as her eyes could focus, Lesley spotted metal bars and beyond them, an officer sitting at a wooden desk. This place looked like the lockup in a movie set, an old-fashioned country sheriff's cell from the past, before jails became technological nightmares. The cage that held Lesley was a homey nightmare, lacking computerized locks and monitors.

"You!" Lesley called to the beefy man in uniform. "Would you come here?"

"You're awake, are you?" he responded and rose from his seat with a great creaking of springs.

Lesley became weak and woozy in attempting a sitting position. She let herself lie back down on the thin, hard mattress. The necklace around her neck felt like a human organ heated on the griddle of terror until the flame caused the brooch to dilate and contract in frantic throes. She didn't dare touch the pendant.

"What's happened?" asked Lesley. "Where am I?"

"You were apprehended and taken to Wolf's Creek jail," the sheriff informed her. "That's where you are now."

"Who are you?" asked Lesley.

"I'm Sheriff Phil Morton, Chief of the Wolf's Creek Police Department," he announced. Lesley tried and failed to recall what she might have heard about Sheriff Morton. Then, she remembered she'd seen him at the PURITI meeting in the Grange Hall. This man had been sitting at Reverend Were's right hand. Lesley shivered.

"You're in league with the Reverend Were!" she accused. Loathing gave her the strength to rise and face him. "What did you do to Rachel Windsor? Where is she?"

A slow grin spread across the sheriff's face. The malice in his eyes seemed directed at her. Lesley's skin crawled.

"Let me out of here!" she shouted, managing to rise and stagger toward the bars. "I didn't do anything." Her head throbbed and blue streaks shot through her line of sight. She reached back and found a sticky knot at the base of her skull. They'd whacked her with a great deal of force.

The sheriff waggled his finger. "I wouldn't waste time protesting my innocence," he sneered. "We've got plenty of evidence. Enough to convict and hang you!"

"What am I supposed to have done?" demanded Lesley. "You can't keep me in jail without telling me why I was arrested."

The maddening smile never left the fat man's face. "You're charged with a federal crime. The kidnapping of Miss Rachel Windsor. We have eyewitnesses. We even have the letter you sent your husband in which you inform him that you have kidnapped his sister in retribution."

"Retribution for what?" asked Lesley, heart racing, brooch

pulsing.

The sheriff's icky grin deepened. "Michael Windsor felt compelled to file for divorce when he discovered you had deviant tendencies. He has a list of young women who will swear you propositioned them. You're obviously an unfit mother for a small boy, so Michael was forced to request sole custody of your son. You're not going to be seeing much of that boy. No court will let you have unsupervised visitation with a little guy at such an impressionable age. Not with your track record. Of course, custody is beside the point with the boy lying in the hospital. Injured, I might I add, as a direct result of your negligence.

"The court won't look favorably on your perversion and they won't like it that you're a kidnapper either. You kidnapped a mentally deficient person, your husband's addled sister, and took your anger out on her. Michael was always so devoted to her. It's a crying shame."

"Oh, my God," said Lesley, so stunned by his recitation that the pain in her head and the brooch's emanations receded.

"You'll get life without parole for the kidnapping. The only thing you have left to hope for is a bunk with the Feds. State prison isn't nice, Lesley, even for gals."

Tears of rage filled Lesley's eyes. "Do whatever you want with me," she begged. "Just let Rachel go! She's endured too much already. Please don't imprison her any longer. And don't harm her."

Sheriff Phil Morton walked toward the cell, his awful grin spitty like a rabid dog's. "That little lady won't be a prisoner much longer. Now that we've got you safely behind bars, you're going to confess what you did to her. Too bad you turned down the chance to have a lawyer present. A lawyer would've told you not to talk so much."

"Just let Rachel go," pleaded Lesley. "I don't care about a lawyer."

"You'll care about a lawyer when you face the charges against you," sneered the sheriff. "You'll be crying for help when they bring you before the judge for the ultimate offense against God and fellow man."

"What do you mean?" Lesley asked. "Rachel's not crazy and

she'll tell everybody what really happened."

"Rachel won't be talking much," laughed the sheriff. "You murdered her in the course of the kidnapping. We take murder real seriously here in the mountains."

Lesley grasped the bars in both hands where they stuck as if frozen to the metal. "Rachel," she murmured. The woman with whom she'd experienced real physical love for the first time could not be dead, not while the impression of her living hands still warmed Lesley's skin. "You killed her," moaned Lesley.

"No. You killed her," gloated the sheriff. "Her body will wash up downriver with physical evidence linking you to the crime."

"Is she dead then?"

"They'll dispatch her any time. She doesn't serve a purpose anymore."

"I'll say anything you want," offered Lesley. "Just don't hurt Rachel. I'll leave Deerhaven Forest Hall and never come near Deerhaven Pines again."

"You should have thought of that before," Sheriff Morton grinned. "It's too late now. You've rubbed the Reverend the wrong way. He wants both you and Rachel Windsor gone for good. And he's not the only one. The Others don't like Miss Windsor either, and they don't like the two of you together."

"Who are the Others?" asked Lesley, trying to grasp the situation in time to save Rachel. The ghost of Richard hadn't really been able to explain about the Others.

Sheriff Morton, for the first time, lost his smile. "The Others stay behind the scenes. They're part of the Reverend's innermost circle. He says they come from old Sierra families." The sheriff grasped the bars and his eyes narrowed. "You never heard any of this from me. I'm done talking. You and Rachel Windsor are history."

The necklace around Lesley's neck, always possessed of a life of its own, swung back and forth, burning an arc into the delicate skin above her brassiere. Lesley lifted the heated chain and let the brooch drop against her bodice.

"You can't have that," barked the sheriff. "Prisoners must surrender all personal property. A person could hang himself with a thing like that!" The sheriff stuck his hand into the cell and reached for the pendant.

Zack, ssssssssssss, a crack and sizzling sounds sent Lesley reeling backward. When she righted herself, she saw a bulky hillock on the other side of the cell door. Sheriff Morton lay dead or unconscious on the floor of the jail, one blackened hand curled against his body. Contact with her brooch had struck the sheriff like a lightning bolt, and Lesley knew this was her chance to escape. How maddening that the bars remained locked against her!

"Help! Somebody help me!" she screamed. Once again, she sat down on the sleeping bench. Without thinking, she grasped her necklace. No bolt of energy struck her down when she touched the necklace but a wisp of smoke arose and hung in midair. As she watched, the smoke thickened into a winter cloud. Then, the milky-eyed fogginess grew darker and more substantial.

The bump on her head must have been worse than she thought. Even after all she'd been through since ringing the bell at Deerhaven Forest Hall, she could not believe what she saw. The fog took shape and an old woman in a long, black skirt and cape materialized out of the dark vapor. Lesley frantically blinked, trying to regain her right mind, but when she looked again, she found the old woman staring at her with a foreboding expression. Lesley uttered the first thing that came to mind, a line that had already been used by screenwriters at MGM Studios.

"Are you a good witch or a bad witch?" Lesley asked.

"Why, I am not a witch at all," replied the old woman. "I am a librarian. You must be a very fanciful young woman," she added in a school-marm tone.

"Who are you? Where did you come from?" asked Lesley, less afraid now that the woman turned out to be a ghost and not a witch. Lesley had grown comfortable with ghosts and was relieved that she wouldn't be consorting with an entirely different occult entity.

"I can answer your first question," the old lady replied primly. "My name is Ursula Smith, and I am the former librarian at Deerhaven Forest Hall."

"Were you Jane Copley Windsor's friend?"

"Yes, I was and am," came the answer, unabashed.

"Ursula," Lesley paused, "may I call you Ursula?" The woman nodded. "Ursula, why are you here? Can you unlock the door?"

"Now that you have developed an affinity with me and Jane, we will help you as much as we can. I do not have the physical ability to open a door, however. Please pardon my limitations." Rather than flowery Victorian phrases, Ursula seemed to be providing remarkably direct answers to Lesley's inquiries. Upon closer observation, Lesley noticed that the ancient librarian must have been handsome once. Except for being under great duress, Lesley would have smiled.

"How can you help me?" Lesley asked. "They're about to kill Rachel and I can't get out of here."

"You have the power to escape," said Ursula, "you can wield the power at any time."

"I don't understand," said Lesley, wearily.

"The Windsor Pendant," Ursula replied. "Look at it. Although vulgar and ostentatious, the necklace offers you unusual powers. Hold the brooch in your hand."

Lesley obeyed. Oddly, the necklace felt cool and dead to the touch now. Lesley traced the curlicues with one finger and then found herself propelled forward. Her brooch, acting as a magnet, attached itself to the steel bars.

"The sheriff's keys spilled onto the floor when he fell," reported Ursula. Lesley nodded, stooped, and thrust the pendant through the bars. Sheriff Morton's key ring jumped and inched its way toward Lesley until she could retrieve the whole bunch.

"Always remember the power of natural forces," suggested Ursula "gravity, velocity, heat, magnetism. They can accomplish what dead people cannot."

Lesley tried one key after another in the old-fashioned keyhole on the jailer's side of the door until she found the one that freed her. Stepping over the prostrate body of Sheriff Phil Morton, she drew close to the almost-solid looking presence of Ursula Smith.

"Jane told me that I should go to the library," she said. "Will you come with me, Ursula? Jane thought I would have to search the library without the assistance of a librarian. With you on my side, I know I'll find what I need."

"Friends will be coming to your aid. Take courage, Lesley."

"But what about you? Can you come with me?"

"I cannot ride in modern conveyances and remain present," said Ursula. "Should you have need of me, however, I will return to you. After all, you and I have established an affinity. Only my complete extinguishment could sever our bond." The ghost in black extended an arm as though, by old habit, like her friend Jane, she felt moved to touch Lesley. The ghost then let her arm fall without a sound.

"Remind Sula to remember the essential magic," said Ursula Smith, and blinked out like a snuffed candle.

Lesley sorted out the sheriff's car keys and ran from Wolf's Creek Jail. Sheriff Morton's long black-and-white car bore the portrait of a snarling wolf, long white fangs and hideous fluorescent eyes, but Lesley did not let the anthropomorphized mascot scare her. The gigantic engine of the sheriff's car purred like a kitten, and Lesley pointed its nose toward the library at Deerhaven Forest Hall.

CHAPTER NINETEEN

"Stand back, Mrs. Woolf!" ordered Sula, brandishing the letter opener. "We're leaving this room even if it's over your dead body!" Sula could hear Valerie hyperventilating and wished that the nurse would get a grip.

Mrs. Woolf raised a fist. "What are you doing in Mrs. Windsor's morning room?" barked Mrs. Woolf. "Mrs. Windsor doesn't like anyone coming here but her." Clearly, she hadn't adjusted to Cosette Windsor's death.

"We needed to make a phone call," Sula informed the seething housekeeper. "Your leader has been holding me prisoner in rooms above. I've called in reinforcements who will make him pay for all that he's done to me, to Rachel, to Ryan, and whoever else he's kidnapped, brainwashed or injured."

"My leader?" repeated Mrs. Woolf.

"The Reverend Were. Valerie has told me a bit about his evil ways. Haven't you, Valerie?"

"Why, yes," began Valerie with temerity.

"Did Valerie tell you that I followed the Reverend Were?" Mrs. Woolf inquired. "Did you say that, Valerie?"

"No, I didn't say that," answered Valerie.

"What?" Sula shouted. She turned to Mrs. Woolf. "Do you mean to say you aren't a member of the Reverend's group?"

"I would never stoop that low! Mrs. Windsor always called him a fiend," Mrs. Woolf asserted indignantly. "I'm a Jehovah's Witness but I don't practice nowadays."

"I just assumed," Sula began and stopped when she couldn't decide how to finish her sentence.

"It's my name," complained Mrs. Woolf.

"Excuse me?" said Valerie.

"People don't have a good association with the name, Woolf. Wolves have such a bad reputation in human history. In Russian folklore, wolves attacked newlyweds before they could enjoy the wedding night. They carried tiny babies away in their great gaping mouths and savaged the bodies of skinny, old people in the coffin. Russians don't care for wolves. They've turned the general population against them. The Russians and whoever made up the Red Riding Hood story. Red Riding Hood is nothing but anti-wolf propaganda. That fairy tale works against those of us who share the name."

"I'm not sure wolves have been completely blameless," Sula interjected in the interest of fairness. She needed time to reevaluate her assessment of Mrs. Woolf.

"Maybe not," agreed Mrs. Woolf. "I still don't see why *I* should be held accountable."

A sudden thought struck Sula. "Do you know what, Mrs. Woolf?" she exclaimed. "I've been associating you with the PURITI Party's Reverend. My mind automatically put the Were together with Woolf. Anyone would make that connection, under the circumstances."

"Well," sniffed Mrs. Woolf. "I think I'm owed an apology. I've been loyal to the Windsors all my working life. Loyal to the family librarian too, I might add. Both you and your mother before."

"I'm sorry," responded Sula. Valerie seconded Sula's apology and then Sula added, "Let us make it up to you. We plan to get rid of the Reverend Were once and for all. Will you assist us?"

"Yes, indeed," agreed Mrs. Woolf. "As a tribute to Mrs. Cosette Windsor, may she rest in peace. Who are those reinforcements you needed to contact by telephone?"

"My mother. She'll be arriving as soon as possible."

"I hope she remembers to bring a regular human being with her," Mrs. Woolf commented. "Someone not related to the family circle or the family library."

"Why would she bring someone else?" asked Sula.

Mrs. Woolf looked surprised. "The lore that goes with the Hall tells us," explained the housekeeper, "an innocent outsider will vanquish the foes of the Hall. Your mother would know that. The Hall's librarians carry knowledge of the essential magic within them until they die. I gather the knowledge hasn't been passed on to you?"

"Mother's not dead yet," Sula pointed out. "Far from it. She's back on salary in San Francisco."

"We could have used the services of a Senior Librarian here at the Hall," sniffed Mrs. Woolf, "long before things this bad came to pass."

"Mother didn't know how much we needed her," countered Sula. "And I didn't know the extent of my ignorance about the library's inner workings."

"You couldn't have known," gushed Valerie in Sula's defense. The nurse's allegiance to Sula seemed absolute.

"Now that we've all clarified where we stand," Sula said to Mrs. Woolf, "we should stay alert."

"I'll help in any way I can," promised the housekeeper. "Mrs. Windsor would have counted on me to do so."

"Can you try to keep the Reverend and his followers out of the house, Mrs. Woolf? Call Deerhaven Pines Security Service if necessary. Just don't call the local sheriff. Phil Morton of the WCPD is definitely in cahoots with the Reverend Were."

"We can't keep Reverend Were out of this house," returned Mrs. Woolf, pacing in anxiety. "The Reverend and his followers can enter Deerhaven Forest Hall at will. I don't why. Any member of the Windsor family can gain admittance to the house at any time they wish. I don't know why the Reverend Were can come and go whenever he wants. He must be entitled or invited by a family member."

"Have Kelvin and Michael Windsor been here? Could they have invited the Reverend?" asked Sula.

"1 haven't seen the Windsor boys for a few days. Michael might have gone home to the Bay Area. I don't know what's happened to Kelvin. He might be with the Reverend. He used to be such a nice young man. His mother was once so proud of him."

Mrs. Woolf then exclaimed, "You know what? I just remembered. The police came here earlier. They got a phone call that our Rachel had been kidnapped. I told them that Rachel ran off on her own two feet; I had no reason to think she'd been kidnapped. Then, Mr. Russell came downstairs and sent them away. Mr. Russell didn't seem quite right in the head. His dead wife told him that Rachel is nearby and being looked after. His dead wife, I tell you!"

"Where is Russell Windsor?" asked Sula, realizing she'd forgotten to ask after the old man. "I do hope he's all right."

"I'm here," proclaimed a thin voice at the door.

Sula turned and saw Russell Windsor supporting himself on a wooden cane. Had he needed a cane before?

Russell's quavery voice continued, "I've heard you plotting against the Reverend. Don't ask me to act against him! I must do what the Reverend tells me. He will extinguish Cosette if I make him angry. I long for the day that my spirit will be reunited with hers. I'm very tired since she departed."

"Cosette's dead," protested Sula. "The Reverend can't do anything do her."

Russell waved her off. "Cosette's much weaker already," he whimpered. "The Reverend uses the Others to torment and distract her."

"Russell," said Sula in alarm. "You're overtired. Perhaps Mrs. Woolf could take you to your room?"

"Maybe that would be best," Russell acquiesced. "I feel a storm brewing. I must save my strength."

"Valerie," said Sula, after Mrs. Woolf led Russell away, "you and I have preparations to make before my mother arrives."

The roar of an engine outside the Hall interrupted their plans. They went to the front door.

****

On the wide wooden porch that ran around the house stood Michael Windsor. The Reverend Were lurked in the shadows behind him. They'd been coming and going through the back entrance in recent days, but a sixth sense had alerted the Reverend to the arrival of an intruder. Michael could see a car coming down the road at a distance.

Michael had not enjoyed this phase of his life, the days since his mother died. He had submitted to the Reverend and his group but he couldn't remember how he'd come to choose such treacherous companions. They, at least, provided guidance and direction. They made him nauseous and shaky too, though. Michael sensed that the careening car coming toward him signaled disintegration, and his descent into the abyss.

"The visitor must be dispatched," came a smooth whisper in Michael's ear. "A civilian who does not belong to PURITI, or to the Windsor family, could cause immeasurable trouble. Michael! You must not forsake the Hue!"

The large, long, silver Jaguar zooming up the drive toward Deerhaven Forest Hall reminded Michael of a piece of his old life, the life he'd so happily shed. Who did he know who drove a low, silver car like that? His head swam.

"What should I do when the car gets to the house?" he asked, feeling stupid and ineffectual.

"All you have to do is point your gun and pull the trigger," sneered the oily voice.

"What does Ronald Chaney think I should do?" sniveled Michael.

"Ronald thinks you should point," commanded the voice.

"I don't want to do the wrong thing," Michael whined. "Ronald might get mad and hurt me." He feared the Reverend

Were's friend, Reverend Ronald Chaney, more than anything in this world or the next. The Reverend Were claimed that Michael had chosen his affinity to Ronald Chaney, but Michael didn't remember doing so.

"Your affinity shall never be an affliction," thundered the Reverend Were. "Your affinity shall bring you tranquility."

Michael thought of Kelvin and what his affinity had brought him. Once a menace to birds, chipmunks, raccoons, Kelvin would never be a menace to anyone again. Reverend Chaney had arranged a terrible end for Kelvin Windsor. Shuddering, Michael stepped out of the Hall and into the day. He shielded his eyes. He could make out the identity of the driver now.

"That's my wife's friend, Pauline Walden. I can't hurt her. Her husband, Dan, would massacre us. He collects semiautomatic weapons as a hobby. You wouldn't believe how much firepower a civilian can purchase legally. Dan pretended to be mellow but once, when we met at a Little League game, he threatened to blow me off the planet if my son pitched instead of his daughter. I don't want to mess with Dan Walden."

"You don't have to shoot the woman," the Reverend's voice repeated implacably. "Your target is that boy."

"What boy?" screamed Michael.

"See that boy down by the river? We've played a trick on that youngster. We never liked him so we sent him down to the river to look for his mother. He won't find her and his despair will deepen." The Reverend Were chuckled. "You can't hurt him, Michael. He's been dead for many years."

"Ryan!" breathed Michael.

"No. That's Richard Windsor who perished before he could attain his majority. Reverend Chaney, leader of the Others, wants your visitor to think it's Ryan and run down to the river. Mortal women are so predictable."

Distracted by the Reverend Were's whisperings, Michael failed to keep track of Pauline Walden's progress until a car door slammed. "Michael!" called Pauline, striding toward the house. "You can't go on like this. I'm not going to let you hurt Lesley or Ryan."

Champion The Hue, Choose Your Affinity, ordered the voices in

Michael's mind. Don't be disloyal, don't make the wrong choice, they cautioned. Michael reached for the gun in his shoulder holster, slid the weapon out, and dropped it on the ground.

"Don't pick up that gun," Pauline ordered.

Michael hated her. He hated her and her overprivileged husband. In a flash, Michael figured out where he should point. He pointed first at Pauline Walden. The voices told him to aim at the figure down by the river. Michael turned and pointed toward the river, swollen from yesterday's drizzle and snow.

"Michael, what are you up to?" Pauline shouted. Michael saw the shade of Richard Windsor, hovering at river's edge. Richard might be taller than Ryan but they looked much the same from a distance. The boy neared the roaring water of the Stanislaus River, appearing to teeter on a log. This time, Pauline turned to see what Michael might be pointing at.

"Ryan!" screamed Pauline.

The Danville matron did not hesitate for a moment. She galloped across country lawns, over two low fences, and kept running toward the rushing water. Her kind of woman could be counted upon to intervene in a case of child endangerment. Pauline Walden's predictable behavior amused the Reverend Were, but Michael gasped in fear.

"Excellent work, Brother Michael," said Reverend Were in the heavy sententious tone that Michael had grown to despise. He stood in silence watching Pauline Walden approach the ghost boy. Had he known Pauline well? He knew somehow that she would die soon. Michael couldn't remember. To his surprise, he regretted her passing.

Pauline paused, confused, just before she reached Richard Windsor's shade. She'd noticed that the boy wasn't exactly Ryan. Still, the force of evil pushed her forward. A cold, dark wind blew down the slope, over the river, and into the forest. The Others had flown along with Pauline. Michael watched as black storm clouds swirled around his wife's friend and carried her into the river. He couldn't hear her screams but he could imagine the sound. Pauline hit the water and the current dragged her away. A ragged sob escaped Michael.

"An accidental drowning won't attract any attention

whatsoever," the Reverend pronounced with satisfaction. "You're safe from your gun-toting friend, Dan."

"Pauline!"

Michael heard a terrible cry from the driveway. Lesley, bolted from the police car and ran at full tilt toward the river. Lesley Windsor had arrived in time to see Pauline plunge into the Stanislaus and disappear.

"Your wife is a danger to the Hue," whispered Reverend Were. "She chose a weak and inferior affinity. Keep her in check, Michael. Turn her away from Deerhaven Forest Hall. Get rid of her for good."

"I can't harm Lesley," stammered Michael. "We're married. Ryan needs her."

"Your son resisted us and he shouldn't have. He accidentally got in the way of a bullet. The boy's instincts aren't good and this is due to poor maternal influence. If your son recovers, we're counting on you to keep him in line."

"I will," promised Michael.

"See that you do. For the boy's sake, see that you do. Come with me to the church, Michael. The congregation will be assembling. We'll be back soon."

****

Evening's dimness turned to dark and Mrs. Woolf lit the electric lights. The household staff dwindled. Lena Suarez, once a stalwart household worker, had seen too many gruesome shadows flitting from room to room. Under cover of night, she had packed her possessions in a canvas duffel bag and fled the Hall. The cook had called from Wolf's Creek feigning illness, but no one wanted dinner anyway. Russell Windsor, flattened by time and grief, lay motionless upon his wife Cosette's cold, vacated bed.

Rachel Windsor, confined for so many years in those unfinished rooms above the Hall's main floors, lay chained in the lower chambers, drugged with tepid chocolate until she could no longer tell up from down. Pauline Walden's stiffening body was lodged against the riverbank at the junction of a small but wildly ruffled creek. Her arm had become wedged between boulder and log and there, she would be found and returned to the husband who would mourn her. William Roe, the gatekeeper, for the first time in his working life, had deserted the front gates early. He now reclined in his burnt sienna armchair sipping hard liquor before the fragrant fire. These defections left Lesley, the housekeeper, the nurse and the librarian, to confront the depraved spirits of the departed. Wicked beings gathered to converge upon the Hall. Reverend Were called upon the living and the Reverend Chaney conspired with the supernatural followers of the same dark faith.

Reverend Were had kept Michael Windsor at his side. Michael became more disoriented as the hours went by. He would need to be removed but only after serving his purpose. Soon, the Reverend Were would be sovereign of Deerhaven Pines. Vanquishing his foes and seizing their assets would augment his power beyond human comprehension, and he would use that power to defend the hue and master the Hall.

As the Reverend circulated below stairs, issuing orders and dispensing guarded bits of information, he considered how to excise the last remaining enemies of the Hue. He enjoyed planning the sequence of their execution. The Others chanted, summoning any spirits with affinity in this matter. These dark souls gathered among the trees in Deerhaven Forest. They all knew that the library would be the scene of the coming denouement.

"Where's Pauline?" Lesley Windsor muttered to herself. "I hope she swam to safety. What's happening to us all?" She could still not comprehend the magnitude of the evil forces ranged against her, but she'd begun to realize the enormity of their power. Standing beside the roaring river that had carried her friend away, Lesley fought tears of anguish. Then, she drew a deep breath of night air laced with river spray. She would not let the Stanislaus drown her newfound strength and courage. She must gather her courage and enter Deerhaven Forest Hall no matter what might be lurking there. Calling in authorities to report Pauline's terrible dive into the water seemed the only thing she could do for her friend before proceeding with the fight to save Rachel and Ryan.

The look of Pauline's body as she'd hit the water did not give Lesley hope but she must contact someone with the ability to initiate a search and rescue effort. She did not know whom to call. Any law enforcement agency she alerted to the situation might potentially call Sheriff Phil Morton of the Wolf's Creek Police Department, and she hoped she'd never see Sheriff Morton's leering face again, in this lifetime or the next. Then, before she could proceed, a breeze through the bushes startled and distracted her. The wind took the shape of a boy.

"Richard!" Lesley embraced the boy with her words.

"Missus Windsor!" cried the ghost of Richard Windsor. "The Reverend Chaney, my mother's greatest enemy in life, used me to do harm. His henchmen pushed me down to the river and tormented me until I grew visible. A lady with golden hair thought I needed her to save me from the fast-running water. She came to my aid and they sent her into the ice stream. I fear she might be dead. Oh, when will the pain of my earthly existence come to an end? I beg you to help me find my good mother who will help me away from here."

"I'm so sorry, Richard," Lesley soothed him. She turned and pointed northeast. "Go that way, Richard, you will find your mother. She's sitting with my son, a boy just a little younger than you, at Sonora Sierra Hospital. Can you find your way there?"

Richard's eyes grew even wider. "We spirits can often find living beings if we so desire. Because you and I are bound in some deep way, I can perhaps find my way to the bedside of your son. I will try. Wish me well, Mrs. Windsor. I wish you all good things in this life and ever after." With that, the shade of Richard Windsor evaporated like river water.

"Good luck," Lesley whispered. "Farewell." She hoped that Richard Windsor would be able to depart Deerhaven Forest Hall for good. He'd lingered there long enough in loneliness and despair.

Lesley tramped back to Deerhaven Forest Hall. As she came through the front doors, she found no spirits and no people in evidence. The Hall's heavy doors swung open when she touched the handles and swung shut after she entered the house. As soon as she crossed the threshold, the pendant around her neck grew warm, and she took this to mean that she should hurry. She remembered a square black telephone sitting in an alcove near the dining room and headed that direction, her footsteps echoing in the wide, empty corridors. Although she'd expected Mrs. Woolf to pounce upon her the minute she returned to the house, she didn't run into anyone.

Finding the phone where she remembered, she picked up the receiver. Information gave her the number of National Park Service headquarters. The Park Service controlled the forestlands bordering the Windsors' property. You could trust a forest ranger more than an ordinary police officer. Rangers, good-hearted people who loved wildlife and led campfire songs, would stand up to Sheriff Phil Morton.

The Forest Service's telephone operator offered to connect Lesley to an after-hours emergency number and Lesley accepted. She waited through a series of clicks and jangles for the call to go through. The receiver emitted a hollow howling and a tinny whistle. The next sounds made Lesley jump. Her skin crawled.

"None shall rest until we purge filth and degradation from our community," an ugly threatening voice spoke over the telephone line. "Telephone service to this house is discontinued. There shall be no contact with the ignorant general population until Deerhaven Forest Hall is purified by the blood of the corrupt."

Lesley's heart sank. Clearly, no friendly rangers would be coming to her aid. The speaker, whose harsh voice dripped with rancor, probably considered Lesley to be one of the tainted whose blood should cleanse the Hall.

"You will be offered one last chance to champion the hue. Should you fail the trial, you must perish. An epoch is over and a new era is at hand. Prepare for judgment!"

"Who are you?" Lesley demanded. "Speak with me face-to-face, if you can talk like a human being."

"I am no longer a human being," growled the voice.

"Ghost or human, I don't want to talk with you," answered Lesley and hung up.

"Then, I suggest you speak with me," ordered a quiet but authoritarian figure down the hall. Lesley whirled.

"Reverend Were!" she exclaimed. "Why have you come to the Hall? Who let you in?" Lesley forced herself to breathe normally even though she was alone in the corridor with the wicked minister.

"I am here to save your soul," the Reverend Were reported, "and the souls of many."

His menace silenced Lesley for a moment. "I have confidence in the purity of my soul," she replied, at last. What she said felt true. Her sweet, placid parents used to tell her that she'd been born an "honest soul," and Lesley trusted their assessment.

Where were her parents? Lesley wondered, out of the blue. Why had she encountered departed residents of Deerhaven Forest Hall but not the spirits of her own loved ones? Something told her that her own parents would not be returning from the great beyond. Those humble bespectacled people, her parents, would have no reason to wander in purgatory. The Windsors and their retainers had lived lives of great uneasiness and exited this life scratching and clawing at the walls of their coffin. The old wives' tales must be true. Ghosts were souls with energy for unfinished business. Those who make their peace before dying go someplace else. Her parents inhabited some better place, and she would not see them until she went there herself.

"False confidence can lead to a fall," the Reverend answered Lesley.

She stared at the minister, fascinated. Reverend Were looked different close up. Rather than dark and portentous, he struck Lesley as natty and stylish. Well-cut, shiny, black hair crowned a small, dark face with handsome Eastern European features. Could this man be the source of all the evil at Deerhaven Forest Hall? His looks didn't convince Lesley of his guilt or innocence. An actor with those looks could get parts as villain or hero, he could go either way.

"What do you want from me?" she demanded.

"To make you pure," the minister answered. "You've been consorting with the depraved. We must break you of that."

"What do you mean?" cried Lesley. "Are you talking about Rachel? Did you take Rachel?" Could this dapper man, who could pass for a Greek stockbroker or a French rabbi, be the one who shot Ryan? The thought was so excruciating that she could not ask. She fully expected the Reverend to dodge her questions, but he answered with a smooth smile.

"Rachel Windsor must be confined. She hears voices and offends normal untrained citizens with her fantasies, which have a libidinous and deviant element. She probably should have been sent to a private facility years ago, but her mother insisted on keeping her at home."

Even though the content of Reverend Were's words provoked Lesley to anger, his voice had a strange effect. She felt him lulling her into unconsciousness. With a painful effort, she shook off the sedation induced by the Reverend's voice.

"Rachel Windsor is totally sane," Lesley argued. "If you've stolen her against her will, you're guilty of kidnapping!" Her rebuttal strengthened her grasp on the present. Then, she heard familiar words.

"Champion the hue! The day of reckoning is at hand! You must champion the hue or die!" came a chant from the dim hallway behind Reverend Were. The Reverend's lips curled into a leer.

"Who's speaking?" called Lesley, craning her neck to see behind the Reverend Were. "I can't see you!"

"You're hearing voices," said the Reverend, sneering. "Nobody's there."

"Who's that down the hall?" Lesley demanded to know. "I heard you on the phone. Show yourself."

"You may call me Reverend Chaney," came the voice, fluid and unctuous as the Reverend Were's.

"Come out," Lesley ordered and a purple wraith glided forward.

"Here I am, my dear. Ready to help you embrace the hue. I've looked after the spiritual needs of the Windsors for two centuries. Put yourself in my care and you need not fear for your immortal soul."

"I have no such fear," retorted Lesley.

"Talking to yourself. Tsk, tsk," the Reverend Were interjected. "You and I are the only living creatures here."

"Lesley Windsor, we must conduct your trial before you

lose what's left of your good reputation," intoned the Reverend Chaney.

How much power did the dead minister wield? Could he keep her from finding Rachel and getting back to Ryan?

"What trial are you talking about?" Lesley asked, trying not to look upon the specter's dark purple aspect. She grasped her brooch for comfort and felt a warming pulse of electricity course through her palm and up her arm.

"You must prove yourself before you become the Windsor wife," the two reverends recited in unison.

"Don't you hear him?" Lesley asked the Reverend Were who was at least, presumably, alive.

"I fear you're losing your grip," the Reverend Were intoned. "How sad that you and your new friend, Rachel, should fall victim to the same affliction. You, and Rachel, both hearing nonexistent voices. I find your plight sad and ironic."

Lesley slowed her respiration again. She must avoid falling prey to Reverend Were's paralyzing voice. "Why is this happening? Why are you visible to me?" Lesley asked the Reverend Chaney.

"The answer to your question is not simple. In life, Cosette Windsor controlled admittance to Deerhaven Forest Hall and even determined who entered the surrounding forest. When Mrs. Windsor died, the forces of good and evil fell into disequilibria. Did you not recognize the nature of the struggle that enveloped you from the moment you entered Deerhaven Forest Hall? Your ability to sense the true nature of discord must be stunted. I attribute this disability to the ill effects of technology and loose living.

"In the nineteenth century, people recognized the fight for dominance between goodness and evil. Gladly, we entered into the fray. You modern folk, who will be citizens of the twenty-first century, must be conscripted before you choose a side. You *should* choose of your own volition." The Reverend Chaney's plumed shape emitted a gaseous vapor and swelled into a horrible-hued cloud which took the shape of a bear too huge, fierce and wild to be trapped in this stifling corridor. Lesley hung onto her brooch for dear life.

"The hands of time have turned against you, Lesley. We will now convene your trial!"

This ominous proclamation shook the walls. Once again, the two ministers seemed to be preaching in unison. Overcome by the Reverend Were's voice or the Reverend Chaney's form, Lesley's eyes rolled inward. The Others, in the form of darkness, rushed forward. They encircled Lesley and conveyed her below, into the bowels of Deerhaven Forest Hall, a darkness that predated modern man.

CHAPTER TWENTY

After several murky seconds in limbo, Lesley felt a floor beneath her feet. Her eyelids admitted light, and she opened them. She found herself in a dim Victorian sleeping chamber, decorated in maroon and gold. The flocked wallpaper, heavy, floral upholstery and carpeting, the huge high-canopied bed, overwhelmed Lesley's modern sensibilities. Her mind didn't focus for a few seconds and only then did she spot a human figure under the gold and red ruffled coverlet.

Without stopping to locate any enemies who were around, Lesley stepped forward to see who lay against the garish pillow sham. The bone-whiteness of the face struck her before the features revealed the sleeper's identity. She put her hand over her heart and staggered.

"Rachel!" she cried out, leaping forward to snatch her lover into her warm arms. Before she could take Rachel against her, she forced herself to pause. A whiteness surrounded Rachel and Lesley wondered if the light could be protective. Clear mist of the same quality encircled Ryan when she'd seen him in the hospital. When Lesley touched her son, she'd gotten the feeling that she'd lessened the power of the aura. Perhaps the brooch gave her a new intuition about things supernatural. She resolved not to touch the woman she treasured, lying so close to her.

The two reverends and their awful band of consorts had brought her to Rachel's prison room. Were they hoping that her touch would dissipate the whiteness that shielded Rachel from their machinations? Did they intend to keep her a prisoner here too? She guessed that these rooms lay underground. Were they still within the confines of Deerhaven Forest Hall? Surely the Reverend Were would think it dangerous to incarcerate two women in the Victorian basement of Deerhaven Forest Hall. Someone would discover them there. She glanced around the bedroom and the dressing room beyond, for a clue. A wall hanging caught her eye.

The piece of tapestry looked, at first glance, identical to the one that hung on the wall of her bedroom upstairs in Deerhaven Forest Hall. The weird circular patterns of light matched those in the section that she had studied. A few mighty bears, deer, horses and riders milled in front of the same caves pictured in the background of the other wall hanging. The necklace around her neck sent currents of heat and electricity down her body and the tapestry seemed to intensify the sensation. She knew she must respond to the electrical urgings but what should she do? What if her theory about whiteness proved wrong? Should she save Rachel by carrying her up the stairs?

"We're beneath Deerhaven Forest Hall," she said. "If I get Rachel upstairs and to my car, I'll be able to take her to the hospital. Dr. Riemer would help us!" A booming noise disrupted Lesley's chain of thought.

LET THE TRIAL COMMENCE!

The rooms seemed to have a public address system. The announcement erupted from the ceiling and rebounded from the fuzzy walls and carpeted floors. Lesley reeled, searching the apartment for the person speaking to her. She could find nobody but herself and the sleeping Rachel.

"What trial? Why am I on trial?" Lesley asked, turning her face upward to address the ceiling or the heavens. No one answered. The room became silent as a grave. Sickening anxiety, a state she had only recently cast off, overtook her for a moment. She fought to regain her courage by focusing on the energy and heat generated by her brooch and, sure enough, the talisman brought her new resolve.

"Rachel!" Lesley called. "We've got to get out of here!" Moving toward Rachel's latest resting place, its gold canopy billowing in a draft, Lesley stretched out her hands and then, willed herself to desist.

"Rachel, wake up," Lesley begged.

The draft intensified and the lights dimmed. A chorus of hoarse whispers, which might have been cold air, agitated Lesley. "The Others," she murmured. Lesley didn't know who the Others might be, but the knowledge that they hovered here, watching, commenting, on her every move, forced her to move away from Rachel's bedside. The milky vapor, a fog, a cocoon, grew thicker.

"Oh, Ryan!" Lesley exclaimed. Ryan's condition had seemed no better or worse when she saw him last, but her every intuition verified that she'd committed an error when she touched him. Had Ryan remained stable after she left? She thought not. She sensed that her son had taken a turn for the worse, that he needed her. She pictured herself brushing back Ryan's soft, brown hair and despaired.

"Sometimes, the things you want ARE NOT TO BE TOUCHED!" Lesley remembered the line from a play she'd seen at the Amador Valley Theater and spoke the words out loud. She stepped back without laying a hand upon Rachel.

Monstrous hissing and spitting echoed from the room's every corner. The Others threatened and protested. With a shock, Lesley realized that she'd disappointed them by not siphoning the spiritual energy that blanketed Rachel. Her restraint allowed Rachel to continue slumbering in relative safety.

"Was that the trial?" Lesley called out.

"The first but not the last," a demon voice answered.

"Haven't I acquitted myself?" she demanded. "I didn't fall into this trap, and I won't be ensnared by your next trick." She spoke with a bravery that she did not feel. The pretense of bravery could be almost as good as the real thing, she realized.

"This time you avoided a pitfall, but the forces of purity gathered tonight will fell you next time," returned the voice.

"Why are you doing this?" asked Lesley. "What do you see in me as a threat to you?"

"You came to Deerhaven Forest and developed the ability to see too much," came words which surprised her. She had expected to hear ranting about deviance and lack of purity.

"What if I promise to take Ryan and Rachel and leave here forever? Will you let me go?"

"You are the Windsor wife," the voice pronounced. "You will never leave."

"I didn't ask for a position at Deerhaven Forest Hall. Let me and Rachel go!" she shouted. The gruesome, whispery voices swelled in response. The walls whirled and the lights faded again. Lesley's vision transmitted darkness for several long minutes, and then she felt herself transported. She landed in a lighted room. She'd been removed to the bedroom in which she'd been installed when she first came to the Hall. She swayed and then oriented herself. Her suitcase and Ryan's big canvas tote bag still sat under a wooden bench where she'd stowed them.

The tapestry on the wall glowed as though the needleworker who'd created the thing had used fluorescent threads. The figures in the tableau, wild animals and ferocious humans, seemed to have acquired the power of motion. Lesley watched the hanging like a television screen until she became almost mesmerized. The necklace resting on her bosom vibrated with electricity like a remote control for the tapestry. After a while, she grew familiar with the creatures in the tapestry and accustomed to their motility.

A new intuition formed in her mind concerning the necklace and the tapestry. Perhaps the brooch and the wall hanging did not exist to benefit the two fearsome ministers and the chorus of Others. The creator of these artifacts might not have been neutral. These two talismans might have been designed to help Lesley and her loved ones. Her eye traced the loops of light in the tapestry and, for the first time, she noted that the circular lines on her necklace mirrored the bright swirls in the wall hanging. What should the pattern convey to her? She'd missed something important.

She thought about her primary mission. She must get to the library and attempt the research she needed to free Rachel and help Ryan. Maybe she would discover information relating to the tapestry or the brooch, instructions for how to use them. Or should she make her way to the bottom of the house of her own volition and try to rescue Rachel from enemy hands? No. Every instinct assured her that Rachel was not in immediate danger. She should go to the library. Moving to the door, Lesley planned the shortest route from bedroom to library.

Circumstances thwarted her once again. She found her heavy bedroom door locked. She wrenched the handle, but the brass fixtures and the door remained solidly in place. The brooch in her palm began to swell and burn. Why now? For a piece of gold jewelry, the thing exercised surprising self-will.

The strength of the emanations from the brooch reminded her of how an assault by this same necklace felled Sheriff Phil Morton. Perhaps her necklace could do more tricks, perhaps open a locked door!

She leaned forward. She planned to touch the necklace to the door handle and see what results the application of metal to metal produced but she didn't even need to go that far. A crack and sizzle issued from the brooch and a puff of acrid smoke stung her eyes. A muffled creak signaled success. The door swung open like a garage door charged by an electronic opener.

She bolted out and down the corridor. Without applying any conscious thought, she found the path to the library etched in her mind. Hissing sounds sent shivers down her spine. Awful whispers indicated that the Others followed her. When a door opened in front of her, Lesley expected a shape in a dark, peaked hood. Instead, Russell Windsor staggered into the hallway.

"Lesley, my dear," the old man began in a soft croak as

though he'd been sleeping for many days. "The boys tell me that you're endangering us. They say that public sentiment has turned against the Windsors because you haven't been faithful to your husband. Michael claims that you embody the impure qualities that PURITI preaches against. Your own husband accuses you of gross impropriety. I don't understand. I liked you so much."

"Russell! You haven't known me for long but I want you to trust me. Don't listen anymore, not until we rid Deerhaven Forest Hall of Reverend Were. Cosette didn't trust him. She didn't even want him at her funeral. Remember?"

"That's right," said Russell, quivery and bewildered. "Cosette called him a scourge upon the community. How could I have invited him into the Hall?"

"That's all right, Russell. He uses devilish tricks to confuse us. He's told you lies about me. I'm not a bad person."

"I know, Lesley. My daughter Rachel never did anything wrong either. There's nothing deviant about her. I don't know why I thought the worst of my own daughter. I let strangers convince me that my child should be confined like an animal. I trust you and will let you run Deerhaven Forest Hall as you think best. Maybe Rachel will assist you. The two of you would like each other, I think. Cosette would have wanted it that way. Still, you must be careful about appearances."

Russell fell silent, looking at Lesley with the fondness he'd displayed when she first came to the Hall. While Lesley contemplated what she should say, whether she should tell him about her relationship with Rachel, Russell's face contorted and he choked.

"Champion the hue! Champion the hue!" he uttered. "Death to deviants. Beware a wrong choice of affinity. Champion the hue!" With this last phrase, he sagged against the doorframe, no longer able to stand.

"Russell!" said Lesley. He could not make eye contact. The grief-stricken old man could not withstand the Others' puppetry. She feared for Russell. The forces manipulating him against her did not care whether he survived or not. She guided him to his chaise lounge and lowered him into a reclining position.

Her son's grandfather collapsed like an old-man doll. She would protect him if she could.

"Stay here," she ordered Russell. "Get some sleep. Don't leave this room until I come for you. There may be intruders in the house. I'll be back when it's safe."

The old man nodded and his eyes slid shut. Lesley covered him with a light blanket. Did a light, shimmering whiteness envelop Russell as she shut the door behind her? Perhaps Cosette enshrouded him. He would like that. Lesley hoped he would be forgotten in the upheaval she knew would be coming.

Progressing on her planned route to the library, she remained alert to danger. An enemy might be lurking anywhere and soon, she spied one. A shadowy figure loomed before her at the end of the corridor. When Lesley recognized the man, she stopped in her tracks.

"Russell!" she exclaimed. "How did you get out of your room?" Her father-in-law smiled but not his usual nice smile, this expression struck Lesley as predatory.

"I can't desert you, Lesley," Russell said in a solicitous tone.

Her confusion deepened. Russell seemed to have recovered and no longer exhibited confusion or weakness. He carried himself erect.

"That's kind of you, Russell," she said.

Russell linked an arm through Lesley's elbow and escorted her toward the stairs. Why did something strike her as awry? Her muscles tensed. Did her suspicions involve whiteness in some way? Her gut told Lesley that the white haze of Cosette had settled over Russell as she left his room. She had made sure not to touch him after that. He should still be sleeping with the protective cloud of his dead wife. Yet, Russell touched her now with no hesitation and his grin had become toothy and wide.

"You're not Russell!" Lesley shouted without premeditation. She yanked her arm away and stepped back.

"You think not?" growled the image of Russell. Hair bristling, fingers extended like claws, the man-beast advanced upon Lesley.

The necklace around her neck shocked Lesley with electrical impulses. She grasped the brooch in order to absorb the shock with her hand and not her body and CRACK! Sparks flew and the acrid smell of burned fur clouded Lesley's senses.

"You'll regret this," the creature howled and dissipated into a thick, black cloud of smoke. Lesley took several shuddering breaths. An Other, he must have been.

"Hang on, Ryan! I'm coming for you, Rachel!" Lesley murmured and resumed her pilgrimage to the library.

The gasping, moaning, hissing, utterances of the Others followed her up and down the halls of Deerhaven Forest Hall, rustling the small hairs at the nape of her neck. She walked the empty halls unassailed, however, and came to the library without encountering another specter. Considering that two reverends and the Others, lurked within the house, Lesley expected that one of them would have locked the library doors, but she found the portal to the library open. The doors, when she pulled them shut behind her, glided on well-oiled hinges. The Others, upon occasion, seemed stymied by closed doors. The frightful chorus of voices shut off once she entered the library, as though a higher power had pulled the plug.

Stepping away from the entrance, she braced herself for a new assault but the library lay in deep silence. She looked around and, finally, up. The building's high glass ceiling admitted a view of the night sky. The staff of Deerhaven Forest Hall kept the glass so clean that she could see the full moon and the constellations of mountain stars beaming from the heavens above Deerhaven Forest. Subtle lights supplemented the lights of the firmament so that the library's catalogues and rows of leather volumes gleamed. The sky struck Lesley as preternaturally clear and the lighting inside the library seemed oddly alluring. She felt drawn further and further inside the storehouse of mysteries.

She wondered what she should attempt to find in the library. Before approaching the catalogues, a library user must know a subject or author for which to search. She knew that the Deerhaven Forest Hall Library's collection included extensive holdings of material about natural history, local history, family history and adjunct English history. How, though, could she determine what books or documents might help free her and her loved ones? That wonderful antique librarian, Ursula Smith, had told her that the library held something relevant to her predicament. But what?

She found the library's middle sanctum and absorbed the seductive atmosphere under the high transparent dome. Scanning the spines of books and the labels on Princeton files, she tried to relate them to the plight in which she found herself. *History of the Sierra Nevada Range* volumes 1-12, *Legends of Tuolumne County, National Archives Microfilm Publications—Pacific Sierra Region, she read, and even some she knew such as, My First Summer in the Sierra* by John Muir. Having spent the last few days in this wild mid-elevation called the Gold Country, she would have loved to choose titles and read, but she did not know which of these works related to what she needed to accomplish. The library's exquisite detailing began to entrance her in spite of herself. The floor beneath her boots gleamed and streaks of white beech inlay within the red oak boards directed her vision toward the library center. Her necklace felt alive in her palm, a warm, beating heart with passions independent of hers. She navigated the high oak shelving and library furniture, following the curving lines of light.

When she recognized the design, she exclaimed in surprise. The fluid lines set into the floor matched the pattern she'd seen in the tapestry upstairs and also the one downstairs and on the necklace in her hand. The library's slanting windows, inset above the cornice that topped the walls, refracted light from the sky to create the same insignia. These had been contrived as a device, the purpose of which was to function as a map into the library's interior. Each time the map appeared, the view presented seekers with a new chance to find their way into the heart of the library.

Lesley felt sure that the way to what she needed had been revealed. She followed the concentric circles around the library floor, confident that she would arrive at the solution to her dilemma. Glancing down at the brooch she wore, bearing a reduced-size version of the key to the library, Lesley guessed that she would soon reach a buffer zone that she must penetrate in order to reach the core. Leaving behind the shelter of book stacks, brass-lit tables, and oaken cabinetry, she entered an unfurnished zone and experienced renewed trepidation. Like a forest creature, she felt more vulnerable in the open, but she shook off her fear and emerged. From the broad circular aisle in which she stood, she could see what the zone encircled: a seamless convex wall of highly polished exotic wood from some eighteenth-century tree not native to California. She went to the lustrous wall and ran her hands along the wooden siding. Not the smallest nail hole alerted her fingers to a joint. She continued round the camouflaged central septagon.

"Lesley!" called an alluring throaty voice.

Lesley whirled and found Sula Smith, guardian of the library, in her path. Sula held a massive ancient volume with a scarlet ribbon marking her place in the book. Behind the librarian, Lesley saw two of her other nemeses, the feral housekeeper, Mrs. Woolf, and Rachel's traitorous nurse, Valerie Kemsley.

"You!" cried Lesley. "Have you come to make my life a worse nightmare than you already have? The three of you are beyond evil!"

She pointed at Sula. "My child was shot while in your care and hasn't woken up. And you," Lesley addressed Valerie, "you betrayed Rachel who trusted you all those years." She turned to Mrs. Woolf and took a breath. "You, Mrs. Woolf, worked for my mother-in-law your whole adult life. And now you're helping monsters attack me and her grandson." Hot tears ran down her cheeks. She clutched her protective necklace but the thing stayed cold and still.

For the first time, Lesley realized that she had no allies among the living except her comatose son and her unconscious lover. Her new sense of strength and self-reliance wavered and she felt more alone than a human being ever should. Every living person deserved support from community, family, or, at the very least, from paid public officials. She knew of nobody who would come to her aid. The only being that she really trusted was a long-dead librarian, and the librarian didn't seem to be at her former post.

"Stay away from me!" Lesley threatened. "Sane people from out in the world will come after you if I'm harmed." With that, she took a breath.

Sula Smith's vivid face, in particular, convulsed with emotion. The nurse and housekeeper opened their mouths as if to protest, but the librarian spoke first.

"The three of us will do anything to protect you, and Rachel, and Ryan. You've been misled, Lesley." Before any of the three could continue, a malevolent spirit intruded.

"Do not attempt to flee, Windsor Wife!" thundered a terrible, hoarse voice that Lesley recognized as that of the deceased Reverend Chaney.

"You have no power over me," Lesley answered, speaking with bravado. The Reverend, in sooty black clerical robes, materialized out of the book stacks.

"Do you think so?" the Reverend Chaney snarled. "You chose a weak and defective affinity and then switched your affinity to known deviants. You identified yourself as an enemy of the Hue. By authority of the old tenets, I may requite the wrongs against purity and decency perpetrated by you and your like. Resisting will only intensify your wounds. The wounds will, of necessity, be mortal but better for you if they are neat, far better!"

Lesley's skin crawled. Her hands, in spite of herself, flew up in a gesture of supplication. "Please leave me and the people I love alone!" Lesley begged. "We'll leave Deerhaven Forest Hall forever. You can have the house for your own."

Before she could say more, a woman's voice gained ascendancy. Sula Smith shook her head. "No, we won't leave the Hall. Lesley has no way to understand the importance of guarding the library in the Hall. I too invoke the authority of the old tenets," proclaimed Sula Smith, librarian. "As an inhabitant of this Hall and a visitor to this library, you must abide by the founder's directives. You need only read this Canon to see that I speak the truth."

"What would you bid me do?" demanded the Reverend Chaney.

As Lesley watched, the Reverend Were appeared at the elbow of his fellow cleric.

"Leave Lesley Windsor alone," answered Sula.

"We intend to exact retribution from purity's assailant,"

stated the Reverend Were. "We have that right, indeed, we have that obligation."

"I have rights too," returned the young librarian. "And I have familiarized myself with the rights of those who inhabit Deerhaven Forest Hall. Don't forget, I've had the knowledge at my disposal without knowing what lay within my library. Tonight, I reaped a reward for my stewardship. I used the library to figure out what I needed to know. I know my rights and Lesley's."

"What rights do you demand?" inquired the Reverend Were, his words couched in a snarl.

The librarian, her magnificent color and unusual height intensified by the gravity of her invocation, stepped up against the seamless wall between two podiums bearing thick dull green volumes. Sula's arms spread wide as though she might fly away. Lesley's fear for her personal safety dissipated in her absorption with what transpired before her eyes.

"May the governors of Deerhaven Forest hear this prayer!" chanted Sula. "I entreat you to grant us the right of proxy. Let the wounds you intended to inflict upon Lesley Windsor be dispensed to me."

A silence ensued. By the time Lesley's eyes fell upon them, the Reverend Were and the Reverend Chaney sported ugly expressions of greed and malice.

"So! You will die in her place, will you, Sula Smith! How worthy! How unexpected. How repellently pious. How like a librarian!"

With a horrifying roar, the Reverend Chaney lunged at the unresisting librarian. Cries of terror arose from Valerie Kemsley and Mrs. Woolf, but the Reverend Were fixed them with poisonous darts from his yellow eyes. The two women shrank back into the shadow of the natural history collection. Lesley found herself unable to move, frozen where she stood. Forced to witness this terrible spectacle from an orchestra seat, she wished she'd never been born.

"You must give yourself to me," the Reverend Were ordered Sula.

The librarian staggered for a moment and then assumed the flying position once again. With anguish, Lesley looked upon claw-like slash marks where the Reverend Chaney's hands raked at Sula. The slashes dripped rose-red blood. Lesley discovered she could not even speak. A mute observer and bodiless, Lesley admired Sula's courage.

Sula Smith unbuttoned her collar and pulled back her shirt to expose creamy white flesh, which shone like stars reflecting through glass. The sight of that intimate area would have caused Lesley to gasp if she could still articulate. What happened then shocked Lesley as much as anything she'd witnessed since departing the Blackhawk housing development.

"I won't resist you," Sula told the Reverend Were. Her face wore an expression of devotion and her head bowed slightly. Sula's eyes closed.

Two fangs of yellowed white materialized, two points of evil. Lesley heard Mrs. Woolf and the nurse screaming in horror, but Reverend Chaney moved his hideous bristled purple-black bulk close to them and they fell silent. The Reverend Were, having bared his hollow teeth, punctured the motionless librarian's neck. He drank deep.

CHAPTER TWENTY-ONE

"I drink the draught of my forefathers," howled Reverend Were, throwing back his head. Behind him, the ghostly Reverend Chaney shrieked with loathsome voyeurism.

"Please don't hurt Sula," begged Valerie Kemsley, breaking loose from Reverend Chaney's beastlike shadow and rushing toward the librarian. "Sula's worth ten of anybody I've ever met."

Lesley had misjudged Valerie Kemsley. The nurse, whom Lesley had assumed to be a traitor to the Windsors, the library and all that was good, seemed deeply smitten with Sula. Maybe Valerie, a caregiver, could save Sula from the evil fate for which she'd volunteered. The librarian meant to give her life in exchange for Lesley but Lesley did not want the sacrifice in her name. When Sula spoke, however, her words belied the atmosphere of tragedy.

"Don't stand so close to me, Valerie. You'll get blood on your uniform."

A sob racked the nurse's body and she staggered back. When the Reverend Were drew near Sula, his physical presence sent the nurse flying back across the river of flooring toward the book stacks. The Reverend Chaney's beastly sphere grew wider. All hope failed and more unnatural events unfolded.

Although tongueless and bodiless, as far as she could tell, Lesley participated in a gruesome bloodletting against her will. The library grew bright as though a forest fire might consume the books and statuary but, quite the reverse, thick luminous gray clouds appeared, blocking the towering windows. Light snow began to fall upon the glass. Like a movie vampire, the Reverend assumed a romantic pose of ordination and bent his dark head against Sula's white neck. Lesley could see clearly as his teeth pierced the librarian's glowing pink skin and watched when the Reverend inserted them again and again. The enamel of his teeth darkened as Sula's red blood coursed through the sickening incisors, into the Reverend's mouth, and down his throat. Lesley wished she could abandon her grisly vantage point, but she remained fixed in some amorphous limbo.

The rose-red in Sula's cheeks faded as the Reverend slurped and gulped. The memory of that gluttonous soundtrack would haunt Lesley with auditory flashbacks for the rest of her life. When the roses withered to snow-white blooms, Lesley wished she could scream or cry but remained without power of speech. The librarian, at the end, parted with her life in the library. The Reverend Were fully blighted the flowers that once bloomed in Sula's face and Sula sank to the ground, obscuring a piece of the light flooring that pointed into the library's heart.

A sick sensation in her chest and stomach signaled to Lesley that she'd returned to her body. If she didn't have an obligation to save Ryan and Rachel, she would have attempted to return to the state of nonbeing where she'd been held captive. Existing in her body created more pain than she could have imagined. She wondered which was worse, dying or letting someone else die for you.

"Reverend Cooper Were!" a forceful voice called out.

All creatures in that sector of the library, living or long dead, all except the newly dead, turned to see who challenged the Reverend's authority.

"Who's there?" demanded the Reverend, his voice greased with blood, his face altered by sated slackness.

"You know me, Cooper. I am Ursa Smith, librarian. I never really retired, only went to San Francisco where I can enjoy the opera and excellent Thai food. Now that you have decommissioned my daughter, I intend to reassume my post. I do so as of now. Beware! Your transgressions will be addressed by me."

"And I am here to obliterate you, Reverend Chaney!" called another voice, deeper and more commanding. "You glutted yourself on innocent blood, and now you must be annihilated. For that purpose, I have wandered among the living these many barren years."

"Who are you?" grunted Reverend Chaney, failing to remain level with the earth as he spoke. His specter levitated off the ground. With fear, Lesley noted.

"I am Ursula Smith, librarian 1858 to 1873. Once upon a time, I helped build a wing of this library and construct the safeguards insuring the building's survival. The library's founders intended your religious trappings to deflect the eye of the community from the library's true purpose. Unfortunately, your pretense of evil became true evil and must be erased. You were intended to protect this revered institution but you became a threat. You must be exterminated along with your modern protégé. He too failed to champion the Hue." The two reverends, one an unsecured shadow of the other, faced the librarians with the look of predators cornered by hunters of undetermined prowess.

"We will snuff you out," threatened the Reverend Were, "the same way we did your descendent, Miss Smith."

"I think not," replied Sula Smith's mother.

Lesley saw that the three librarians looked almost identical in appearance. Ursula Smith, the ghost librarian, wore the mantle of her time, a stately posture and a formal expression. Ursa seemed to have gained some weight in San Francisco's three- and four-star dining establishments, but Sula's resemblance to her relatives could only be called remarkable.

"You have lingered on this earth long enough," Ursula told the man who was once her contemporary, Reverend Chaney. "Both of you false ministers must depart this place."

"What are you going to do? Take away our library cards?" sneered the Reverend Were with an obscene gesture.

"That's right," Ursa replied. "Your borrowing privileges we hereby revoke! Don't move or I'll shoot." A flash of silver leapt from Ursa's coat pocket and into the air. A gun had materialized in her hand. Ursa pointed the weapon at the Reverend Were.

"What do you intend to accomplish by pulling a gun on me?" asked Reverend Were.

"First off, I intend to make you answer some questions," Ursa informed him in a level voice.

"Such as what?" the Reverend responded. "I thought librarians had all the answers."

"How do you come and go from Deerhaven Forest Hall? No enemy can enter Deerhaven Forest Hall unless invited by a member of the family."

"I thought you had the answers! You understand nothing," the Reverend Were replied with world-weariness.

But Lesley sensed that the answer to Ursa's question would bring her some kind of enlightenment.

"We don't need the Reverend to answer this particular question," said Ursula Smith, unexpectedly. "I can supply this fragment of the Hall's history. The truth lies in my time, the eighteen hundreds."

"Tell us, Ursula, my dear great-grandmother," begged Ursa.

"You know, don't you, that Jane Copley Windsor bore a son who died young?" said Ursula.

"I met her son in the woods searching for his mother," said Lesley. "And I saw Richard Windsor again today, down by the river. He lured my friend to her death, but I don't think he meant to hurt her. Pauline drowned in the Stanislaus trying to help Richard, who she believed to be my son, Ryan. The Reverend Chaney or the Reverend Were used Richard to destroy Pauline who would have fought to help me."

The two Reverends looked as though they would have

preferred that the assembled company not hear this unbecoming story. Or did the Reverends have any conscience at all?

"Richard used to be a lovely boy," said Ursula, "who would never harm anyone. I have mourned his early death these long years. What I need to disclose doesn't concern sweet, young Richard. You see, Jane gave birth to another son and not of her own volition. An evil man stole Jane from her home and forced his seed into her. The child of that foul union she named Robin and Reuben, known as Ben Windsor, became the father of all living Windsors."

"Oh, my God," Lesley gulped. "Poor Jane." Then she asked, fearing the answer, "What does this terrible piece of history have to do with the Reverend Were's access to Deerhaven Forest Hall?"

"The monster who took Jane Copley Windsor against her will was the man who in life was," Ursula pointed her finger at the shadow behind Reverend Were, "HE! The Reverend Chaney. In that way, Reverend Chaney made himself the ancestor of every living Windsor. Reverend Chaney also married a sinister woman called Nell Cross and that union eventually produced Cooper Were. Since Reverend Were is also a direct descendant of the Reverend Chaney, he may enter Deerhaven Forest Hall at will and invite whomever he wishes. The Reverend Were, whether we like it or not, can claim a blood kinship with the Windsor family."

"So often, when people think of a family, they imagine a single entity bearing one name," intoned the Reverend Were with what might even be sadness. "A family includes many branches of a common tree and may be known by many names. You made that error, Lesley, and failed to see connections and affinities. Without you, Lesley, and without Michael, Rachel, and Kelvin Windsor, a wife of mine would be the Windsor wife, mistress of the Hall. I am next in line, after Cosette's children, and my wife would assume the running of the Hall."

A piece of the puzzle fell into place, a part of what motivated Lesley's enemies to work against her.

"Where is Kelvin Windsor?" demanded Lesley. "I haven't seen him in days."

"Kelvin Windsor got his due and faced his Maker," answered the Reverend Were. "He died an agonizing death, God rest his soul. A rabid animal bit Kelvin in the leg, and he failed to seek medical aid in time. The county hospital recorded his death at 6:66 yesterday. I managed to be present in time to administer my church's version of the last rites. I'm afraid he didn't pass away with peace of mind, however. He died screaming vituperation at God's small, furry creatures, particularly the one that infected him with the fatal malady which killed him." The Reverend Were's harsh, malicious dialogue slowed and then resumed. "Actually, by the time he died, his jaw locked and foam poured from the corners of his mouth."

"Stop," cried Lesley. "Every further moment in your company proves that you're a worse fiend than I could have imagined. Ursula, Ursa! Please help me fight this terrible man and the evil spirit who created him. There must be some way to protect ourselves from Reverend Were and Reverend Chaney."

"Aren't you interested in the fate of the man you promised to love, honor and cherish, for as long as you live?" quizzed Reverend Were, with a flash of his long maroon teeth.

"My marriage turned out to be a horrible joke," responded Lesley. "But Michael is my son's father. I never wished for anything bad to befall Michael! If you've brought him to some horrible end, exposed him to a rabid animal or drowned him like an unwanted kitten, don't tell me."

"Oh, he lives," the Reverend Were replied. "Michael will execute a crucial part of my plan. The husband who you annulled in your mind will make himself useful. He will be the one who removes your son from the equation. Little Ryan is legally and obviously a Windsor. I can't afford to let him live."

Mrs. Woolf and Valerie found their voices then and begged mercy for Ryan. Lesley could feel her body ready to explode like a dry pine tree struck by lightning. Her necklace blazed with terrible heat.

The two reverends looked irritated by the clamoring voices of Mrs. Woolf and Valerie. Perhaps they'd counted those two women as potential confederates. The Reverend Chaney surged forward in a swirl of purple and encircled the nurse and the housekeeper. He swept them back into the tall forest of book stacks. Sinking to their knees in a supplicating posture, the women ceased moving and speaking. A coating of light ash seemed to blanket their skin and clothes. When the Reverend Chaney moved away from the two women, he looked diminished. Chaney resumed his position behind the Reverend Were and assumed his habitual nasty leer.

"Touch the nurse or the housekeeper and they'll be as dead as your son," the Reverend Were warned Lesley.

"You monster!" Lesley screamed. Her accusation could not be considered hyperbole, she realized. The Reverend Were lived his life like a monster, a Bela Lugosi type, an Anne Rice bat/man without the intellectual energy of Lestat. Remembering the necklace's powers, Lesley grasped the searing object and spoke to her pendant. "If you have the power to strike down one more living person and one more ghost, please crush this evil man and his horrible ancestor." She shook the brooch in the reverends direction as though she could aim the locket like a gun. The necklace grew cool and heavy in her hand.

"That talisman would never harm a member of the Windsor family," the Reverend Were informed her, his eyes narrowing with annoyance. "You forget. Deerhaven Forest Hall provides a fortress for me and all who champion the Hue."

"The Hue," repeated Lesley. "What is the Hue? I've never understood." She must keep the Reverend talking until she figured out how to prevent him from harming Ryan.

"The Hue is the cloak of decency," answered Reverend Were. "I represent the tradition of moral life in this part of the world and all citizens pure of mind and body. No matter that the higher powers invested me with this mission in order to distract the eye of the world from the central purpose of Deerhaven Forest Hall's library and the carnal knowledge contained within."

"Enough!" cried Ursa Smith. "Reverend Were, you're a foul and sloppy man. You've misinterpreted your calling in life and violated the legacy of your forebears. I despise a person who fails to do a careful reading of a book or a situation. Look what you've done to my daughter! You gave yourself license to destroy a person of beauty and integrity. I should fire this gun and do away with you right now. I've never harmed a living thing, and I don't wish to, but if a bullet will rid Deerhaven Forest Hall of you, I will."

The Reverend Were relaxed at hearing Ursa's pacifist sentiment and the Reverend Chaney, floating behind him, seemed relieved also. How would Lesley prevent these evil beings from carrying out their plan to kill her innocent son? When Ursula addressed the Reverend Chaney, Lesley thanked the ghost librarian for the further distraction.

"I have been obliged to remain in this vale of wind and tears past my natural time in order to keep YOU in check, Reverend Chaney! As God is my witness, I will keep your evil subdued."

"Miss Smith," Reverend Chaney replied. "I plucked what fruit I desired from the tree of life and that included, your," he halted and his eyes grew red with devilish greed, "your friend, the Mistress of Deerhaven Forest Hall."

"Yes," answered Ursula Smith, through ghostly clenched teeth, "and you deserve a fate worse than death for what you inflicted on the loveliest flower in all the forest."

The dead minister bragging of rape brought Lesley another body blow of horror, and she could not endure any more. Only the advent of racing footsteps kept her from throwing herself at the two ministers. Who would come to the library at such a time?

"Michael!" called Lesley when she saw who entered.

"I know you can never forgive me," began Michael, and Lesley saw that he was speaking to her, "the same kind of insane voice that haunted my sister made my life into a waking nightmare. A cruel madman who called himself John Bennett has become a snake curled within my brain. John Bennett orders me to follow the orders of the Reverend Were." Michael's pitiful, hoarse voice sheared off and a whispered croak issued from his lips. "He wants me to hurt you and Ryan. Over the years, I've lost the strength to resist him. Please understand. And grant me a small piece of the charity you've extended to my sister, Rachel." Michael looked more decomposed than the Reverend Chaney or Ursula, but Lesley felt no stirring of pity for the man assigned to kill her son.

"Your sister didn't need charity from me, Michael," Lesley replied in a voice so cold that Michael might not recognize the words as hers. "Those same voices hissed terrible things to Rachel, but she remained a decent human being. Don't even talk about Rachel. I love her without restraint and she loves me in return. You listened to the sickening voice in your mind and never registered a word of what I said. I know that now."

Michael extended his hands as if appealing for clemency but Lesley backed away, repelled by him. Her former husband saw that he'd exhausted Lesley's tender feelings and could expect no mercy from her.

"We can use your help, Michael," said the Reverend Were. "Our first task will be to bury the librarian deep in Deerhaven Forest where nobody will ever find her." The Reverend Were spoke as though Sula's mother weren't three feet away, holding a gun.

"Don't touch my daughter," ordered Ursa. "Or, I'll overcome my squeamishness about guns."

"It's nothing to you, really. I intend to dispose of the evidence before civil authorities arrive. Your daughter's body provides evidence. You can't hinder me any more than your daughter could. My cause would be doomed if I weakened and let myself become implicated in the sordid murder of a librarian. A librarian might capture the public's sympathy, even a promiscuous, lesbian librarian." The Reverend Were stepped forward again.

"You don't seem to have heard me," said Ursa, in the sternest of tones, designed to render library-goers mute. "I told you not to go near my daughter."

The Reverend's lips curled in the smile that exposed his tubular teeth. "Threats won't bring back your dear departed daughter, the gay playgirl of Deerhaven Pines. Sula Smith chose to die. Remember? Return to your retirement home, Mother Ursa, and I won't sic the Others on you. The Others formed out of derelict souls. They make for quite unpleasant company. What do you say? Do we have a deal?"

"Any last words?" said Ursa, the last living librarian in the room, her syllables icy.

"That gun isn't big enough to kill a fat pheasant," the

Reverend scoffed. "You could make me uncomfortable at best."

"It will do the trick, though," Ursa informed him. "I melted down a sterling silver bookmark my mother gave me. The marker had an inscription on the handle written by Walt Whitman, an unpublished passage. Believe me, I didn't disfigure a possession like that without determining that this was a matter of deepest urgency."

The librarian sounded like the school librarians of Lesley's childhood. Lesley felt hopeful for the first time.

"Go to it, man," the Reverend Were ordered Michael. "Take the dead librarian into the forest and bury her."

"I can't, Reverend. When I found that my brother had died, I began to see PURITI in a different way. I no longer champion you. I reject John Bennett Windsor for making me into a pestilent vessel."

A bolt of yellow from the Reverend's eyes drew Lesley's eyes to his face. The Reverend Were's teeth appeared to grow. They protruded from his mouth, dripping foam. Lesley's throat constricted as the Reverend raised his arms within the heavy, black wool cloak he wore and the cloak settled over his shoulders. Rather than ministerial garb under his outerwear, the Reverend sported a neat brown business suit with white shirt and tasteful tie. The Reverend Chaney inched behind him, a hibernating shadow.

"I've lost patience," barked the Reverend Were. "I've battled against the impure tendencies of the Windsors all my life and gotten no appreciation from inside Deerhaven Forest Hall. No more. Let's end the Windsor line and destroy whatever's harbored within the library. I will be master of the Hall and my progeny after me."

"Destruction of library materials?" Ursa repeated, in a whisper so fierce the sound could only come from a trained librarian. "I think not!" she pronounced. The librarian, rose-red cheeks blazing, pulled the trigger and an explosion louder than seemed possible reverberated throughout the library.

Black blood spouted from a hole in the narrow chest of Reverend Were, staining his fancy bleached shirtfront. Pain and shock registered on his natty face. The Reverend touched both hands to the wound above his heart and his knees folded.

"I never believed that garbage about stakes and silver bullets," the Reverend Were whined. And died.

"Just as I said! He didn't comprehend what he read," said Ursa Smith, wiping her forehead with her sleeve. "The danger of silver bullets and wooden stakes, to folk such as he, has been clearly documented in the literature."

The library fell silent until Ursula's voice, stern and ghostly, loud enough to be heard but not so blaring as to be inappropriate in a library, rang out. "Now! I will mete out retribution to you, Ronald Chaney," said Ursula Smith. Ursula turned to her forebear and nodded goodbye. Lesley raised one hand in an instinctive farewell to the good woman. Ursula Smith did not fly; she paced gracefully toward the cowering specter who used to be the Reverend Chaney.

Chaney's yellowish eyes seemed fixed upon the heap of dark clothing which once housed his descendant, the Reverend Were. When Ursula reached the former minister, she glowed with eerie supernatural light. Without further warning or threat, Ursula enfolded him and the envelopment sent them both upward and onward. The Reverend Chaney lost form and crumbled like burnt paper. Fine dust fell to the library floor in a tiny pile. Lesley could not tell what Ursula became, but she did not turn to dust. The light of Ursula just disappeared.

A luminous spray of snow wafted down from the heavens. Outside, voluptuous-eyed snow clouds had begun to deliver a fine fall of white powder.

The violence of our struggles must have cracked the high glass, thought Lesley. As she turned away from the white lace floating down from the sky, she saw thick, dark vapor swirling along the floor.

"Where are they?" guttural speakers demanded. "Where are the reverend leaders whom we followed?" The smoke became menacing shadows. The Others had found a way into the library.

"That heap of ashes used to be the Reverend Chaney," began Michael, his speech halting. "The Reverend Were lies here!"

At his words, the Others converged upon Michael Windsor until a darkness too intense to be of this world obscured the sight of him. Trickles of the finest black ash materialized in the air and floated to the floor. The black cloud surrounding Michael lost hue and then density. A layer of cinders blanketed the library floor, finally, and the Others' shrill, nasty voices faded, and they departed this earth for their next destination. Michael Windsor served his wife and son well at the last.

After all traces of the Others dissipated, Michael's tall, slender body hung suspended in the air for a few seconds. Eyes closed, his face looked peaceful. He looked different from the man he'd been for years. He resembled the earnest young man who'd courted Lesley, and his beatific expression never changed when gravity exerted its hold on him and his body fell to the oaken floor.

"Michael must have been suffocated by the death throes of the Others," Ursa gently told Lesley, after feeling for a pulse. Ryan's father lay drained of all color, a crumpled piece of parchment. "I'm sorry, honey," said Ursa, rising and coming to Lesley's side.

Lesley felt that she should touch Michael and see if her touch restored him. No, that would do no good. The time had long passed when Lesley's touch was what Michael needed. Tears sprang to her eyes. "Ryan's lost his father, and you've lost your daughter! I'm so sorry, Ursa," choked Lesley, a sob strangling her. "Poor Sula! I should have trusted in her goodness. She would never have let harm come to Ryan if there was anything she could do. I wish I could thank her. She gave her life for us all."

"Please don't blame yourself!" said Ursa. "Sula wouldn't want you to grieve on her behalf. I myself feel worried but not grief-stricken."

"My visit to Deerhaven Forest Hall brought your daughter to this terrible end!" replied Lesley, unable to comprehend why the older librarian seemed so unmoved by her gorgeous and talented daughter's death.

"In the Deerhaven Pines reference area, you will find writings which predict the events that just occurred. What Sula gave, she gave freely and that makes all the difference."

"Why?" asked Lesley, straining to understand.

"Why?" echoed Ursa. "Because the library's principal collection must be maintained and protected. When you married Michael Windsor and gave birth to Ryan, you became a guardian of the library, though you did not know it. Your position, Library Trustee, involves a sacred and lifelong commitment."

"I'm so confused." Lesley's words tumbled out. "I don't understand why this library is so important. Most of the volumes and maps can probably be checked out of the Stanislaus County Public Library."

"Definitely not," Ursa contradicted. "The most valuable primary sources housed within the library at Deerhaven Forest Hall will be found nowhere else on earth."

"Where are they kept?" asked Lesley, looking around.

"You'll need the assistance of me or of the librarian in charge," said Ursa. "You could use the self-guiding signs, some do, but you have been too distracted to notice them."

"The librarian in charge was Sula," moaned Lesley. "She's dead and can't provide me with answers anymore."

As if in answer, Ursa Smith went to the shelves of books near where Mrs. Woolf and Valerie Kemsley sat in suspended animation. The librarian moved with purpose and grace. She tapped the women's shoulders, and they shook their heads. Both women rubbed their eyes. Ursa turned to Lesley.

"See, these women are restored and may even go on to be better human beings than before. The Reverend Chaney's spirit can no longer sap the psyche of a living person. He is gone. More importantly, for me, I found justification for vanquishing the Reverend Were. He disobeyed the tenets of the Hall when he let my daughter offer her life in place of yours. He neglected the most arcane magic. A librarian who did her research well would never ignore the deeper, more abiding principles. The Reverend Were learned what he knew about magic and faith during our time. If he wanted to triumph over me, he should have delved deeper. My daughter found her way to the right sources of information. She didn't even need my help, although I came prepared to guide her.

"What Sula discovered today proved to her that Deerhaven

Forest Hall rests upon ancient holy ground. We are only indirectly descended from the beings who consecrated this place originally, but their religion prevails here. So much was lost when the immigrants of the 1800s and 1900s imposed their ruder way of life upon this forest. We must try and emulate, as best we can, our earlier forebears who embraced a more elegant and gentler philosophy."

"What do you mean?" asked Lesley, her voice still shaking.

"That nothing valuable has been lost. Affinities and deaths may have been preordained, but the first people who lived here predicted resurrections too. Go and look at my daughter. See? She's as beautiful now as ever."

Lesley crept forward and sank to her knees beside the motionless body of Deerhaven Forest Hall's librarian. Although the Reverend Were had extracted rivers of blood, Sula's face once again glowed as brightly as though she readied herself to revel in the attention of vivacious women.

"She looks alive," mourned Lesley and hot tears rolled down her cheeks. She reached out and took one of Sula's lovely white hands in her own.

As she knelt beside the slain librarian, cloudy tears fell onto the radiant forehead. To Lesley's amazement, Sula's slender fingers warmed her palm. Then, Sula's bright sapphire eyes opened and blood returned to her generous mouth. Lesley gasped and dropped the librarian's hand.

Behind Lesley and Sula, Ursa Smith laughed with relief.

CHAPTER TWENTY-TWO

"My darling Sula!" said Ursa, kneeling to help her daughter sit up. "I trusted that you would return, but one never knows for sure. Putting so much credence in myths and legends can be nerve-wracking even though they tend to be as valid as science."

"How can this be?" stuttered Lesley. "We saw Sula die."

"I hope I don't experience death again for a long time," commented Sula, some of her normal vigor already returned to her voice.

"The deep magic demands that no completely innocent person who dies at the hands of a traitor to the Hall shall remain dead," Ursa assured Lesley. "Your sweet tears brought her back. You've read about such things in fairy tales, haven't you? Princesses brought back to life with a kiss? Prince turns into frog and back, that kind of thing?"

"Fairy tales?" Lesley repeated in wonder.

"There's excellent material in those ancient stories. Most people don't think to apply what they read. Don't stand up, dear. You look faint. Not you, Sula. It's Lesley, here, who looks a bit worse for wear."

"Mother?" Sula began, stretching like a cat who'd spent the afternoon sleeping on a library chair. "Why did you make such a point of asking me whether the sky would be cloudy or clear? What did that have to do with anything?"

"I thought you might be able to complete your reference search without my assistance if you could read the signs by good natural light."

"Yes," Sula admitted. "Light from the heavens above did direct me to an ancient volume with a cover of bark and pages like leaves. I found, in the book, an early healer's description of the essential magic that prevails in this library. Beyond the library perhaps! The writer suggests that the deep magic might transcend philosophy and religion. Where did I put that book? I don't see it now. Can't we install better lighting in the side recesses of the library so we don't have to hope for a clear sky?"

"Perhaps," Ursa replied, "but those volumes might stay better preserved if they don't see much light. Anyway, all's well that ends well."

"There are two things that librarians love most," Sula explained to a dazed Lesley, "knowledge and self-sufficiency. The American Library Association promotes them both, with posters, T-shirts and buttons."

"Are you feeling any better, Lesley?" asked Ursa.

"I'm all right but tell me, will Michael recover the way Sula did?" Lesley inquired in a faint voice.

"I'm afraid Michael actually got injured," replied Ursa, examining Lesley's husband. "But modern medical science might pull him through. His pulse and respiration are getting stronger."

"The phones are out," said Lesley. "We can't even call 911."

"My lover, Coral, is waiting in the car," said Ursa. "She'll help."

The librarian from San Francisco turned around to face the slumped figures of Mrs. Woolf and Valerie Kemsley, leaning against one another. "Valerie! Mrs. Woolf! Try to pull yourselves together. You two drive into Deerhaven Pines and call the paramedics. Tell them that Michael Windsor fell from a tall ladder while retrieving a library book from a high shelf. Send Coral inside. She's a doctor."

Ursa prodded Valerie and Mrs. Woolf with the toe of her boot until they stood and departed.

"Before they reach the paramedics, we have to work fast," Ursa told Lesley and Sula. "There's a lot to do before people arrive from the outside world. Only those who champion the Hue will be allowed to learn of today's events. We need to discard the Reverend Were's body and rid the library of this dust created by the departure of Reverend Chaney and the Others. Coral won't mind helping with the cleanup. She's tidy and competent. If we all pitch in, everything will be in order by the time an ambulance can arrive."

"I have to find Rachel before I do anything else," cried Lesley. "The Reverend Were and those Others kidnapped her, and she's unconscious. I think she's below us, in a subterranean part of this house. Does Deerhaven Forest Hall have a basement?"

The librarians knew the answer. "Beneath the house is an apartment where a former housekeeper once lived. She feared winter storms and felt safer below ground. That's where Rachel lies right now. Don't worry, Lesley. No harm can come to her. As you probably guessed, Cosette Windsor wrapped her spirit around Rachel to protect her. Cosette visited me in San Francisco to tell me that she would expend the last of her spiritual substance to ensure her daughter's survival."

Ursa paused and studied Lesley with a severe expression. "Cosette told me that you and Rachel shut her out. Your coldness almost extinguished her. She used some of herself to defend your son, Ryan, but when Jane Copley Windsor took over the protection of Ryan, Cosette formed a cocoon around her daughter. You didn't touch Rachel did you?"

"Almost. At the last moment, something told me not to," admitted Lesley.

"Your touch might have sapped the last of Cosette's strength, but your good instincts kept Rachel safe," said Ursa approvingly.

"And Cosette?" asked Lesley. "Will she be all right?"

"Cosette will most likely pass on to another plane when her work ends. I hope that you and Rachel will send her on her way with love and forgiveness. All good souls deserve that much from those they leave behind."

Lesley nodded, new tears in her eyes. "Now that Rachel understands the real evil in her life, bigotry and hatred as represented by the Reverend Were, I know she'll forgive her mother," she said. "And, as for love, there's no more loving person than Rachel. I think Cosette must know that." She blushed, wondering if she sounded like a schoolgirl with a crush.

Ursa smiled, satisfied that Cosette, her old employer, would receive decent treatment from Rachel and Lesley before leaving the physical world behind.

"How are you feeling, Sula, my dear?" Ursa asked, turning to practical considerations.

"Quite well. Willing and able to be a Champion of the Hue," replied Sula, throwing back her long, tangled, black curls and stretching.

Ursa Smith jogged toward the librarian's station at the front of the library. Lesley helped Sula to a reading chair, took her hands, and rubbed her wrists as though she could restore circulation to the newly risen librarian. Ursa returned with bucket, broom, towels and blankets. The women began the cleanup, but Lesley could not work in silence. She had too many questions for the senior librarian.

"Champion the Hue?" said Lesley, confused by Sula's earlier statement. "The Reverend Were used that slogan and, I think, the Reverend Chaney did too. Why do you and Sula seem so comfortable with the words?"

"The two reverends adopted the phrase and twisted the meaning," Ursa explained to Lesley. "Think about it. 'Hue' can connote darkness and the dark but all colors have a hue. The words were originally intended to serve as a reminder that the Windsors must always protect the rights of those whom their library was built to serve. Gay people everywhere know in their hearts of this library's existence."

"The phrase sounded so menacing when the Reverend's PURITI group chanted the words," said Lesley, with amazement.

"The two reverends stole the words and used them as a smokescreen, just as the founders meant them to do. The same words, crafted to represent the library's constituency, rallied the groups that hated those whom the library celebrates. So much can be ignored in the confusion. This library is not open to the general public, after all. Only gay people get borrowing privileges."

"It always seemed like a clever ploy. The founders of the library elected the reverends to serve a purpose. The mission of both the Reverend Chaney and the Reverend Were was to distract the community from scrutinizing the function of the library at Deerhaven Forest Hall. To that end, the communities around Deerhaven Pines achieved a reputation for intolerance and bigotry. This reputation made the existence of the library so unlikely that enemies would never look here."

"But the Reverend Were became truly evil," Lesley protested. "He injured Ryan and tried to kill Sula. He stole Rachel and held her prisoner. Did he know he functioned as a guardian of the Windsors' library?"

"The milieu in which he operated corrupted the Reverend Were," explained Ursa. "He strayed from his original purpose long ago. It's a common phenomenon, Lesley. The intelligence agent planted in a foreign country develops an allegiance to that country and betrays his own. Also, you will have noticed his anatomical differences from other people. Dental differences, at any rate. And the aberrant taste for human blood."

"Yes," said Lesley and shuddered. "What about 'Choose Your Affinity'? Why do those words also appear on emblems of the Windsor family?"

"That phrase came from an early member of the lineage, before the family acquired the name Windsor. The motto should remind the family that they may choose what elements of the past speak to them. Everyone should be entitled to embrace those fragments of history that give them sustenance, and every person should be able to choose their orientation too. That's why the library must be perpetuated."

Lesley fell silent, deep in thought.

With Lesley's and Sula's assistance, Ursa Smith swept, scrubbed and hauled. When Ursa's partner appeared, she joined them in the clean-up effort. Lesley tried the library phone and found the service reestablished. She immediately called the hospital. The nurse at the station nearest to Ryan's room related some of the drama that had occurred after Lesley left the hospital. The account agitated Lesley, and she begged for an up-to-date status report on Ryan. After what seemed like a long wait, sulky Nurse Horvath took the phone and assured Lesley that Ryan's condition had been upgraded to stable once again.

"The doctor has been puzzled by a white-looking film coating the child's skin, but the lack of coloration doesn't seem clinical and doesn't restrict his breathing," reported Nurse Horvath and added, "I personally believe that it's fluorescent lighting in the room that creates the impression of whiteness."

Lesley recalled the protective essence of Cosette enveloping Rachel and smiled. She could only assume that Jane Copley Windsor guarded Ryan in the same way. Lesley thanked him, hung up and returned to the tasks at hand.

Coral turned out to be a good-humored woman wearing jeans and a ski parka. The presence of this pleasant, ordinary person, a pediatrician by trade, encouraged Lesley to voice the question she'd squelched earlier. Lesley moved closer to Ursa Smith and cleared her throat.

"Ursa," Lesley began. "When you use the word 'orientation,' what do you mean? You don't mean sexual orientation, do you?"

"Why, what else would I mean, Lesley? Do you know nothing about the library at Deerhaven Forest Hall?"

"Not much," answered Lesley, wondering how the library related to her question.

"You really don't understand the function of the library at Deerhaven Forest Hall?" chorused Sula and Coral.

"Michael should have told you before he asked you to marry him," Ursa informed Lesley. "The Windsor wife assumes responsibility for overseeing the library. She must provide the stage that screens the library from the eyes of the unenlightened in the world. Michael let you enter into a contract with clandestine clauses and never told you."

"Clandestine?" repeated Lesley, as out of sync as ever. "Tell me about those clauses. For all I know, I object to them."

"Oh, no," said Ursa, complacently. They finished sweeping the ashes of the long-ago departed into paper sacks. Coral began ferrying the sacks out to her van. "I have no doubt that your union with Rachel will prove more permanent than your marriage to Michael, and the nature of your feelings for the Windsors' daughter guarantees you will work for the library's continued existence."

Lesley felt herself blushing again. "How do you know?" she asked. "About me and Rachel, I mean."

Ursa smiled. "Cosette shared the happy news with me. You and Rachel have her blessing. She hopes the two of you will raise her grandson together and you will know joy and security. She assumes you will live at the Hall and stay near the library. You will be her daughter-in-law by virtue of your relationship to her daughter. Cosette grew much more enlightened the second she died." Ursa's mouth turned down at the corners as she added with sadness, "Cosette foresaw the death of her son Kelvin but not the demise of Michael. When I spoke with her earlier today, she hoped Michael would be a part of the Windsor family and a father to his son. We shall see."

The ambulance carrying emergency medical technicians had met with traffic delays because of the ever-thickening fall of snow. By the time the stretcher bearers entered the library and tended to Michael, no sign remained of the cosmic struggle which pitted the Champions of the Hue against those who meant to champion the hue but went astray. The library floors gleamed except for where the huge canvas boots worn by paramedics left puddles. Where the Reverend Were's black-draped body once lay, spurting his blood and Sula's, only a thin film of bleach and ammonia marked the desecrated spot.

After emergency medical technicians loaded Michael into the ambulance and drove away, Lesley sent Mrs. Woolf to her room.

The old housekeeper looked white and in shock. The days since Lesley's arrival at Deerhaven Forest Hall had taken a terrible toll on the formerly formidable woman. When Lesley suggested that Valerie Kemsley retire to her room, the nurse protested.

"I should find Rachel and look after her," said the nurse. "She's been my patient for many years, and I let her down." The nurse cast sheep's eyes at Sula. "Besides, I should stay near Sula. There's safety in numbers, as they always say."

"If Rachel were to see you," Lesley said as gently as possible so as not to injure the nurse's feelings, "I'm not sure she'd know you're on her side now. You regret your part in all that was done to Rachel, I can tell, but Rachel doesn't know yet. I think you should let us go and get her. Make yourself a snack and get some sleep."

Valerie hesitated, eyes cast down now.

"Go ahead. You deserve refreshment and rest, Valerie," Sula told the nurse, winking.

"All right, Sula," Valerie acquiesced. "If you say so." The nurse departed for the kitchen, offering to leave hot chocolate warming on the stove.

"No hot chocolate for me," rejoined Sula, blanching.

"Sula, Ursa, do either of you know how to get to the basement rooms?" asked Lesley.

"I could find my way in the dark," Ursa assured her. "When I was a child we would take shelter down there when the mountain winds grew strong. Since that time, engineers have replaced the glass in the house with high-tech safety glass, reinforced the foundation and braced the walls internally. This house could withstand a tornado. Follow me. Let's find Rachel and tell her she's free to live among us!"

True to her word, Ursa led them right to the Victorian downstairs room where the Others bore Lesley earlier.

Once Lesley stood beside the tall, old-fashioned bed, she looked down upon her lover and sighed. Rachel's trance appeared so deep that Lesley thought of accident victims who lingered in a coma for years, only to die. Sula, Ursa and Coral stood at a respectful distance.

"Are you sure we shouldn't call the paramedics back?" asked

Lesley. "Ursa, how can you be sure that Cosette is taking care of her?"

"I've read the old accounts," Ursa replied. "They cite instances in which a resident of Deerhaven Forest Hall slumbers in a milky-hued cocoon, wrapped within the ghostly essence of an ancestor who shields them. Besides, Ursula told us so and my great-grandmother never made mistakes."

"Will tears bring her back?" asked Lesley eagerly. "Like Sula?"

"I'm not sure what applies," mused Ursa. "There's deep magic at work here too. But is it the same?"

"I don't want to make a mistake," said Lesley. "Maybe I should go upstairs and read the earlier reports."

"I think you'll find the way," Ursa encouraged her. "Concentrate on Rachel."

The four women fell silent. Lesley bent over the woman she loved and thought of the time they'd spent together. The interlude had been astounding but the circumstances had not been perfect. Enemies had ranged nearby while Lesley's son lay wounded.

Tears formed in Lesley's eyes as she wondered when Rachel would hold her again. The day-old imprint of Rachel's gentle hands on Lesley's skin, and the remembered softness of her body amazed Lesley still. Lesley felt her lips tremble. The urge to kiss Rachel's pale mouth became a fever that stole her senses.

"I must! I must touch her." She bent and touched her mouth to Rachel's.

The white cloud surrounding Rachel stirred and coalesced. Soon, the whiteness began to dissolve. Lesley touched Rachel's hand and, as she did so, a sweet, ghostly voice sounded in Deerhaven Forest Hall for the last time.

"Worms are the words but joy's the voice. I need to go. Don't forget what we've learned these past days. Embrace the Hue and champion your affinities," murmured Cosette.

Rachel's eyes opened.

"Mother?" Rachel asked. "I dreamed that you gave your life for me."

"No," came Cosette's voice. "I'd finished my life. But I'm giving up my existence on this earth for you and gladly so."

"While I slept, I felt so close to you," said Rachel with a dreamy slur to her speech. "I used to be so angry."

"All that I am and all that I was, I leave with you." The milky cloud became light rain and soon, mist joined the wet tears on Rachel's face.

"What I did wrong, died with me," whispered Cosette. "My love remains. Goodbye, Rachel. Goodbye, women of the world."

A strange daylight flooded the basement room and then disappeared. The last drops of mist settled, and Lesley sensed that Cosette could not come back to Deerhaven Forest Hall.

"Your tears and your kiss woke Rachel from her sleep, Lesley," said Ursa.

"How could that be?"

"I told you to remember the old fairy tales, didn't I?" Ursa replied. "There's a grain of truth in them all. That's why they get passed down. Remember how the prince wakes the princess with a kiss? Well, we're gay. That makes you the prince. You woke her."

Lesley smiled, and Rachel reached for her hand. Stooping, Lesley touched her lips to Rachel's again and found them wet with the dampness that Cosette left behind.

"I'm a doctor," said Coral. "Let me take a look at you, Rachel."

"Can you sit?" asked Sula.

"I think so," Rachel answered, sounding stronger.

Coral set about checking Rachel's vital signs. Lesley could not stop stroking her lover's arm, and Rachel returned her affection with shy, loving glances. Would Rachel change her mind when she met other women? Lesley hoped not. Somehow, she thought not.

"Now that Rachel's safe, I have to get to the hospital," said Lesley and kissed Rachel's forehead.

Upstairs, she called the nurse's station at Sonora Sierra Hospital to tell them that she was on her way.

"You'll be pleased to learn your son has made significant progress toward recovery," said Nurse Horvath with unprecedented warmth in his voice.

Lesley's heart jiggled under her breastbone.

"Is Ryan awake?" she asked, her voice thin with hope.

"He's awake and alert. The Doctor will fill you in, but Ryan's, prognosis just got elevated to good.

Weak with relief, Lesley hung up and told her friends the news. Coral Montoya offered to accompany Lesley to the hospital as medical advisor. She would check on Michael while Lesley visited Ryan. Rachel and Sula offered to awaken Russell and tell him the good news while Ursa put together a late-night supper.

****

"The funniest thing," said Ryan, propped against faded green hospital-issue pillows. "When I first woke up, I thought I saw a boy wearing old-fashioned clothes. His mother said she'd been sitting with me. I told them how I was afraid I might die and the lady answered me and this is what she said:

"*We will replenish you.* Do you know that passage from the Bible? *He shall come down like rain upon the mown grass: as showers that water the earth.* She said we are all part of that Bible passage. Our love will help you live, Ryan." Lesley stared at her son in wonder.

"The boy and his mother went to each other and joined hands. Then, they became one...person." Ryan's voice trailed off since he didn't have the vocabulary to express what he had seen. "They turned into rain. Warm rain came down on me, Mom, and I was better."

Smoothing her child's still-damp hair, Lesley remembered the sweet clear sprinkle that marked Cosette Windsor's leave-taking.

Gentle Jane Copley Windsor must have finished her earthly duties by saving Lesley's child and finding Richard. Although Lesley claimed to be agnostic, neither Jewish nor Christian, she found that she believed that Richard and Jane had gone to join Ursula Smith. Somewhere. Some better place. She didn't believe that the others had gone to hell, though; they'd just disappeared. You can only push a Jewish agnostic so far.

"Thank you, Jane," Lesley whispered. "I hope we meet again someday."

"Mom," asked Ryan. "Did Dad visit me while I was asleep?"

"Yes. He's been here," she said. "Dad's not feeling well, but he'll come as soon as he's better."

She sat with Ryan until he fell into a natural sleep. Pink had returned to his cheeks and the corners of his mouth tilted upward. Lesley thanked Mother Fortune, or whoever was in charge of these proceedings, for her son's restoration.

Coral appeared with a report on Michael's condition. "Michael sustained a broken pelvis, a couple cracked ribs, and a dislocated shoulder but he'll recover. He's medicated right now. You can see him tomorrow."

"All right," said Lesley. Tomorrow would be soon enough to begin building a new relationship with her son's father.

A soft fall of snow continued as Lesley and Coral drove back to Deerhaven Forest Hall. A few windows glowing with light promised that Rachel and the Smiths had waited up for them. The library radiated illumination. The Windsors never let the library go dark, Lesley realized. Floods of light from Deerhaven Forest Hall turned falling snowflakes to stars in the night sky and warned predators not to come near. Would this be her home now?

She entered through the heavy front doors that Cosette had opened for her when she first came to Deerhaven Forest Hall. After the doors swung shut behind her and Coral, Rachel appeared from the kitchen, flanked by two generations of tall, raven-haired librarians. Rachel's face lit with unmitigated warmth.

"We made fondue and toasted chunks of stale sourdough bread to dip in it," reported Sula.

Lesley felt her stomach contract in reaction to the day's events. "I can't eat until I understand what's happened," said Lesley. "I can't stand being here at the Hall until I know everything about why Rachel had to suffer so terribly, and why the Reverend Were felt that he needed to shoot my son. You told me that before they went astray, the Reverend Were and the Reverend Chaney were meant to provide a smokescreen for gay people. What's hidden here of such importance?"

Silence ensued as each woman contemplated dangerous secrets. Ursa, eventually, waved her hand in a devil-may-care gesture.

"Everything that has transpired in this house, ever, concerned one thing," said Ursa.

"What?" asked Rachel. "There's so much I've never understood. That's what drove me crazy."

"Your 'craziness' grew out of Deerhaven Forest Hall," Ursa replied, with a sad smile for Rachel. "Everything that ever happened arose from the roots of the Hall. The Reverend Chaney's rape of Jane Copley Windsor, the Reverend Were shooting Ryan in the name of the PURITI party, served to perpetuate the guardian family and to distract the public's eye from the real purpose of the Hall's founders. The plan went awry in those instances."

"What plan?" asked Lesley, bracing herself to hear something strange.

"The plan for the preservation of the library."

"The library?" Lesley and Rachel repeated. "What does the library have to do with what's happened?"

"Everything," replied Ursa.

CHAPTER TWENTY-THREE

The septagon centered within the body of the library shimmered in a conjured light composed of falling snow, occasional moonbeams and the aura of imagination with which every library glows. When Ursa approached the ashen walls surrounding the center, Lesley half expected a concealed door to open. The library within a library, however, had been built by people not technologically advanced enough to construct an aperture with a sensor device. Opening this door took muscle. Ursa positioned her two palms on the wood and pressed until a crevice appeared, grew, and became a portal. A warm, golden radiance, unlike the clear perimeter light, poured from the opening.

"Come," said Ursa and motioned them forward. Lesley and Rachel went first, followed by Sula and Coral. Ursa entered last and sealed the thick wall behind them.

Inside, Lesley drew a startled breath and heard Rachel's companion gasp. They stood in a cosmos lit by lamps, which emitted an amber light like a warmer sun than the one she knew. Rich woods, cherry, mahogany, oak, decorated the walls. This interior building hummed like a forest, the quietest forest Lesley could imagine. No birds, no insects, no wild animals, and no wind, disturbed the silence and yet she could almost feel trees growing. Although constructed from felled wood, this forest remained alive and Lesley felt stronger, more alive, than ever before.

The square wooden beams curving upward to frame the room reached ceiling-high to form branches that framed a circular window. The pinnacle of window glass, Lesley realized, could be seen to be contiguous with the clear, aerial ceiling of the library proper. This porthole at the library's zenith conducted moonlight, a silver spray fusing with the room's golden torchlight like striations on a burning candlewick.

"Where are we?" breathed Lesley.

"At the crux of what matters," explained Ursa. "This is the reason for you and me and Deerhaven Forest Hall."

Eyes and mind adjusting to the rich, strange atmosphere, Lesley walked forward. For the first time, she saw that the carefully crafted wooden shelving housed bound volumes, books and papers. Gold script on the spines of the books nearest her appeared to be titles, but she could not read the letters. She didn't presume to touch oiled leather, vellum or paper.

"Some of these books predate Shakespeare," Ursa told them. "We have pictures and stones from before Western civilization."

Lesley groped for the appropriate questions.

"This library serves some high purpose," said Rachel, stating the obvious. "I've never been to an exalted place but now that I've come here, I wonder what place could feel as important?"

"Words could never express the value of what this place holds," Ursa began, speaking with great care. "I can only present you with vague generalities."

Glancing at the line of volumes opposite her, Lesley's eye finally caught a familiar name. "Sappho," she murmured, able to identify the writer as an ancient author, but unable to recall anything about her writings.

"Sappho's work belongs in this library," said Sula.

"Tell them," Ursa encouraged her daughter. Coral, smiling, nodded agreement and Sula began to speak.

"The library exists to preserve the lives, the collective knowledge, and the creative power of women who choose to love women and men who choose to love men. To understand you start by reading your way along the bookshelves and begin absorbing the magnitude of this treasury." Lesley and Rachel looked around in fascination. "Who created this place?" asked Rachel. "My mother ran the house, but she didn't know about this part of the library. I'd bet on it."

"Throughout history, the Windsor wife in residence retained knowledge of this library's existence only if she chose to love women. Cosette Windsor loved her husband, Russell, and so this part of the library did not stay real for her."

"Cosette never questioned why the library's interior appeared to be sealed behind these seamless walls?" asked Lesley, her mind struggling with the practical details of Sula's revelation.

"Cosette came to believe that the Hall Librarian toiled behind the wooden panels, maintaining the library's catalogue and mending books and manuscripts pertaining to local history," said Ursa. "First I, and then Sula, perpetuated this subterfuge."

"Sula," asked Lesley, "didn't the Reverend Were notice this structure when he entered the library to kidnap you and injure Ryan?"

"The Reverend Were, as a descendent of the Windsor line, felt a calling: to protect this library even though he didn't recognize the forces which impelled him. Although he operated in moral darkness, Reverend Were could not dismiss the library's existence since he would have chosen to love men if he'd given himself a choice. He should have been a gay man. Then he could have found a less convoluted way to carry out his imperative, to protect the library."

"The Reverend Were?" exclaimed Sula. "How would that skinny vampire have found a lover? The guys around here are buff, they work out with weights, and they keep themselves nice and tan. They avoid activities that involve exchange of bodily fluids and the Reverend...well, you know."

"The Reverend never found sexual or emotional fulfillment, and his physical countenance reflected the sadness of his disassociated existence," Ursa reproved her daughter. "Let us hope his spirit has found peace."

Lesley moved to a corner of the septagon. A bank of networked computers hummed and glowed. "Ursa? Does modern technology belong in the library?"

"You don't think we'd let the library become an anachronism, do you?" laughed Ursa. "Move about freely, Lesley, Rachel. You need to learn how to navigate the library. Find yourselves something good to read. A small segment of the materials can be removed on a temporary basis although most items must remain inside these walls."

As she walked the aisles, a warm, matchless joy flooded Lesley, and she could see Rachel experiencing a similar sensation. The unparalleled romance of the life that she had chosen when she first set eyes upon Rachel seemed validated and amplified here at the library's core.

Then, they skidded to a halt. A shrill shriek interrupted the rapture of their introduction to the library. The four women called to each other and found their way to the door where Ursa had admitted them. Standing in the entrance, letting temperate, gold air leak out the opening, Lesley saw Valerie Kemsley, holding a long, blue candle aloft.

"Get out if you value your lives," Valerie screamed. "I will not see Sula debased by the evil smut that you house in here. I intend to destroy the vile pornography within these walls, and deliver Sula from the pornographers who have tried to steal her away from all that's good and wholesome!"

"Valerie, I'm a librarian," Sula began. "I love this library. If you damage the library, you destroy me."

"You've been corrupted by enemies of the hue!" screamed Valerie.

"She's chosen a bad affinity," whispered Ursa.

"What do you mean?" Lesley whispered back.

"A malign spirit must have attracted Valerie and settled

within her. I suspect the Reverend Were. Perhaps he didn't pass on."

"Leave now!" Valerie cried with a shriek that must have been painful for her vocal cords.

"We can't let Valerie burn down the library," Rachel cried in terrible distress. She ran forward.

"Rachel!" screamed Lesley.

Rachel reached for the midnight-colored taper in Valerie's hand but the nurse fought her off. As they struggled, Rachel lunged to the left. A metallic glint caught Lesley's eye, and she saw Rachel pick up a long, wicked letter opener from an oak and cherry wood dictionary stand and defend the library using the opener as a weapon.

"Rachel, don't," Lesley called. She picked up her brooch as though the necklace could control the actions of Rachel or Valerie. The brooch remained static, a cumbersome piece of heirloom jewelry.

Rachel righted herself, and Valerie swung her taper. The candle grazed Rachel's face leaving a black caterpillar of burn.

"Valerie!" came a harsh but commanding voice from outside the door. Mrs. Woolf loped into sight. The nurse's stiff and agitated posture relaxed at the sight of Mrs. Woolf.

"Yes, Mrs. Woolf!" Valerie responded, her tone now subdued.

"Tell them why you're acting this way, Valerie," demanded Mrs. Woolf.

Valerie, for the first time, scrutinized the clutch of women in the library.

"Make her tell us, Mrs. Woolf," answered Sula. "If the Reverend Were snuck back and seized her, we'll exorcise him."

"You can stop talking that kind of nonsense, Sula Smith. Despite what I've witnessed today, I believe in the here and now. The girl's problem seems obvious to me. The poor thing hasn't admitted her affinity. I don't mean an affinity with them from the past, that rubbish that Mrs. Cosette always spoke of as she lay dying. I mean that Nurse Valerie here needs to choose whom she will have an affinity with in this lifetime, men or women."

Lesley watched Ursa Smith startle when she heard Mrs. Woolf state the obvious. Coral smiled and nodded.

Mrs. Woolf continued. "I started to hear those godawful voices teasing at me, nights when I lay in room upstairs as a young woman when I first took the post of housemaid. When I acknowledged my real and true affinity, the voices left me alone to do as I please."

"You?" gasped Sula and Rachel. "You're a lesbian?"

"What? Did you think you could tell by looking?" demanded Mrs. Woolf. "You shouldn't stereotype people based upon appearance."

Valerie Kemsley blew out her candle and bowed her head. With an apologetic and embarrassed shrug, Rachel lay down the letter opener. Lesley moved to Rachel's side and took her hand.

"I wouldn't have hurt you, Valerie," said Rachel. "You treated me well during all those years when my family held me prisoner and forced you to be my jailer. Finding the library meant so much to me; I picked up the letter opener to scare you away. Forgive me."

"I know, Rachel," answered Valerie.

"The library wouldn't actually have burned," Sula volunteered. "The smoke and heat would have triggered the remarkable protection systems designed by the library's most recent architects. The temperature inside the library would deviate only if the entire building went down in flames. The library would still be saved in that worst-case scenario because the architects who worked here in the year 2000 shielded the walls of the library with high-tech, anti-inflammatory material and installed external and internal sprinklers that operate independently of the rest of the house, on a generator."

"I'm glad the library can withstand so much," said Mrs. Woolf. "But we need to help guide Valerie. Are you ready to consider who you want to become?" Mrs. Woolf asked Valerie. Valerie lifted her eyes to view her surroundings, bounded by priceless papers and books, peopled with two pairs of lovers, Lesley and Rachel, Ursa and Coral, and two women who had always been strong and clear about their affinity, Sula and Mrs. Woolf.

"I don't really need to think, now that you've brought the matter to my attention," said Valerie with dignity. "I'm ready to admit my true self." She cast longing eyes upon Sula Smith.

"You're sure to meet the right woman," said Sula hastily, thinking of the proprietress of the Fruitful Arbor Bed-and-Breakfast in Jackson, the one with those arched black eyebrows, whom Sula planned to approach by tomorrow night. "I'll take you to a very nice place in Sonora where the women are easy to talk to, Wildflowers. You'll love it."

The room took on a red tinge but no one noticed.

When they closed the library for the night, Lesley noticed a brass plaque on the wall that read, *Simon Chalmers Memorial Library*. Where had she heard that name? Lesley almost found the energy to ask. Then, she reminded herself that she would have a lifetime to research the infinity of questions she would like to ask. And a happy ever after to make peace with the questions whose answers would defy even the most celestial librarian.

Publications from
Bella Books, Inc.
Women. Books. Even Better Together.
P.O. Box 10543
Tallahassee, FL 32302
Phone: 800-729-4992
www.bellabooks.com

CALM BEFORE THE STORM by Peggy J. Herring. Colonel Marcel Robicheaux doesn't tell and so far no one official has asked, but the amorous pursuit by Jordan McGowen has her worried for both her career and her honor.
978-0-9677753-1-9

THE WILD ONE by Lyn Denison. Rachel Weston is busy keeping home and head together after the death of her husband. Her kids need her and what she doesn't need is the confusion that Quinn Farrelly creates in her body and heart.
978-0-9677753-4-0

LESSONS IN MURDER by Claire McNab. There's a corpse in the school with a neat hole in the head and a Black & Decker drill alongside. Which teacher should Inspector Carol Ashton suspect? Unfortunately, the alluring Sybil Quade is at the top of the list. First in this highly lauded series.
978-1-931513-65-4

WHEN AN ECHO RETURNS by Linda Kay Silva. The bayou where Echo Branson found her sanity has been swept clean by a hurricane—or at least they thought. Then an evil washed up by the storm comes looking for them all, one-by-one. Second in series.
978-1-59493-225-0

DEADLY INTERSECTIONS by Ann Roberts. Everyone is lying, including her own father and her girlfriend. Leaving matters to the professionals is supposed to be easier! Third in series with *PAID IN FULL* and *WHITE OFFERINGS*.
978-1-59493-224-3

SUBSTITUTE FOR LOVE by Karin Kallmaker. No substitutes, ever again! But then Holly's heart, body and soul are captured by Reyna... Reyna with no last name and a secret life that hides a terrible bargain, one written in family blood.
978-1-931513-62-3

MAKING UP FOR LOST TIME by Karin Kallmaker. Take one Next Home Network Star and add one Little White Lie to equal mayhem in little Mendocino and a recipe for sizzling romance. This lighthearted, steamy story is a feast for the senses in a kitchen that is way too hot.
978-1-931513-61-6

2ND FIDDLE by Kate Calloway. Cassidy James's first case left her with a broken heart. At least this new case is fighting the good fight, and she can throw all her passion and energy into it.
978-1-59493-200-7

HUNTING THE WITCH by Ellen Hart. The woman she loves — used to love — offers her help, and Jane Lawless finds it hard to say no. She needs TLC for recent injuries and who better than a doctor? But Julia's jittery demeanor awakens Jane's curiosity. And Jane has never been able to resist a mystery. #9 in series and Lammy-winner.
978-1-59493-206-9

FAÇADES by Alex Marcoux. Everything Anastasia ever wanted — she has it. Sidney is the woman who helped her get it. But keeping it will require a price — the unnamed passion that simmers between them.
978-1-59493-239-7